ATLAS

Speed Demons MC: Book Three

Jules Ford

ISBN: 9798377439318

Copyright 2023 by Jules Ford.

All rights reserved.

This is a work of fiction. Names, characters, business, places, and incidents are either the product of the author's imagination or used in a fictitious manner. Any resemblance to actual living persons, living, or dead, or actual events is purely coincidental.

ALL RIGHTS RESERVED

This book contains material protected under International and Federal Copyright Laws and Treaties. Any unauthorized reprint or use of this material is prohibited. No part of this book may be reproduced or transmitted in any form, or by any means, electronic or mechanical, including photocopying, recording, or by any informal storage and retrieval system without express written permission from the author/ publisher.

Cover by JoeLee Creative

Formatting by Md Foysal Ahmed

www.facebook.com/foysal.rumman1
www.fiverr.com/foysalrumman

Editing and proofreading by Ellie Race

With thanks.

Dedication

Nicola Thorpe You rock!

A special shout out to Kirsty Bartlett, who won an LLMC: book club Facebook competition. Thank you for choosing Boner's road name. I love it.

Thank you Christina and Rose for all of the time you dedicated.

XOXO

Other Books by Jules

Speed Demons MC
Bowie
Cash
Atlas
Book Four ~ Coming Soon

Soulless Assassins MC
Tyrant's Redemption (Co-author Raven Dark)

Note to Readers

This book has detailed scenes of domestic violence, drug use, abuse and other dark themes (including death) that may offend.

Domestic violence can happen to anyone.

There is no discrimination.

If you need to talk to somebody, please call the number that's relevant for you.

USA National Domestic Violence Hotline (800) 799-7233

Domestic Abuse Helpline UK 0808 8010327

Domestic Violence Support Service Canada (204) 945-6851

Family and Domestic Violence Helpline Australia 1800 737 732

Table of Contents

Chapter One 1

Chapter Two 21

Chapter Three 35

Chapter Four 52

Chapter Five 67

Chapter Six 74

Chapter Seven 85

Chapter Eight 100

Chapter Nine 115

Chapter Ten 131

Chapter Eleven 145

Chapter Twelve 158

Chapter Thirteen 174

Chapter Fourteen 182

Chapter Fifteen 194

Chapter Sixteen 205

Chapter Seventeen 210

Chapter Eighteen 222

Chapter Nineteen 232

Chapter Twenty 242

Chapter Twenty-One 265

Chapter Twenty-Two 284

Chapter Twenty-Three 291

Chapter Twenty-Four 301

Chapter Twenty-Five 309

Chapter Twenty- Six 316

Chapter Twenty-Seven 334

Epilogue 340

Acknowledgements 350

Chapter One

Sophie ~ Three Years Earlier.

The hospital speakers crackled and squealed.
"Code triage. Available doctors to the ED. Code triage. Available doctors to the ED."

I glanced up from the iPad I was making notes on, handed it to the nurse, and quickly silenced my beeping pager. "Helen, can you make sure Mr. Wilkins is comfortable? I'll be back as soon as I can." I swept out of the room and down the corridor toward the Emergency Department.

Vegas was notorious for car accidents, usually caused by drunk drivers who over-indulged while they gambled and then stupidly decided that it would be a good idea to get behind the wheel of a car. The fallout from that wasn't something anyone should get used to, but I was desensitized to it nonetheless.

A deep voice called out my name, "Sophie!"

Looking up, I saw Ty Hollifield jogging toward me from the opposite corridor. He slipped his cell phone into the pocket of his white coat. "There's been an armed robbery at the jewelry store on Bullion Drive. I've heard reports that a cop, two civilians, and a perp all have GSWs."

My stomach gave a hard jolt. "Cop? Any names?"

Jules Ford

Ty shook his head just as we turned the corner and pushed hard on the doors that led into the Emergency Department. The room was noisy, people running back and forth shouting instructions as stretchers of injured people were wheeled in from the ambulance bay.

Immediately my eyes were pulled across the room. Ty's strong hand rested on my shoulder, and I froze. "Catch you later, Soph," he said softly in my ear and disappeared.

My heart sunk as familiar cold, blue eyes flicked over my face, then to the spot on my shoulder that Ty had just touched. I tried to clear the lump in my throat as my husband made his way toward me, but my mouth was too dry.

I pressed a hand to my racing heart. "Thank God you're okay," I croaked as he got closer. "Ty said that a cop's been shot. I was worried."

Luke sneered, gripping my arm. "You'd have been rejoicing in the streets if it was me, wouldn't you? Sorry to disappoint you." His eyes snapped toward Ty, who was checking a patient's vitals across the room, then looked back down at me and sneered. "Are you fucking him?" His hand squeezed my arm roughly.

I winced. "Don't do this, Luke," I pleaded quietly. "Not here. We've talked about this."

He leaned down close to my face with gritted teeth, eyes flashing with anger. "Don't lie to me. Are you two fucking aroun-?"

He was interrupted by the double doors crashing open. Two paramedics rushed through, pushing a stretcher. One of them shouted, "Male, age thirty-nine, GSW to the right lower quadrant, no exit wound. BP's seventy over fifty and dropping. Already started chest compressions."

Luke's face jerked toward the commotion. "That's Hobbs." He thrust a hand through his dark blonde hair.

Atlas

"I'll deal with it," I said reassuringly. "Go to the waiting room. Be there for Maggie."

My head flew around as the main doors flew open again, and a Paramedic shouted, "Female, twenty-five, head injury, unresponsive."

Another stretcher followed, and more shouting cut through the room.

"I need to treat Hobbs," I snapped, pointing at my arm. Luke's grip loosened, and I took a deep breath, pulling away from my husband.

Then I went to work.

Exhausted, I pulled off my surgical cap and stalked out of OR while fighting back the tears that burned my throat.

Yet again, I'd been reminded how life was tragic and cruel and how easily it could break you.

From what I knew of Andrew Hobbs, he was a good man and a good police officer. He had a teenage boy, a girl, and a wife of twenty years. I'd met her a few times at parties and celebrations. I was nauseous because I had to go and make her entire world crash down around her.

The waiting room was wall-to-wall blue uniforms. Stalwart men, the County's finest, all showing support for one of their own. A blonde head popped up, and grey eyes met mine. Maggie Hobbs, once a wife, suddenly a widow.

My knees trembled as I moved toward her, dreading the conversation I was about to have. Luke's angry stare burned into my face, but I didn't look at him; I couldn't. Instead, I walked toward Maggie, my eyes never leaving hers.

She stood, tilted up her chin, and stumbled toward me. She knew, she could see it in my face, and she wasn't a stupid woman. Maggie faltered slightly, then recovered. "Sophie?" Her voice cracked as she said my name.

I swallowed down my tears and grabbed hold of her hands. "I'm so sorry, Maggie. We did everything we could, but Andrew's injuries were too severe. He didn't make it."

Her face crumbled, and she let out a pain-filled moan. "No!" she wailed and went down on her knees. Two officers grabbed her and pulled her up, but her head lolled downward and rested on her chest, her face contorted with pain.

A single tear trailed down my cheek.

Heat suddenly hit my back, and a hand roughly squeezed my shoulder. "I'll be with the boys. Doubt I'll be home tonight."

My stomach froze at the coldness in Luke's voice, but I inwardly breathed a sigh of relief. It was a good thing. I knew he'd be angry and take his shit out on me. I couldn't face that drama tonight.

Spending time with his colleagues, and remembering Andrew, was the best thing for us both.

A shiver skated down my spine just as Luke's mouth brushed my ear. "I'll see *you* tomorrow," he hissed. "We're going to talk about what happened with Andrew."

I tilted my chin and frowned when I saw his face lined with fury.

Was he blaming me for this? I spent four hours fighting a losing battle trying to save Andrew's life when it was evident that it was a hopeless cause.

I took his arm and pulled him out into the empty corridor. "Luke," I whispered so that Maggie couldn't hear me. "The bullets did too much damage for me to repair. He bled out internally. As I patched one, bleed another one started. I was plugging him fast, but I couldn't keep up. Nobody could've saved him; his body was too damaged."

My husband folded his arms across his chest. "You're supposed to be a hot shot, genius surgeon, Sophie. How the fuck did Andrew end up dying?" He swept a hand toward the room from which we'd just come. "Maggie lost a husband, and we lost a brother because you're too distracted cozying up to that Hollifield asshole when you should be focusing on saving an officer's life."

I closed my eyes, trying not to be affected by his cruelty, but it still made my breath catch and my stomach sink.

My husband had changed in the two years we'd been married. Gone was the man who used to talk to me for hours about my day. The caring man who brought me flowers to cheer me up when I lost a patient had disappeared, and I didn't recognize the stranger in front of me.

He'd become paranoid and accusatory. I was starting to realize that the sweet guy I married didn't exist. The real Luke had begun to peek through the mask, and I didn't like this version of him.

"I'm sick of this," I murmured. "It's all bullshit."

He reared back slightly, looking at me with narrowed eyes. "What are you saying?"

"This. You. Us. The way you're being, constantly picking fights and pushing me around all the time. I meant it when I agreed to try, but it's not working, Luke. I think we should take a break."

He looked at me like I was crazy.

I chewed my lip nervously.

We hadn't been happy for a long time. Luke talked me into staying so many times, but things between us weren't getting better; quite the opposite. I felt sick to my stomach at the thought of living with him for one more day. Of him shoving me across the room in frustration.

Of his face lowering to mine and his eyes spitting more and more hate.

Enough was enough. I couldn't do it anymore.

I closed my eyes exasperatedly. "We've talked about this, Luke."

"No!" His hand jerked up and grabbed me by the back of my hair so roughly that the sharp pain brought tears to my eyes.

His face lowered to mine, contorted with fury. "I'll be home tomorrow, and we'll talk then, right? You're my wife," he said through clenched teeth. "We're not separating."

"Luke, you're hurting me!" I cried.

His hand suddenly released me, and I slumped back against the wall. My eyes sliced to his. "Put your hands on me again, and you'll regret it."

"Sophie-" he began, but I cut him off. "-No! There's no excuse for what you just did. I'm going home after my shift, I'm packing your shit, and you're leaving. We're done."

He scrubbed a hand down his face, suddenly contrite. "I'm sorry, Pet. I'm losing my head because of Andrew. You know I'd never hurt you."

A figure loomed in the doorway. "Detective. Lawson's taking Maggie home. We're going to head back to the station."

My husband looked down at me pleadingly. "We'll talk tomorrow, Sweetheart."

No, we won't, I thought as I watched him walk away without a backward glance.

I slumped into my driver's seat the next morning and let out an exhausted sigh. "Siri, call Ned." I hit the ignition button, checked my mirrors, and pulled out of my parking space.

I'd known Kennedy Carmichael for ten years; she was the closest thing I had to a sister. I was adopted and an only child. My mom had passed away three years before, and Ned and her twins were the only family I had left.

"Morning, beautiful," she greeted me chirpily. "Good shift?"

"No." I paused while I thought about what to say. Ned had probably crossed Andrew's path back when she worked in the DA's office. "Look, you'll hear about it at work today. Last night there was an armed robbery that turned into a shootout. Andrew Hobbs died. I lost him in surgery."

"Shit," she said with a breath. "Did they catch the perps?"

"Yeah," I replied. "One's injured. He's in hospital under armed guard. The other two are in county." I let out a quiet snort as I stopped at some lights. "Bet you're happy you left the DA's office now. You'd've been called in last night."

Ned was one of the top criminal defense attorneys in Vegas. She may have looked like a Barbie doll, but she was scary smart. People consistently underestimated her, and she used it to her advantage.

She made a gagging sound. "Fuck that. My days of working until four in the morning are well and truly over. I'm home for my kids by six now, and that's the way it's staying." She paused for a few seconds before her voice lowered. "Are you okay, Soph?"

The lights turned green, and I pressed my foot to the gas. "I'm leaving him today, Ned. He blamed me for Andrew's death. His paranoia's getting worse, and so's his temper."

The lengthy silence told me Ned was trying to get her shit under control. She had some major big dick energy.

It was a running joke; Kennedy strutted like she was hung, whereas I was much more understated.

"If he's laid a hand on you, I'll rip his balls off," she murmured.

"No, he hasn't, not entirely," I assured her with more bravado than I felt. "Regardless, I'm not going to stick around to risk it. I was going to pack his shit and make him leave the condo, but I'm going to pack my stuff today instead and get out of there. The condo belongs to me, so I can sell it from anywhere if I get agents to list it. I'll even get renters if I have to."

"Why don't you stay with me and the kids for a while?" she offered. "We've got plenty of room."

My shoulders relaxed, and I let out a sigh. "Are you sure?"

"Yeah," she scoffed. "You can have the pool house. I've just had a new security system fitted. We'll know if asshole comes creeping around."

I smiled. "You, Ned Carmichael, are a dream come true. Do you know that?"

"Well, duh," she let out a soft laugh. "Pack what you need, get your mom's keepsakes, and get your ass over to my place. The kids have their clubs this morning. If you're not here in a couple of hours, I'll come help you."

I couldn't help the smile that curved my mouth. My life was falling apart, but all I could feel at that moment was safety and comfort.

"Soph," Ned prompted.

"Yeah?"

"I've got you," she promised. "It's all going to work out."

I zipped up the last suitcase and looked around our bedroom while memories flashed through my mind like

Atlas

a movie reel. Staring at the bed where we spent hours together, I couldn't help wondering where everything had gone so wrong.

We were happy once. Maybe we could get back to that one day? A small part of me couldn't help worrying that perhaps I was giving up too soon. But then I remembered Luke's hard, blue eyes and the accusations he spat at me in the hospital. It was like he'd turned into a different person.

That thought made my spine straighten and my chin jut up.

Leaving was the best thing for both of us. Separating didn't mean divorce. It meant taking time to see if we missed each other enough to fight for our marriage. He needed a wake-up call, and this was it.

I grabbed my two pieces of luggage and hauled them to the top of the stairs. Then I went back for my carry-on bag and purse. That was when I heard the front door slam.

"Hi honey, I'm home!" Luke called out and started laughing maniacally.

I closed my eyes and began to count to ten. He'd been drinking again.

Heavy feet started to thump up the stairs. Stomach pitching, I picked up my purse, put it over my shoulder, put on a blank face, and waited.

After a minute, he appeared in the doorway. His hair was messy from where he'd been running his fingers through it. He'd looked smart when I saw him at the hospital, now his jacket was rumpled, and his tie was askew.

His gaze fell on my cases, and he froze, staring at them. "What the fuck's this?" he demanded, slurring slightly. His eyes darted up to meet mine, and it was my turn to still. They were overly bright, and his pupils had blown huge, taking up most of his blue irises.

I'd seen blank eyes like that hundreds of times as an intern and a resident during late nights working in the

ED. "Have you taken drugs?" I asked incredulously. "Luke, you're a cop. What if they do a random test?"

He stumbled toward me. That was when I caught the smell of strong, cloying perfume. My heart sank into the pit of my gut. My perfume was lighter, more subtle. I couldn't wear strong scents like that. They gave me headaches.

I stared at him, shocked.

He'd been with another woman.

"I asked you a fucking question," he snarled, interrupting my racing thoughts.

Hand to hip, I looked him up and down. "Whose perfume is that? You smell like a brothel."

His stare blanked, like shutters snapped down over his eyes. I marveled at how easily he could hide his thoughts, his truth.

"Don't be fucking stupid," he grated, gesturing to my cases. "You better answer me. What's going on?"

It wasn't lost on me how he was trying to change the subject. It also wasn't lost on me how I suddenly didn't care what he'd been up to. We were over. It was the final straw.

I brought my hand up to rub my temple. "I'm leaving." My voice dropped, suddenly defeated. "It's not working, Luke. I'm not happy. I haven't been happy for a long time. You reek of another woman's perfume, for God's sake. I'm going to stay with Ned while we work out if we can save this marriage."

He began to laugh maniacally again. A small dot of spittle gathered at the corner of his mouth.

Something dark and cold slithered through my chest.

What the hell had he taken? His entire aura had changed. It was like he was a different person.

Or maybe this was the real him, and I'm only just starting to see it.

"Should've known you'd go running to that slut." His face hardened, and he took a step toward me. "You're my fucking wife. You're not going anywhere. Fuck you, Sophie. How could you do this to me after Andy?" A strong hand shot out and gripped my upper arm painfully.

"Get off me," I demanded. "What the hell do you think you're doing?" I tried to shake him off, but he held me too tightly. "Luke." My chest clenched, and I started to beg. "Stop. Please. You're hurting me."

He glared down into my face, but it was like he didn't see me. His eyes were vacant, blank like he didn't know me. Like I was nothing.

A bad feeling squirmed inside my belly; it felt tangible, real. "Get off me. Please, Luke." A cry escaped my throat as he began to shake me, harder and harder, until my head rattled.

"Why are you making me do this?" His hand came up to grip my neck, and he squeezed.

My entire body went cold with panic. I felt my eyes bulge as his strong fingers contracted harder. A hiss escaped me, and my hand came up and clawed at his wrist, trying to get him away.

He shoved me from him. I tripped, my feet got caught in the carry-on, and I fell into a heap on the floor, landing on my shoulder. I moaned at the stab of pain that burned through my arm. My eyes sliced to him, and I looked at his face, shocked. Who was he? Even at his worst, he'd never been physically abusive before.

I began to scramble across the floor toward the door.

Luke laughed again as he strode toward me. "Get the fuck up." He bent and grabbed my hair, pulling hard.

My scalp felt like it was on fire. His hand flew out and backhanded me hard across the face.

I let out a cry.

Sharp pain radiated through my mouth, and I tasted the tang of blood. My hand came to my lips, and I stared wide-eyed at Luke, frozen with shock.

Something inside my soul cracked. Nobody had ever hit me like that before, not even my mom, especially not my mom. As an ED doctor, I'd seen women come in needing help, victims of violence and assault. I knew the world could be cruel, but its darkness had never touched me like that, not until then. How could it be happening? This wasn't my life. I was a doctor. I was married to a cop.

Nausea stirred in the pit of my stomach. That one punch had changed *everything*.

Luke's face twisted harder, his expression flat and hard. Blown pupils made his eyes appear like black voids as he looked down at me, his mouth a snarling grin.

At that moment, my handsome husband was nothing short of demonic. Hatred rolled off him in waves so forcefully that the air seemed to crack around him.

Icy fear stabbed through me, and I jerked back. My heart sank because I knew I was in deep shit. My mind whirred, trying to think through the confusion. I needed a plan to get out of there. I couldn't physically overpower him. I had to think of another way out.

I backed up slowly toward the door, lifting my hands like I was trying to soothe a rabid animal. "It's okay." My voice was soft, reassuring. "It was an accident. I know you'd never hurt me intentionally. Let's go downstairs. We'll tal-"

Like a cobra, he shot forward and struck me again, but that time across my temple. The force of it made me stumble backward. I felt myself falling. Then my skull cracked off the corner of the dressing table, causing a sharp, shooting pain to explode through my head.

My wail was horror filled. I tried to lift from the ground, but the dizziness made me so disorientated that I collapsed. My limbs were like jelly, probably from the pain or the shock.

The sounds of him shuffling around, muttering to himself registered in the back of my mind, but I blocked it out, trying desperately to think straight. I tried to remember some Krav moves, but my mind blanked. I couldn't get my head right. Shit, maybe I was concussed.

"Luke," I croaked. "I need a hospital. My head hurts."

"Fuck. Fuck." He paced the room, thrusting his hands through his hair. At least he had the good grace to look sorry, not that it made anything better. "I can't take you to the hospital, Soph," he whined. "I'll lose my job. You're the doctor. Tell me what to do."

He stopped pacing and got down onto the floor, grabbing my hands while trying to straddle me. I turned my head to the side, but his fingers gripped my chin, forcing me back around to face him. "I'll look after you. You'll be okay."

I winced as he ran his fingers down my cheek. He lowered his face to mine, and I shrank back into the carpet, letting out a quiet moan.

"I love you," he muttered against my skin. "I'm sorry."

A banging noise registered, and someone called my name, but my skull throbbed so severely that I couldn't concentrate.

Luke stiffened and cursed under his breath. "Who the fuck's that?" he snapped.

Relief prickled through me as his weight disappeared. I cracked an eye open just as my cell rang loudly inside my purse. The ringtone suddenly cut off, and the banging noise resumed.

"Fuck!" Luke bit out. "Bitch."

Somebody banged hard on the front door. Tears hit the back of my eyes as I heard Ned shout my name. A recollection of her telling me that she'd come and help me pack rushed back at me. I tried to call out for her to get away, but my voice was just a croak.

Then I could hear voices. Ned yelled my name, and I realized she was in the house. My heart seemed to freeze.

What if Luke hurt her too?

Get up. Get up. Get up.

I couldn't tell if I was thinking the words or chanting them out loud, but they helped motivate me because I laid my arms on the floor and pushed, trying to haul my body to a sitting position. After several attempts, I managed to pull myself up, but the room was spinning so much that all I could do was put my head in my hands and groan loudly.

"Soph!" I could hear the panic in Ned's voice even though it sounded like she was miles away. "He's gone. Where are you?"

"Up here," I tried to call out, but my head throbbed so much that it was painful to speak. My stomach lurched with nausea, and I knew I was about to throw up. I couldn't move. All I could do was turn my head to the side and vomit on the carpet next to me.

I moaned as I continued to retch, the pulling sensation making my head pulsate even harder.

"Jesus," Ned cried. "There's blood everywhere."

I looked up to see her staring at me wide-eyed, then she was next to me, holding me as I heaved and coughed. When I finished, she gently laid me back down. "It's okay," she reassured me. "I'm getting help."

I closed my eyes and prayed for Luke not to come back. If he did anything to Ned, I'd never forgive myself. I let out a moan because the thought of it made my heart ache.

Snippets of her conversation registered. "Hurry up, please... She's got a head injury, and it looks bad... She can't keep her eyes open."

I must have kept losing consciousness and then coming back around because Ned seemed to be talking to different people all at once. Soothing voices reassured me, and bright lights shone in my eyes.

Atlas

I tried to talk and say that I was a doctor and needed a CT scan, but nobody understood what I was saying. Maybe my words were all jumbled up; I didn't know.

Suddenly, I was being lifted and carried, and I knew I was on a stretcher. Ned whispered in my ear, "We're on our way to the ER, Soph. You're going to be okay."

Was time all screwed up, or was I going crazy?

One minute I felt myself being carried out of my house; the next, I was being rushed somewhere on a stretcher. I recognized the sounds of an ED, of doctors barking out orders. I began to shake because I thought I was back in my bedroom and Luke was there.

The sounds of Ned's soft cries and the pain throbbing through my head startled me awake.

One lamp lit the room dimly, but it still made me wince to look at it. "Ned?" I croaked. "What happened?"

She softly stroked my hair back from my face. "You've got a serious concussion and a hairline skull fracture. They want to keep you in the hospital for a few days and monitor for brain bleeds, but they're hoping it will heal."

My eyes burned with tears from the pulsing ache in my scalp. "The dresser. He hit me. I fell and banged my head."

"We know," she squeezed my hand reassuringly. "I got the firm's investigator in your condo. He was a CSI for twenty years. It didn't take him long to pinpoint what happened exactly."

Sickness washed through my stomach. "Luke?"

"Nobody can find him," she informed me, a hard edge to her voice. "He won't get away with this. I'll make sure of it. I'm gonna nail his balls to the wall. Nobody fucks with my family."

My eyes began to droop. It took too much energy to keep them open. A memory hit me, and my stomach jerked. "I need to pack up the condo. I can't…" My voice trailed off as the magnitude of what had happened finally hit me, and my face suddenly became wet.

Life would never be the same after what he did.

I would never be the same.

"Rest, Soph," Ned whispered. "I'm not leaving you." Soft fingers wiped the tears from my cheeks.

And that was all I needed to fall asleep.

"My client's not the one under suspicion here, Captain." Ned's voice had a steely quality to it that almost made me shiver. I'd heard she was a ballbuster, but it was more than that. She was legit scary.

"You had our conditions in writing a week ago," she continued. "What you tell my client in the next minute will determine if she presses charges against your officer." She leaned forward, her long, glossy blonde hair falling over one shoulder. "Have you thought about the publicity this could generate?"

Captain Cooper's eyes narrowed as he glared at her angrily.

Ned let out a derisive snort. "Still, it would be nothing compared to the reign of holy terror I'd rain down on this station. You forget I've still got friends in the DA's office." She threw a file on the desk. "Detective Price has twenty-four hours to sign the divorce petition. There are waivers in that file that he needs to sign in order to relinquish his interest over any of my client's financial assets."

Luke's boss took the file and flicked through it. "This isn't fair," he muttered. "Luke's being treated in a mental facility. If he signs this now, it won't hold up in court."

Ned curled her lip. "Looks like I'll have no choice but to call my friend at the Gazette then." She bent down to get her briefcase. "Come on, Sophie, this is a waste of time."

"Wait!" Captain Cooper held his hands up resignedly. "Okay, okay, you win. I'll take them to Luke myself and stand over him while he signs, and I'll initial them." His stare came to me, and his eyes softened. "He wanted me to tell you he's sorry, and he'll regret his actions for the rest of his life. He just lost his head. Nobody knew he'd been spiraling, and then when Andrew-. Well - I guess it pushed him over the edge."

I stared at him blankly.

It felt strange. On the one hand, I wanted my ex-husband to get help. It was right that he got himself straightened out and looked after himself mentally. Being in the force was a challenging career. Officers saw the worst of humanity, which was bound to take its toll. He'd had a breakdown, and I felt terrible for that.

But he was still dead to me.

Luke deserved to be in jail for what he did, but I was willing to refrain from pressing charges as long as he got help and left me the hell alone. Captain Cooper assured me that Luke would never hurt anyone again. After thinking long and hard and talking it out with Ned, I let him sweep it under the rug.

I wanted a quick divorce and to leave town. The thought of a long-drawn-out court battle filled me with dread. Luckily, I lived in the perfect place to get a quick divorce, and it also helped that my best friend could pull strings with lawyers and judges.

It was over, and it was time for me to start again somewhere else.

What happened changed the core of me. The Sophie from a month ago didn't exist anymore. It was like the hand of evil had touched me and marked my soul. I needed a change of scenery so that I could think long and hard about my life.

I glared at the man sitting on the opposite side of the desk from Ned and me. "If I hear that he ever abuses another woman, I'll hold you personally responsible. I may be leaving, but Ms. Carmichael isn't, and she'll have her ear to the ground."

The captain jerked a nod.

Kennedy stood, smoothed down her skirt, and grabbed her briefcase. "I'll send a courier for the papers at noon tomorrow. Make sure they're signed."

I rose from my chair and followed Ned as she opened the door to the captain's office and swept out.

Together, we began to stride through the large bullpen where the officers were working. Silence fell over the room as we walked toward reception and the main doors.

I could almost feel the heat from all the hard stares scalding my skin as we strode through.

"Head up," Ned hissed, pulling her shoulders back. Confidence oozed from every pore as she strutted past the men. "You don't show those fuckers any weakness. You're the one with all the power here."

I jutted my chin and kept my eyes fixed ahead.

Ned was right. These men had shown their true colors in the six weeks since Luke beat me.

They'd hidden him, protected him, and when Ned finally pulled enough strings that they had no choice but to give him up, they checked him into a mental facility that specialized in treating PTSD.

I didn't doubt that Luke was sick. His entire demeanor that night proved that something in him was wired wrong. I knew he'd been struggling for a long time, but still, it seemed to me that they wanted to protect him no matter the cost.

They looked at me like *I* was in the wrong. Like *I* was the one who raised a hand to him. Maybe they blamed me for Andrew's death. Maybe they thought I deserved it. Or perhaps they were just misogynistic

Atlas

assholes that didn't like to allocate blame on one of their own. I mean it couldn't be Luke's fault. I must have done something to push his buttons. I must have set him off.

Assholes.

We pushed through the precinct doors and into the hot Las Vegas sun.

The wind had picked up, casting a sheen of red sand over the sidewalk. It was weird that everyone from Vegas hated the sand. They thought it was annoying. But I didn't because it represented home to me.

I was going to miss it.

Slowly, Ned and I walked toward my car.

Saying goodbye to this woman who'd protected me so fiercely was going to rip my heart out, but I knew I couldn't stay.

What he'd done to me had changed everything. I was a thirty-year-old woman, but it felt like he'd somehow ripped the last of my innocence away. The world was different now, I was different, and the thought of staying in a town where I could run into Luke or one of his cronies made me want to die.

Ned grabbed my hand as we reached my car. "So, London first?"

I smiled through my tears. "Yeah. I have a friend there from med school so I'm going to visit with him, then Scotland and Ireland."

"And we'll see you in Paris on Christmas Eve." Her eyes were suspiciously wet.

"I'm going to miss you," I murmured.

She smiled. "Not for long. Me, you, and the kids will all spend Christmas in Europe together, and then we'll take it from there, okay?"

I nodded, unable to speak.

"Sophie," she scolded me gently. "You're going to be fine. Go, find yourself again. After your mom died, you threw yourself into work and Luke and stopped looking after yourself here." Her fingers tapped my heart.

"Don't use what he did as an excuse to close yourself off even more. Eat tapas in Greece. Fuck a hot Spaniard on a beach in Ibiza. Sit outside an Italian café drinking expresso and watch the world go by. This is your time, so make it count. Just fucking live."

I swiped at my face. "I'm going to miss you."

Ned grinned. "Nah. You won't get a chance to. We'll speak every day. Now get in that rental and go before you miss your flight. And don't worry about anything here. I've got it under control."

She opened the car door and ushered me inside. "Remember to fuck all the hot European men." Her voice was full of humor, but I could tell it was forced.

I closed the door and wound down the window before putting on my seatbelt. "I'll call you as soon as I get to Heathrow."

She smiled her beautiful smile. "Make sure you do."

I pressed the ignition button and turned to take in Ned. I knew I was going to see her and the twins soon. I just needed a mental snapshot before I left.

"Be good," I gave her a watery smile.

She laughed. "No fun in that."

I looked at her earnestly. "Thank you. I would've died if it wasn't for you."

"Fuck off before I cry." She swiped quickly at her face before banging twice on the roof.

I put my foot on the gas and pulled away, glancing back in the rear view to see my best friend watching me, one hand on a cocked hip, all long gorgeous blonde hair, perfect boobs, and pouty lips.

I already missed her.

Chapter Two

Atlas ~ Six months earlier.

You could cut the tension in the waiting room with a knife.

Bowie was lying fifty feet away in a hospital bed after comin' outta surgery.

My chest burned with cold, brutal fury and stabbin' guilt.

I'd let my club brothers down.

My job as SAA was to make sure everyone played by the rules, implement changes, and ensure everyone was happy and healthy.

'Cause of me, the club ran like clockwork until now.

"Stupid fuckin' idiot," I ground out under my breath as I paced. Bowie owned a bulletproof vest. I wore mine out on patrol; why didn't he? Jesus, it was safety one-o-one

I cursed for the hundredth time that night. He was at death's fuckin' door. We could lose him at any time.

Again, I thought about the trainin' I'd taken him through a few years earlier when he made Enforcer. He was a fuckin' good fighter. He could'a been a pro boxer if he hadn't enjoyed the MC life so much. But you could box like Mike Tyson all day long; it wouldn't stop a bullet.

He'd literally taken his fists to a gunfight, and I couldn't for the life of me work out why. I thought about our trainin' again, goin' over and over it in my head.

BPV. Check.

Weapons. Check.

Cell. Check.

When you corner a wild animal, wait for backup. Check.

And definitely don't approach any fucker you cannot see. Check. Check. Check.

I was furious because I'd been sayin' for a while that we should've brought back weekly training sessions. Since the club had gone legit, we'd let things slide. The men were too busy workin' for the club's construction company and bar to worry about fightin' and target practice. Bowie getting hurt just proved that I should've insisted.

"What the fuck was he thinkin'?" I muttered quietly, still pacin' the room.

That's when I heard alarms begin to wail and a woman's scream.

Every cell in my body froze for a split second, then I turned toward the corridor and began sprinting toward Bowie's room.

The screech of the alarms wailed louder, and my heart thudded painfully.

Bowie was one'a my boys. A talented mechanic who was looked up to by the men. The thought of him not bein' on the earth didn't make sense. He was at the heart of the Demons; if he died, that organ would've been ripped out of the club.

I wasn't sure if we'd survive it.

"Get them out of here," an authoritative voice ordered as I ran toward the room. I noticed the husky quality of it even through my grief.

"Let the doctor do her job, Dad," Freya begged before she pulled Prez out of a room and into the hall just

Atlas

ahead of me, closely followed by Breaker, then Bo's ol' lady.

Layla spun toward the windows and rested her fingers on them. Even from the side, I could see tears streamin' down her face. "Please, Bowie, don't go," she cried as she watched the doc work on her ol' man.

I watched Prez clasp his head in his hands as he turned to stare into the room, and my heart seemed to wither and die inside my chest.

He looked broken, lost.

I went to him and squeezed his shoulder. "He'll be okay, Prez." My voice reeked of confidence that I wasn't feelin', but I continued. "That fucker's a fighter. He'll be up walkin' in a couple of days." My gut roiled 'cause I knew I was tryin' to convince myself as much as him.

God must've heard me 'cause at that second, the alarms quieted, and the beeps slowed in time with Bowie's heartbeat again.

I scraped a hand down my face. "See?" I said, lettin' out the same collective sigh as everyone else.

I glanced through the windows into the room to see the doc standin' over my brother with her head bowed.

My gut gave a tug at the forlorn expression on her face before she visibly pulled her ass into gear and began to check his vitals.

She was beautiful, hard but soft at the same time. There was an air of sadness about her. Her eyes were world-weary, and it was obvious that there was a story behind their whisky color. She heaved out a loud sigh filled with relief. Her face was pale and tired, and I remembered someone saying she'd pulled a double shift to do Bo's surgery. The doc must've been exhausted.

My eyes slid to Bowie fightin' for his life and my shoulders stiffened.

Tired or not, she was here to save my brother, and I was gonna make sure she did her goddamned job.

Whatever bullshit she was goin' through would have to take a back seat.

She looked up at us through the window. "You can come back in now. Gage has been stabilized."

Slowly, everyone filed back into the room and sat. Layla took a hold'a Bowie's hand and began quietly talking to him.

The doc's eyes swept to her. "Keep talking to him. I've seen patients respond better when their loved ones are around them. It's not science, and it's not proven to work, but feeding a man's soul can lead to miracles. I've seen it."

"Thank you, Doc," Dagger murmured. "I appreciate everythin' you're doin' for my boy."

She jerked a nod before makin' her way outta the room.

I tried to catch her eye as she walked past me, but her mind was a million miles away. She didn't even shoot me a glance before she stalked through the door, turned right, and started down the hall.

"Be back in a minute," I muttered before I walked out and followed.

A door closed further down the corridor, and I walked toward it.

My mind whirred. I got that the doc was tired, but she should'a been in that hospital room with Bowie, especially since he just fuckin' coded. Instead, she'd disappeared into her office for a little rest. My chest ached with the need to school a bitch and let her know my expectations. I didn't know what hospitals she'd worked at before, but we were short of surgeons in Hambleton.

She was the only person who stood between Bowie and the reaper. I expected more from her.

I got to the door and pushed it open without botherin' to knock. "Doc-" I said, makin' my way into the room. My eyes caught sight of her, and I froze.

Atlas

Her ass was perched on the desk, fingers over her face, sobbin'. Her hands dropped to her sides, and her teary eyes sliced toward me. "Don't you knock?" she demanded, swipin' at her face.

I folded my arms across my chest. "What's wrong? Why ya cryin'?"

Her dark eyebrows snapped together confusedly. "Who are you?"

"Atlas," I retorted. "Sergeant at Arms of the Speed Demons MC. You've got my brother out there with a hole in his chest. Don't you think you should get back to him and do your fuckin' job, *Doc*?"

Her eyes narrowed to slits. I could almost feel the frustration behind them. She glared at me like she wanted to drown me in a vat of acid, balls first.

My cock gave a tiny kick.

She was a fiery little thing.

"Get out of my office," she ordered, teeth clenched.

I cocked my head.

She got to her feet and pointed toward the door. "Get out before I call security."

One eyebrow quirked. "Just wanna little chat."

"Is this what you do?" she asked, lip curlin'. "Are you one of them?"

Woman was speakin' in fuckin' riddles. "Come again?"

"You know? One of them," she reiterated. "A bully. Coming in here uninvited and throwing your considerable weight around."

I folded my arms across my chest.

I only came in to tell her to do her job. I'd been relatively well-behaved. "Look here, Toots, I just want my brother looked aft-" I began, but her hand sliced through the air, and she cut me off.

"-No. *You* look here, *Toots*. I've been awake for thirty-two hours. Five of them were spent operating on Gage. I don't know if you noticed, but he's in a bad way.

I need five minutes to regroup, so excuse my lack of professionalism but do me a favor and get lost so I can cry my goddamned eyes out for five lousy minutes and release some stress."

Well hell. When the Doc put it like that, I felt like a bit of an asshole.

I caught her eye, ready to give her the death glare that usually put grown men on their asses, but my mouth clamped shut when I noticed the hurt behind her expression.

Something silky glided through my chest, and a sudden urge gripped me to take her in my arms, lay her down, pull her in close, and let her lean on me.

I tamped that shit right down. I was here for Bowie, not my dick.

"Either treat my boy or go the fuck home and let someone else see to him," I demanded.

She looked at me like I was crazy. "Huh?"

"Get your shit and fuck off home." I made my way closer to her.

"I can't. You saw what just happened. I need to be here. What if Gage crashes again?"

I took another step toward her. "There are other docs."

"I'm head of general surgery, and he's my patient. The hospital doesn't have a trauma surgeon, so I'm his best hope. The only other doctor on call is Doctor Sullivan, a resident."

The catch in her voice got my attention.

She was pretty, but it was an understated beauty. About five-three with thick, dark brown hair that had escaped the ponytail she had it tied up in. Her eyes were the color of fine whisky, her smooth skin the color of porcelain, and her body toned to perfection. My gaze rested on the tiny little mole on her top lip, and my throat ached with the need to lick it.

Atlas

There was so much goin' on behind her eyes, so much damage tucked deep inside. I wanted to know her story.

"What's his prognosis?" I asked.

She tilted her head to one side and glared. "I'm sorry. Are you family?"

"Told ya, he's my brother."

She blew out a sigh. "In laymen's terms, his lung collapsed. I've fixed it, but it's touch and go. The longer we can keep him stable, the better his chances are. I can't give you the promises that you're looking for. I can only say that he's in the best place and being cared for by excellent people."

"Why are you in here when I saw you doin' CPR on my bro five minutes ago? Shouldn't you be takin' care of him?"

"He's stable now," she explained with an edge to her voice. "And I'm ten seconds away."

"Get your ass back out there," I ordered.

"Get out," she whispered.

"Get your prissy ass back out there," I repeated.

Silence.

"Go see to my brother." I grabbed her shoulder. There was no intent to hurt her, just the intent to fight for Bowie.

Her head snapped up before a hand flew out and knocked mine out of the way. While she did that, her other hand whipped behind her, grabbed a silver letter opener, and lunged it toward me.

Quick as a flash, I caught her wrist and squeezed until she dropped the weapon. "What the fuck are you doin'?" I rasped. "You could'a fuckin' stabbed me."

Her eyes flashed, and she got up in my face. "Get off me before I kick your ass."

I stared down at her, all angry eyes, sassy mouth, and tiny heavin' tits. Up close, she was even more stunnin'. My cock thickened behind my zipper. Our eyes locked. I watched hers dilate and felt my heart tug inside my chest again.

Without a thought, I lowered my head and smashed my lips against hers. I didn't think, didn't plan, didn't fuckin' care. I just went with the urge.

She made a sound in the back of her throat like she was about to fight me, but the second my hand slid into her hair and my thumb stroked her face, I felt her body melt against mine.

My lips moved against hers, kissin' her fiercely. She moaned as I gently nipped her bottom lip before I retook her soft, warm mouth. My hand moved down to her ass and pulled her into me so I could grind my rock-hard dick against her hot little pussy. Fuck me, I nearly jizzed in my shorts right there and then.

My hands slid up to the front of her white coat. I ripped it open, looked down, and moaned at the sight of her firm little tits encased in a black lacy bra.

She squirmed on the desk, cupped the back of my neck, and pulled my mouth down to hers again.

My brain began to have a powwow with itself.

Get off her.

Nope.

You don't know her.

Never stopped me before.

What about Bowie?

The thought of my injured brother hit me in the solar plexus.

I released her lips and slowly lifted my head to see tears fill the pretty doc's whisky eyes. My gut dropped, and a burnin' stab of guilt made my chest heat.

"Never made a bitch weep by lockin' lips before," I muttered, tryin'a make light of the situation.

She stared up at me with swollen lips and a shocked stare. "I've had a bad day," she whispered.

"Go out with me," I demanded gently.

Confusion made her forehead furrow. "I don't date."

Atlas

A need took hold of me, a yearning to alleviate her tears and make her smile. "Cool," I smirked. "We'll just fuck then."

Her eyes widened in shock, and then she began to laugh from her belly. "Jesus. You're ridiculous."

Emotions I'd never felt before coursed through my blood. Couldn't say I'd ever yearned for a woman before. They came, and they went. No feelin's no connection. But this felt different.

I gently tucked a lock of hair behind her ear. "And you're gorgeous."

Her eyes went soft, and a smile played around her plump lips. "Why did you kiss me?"

One side of my mouth hitched up. "Just helpin' you relieve that stress. You feelin' better now, Doc?"

She just gazed at me.

My eyes flicked between hers. "See to Bowie. We'll talk after." I stepped back and made my way to the door. Just before I reached for the handle, I turned around. "I'll be out there waiting." I turned and left; a huge smile spread across my face, and my heart racin'.

Sophie

I stared at the door, unable to quite believe what had just happened.

Never before had a member of a patient's family walked into my office, given me shit, and then kissed me. I touched my bottom lip with my finger as I recalled his soft mouth, hard body, and sexy grin.

My hands went to fasten my white coat, cheeks burning at the memory of Atlas ripping it apart and staring down at me with heated eyes.

I hadn't been with a man since Luke. Hadn't had sex, hadn't kissed, hadn't even dated. After what happened, I consciously made a vow to myself that I needed to heal and get my juju back so I could choose better next time.

After a while, being alone became a habit. The thought of going through the dating scene again left me cold. I guessed that it came down to the fact that I was happy on my own. Being independent made me stronger. Self-reliance meant that nobody could hurt me again.

Admittedly, I'd seen Atlas around town occasionally and gave him furtive double glances. He was a striking man, tall, muscled, and tattooed. What appealed to me most, though, was his quiet confidence.

I could appreciate a good-looking man, but he didn't jump out at me as my type. He was rough and tough and probably too much for the likes of me. Also, after seeing him with a few women who didn't wear much in the way of clothes, I didn't think I was remotely his type either, seeing as I liked jeans and tops that covered my boobs.

Because of that, I wrote him off. It was easier that way. I had to be real with myself; if I was alone, there was less chance of my skull getting smashed off a dresser.

Luke had done more damage to me mentally than physically. What happened made me generally more skittish. I had no clue why, but I didn't feel that way around Atlas.

The kiss flashed through my mind, and I smiled when I recalled how I responded.

I'd had no sexual urges since I left Vegas until today.

Interesting.

My hand went to my pocket. I pulled my phone out, stabbed at the call log, and waited.

Ned answered after a couple of rings. "Hey."

"Remember when I told you how doctors often need some kind of sexual release after a big surgery?" I blurted out. "Well, I just got kissed, and it was fabulous. I could've jumped a man's bones for the first time in a long time."

She laughed. "Way to go, Babe. It only took you two and a half years. Who the fuck is he?"

Atlas

"He's a biker with no manners," I explained. "Every time I've seen him, he's been wearing jeans, a wifebeater, and biker boots. He has cropped hair, lots of muscles, and tattoos. When I think about it, he's a bit of an asshole."

She giggled that time. "Okay. So, he may not be your Mr. Right, but he sounds like your perfect Mr. Right Now. Go get some. Be crazy. Don't do anything I wouldn't do. Oh, and make sure he wears protection. Bikers are all slutnuts. I mean, have you seen Sons of Anarchy?"

I smiled. "Don't do anything you wouldn't do? Well, that just opened up the playing field."

"You know me," she murmured. "I like a play."

The line went quiet for a few seconds. "I'm scared," I whispered.

"Babe," she said softly. "While you go through life being scared of taking a chance, you're not living. You've trained like a ninja, and you can look after yourself. Go out, smell the roses, have sex, be free, and most of all, be free of *him*."

My eyes went misty. "I absolutely miss you so much."

"There's no need to miss me, Sophie," she replied quietly. "I'm right here."

"I know. I'll speak to you later." I quickly ended the call before I sobbed down the line. Ned was right about one fundamental thing; I was lonely.

I'd left Vegas and traveled around Europe alone without batting an eyelash at doing it solo. Then I came back to the States, went to New York, and stayed a while with a college friend.

All I had to do all day was train. I joined classes and honed my martial art skills alongside my Krav Maga, determined that nobody would ever hurt me again. Learning how to fight and growing stronger gave me a sense of safety and peace.

I left there, solo again, and came to Hambleton for two reasons.

My mom was born and raised here. She was a nurse at this same hospital when she adopted me. When I was a girl, she used to tell me about the town, the people, and her life here. She loved it but moved us away when she got offered a promotion in Vegas. She said it was for the best because people in Hambleton could be closed-minded, and she didn't want me growing up with the old-fashioned stigma of being adopted.

Las Vegas suited us because nobody there cared.

After I left Luke, I applied for a position here. Maybe I was trying to feel close to Mom again, and coming here was the only way I knew how. It took a while, but eventually, my predecessor left, and I got offered the head of general surgery position.

I'd come full circle and couldn't help believing this was exactly where I was meant to be. I'd arrived here intending to start a new life, make new friends, and eventually even meet someone I could love again.

But I realized after a while that what Luke did marked me in a way that stopped me from trusting my own judgment. I'd picked badly with before. What if I did it again? How could I trust myself when I chose so destructively last time?

I brought my fingers up to my lips which were still swollen from Atlas' kiss. My skin still heated. I remembered the intensity in his eyes when he stared at me, and I felt a sense of excitement that I hadn't experienced in years.

I'd seen his protectiveness over Bowie, and a part of me craved that for myself. I wanted more than anything for someone to be that protective over me. It wasn't that I needed someone to look after me. I could do that myself. I guess I just craved safety and security.

I craved a family.

My stomach leaped with excitement.

Atlas

Maybe it was time to take a chance. Atlas made me feel. That was as good a starting point as any. He was different from any man I'd dated before, but that wasn't necessarily bad, seeing as they all turned out to be duds. My belly jumped and swirled, and I suddenly felt something I'd been lacking for years.

A sliver of hope.

I stood, slipped my cell into my pocket, and went back to the corridor. My hand held a slight tremor as I walked toward Bowie's room. My throat was tight with nerves, but Ned was right. I had to put myself back out there.

Voices echoed in the hallway, and I heard John's deep voice.

"Leave her alone, Atlas. She saved my boy's life. If anythin', I owe her a marker."

I smiled. John didn't owe me anything, but it was nice to hear.

My heart warmed as Atlas replied, "I know, Prez, but if I get close, charm her, she'll go outta her way to look after him better seein' as he's my brother. Did you see how that bitch fucked off and left him?"

My smile froze.

"You're a fuckin' asshole," John grunted.

A short bark of laughter. "I'll take one for the team. The Doc's easy on the eye but not enough ass for my likin'. She's got the body of a fifteen-year-old boy. Never stuck it to a man-bitch with more muscles than me. I'll let you know how that shit goes."

My body jerked like I'd been struck. I raised my hand and leaned against the wall to steady myself. My knees shook, and hot tears burned my throat.

John groaned. "Shut the fuck up with that bullshit."

I sucked back a sob, turned, and ran back to my office. Dazed, I opened the door, slipped inside, and pressed a hand to my heated cheeks. My mind went back to our kiss. The floodgates opened, and a tear slipped down my cheek when I remembered how he brought me back to life.

She's got the body of a fifteen-year-old boy.

I winced as all my old insecurities came surging back. I'd never really thought that there was anything majorly wrong with me before, but at that minute, I hated myself.

I'd always known that I wasn't idealistically sexy like Kennedy. Compared to her, I was petite. I definitely wasn't anything like the reality stars with big butts and sexy pouts, but I'd never experienced a man being so blatantly turned off by me before.

No wonder he couldn't wait to get out of there.

Atlas was out of my league in looks, body, and confidence. Why did I ever think that he'd want a broken woman like me?

The spark of hope that danced in my chest flickered and died. It was evident that I'd been right about something all along.

My judgment was way off.

Chapter Three

Sophie ~ Four Weeks Ago

The ringing of my cell phone startled me awake.
I sat bolt upright and stared ahead, dazedly wondering who the hell was calling me in the dead of night. I rubbed at my burning eyes, taking in the time on my cell, which was lit up next to me on my nightstand.

It was just after one a.m.

My first thought was that something must be wrong. I mean, who makes calls in the early hours of the morning unless it's an emergency?

Jesus, what if I was lying here waiting for my cell to answer itself, and Ned or one of the kids needed me?

I grabbed the phone, stabbed the green button, and held it to my ear. "Hello?"

A deep voice said, "Doc? It's John Stone."

I let out a relieved breath before indignation washed through me. "Do you know what the time is? I've only been asleep an hour."

"Yeah. Sorry, but we have a bit of an emergency here. I'd be indebted to ya if you could come to the clubhouse. Gotta man coming in with a GSW to the shoulder."

I rubbed my eyes. "Are you crazy? If he needs medical attention, take him to the Emergency Department."

"No can do. It's an umm... a delicate matter. You're the only one I trust with it."

My hand went to my aching temple and rubbed it. "John. I could lose my license if I treat somebody under the table." But I was already throwing back my comforter.

"You got my word," John said quietly. "It won't get out."

I sighed. "Okay, but it's going to cost you."

He barked out a laugh. "Ten grand, okay?"

I grabbed my jeans. "The children's ward will be very grateful. What equipment have you got there?"

"Freya says it's basic, but it'll work for what you need."

"Right," I murmured. "See you in twenty."

Eighteen minutes later, I drove through the Speed Demon's compound gates, parked outside the main doors, and turned off my engine.

John was outside the building waiting for me with Freya and an older man who I recognized, but hadn't been introduced to yet.

I grabbed my medical bag, got out of the car, and lifted my hand in greeting. "Where's the patient?" I asked as I walked over toward them.

"They're on their way back now," John informed me. "They got a couple'a kids with 'em too that may need checkin' out."

"What happened?" I asked. "Are you getting me involved in something I'm not going to like?"

Atlas

John looked at the other man and winced slightly. "They ran into some trouble on a recon mission. Some kids were in trouble, and my boys helped them, but Atlas got shot in the process."

My heart jolted. "Atlas?"

Freya nodded. "It's a shoulder wound. He was running around after it happened, so I don't think the bullet did significant damage, but Cash said he's losing a lot of blood.

I chewed on my lip as I remembered what had happened at the hospital. After what I overhead Atlas say about me, I completely ghosted him. Every time he visited Bowie, I made sure I was somewhere else. On the one occasion I saw him in Magnolia's, I avoided his stare. Then a woman came in and started to paw at him, and my chest began to ache, so I left.

I tried not to think about him, but at moments I'd find myself reliving our kiss. As much as I hated to admit it, he hurt me, which was stupid considering I hardly knew him. He just never came across as the type of person who would belittle me like that. Not only did he prove me wrong, but he also proved that I couldn't trust myself to pick someone decent.

The older man shook his head. "Trouble follows that fucker. This is a normal working day for him." He held his hand out to me. "I saw you at the hospital when you treated Bowie. I'm Abe."

I took his palm and shook it. "Sophie."

"I know. We're much obliged that you're helpin' the club out like this, Doc."

I smiled. "It's fine. John's compensating me by donating to a good cause."

Abe grinned. "I'd expect nothin' less. Good on ya."

We turned toward the door, and it opened. A beautiful guy stood at the entrance with an iPad in his hand. I stared up at him, blown away by his piercing blue eyes.

Jesus. I thought to myself. *It's like America's Next Top Biker Model in this place.*

"Just tracked Cash," the pretty man said in a deep voice. "They're a few minutes away."

"Come on," Freya said quietly. "I'll take you down to the infirmary. We can set up."

"You've got an infirmary?" I asked, wide-eyed.

"Yeah," she replied. "But it's pretty basic. It's set up a bit like a field hospital. Not as sophisticated, but you should have everything you need for the injuries coming in." She took my arm and led me toward the doors. "Thanks for coming. I would have dealt with it, but GSWs are a bit out of my league."

"They're not an everyday occurrence for me either," I murmured as I followed her through a huge bar and into a corridor. "But we'll assess the patient and take it from there. We'll have to fill him with antibiotics because we're not working in a sterile environment."

"I disinfected the rooms before you arrived," Freya replied. "They're as clean as they can be, and I've sterilized all the equipment."

We walked inside a room containing a hospital bed. Next to it was a blood pressure monitor and a portable drip holder. Freya had set a tray of instruments up on a table next to the bed. An adjustable surgery light was already shining through the room.

"There's medication in the fridge, and I left Atlas' personal file out." She pointed to a clear plastic wallet. "It holds his stats, blood type, allergies, everything you need to know."

I picked up the file and began to read. "Danny Woods," I whispered. It suited him. "He's type A-positive. He's lucky because he can take blood off almost anyone."

She thought for a second. "Dad and Cash are both O-positive. I can probably drum up some more if you give me a few minutes to check more club members' medical files."

I snapped the file shut. "No, that should be enough if both men donate. Can you set that up for me?" I took my stethoscope from my med bag and positioned it around my neck.

"Of course," she said as she went to open the door. A commotion sounded from down the hall. Seconds later, a huddle of huge men wearing cuts carried Atlas into the room.

"Settle him over there," I ordered, pointing to the bed.

The men complied.

John stalked into the room with another tall, handsome, built-up guy. He had the same golden eyes as - I assumed - his dad. "We've got two kids with us who were in the van when it crashed," he told John.

"Are they lucid?" I asked, snapping some latex gloves on.

He turned to me. "Yeah. Both talking and coherent, but the girl took a blow to the noggin, and the boy's arm's hanging at an angle."

I looked at Freya. "This patient's injuries take precedence. Assist me, then go and do an initial assessment on the other two. You're looking for breaks and concussions."

Her face paled, and she bit her lip nervously.

"Freya." My voice was curt. "Can you do that?"

Her face took on a determined look, and she gave a nod.

The men who had positioned Atlas moved away from the bed, muttering and cursing amongst themselves.

"Everyone out except John," I ordered.

"You stay too, Cash," Freya said to the handsome guy. "We need blood."

"We need to go vein to vein. Can you do that?" I asked, adopting the tone of a surgeon in the ER. I knew from experience that it would subconsciously help Freya focus.

Taking my own cue, I began to morph into doctor mode as I looked down to assess Atlas' injuries. The instant I caught sight of him, all the air in the room seemed to go cold.

His skin was grey and pallid. Blood covered the entire front of his shirt. Some of it had streaked across his face and into his cropped dark hair.

His colossal body looked smaller somehow, his muscles less pronounced. He didn't look like him, which shocked me because every time I'd seen this man before, he was larger than life.

My heart and brain stuttered at the same time. I hated seeing Atlas like that, even though I had every right to detest him. It just seemed all wrong, like the universe was out of whack somehow. This huge character that boomed and barked was now small and muted, and I didn't like it one bit.

I pushed my visceral reaction down into the pit of my gut. Atlas may have affected me, but he was also an asshole.

Assessing him, I focused on his pallor. "We need blood now," I stated, glancing up at John. "Freya said that you and her brother are O-positive?"

John nodded. "I think Bowie is too. Anything you want, Doc."

Freya began to hook Atlas up to the heart rate monitor, and after a minute, it beeped to life. She snapped on some gloves and placed a sterile bandage over Atlas' wound.

"What sedative and how much?" I asked.

Freya rattled off the names of the medication that we had available and suggested which ones we could use. Taking the patient's weight into consideration, she told me the appropriate dosage.

Atlas

"Good job," I said, placing my stethoscope on different areas of Atlas' chest and listening for suspect noises. "Now, start the transfer. He needs blood."

"On it, Doctor," Freya replied.

I turned to Cash. "Can you roll him slightly? I need to see his back."

The man strolled over, grabbed Atlas' shoulder, and shoved him onto his side like a sack of potatoes.

"Jesus," I murmured, checking for signs of the bullet. "You can roll him back now."

The guy grinned and dropped him. He let out a barking laugh at my wince. "Fucker needs some payback," he muttered. "He'd be doin' a lot worse if it was me lyin' there. He'd have drawn a dick on my face by now."

John let out a chuckle. "My boy ain't wrong."

I shook my head, glancing at Freya, who was just about to stick a needle in her dad's vein. "How are you doing there, Doctor Stone?"

"Once Cash sits down, I can draw his blood. Dad's almost ready, but first, I need to set Atlas' needle up."

I checked his pulse. "There's no exit wound, so I've got to fish for the bullet. Can you assist me once you've finished? After I get the bullet out, I can give him more blood. Then while I'm stitching him up, you can examine the other patients."

Cash took his shirt off, sat next to his dad, and held out his arm. "Stick me, Sis." He nodded toward Atlas. "And hurry up. That fucknut's lookin' pale."

I looked up as the door opened to see Bowie poke his head around it. "Need anythin'?" he asked.

"Yeah. We need your claret," John replied. "Sit your ass down and let Freya sort ya."

"What the fuck happened out there?" Bowie asked as he took off his cut and sat next to Cash. "Thought it was just recon."

"Is it ever just recon with that one?" John asked with a snort. "Fucker thinks he's John Wick in a cut."

"Wick's cool as fuck, and his ass ain't that fat," Bowie nodded toward Atlas.

Cash grinned. "His mouth ain't as fat either." He looked at me pointedly, then at his dad. "I'll debrief when we're done. Gotta go check on my woman first."

"Club comes before that, Son," John said pointedly.

"Never before her," Cash retorted. "Don't start, Pop. I've had the night from hell. Just wanna curl up next to Cara and sleep for a week."

Bowie looked at Cash incredulously. "How the fuck did you get Cara to agree to sleep in your room with you? Last time you were together, she was running for the fuckin' hills."

Cash grinned. "She sleeps like the dead. What she don't know won't hurt her."

Freya made a noise in the back of her throat.

"Ow!" Cash yelled, glaring at his sister. "What the fuck did you do that for?"

She held up a needle. "You're a dick. You can't sleep next to Cara without her knowing about it."

"Why?" Cash asked, face confused. "It's not like I'm gonna fuck her."

Freya craned her neck and looked at John. "Dad. Tell him."

John chuckled. "Nope. I'm holdin' out for front-row seats so I can watch Wildcat chop his nuts off."

Cash winced.

Freya and Bowie laughed.

I carried on examining Atlas and kept my mouth shut.

These people were crazy, loop the loop, straight jacket wearing, needed supervision in public places, nutjobs. But something about their banter drew me in. Their closeness and evident love for each other shone

Atlas

through the room and caused a yearning to burn inside my belly.

I'd never had that. Ned was family, but she wasn't blood. My mom was amazing, and I knew she loved me, but it was just her and me after dad died. She tried her best but had to work long hours to keep a roof over our heads because every cent Dad left us went toward my college fund and subsequent med school fees.

I was a latchkey kid, meaning I made my own way home from school, fed myself, and kept my own company. I had friends, but nobody especially close until I met Ned. That shaped me, so when Mom died and left me alone, I looked for a family in the wrong places.

Hence my marriage to Luke.

I was startled as Freya appeared next to me with John and began to slide a needle into Atlas' arm. "I'm ready if you want to go bullet hunting," she said quietly. "I'll hook Dad up to Atlas, and then I'll set up an IV for Cash's blood."

The long tweezers glinted in the bright light of the surgical lamp as I picked them up. "Glad the big man's out for the count. This may hurt a bit." I bent to Atlas' shoulder, took off the sterile strip, and went to work.

The heart monitor began to make a loud noise.

I let out a quiet curse and put the tweezers down.

"His BP's dropping," Freya said urgently.

I checked at his pallor; his skin had turned deathly white. "He's lost too much blood. Get him hooked up to John. Now, Freya."

She did as I told her.

"Don't worry about hurting him," I said urgently. "Get that line in him. You need to get his artery."

The machine seemed to scream at us.

Heart pounding, I jumped on the bed, straddled Atlas, and began CPR. "Is it done?" I demanded.

"Just a second," Freya said. "Just give me one minute... There! It's in." I turned to watch her stand John next to the bed and hold his arm up for the vein-to-vein transfusion.

Turning back to Atlas, I continued chest compressions.

The machines screamed even louder.

I grabbed Atlas' face, opened his mouth with both hands, and breathed hard into it. As soon as his lungs were full, I pulled back and began chest compressions again.

The machine kept beeping loudly.

"Doc?" John demanded.

I ignored him and repeated my actions once, then again. "Come on, come on," I murmured as I pressed down on his hard chest.

Suddenly the machine quietened. After a few seconds, the beeps began to slow down.

I closed my eyes, trying to calm my galloping heart.

"Jesus," John said, his face as pale as Atlas'. "I thought we'd lost him."

"Good job, Doc," Cash muttered. "My ass was nippin' for a minute there."

I climbed off the bed, leaned back on it, and ran a trembling hand through my hair. "Yeah," I murmured. "Mine was too."

An hour later, I was patching up Atlas' shoulder.

John, Bowie, and Cash were umming and ahh-ing over the bullet I'd just removed as they passed it between them.

"It's a twenty-two," John said and looked at Bowie. "Same make as the one that got you."

"We should get it analyzed," Cash muttered. "It'd be interestin' to see if it's related to Bowie's slug. If it was, we could connect the Sinners with Henderson Junior. Especially as his gun didn't turn out to be the shooter."

"Imagine that," Bowie said thoughtfully. "Henderson and the Burnin' Sinners in cahoots. That's a partnership made in hell."

"Wait until you find out what happened tonight, Bo," Cash muttered. "I've got theories coming outta my asshole."

"Boys," John barked. He widened his eyes at the other men before glancing at Freya and me. "Save it for later, yeah?"

Cash and Bowie nodded.

Freya rolled her eyes. "Ignore them, Sophie. You'll learn that we're good enough to bail them out when they need a doctor, but woe betide they tell us why."

"Freya!" John barked.

She shrugged. "It's true. I don't know why I let it bother me. I should be used to it by now."

"It's for your own good," Cash explained. "Pigs can't arrest ya if you don't know anything."

"True," Freya snipped. "They'll just arrest us for carrying out unauthorized surgeries, and then we'd get struck off the medical register."

An awkward silence filled the room.

"Look," I said, trying to alleviate the tension. "I'd rather not know anyway. I'll go home after all this is over and get on with my life." I turned to Freya and tried to change the subject. "You did great. Are you okay with seeing to the other injuries while I stitch up the big man here?"

"Of course."

"Come back if there's anything you're not sure of. I'll make my way in soon and check on them too." I pulled a stool toward the bed and began preparing the sutures. "You'll do great."

Freya lingered by the door for a few seconds. "Thank you for tonight, Sophie. I've learned a lot," she grinned. "I've never done a vein-to-vein transfusion before."

I shrugged nonchalantly. "I wouldn't have known that. You did a good job."

A slight grin played around her lips as she opened the door.

John and the other two men followed her. As he reached the exit, John stopped and looked at me over his shoulder. "Thanks for tonight, Doc. Atlas is important to the club. You'll never meet a more stand-up brother. You did the world a favor tonight by keepin' him in it."

I injected some anesthetic into the area around the gunshot wound. "It's not my job to know about the people I treat, John. I'm just here to try and help them live."

"Right," he said quietly and turned to leave.

"John," I called.

He stopped but didn't turn around.

"Next time one of your boys gets shot, do me a favor and take them to the ER."

He stilled for a few seconds, then jerked a nod and left.

I steadied my hand and began gently cleaning around the wound, taking my time to ensure the area was germ-free. I wiped some iodine over the skin – an old-fashioned technique I still swore by – then began to sew.

The rhythmic rise and fall of Atlas' chest seemed somehow comforting as I stitched his wound, pressing the skin together with the fingers from my left hand while weaving tiny stitches with the right.

He was going to have a scar from the entry point. I could try and make it less pronounced with how I sewed him back together, but I doubted that he was the type of man to care about that.

I let out a quiet snort. Atlas would show it off like a badge of honor.

His scent, leather, and spice settled around me. I couldn't help liking it. He smelled fresh and well, manly.

I'd thought about him a lot over the months. I'd also gone over what he said about me a million times. It was strange how I could feel so let down by someone I hardly knew.

Atlas

He was the first man since Luke to make me feel something. Maybe that was why it was so hard to forget him. It was crazy how one minute he made me feel so beautiful and the next so lacking.

I was so intent on my thoughts that I didn't notice his breathing change. It was only when he let out a quiet groan that I realized he'd awakened.

My eyes flew up and met his almost black ones.

He was staring at me with a soft grin playing around his lips. "Good technique you got there. Those are some nice stitches." His usually booming voice was muted and rough with sleep.

I couldn't help smiling at him, relief washing through me that he was awake.

My eyes flickered between his.

The air around us seemed to thicken. Suddenly I couldn't bear to look at Atlas' intensity. It was too much. My eyes dipped to his shoulder, and I bit the inside of my cheek.

A strong hand gripped my hip, and I shivered slightly as his fingers stroked over my jeans. His touch seemed to burn, and I swear my clit sang the Hallelujah Chorus. My gaze swung back up to his. Our faces were so close that our breaths mingled together.

"It's like you're breathing life back into me," he murmured, his soft lips almost touching mine. His dark eyes locked with mine like he could see down into my soul.

My throat heated because I wanted so much to believe his pretty words, but how could I? He'd proven that I couldn't trust him, even though everything inside me yearned to.

He blinked rapidly, his glazed eyes slowly becoming more aware. His head reared back slightly, and a cocky grin spread across his face. "Stitch," he said in a sexy low voice.

"What?" I asked, still caught under his spell.

His eyes flashed, and he smirked. "Gimme a little suck, babe."

My belly dropped. The air seemed to freeze around me as I stared at him, shocked. "You want me to give you a blow job?"

He lifted his arms and put his hands behind his head. "It may take a minute for me to get goin', but it's all yours, baby."

My entire body went rigid.

He boomed a laugh. "Don't look so shocked, Stitch. I'll give you a second chance even though you ghosted my ass last time." His voice dropped. "S'okay. I won't hold a grudge. You're good to go."

"Good to go?" I parroted.

He suddenly frowned. "Are you simple, babe? Chop, chop. Ain't got all fuckin' night. Got things to do, people to see." He circled his hips off the bed. "Don't stress, won't take long, gotta few days' worth in there. It's been a slow week."

A slight ache gripped my heart as I continued to stare at him.

He was handsome in a rough way with his dark eyes, short, cropped hair, and well-kept beard. He had women everywhere; I'd seen it first-hand. I was stupid to think that I was special. He'd shown me what he thought of me six months ago, and I should have taken note.

I straightened, grabbed the scissors from the tray and finished up.

"You good?" he asked me gruffly.

"Yeah. I am now." I cut the suture and taped a bandage over his wound. "There's a major risk of infection. Ask Freya to change your dressing twice a day. She'll know what to look out for. If you feel faint, tired, or generally unwell, go to the ER." I stood, peeled my gloves off, and went to the basin to wash my hands.

"Stitch!" he barked.

Atlas

"My name's Sophie Green." I craned my neck. "You need to take things easy until your wound heals. Lay off the recon."

He had the good sense to look sheepish.

"I mean it," I continued. "An infection could kill you. Take it seriously." I wondered how I could sound so professional when my insides were trembling so hard. "I'll write you a script for painkillers and give it to Freya. Rest for now. I'll send her in soon to top up your IV."

He sat up and smirked. "Was it too soon to ask for a cock suck?"

I dried my hands.

Asshole.

"How 'bout dinner?" he asked, watching me rub anti-bac gel into my palms.

I dropped the bottle into my medical bag before turning to face him angrily. "How about you show me some respect?"

His lip curled. "How 'bout you earn it."

I grabbed my things, made my way to the door, and pulled it open. "How about you fuck off? I don't need to earn your respect, Atlas because I don't care enough to have it." My eyes traveled from his handsome face, over his tattooed skin, and down to his jeans, then I shook my head disparagingly, turned, and walked out.

Dick.

A half-hour later, I walked back into the hallway with Freya after watching her examine Mason and Sera. Luckily I hadn't had time to think about Atlas and his mean mouth.

"How do we check for concussion?" I asked.

"Watch for signs of delirium and sickness," she said without pause. "Wake the patient regularly to ensure they can awaken normally."

"Good. I'm impressed, Doctor Sto…." My voice trailed off as I caught sight of a woman with fire-engine red hair sauntering toward us down the corridor. She wore a tight, low-cut tee and booty shorts. Her brightly made-up face looked like a ten-year-old had gotten into her mom's makeup.

"Cherry. What are you doing here?" Freya demanded. "This area's off-limits to club girls."

My heart froze. Club girls? Like in Sons of Anarchy? *Jesus.* I thought that was all made up for the TV show.

"Hey," the woman drawled. "Atlas called up for me. He wants, umm, some attention." Her tongue poked at the inside of her cheek, leaving no doubt as to what attention she meant.

My mouth suddenly went dry.

The bastard had got a girl down here to give him oral sex, knowing I'd see how easily he replaced me. I'd come to the club to care for him. All he'd done was mess with me. He really was a disgusting asshole.

I breathed through the ache in my chest.

Stupidly, even after what happened at the hospital, a tiny part of me had still held out hope that he wasn't really the asshole he'd shown me. He was the first man who had caught my attention in years, and like a fool, I'd looked past the countless red flags and still tried to give him the benefit of the doubt.

I'd heard people talk about how great he was, how he protected the club and their families. Somehow, I'd spun a little fantasy in my head that I could have that too. I'd developed feelings for him, but they'd come back to bite me in the ass.

At that moment, I decided something.

No more.

Love wasn't on the cards for me. I kept choosing men who hurt me, not just physically but emotionally too. I was better off alone. At least that way, I wouldn't keep getting so disappointed.

I turned and walked inside Atlas' room.

He was lounging on the bed, not a care in the world. His stare went over my shoulder, and he smirked. "Yo.

Atlas

Cherry. That was quick." His eyes slid to me, and he cocked an eyebrow. "You stayin' for some fun too, Doc?"

Pain stabbed through my heart and suddenly, I was the one bleeding out.

"Atlas. What are you doing?" Freya asked in a confused voice.

He cocked a thick eyebrow. "You know the score, Frey. You're either in or get out."

I slowly opened my eyes, and our stares locked.

Hurt must have been slashed across my features because his eyes seemed to soften for a second. Then he caught himself, and his expression hardened again.

"Get gone," he rasped. "Unless you're joinin' in."

Still staring into his eyes, I nodded slowly. This was precisely what I needed to really move on. He'd done me a favor, and I was suddenly grateful that I hadn't gotten mixed up with him.

"Be careful that you don't bust your stitches." I turned blindly and hurried out of the room.

He called after me, but I didn't look back. What was the point? He was him, and I was me. We were oil and water, and I didn't want another relationship where the man I cared for thought it was okay to treat me like shit.

I just needed to go home, call Ned, talk it out, and move on like I always did because one thing was for sure.

Danny 'Atlas' Woods had shown me who he was, and I didn't care for it.

Chapter Four

Atlas ~ The Next Day

Somethin' didn't feel right. My insides ached, and it felt like I wanted to throw up. It must've been down to the bullet hole in my shoulder.

"No!" Prez barked at me. "You're laid up, and you're on a time fuckin' out, Danny Dickwad. Hendrix can do the honors instead."

I looked up at the heavens and blew out an angry breath. What was up their asses? I was only havin' a bit'a fun with the hot little doc. Anyone would think I'd killed her kitten, though to be fair, I wouldn't have minded takin' a shot at destroyin' her pussy.

My cock twitched.

"You shouldn't be such an asshole then, should ya?" Hendrix snapped before turning to face my brother. "What's your take on it, Cash?"

I dragged my thoughts outta the gutter and back to the conversation I was having with my brothers.

"Sera doesn't seem like she's one of theirs. She's not a drug addict. She's just a kid" Cash explained to the VP. "We need to find out what her and Mason's involvement is and go from there."

Drix nodded thoughtfully. "Right. You ask the questions; I'll back you up. They already know you, and you're the one who got 'em safe last night, so they'll open up to you more."

He was right. Last night, Cash was their knight in leather armor. Out of everyone, they'd trust him the most. "Yeah," I agreed. "If they're gonna talk to anyone, it'll be Cash."

Prez scraped a hand through his beard. "You said it looked like they were takin' her somewhere against her will?"

"Yeah," Cash affirmed. "It didn't look good, Pop."

Prez's eyes narrowed. I could tell he was hatching somethin'. "Offer her protection, him too. If they know the Demons have their backs, they may give us some shit that we can use."

The VP clapped Prez on the back. "Good idea." He turned to Cash and nodded toward the hallway. "Come on. Time to dance." He made his way into the corridor, Cash followin'.

A grimace stole across my face as I watched them leave. "Fuckers," I muttered.

Prez shot me a glare. "What the fuck's that supposed to mean?"

I threw out my arm toward the door and winced when the action pulled my stitches tight. "I'm the SAA. I should be doin' the interrogation."

"They're fuckin' kids, Atlas," Prez snapped. "They don't need the rack and thumbscrews." His hard stare swept over my made-up face, which the girls had done fifteen minutes before. "Anyway, you look like a bad fuckin' drag queen. How you gonna put the shits up someone when you look like you're about to burst into a Judy Garland song any fuckin' minute?"

Ice roared with laughter.

Bowie snickered. "He's right. You look like you're goin' to a trans party."

"Or a gay bar." Ice laughed.

Atlas

Colt began to tap on his iPad. "That's a bit of a generalization, Iceman. Would you believe that many drag artists aren't gay? Many are bi, some even straight. It's purely a career choice."

Fuck me. I dropped my head into my hands.

Fine whisky eyes flashed through my mind. Smooth, porcelain skin, long eyelashes, and bee-stung lips with a sexy little mole on the cupid's bow that I suddenly envisaged my cum drippin' off. I thought about how tight and compact her little body felt when I stroked my thumb across her hip, and my cock began to thicken for the second time.

Annoyingly, the doc's pretty face had been floatin' around inside my noggin since the first time I locked lips with her at the hospital, back when Bowie got shot. In a moment of madness, I'd asked her out and regretted it almost immediately. Luckily, she didn't hold me to it.

Whenever I saw her in town, I managed to avoid talkin' to her. Not that she cared seein' as she never approached me either.

I bristled slightly at that thought, even though I had enough on my plate without addin' a woman into the mix. With my SAA duties and now the Sinners' bullshit, I had to focus on the club. They'd hunted Cara the night before. How could I bring a woman into that shitshow? Nope. It wouldn't be fair.

I ignored the burn that seared through my chest and turned toward the sound of footsteps comin' from the corridor. Everyone whipped around to watch Abe stalk inside.

He saw me, and his steps faltered. "What the fuck happened to you?"

"Gabby and Sunshine gave him a makeover," Bowie muttered with a laugh.

Abe held out a hand and pointed at me. "You're a fuckin' asshole."

Prez smiled wryly. "You only just worked that one out?"

"Just been speakin' to Freya," Abe hissed. "And I've concluded that you need to learn some fuckin' respect, boy. Bet the doc wishes she'd let you die a slow, painful death. Can't say I'd blame her."

Shit, Abe only called me 'boy' when he was ragin'. Suddenly his words registered, and my gut bounced. "Die? What the fuck are you talkin' about, old man? I ain't goin' nowhere."

His eyes swung to Prez. "Didn't you tell him?"

Dagger shrugged. "Thought Freya did."

"Can someone tell me what the fuck's goin' on?" I demanded.

"Oh, I'll fuckin' tell you alright, asswipe." Abe stomped toward my hospital bed, eyes spitting hellfire. "Last night, you lost so much blood that you began to code. Freya just told me that Doctor Sophie leaped on the bed and CPR'd you back to life while shoutin' out instructions for Freya to set up your blood transfusion." His eyes narrowed angrily. "You'd have met your maker if she hadn't got outta bed after workin' a double at the hospital, then driven here in sub-zero temperatures to deal with your gung-ho ass. But what *really* gets me pissed is that Frey then tells me how an hour later, you threw the doc out so you could get a fuckin' blow job off Cherry!"

Prez's mouth thinned to an angry slash. "Already fined him for bein' a cunt." He turned to the club's secretary. "I dunno what's gotten into the fucker.

My stare dipped 'cause suddenly I couldn't look at Prez or Abe. Somethin' crept through my gut, an emotion I wasn't used to feeling.

Goddamned regret.

Down in my bones, I knew I'd done wrong. Sophie was a cool chick. Sweet, cute, and intelligent. She'd done a lot for the club, savin' Bowie's life and comin' to treat

Atlas

my ungrateful ass. She also assisted us with the DNA tests that helped catch that Henderson fucker.

All I'd done in return was act the asshole.

God only knew what had gotten into me. Friends of the Demons deserved almost as much respect as the brothers. Usually, I'd check on 'em, make sure they were good, and extend the club's protection to 'em, but I needed to keep Sophie at arm's length.

I'd seen how she looked at me, sensed her interest, and it was best to stay away from her for the club's sake. So, I'd ensured she did precisely that by actin' the fool and flauntin' women in her face. One time I saw her in Magnolia's, so I called the club and got a girl down there to put on a show.

If I was honest with myself, she unsettled me, and I couldn't afford that.

The second I lost focus, people would get hurt, and that shit was unacceptable. Look what happened to Bowie. I'd already dropped the ball. I couldn't afford to let my brothers down again.

My eyes slid back to Abe's. "I didn't get a fuckin' blow job, alright? The doc was makin' eyes at me, so I showed her that I was a bad bet."

Every eye snapped to face me.

"What the fuck are you whinin' about?" Prez barked. "You? A bad bet?"

Tech boy went back to his iPad, shakin' his head.

"Fuckin' idiot," Abe muttered.

Ice looked at me and shrugged.

I held my hands up. "Don't want a woman. Ain't got time for that shit. We're gettin' hit from all sides. I need to keep my focus."

Prez stared thoughtfully at me for a minute.

"Fuckin' prick!" Abe rasped. "Whiny, good for nothin' little scrotum."

"Fuck you, Abe." I glared. "Keep ya goddamned nose outta my business."

Ice cleared his throat. "Err. Atlas, you sure you're not gonna go there with the doc? It's just that I think she's cool, ya know? If you're not gonna make a play, I will."

A burn swept through my chest, and before I could stop myself, I barked, "No!"

Ice absentmindedly rubbed at the back of his neck. "No, you don't care? Or no, I can't ask her out?"

I sat forward, starin' daggers at him. "You touch her, and I'll rip your fucking nuts off. She's off-limits."

A snarl escaped Abe. "No, boy. It don't work like that. If you don't want her, she's fair game. You can't slap a reserved sticker on her ass and tuck her away from everyone else. Either do a shit or get off the pot."

I turned to Prez, jaw clenchin'. "They're irritatin' me, boss. Tell 'em to stand down."

Dagger smirked. "Nah."

My chest almost exploded. "I'm tellin' ya, Boss, if anyone so much as touches her, I'll-"

"-You'll what? Beat 'em up?" Abe let out a snort. "I've put better men than you on their asses. Horrible little pissant."

"Okay, okay. Let's deal with this like brothers." Prez looked at me. "Are you gonna try to get to know the doc or not?"

Every obstacle loomed large.

It wasn't the right time for me to bring a woman into the fold. I had a club to protect. She was a cutie, no doubt about that, but my needs and wants had to sit down and shut the fuck up.

Bile burned the back'a my throat at the thought of what I was turnin' down. I shook my head jerkily.

Prez stroked his beard. "Then, like it or not, that makes her available. Last night proved she's a decent woman. I like her. She'd be a good friend to the club, and let's face it, havin' a doctor in the fold will be a grade-A addition. Plus, she can keep her mouth shut." He gave Ice a nod. "You got my blessin', brother."

Atlas

My teeth gnashed so hard that I was in danger of cracking a molar.

"Church this afternoon," Prez continued, turnin' back to me. "You good to go?"

"Yeah," I muttered resignedly. "Need a painkiller shot, though."

"Just as well the doc left a couple here then," Prez retorted. "See, she's takin' care of ya even though you acted the fool." He made his way toward the door. "Freya's on her way back to sort ya. When she's done, get your ass up and start movin' around. I want a meetin' in my office an hour before Church starts to go over the offense plan before we put it to the brothers. And we need to discuss any information Cash and Drix get from the kids."

"I'll be there," I said to my brothers' backs as they followed the boss man into the door.

Prez craned his neck. "Make sure you are," he ordered before disappearing down the hallway.

The doc's face flashed through my brain again. That thought morphed into an image of her and Iceman together, and I let out a quiet growl.

I leaned back and banged my head gently on the wall behind me once, then again, deep in thought. One thing was for sure, the pretty little doc had gotten me all bent outta shape.

I'd been a dick to her. It wasn't like me to disrespect good people, and I didn't particularly like that I'd acted that way. She didn't deserve that shit, and after what Abe had just told me, I knew I'd gone too far.

I looked at the table next to the bed and grabbed my cell, then I tapped on the call log and waited. After a few rings, she answered. "Everything okay, Atlas?"

"Freya," I barked. "Get your ass over here pronto and gimme my painkiller shot. There's someone I gotta go see."

Jules Ford

I parked my truck and stared at the doc's cute lil' house.

It had been built in the Craftsman style typical of the area. The outside was painted white with wooden porch steps leading up to a green front door. A painted white decorative iron table sat inside the porch with two white wooden chairs with sky blue seating pads tied on.

If ever a house suited Sophie, this was it. I couldn't imagine living among all the fuckin' cuteness, but I bet the doc loved it.

She'd probably turn her cute little nose up if she saw my room at the clubhouse. She was all diamonds and pearls; I was all motor oil and whisky.

There was no way we'd suit.

I swung the driver's door open and jumped down from my truck. My shoulder jarred as I hit the ground, and I winced slightly.

Couldn't wait for the weather to turn warmer so I could get back on my bike. It had been snowin' on and off for the last month. We had to stick to cages seein' as it was too dangerous to ride, plus bein' on a bike for too long in minus temperatures would make us freeze to death.

I looked up at the house and made my way up the wooden steps. A cold breeze swept through the open porch area, and a shiver ran down my back. Makin' a fist, I banged twice on the door. She was home 'cause her silver Equinox was parked out front. I raised my hand again and thumped hard. "Yo! Stitch!" I bellowed impatiently.

A loud crash and a screech sounded from inside.

I stilled.

My base instincts kicked in. Bending low, I ran around the house toward the backyard in stealth mode.

Atlas

Visions of Sophie bein' attacked by an intruder pinged through my mind. My jaw clenched. Base instincts screamed at me to ensure she was safe.

I slipped my hand into the inside pocket of my cut to grab my Smith and Wesson, which was secure in the body holster I always wore. A quiet curse flew outta my mouth when I considered that I hadn't put my BPV on that mornin' 'cause of my stitches.

Fuck.

I grimaced at the painful throbbing in my shoulder, but I pushed my discomfort down. Stitch could've been in trouble. I forced myself to concentrate on the house, listenin' for any clues. Scufflin' noises sounded, and my blood ran cold when another loud screech cut through the air.

"Vic. That hurt. Get off me. Jesus, you've made me bleed."

My gut froze.

I worked out the entry and exit points as if on autopilot. There were two choices. Either go through the open window, all guns blazin', or creep through the back door and take the fucker by surprise.

My mind whirred, lungs on fire at the thought of someone puttin' their hands on Sophie. I tamped down the burn in my chest. If I swept in there, all guns blazing, I'd be in danger of shootin' Stitch. There was no fuckin' way that was acceptable. It was better to go in soft.

My eyes fell on the back door, and I crept toward it. It'd be game over if the motherfucker hurting the doc saw me. The thought of that sent my gut churnin'.

Another pained shriek pierced the air. My plan flew outta my head. All I could think of was gettin' to her, makin' her safe, and then annihilating the fucker who thought he could lay his hands on a good woman.

I reached for the handle and twisted. It swung wide open to reveal a cloakroom of sorts, containin' coats, boots, and other outdoorsy shit. My fists clenched. That fuckin' door should've been locked.

I inched my way through, keepin' my weapon raised while I crept silently toward the room where Sophie was bein' held.

My heart hammered, my veins thumpin' along with it. Heat rose through my chest at the mere thought of her bruised and bleeding.

Who the fuck would hurt a decent woman like her? A woman who worked hard, who helped people. She deserved some goddamned peace of mind for all the shit she went through on the daily.

The door leadin' to the kitchen was ajar. I glanced around the small room and took a mental note of any obstacles that may have impaired me gettin' Stitch outta there.

It all looked clear.

I froze as another piercin' scream echoed from the next room. "Oh, my God! Stop hurting me!"

My hair-trigger temper unraveled, and a lighting bolt of fury smashed into my chest. Before I could stop myself, I let out a warrior's roar and bolted into the room, gun cocked and ready to fire.

"Get your motherfuckin' hands where I can see them!" I bellowed before heavin' out a pained "Oof" as an arm flew out and knocked my gun outta my hands. Another punch struck my kidneys from the back, effectively winding me.

I sucked in a breath and twisted toward the assailant, completely forgettin' my wound. The stitches in my shoulder ripped apart as I turned to face my attacker. The pain took my breath away, but I ignored it and got into an offensive position.

I bounced on the balls of my feet, pulling my fists up. "I'm gonna kill you, motherf…" The words died on my lips as I caught sight of the doc crouched low with her fists over her face, ready to strike.

Atlas

"Wait," I rasped, droppin' my hands to my sides. "Did you just fuckin' hit me?"

Jesus Christ. She looked like Lara fuckin' Croft dressed in tight, black yoga pants and a fitted black tank held up with tiny straps. A plait ran down each side of her head, accentuating the sexy curve of her neck. My heart gave a jerk at how fucking beautiful she was.

She stood straight and cocked a hip. "What the hell are you doing?" she yelled. "I could've junk punched you."

I looked around the room, tryin' to take my focus away from Doc's tits to where the intruder had gone. The room was empty except for us. "Where'd the fucker go?"

Doc's eyebrows snapped together. "Huh?" She looked around. "Where did who go?"

"The fucker who had his hands on ya." I grated out chest heavin'. "Where is he?"

Her cute face scrunched up, all confused, then her cheeks reddened. "It's not what you think." She pressed her lips together like she was tryin' not to laugh.

My stare darted around the room. "Did he go outta the window?" I lowered my voice. "I won't let him hurt you again, babe." As I spoke, I caught somethin' move outta the corner of my eye. I spun around to see a big grey cat saunterin' toward me with its nose in the air.

Doc snapped her fingers to focus my attention back on her. "Look," she demanded gently.

I turned back to see her holding her arm out straight. Scratches and tiny faint lines of blood covered it.

Doc leaned her head to the left and pointed to her sexy little neck. "She got me there too. Vic's a little demon when she can't get her way."

My heart dropped. "Vic?"

Sophie smiled and pointed at the cat. "Queen Victoria the Second. Queenie when she's sweet, Vic when she's an asshole." Her lips twitched. "I think you may have misunderstood."

I scrubbed a hand down my face.

I'd gone mission impossible over a cat.

Motherfucker.

My skin began to grow uncomfortably hot as I stared at the doc, all tongue tied and twisted up.

This was a first for me. Usually, I was the man with a plan—the capable one. The SAA who commanded respect. Except right then, I felt like a fool. I'd lost control of the situation, and I didn't fuckin' like it. My skin prickled like pins and needles were stabbin' me. The burnin' in my chest was a surefire sign of my anger, but it also held a twinge of humiliation.

I leaned down until our faces were close. "Are you fuckin' crazy?" I snarled.

She shrank back and cowered like she was turnin' in on herself, but I was so goddamned furious that I didn't think about why.

"I thought you were getting beaten," I spat. "I thought some asshole was in here fuckin' abusin' ya." My eyes narrowed. "How fuckin' stupid are you? I could'a fuckin' shot ya."

Her head snapped up, face heated. "How dare you?" she shrieked.

My head reared back. "Don't you get it?" I bellowed back. "I could've hurt ya."

She unfolded her body, her back snapping straight. "Oh, I get it, alright!" she took a step forward. "You break into my house, then you start getting aggressive and shout at me like it's my fault that you jumped to conclusions. Then you've got the bare-assed nerve to blame me because *you* misunderstood what was happening."

I started to retort a reply, but her hand sliced through the air, silencin' me. "No. You've said enough. This is my first day off in six weeks!"

"I don't giv-"

"I said no!" she shrieked.

Atlas

My shoulders tensed 'cause I knew shit was goin' south, fast.

Her eyes flashed, and she shrieked, "Laundry!"

I cocked an eyebrow.

"All I wanted to do today was laundry and play with Queenie. Some days I'm stuck at the hospital for hours, and she misses me. She feels neglected, which is why she's such an asshole." She held her arm out again and pointed to it. "I tried to hug her, but she's giving me the cold shoulder, hence the cat hickeys."

I bit back a grin.

She was cute and goofy as fuck, but what made her even more appealing was that she had no goddamned clue. My eyes flicked over her face, takin' in her pretty features. She was different from the women I usually fucked. I was a big man, so I liked women who had meat on their bones. More petite chicks like her didn't handle me well.

I'd always thought she was good-lookin', but that didn't mean jack in the grand scheme of things 'cause she didn't seem the type to want a no-strings fuck, and it wasn't like I was a man who wanted to go steady.

We were oil and water.

The only ring she'd get outta me was the one up my rear end. If she wanted to go there, that was cool; I'd try anythin' once. But somethin' told me that the doc wasn't an ass chick unless she was holdin' an enema.

There weren't many women I liked, barring family and the ol' ladies, but I liked her. That was dangerous for both of us. The club was at war, for starters, and Prez would see me in the ring if I treated her like I treated my usual fuck buddies. She'd take one look at my lifestyle and run for the goddamned hills. She was an intelligent doctor, for fuck's sake, and I was just a biker.

Time to shut it down.

My lip curled into a sneer. "Are you really that desperate for my attention?"

Jules Ford

Her face dropped.

"You think I don't know when a bitch is panting for me? You wanna fuck, baby? We'll fuck. I'll throw you a bone. Just do me a solid and keep it on the lowdown, huh? Don't want the boys thinkin' I hand out pity fucks. I'd never hear the goddamned end of it."

I heard her sharp intake of breath and suddenly wished I could kick my own ass.

Red stained her cheeks. She blinked a few times before a mask slipped over her face. "Get out of my house," she whispered, voice filled with hurt.

The mangy cat weaved between Sophie's legs. She stooped down, and the feline jumped into her arms. Stitch straightened and cuddled the cat like she was using her as a shield against me.

I forced a smirk onto my face. "Typical prissy bitch, you're all 'fuck me' eyes, but no action. Should'a fuckin' known you were a cock tease."

She stiffened. "I told you to leave. You've got five seconds before I call the cops and have you arrested for trespassing."

I paused for a minute and took her in.

Her smooth, toned body pulled taut like she was ready to strike. Yeah, I was right. This chick took no shit. Even though I was the object of her disgust, I was strangely proud of her.

I gave her a loose salute with two fingers and turned for the door. "See ya around, Stitch baby," I called over my shoulder as I stalked back through the cloakroom.

I heard her let out a brittle laugh. "Unfortunately, you're probably right," she shouted after me. "But when our paths cross, don't bother saying hi, and I'll do the same. I don't need any more assholes in my lif-"

The door slammed behind me, blockin' out her hurt and angry voice. I returned to my truck, got inside, and heaved a breath.

Atlas

Lookin' outta the windshield, I clicked my seatbelt on and fired up the beast. I'd accomplished what I set out to, done the right thing even, but I didn't feel proud of myself in the least.

Her and me were just a fantasy. She was way outta my league.

I switched on my engine, checked my mirrors, and set off to the clubhouse, knowing I'd just saved us both a lot of bullshit.

The question was, if I'd done the right thing, why did I feel so empty?

Chapter Five

Atlas

The Sinners' tatty old compound lit the night like a Christmas tree.

A neon sign above the old wooden door blinked like a beacon leading us to our target. Thumping thrash metal screamed from the tattered old buildin', the wailing echo makin' it appear that the clubhouse was somehow cryin' in pain.

I slowly cracked my neck left then right before droppin' my binoculars and settlin' back in the driver's seat.

"Where is he?" Cash breathed from the back of the SUV. "Come on, Kit, for fuck's sake."

I glanced over my shoulder to see my brother's denim-clad knee bounce furiously as he peered through the window into the night.

His blood brother was alone behind enemy lines. The desperation to get out there and ensure that Breaker was okay almost strangled me, but I tamped that shit down. Rules were rules. We'd thought up a plan and had to stick to it.

"Give him a chance to do his thing," I ordered quietly. "He's good at what he does. Don't underestimate him. He's been trained by the best in this shit."

Cash let out a snort. "It's been thirty minutes. How fuckin' long does it take to set up an explosion? I'd have been in and out in half the time."

"And you'd have probably blown your own ass up, too," I retorted. "Breaker's an expert in explosives. He knows what he's doin'."

"He's been outta the military for years, Atlas. That makes him rusty at best."

"Kit can make and plant a bomb in his sleep," I clipped out. "He worked with explosives for three years. Now, give him some fuckin' credit and stop whinin'." I heaved out a big sigh. "Jesus Christ! It's like havin' a fuckin ol' lady."

A heavy silence fell over the SUV.

Everythin' would explode after this mission – no pun intended. We were about to blow a hole in the Sinners' clubhouse, and it was only a matter of time before they retaliated, probably ten-fold.

The thought of Sophie gettin' targeted 'cause of what we were about to do made me glad that I'd pushed her away.

I kept tellin' myself that she was better off not bein' involved, but a part of me still had regrets.

It had been two weeks since Bear held a gun to Cara's head. Two weeks since I failed my club and allowed those fuckers to storm our home. Two weeks since I let everyone down again. We'd been on the back foot for months, but not anymore. We were about to go on the offense and make some fuckin' noise, literally.

It was time to step the fuck up and think like a one percenter again.

"I'll give him exactly three minutes before I go out there and look for him." Cash pointed toward the Sinners' clubhouse. "Be warned, Atlas. I'll shoot the place up to get him back if they've captured him. I'll die before I leave my brother for those sick fucks to torture."

Atlas

My teeth almost gnashed together. "Give Breaker a fuckin' chance, will ya!"

Cash shook his head frustratedly.

I searched the darkness, looking for signs of movement. As much as I hated to admit it, Cash had a point. Breaker estimated that it wouldn't take more than fifteen minutes to set up the explosions. All he had to do was get into the compound without bein' seen, do his thing, then get the fuck outta dodge so we could detonate.

"Wait. What's that over by the tree line?" Cash asked. "Down on the left. Look!" He pointed toward someone stumblin' away from a cluster of trees.

I squinted, tryin' to make out who was comin' for us, but the shape of the outline looked distorted. "Is that Breaker?"

"Must be," Cash said incredulously, "but what the fuck's he doin'?"

"Only one way to find out." I glanced back at him, shoulders tense. "Ready to rumble?"

Cash jerked a nod and flung his door open so hard that it almost flew off its hinges.

I jumped down into the snow-covered grass with my weapon raised.

The night air was frigid with cold, but I hardly noticed as I followed Cash toward the shadowy figure that was drawin' closer to us by the second.

The moon shone from behind a cloud and lit up the scene. I stared for a few seconds and almost barked out a laugh.

Kit was makin' his way toward us with a big man slung over his shoulder.

"What the fuck?" Cash exclaimed.

I smothered my chuckle. "Looks like your little brother's been busy. It's no wonder he took his time." I slotted my weapon back inside my chest holster.

Breaker moved closer. "Don't just fuckin' stand there like two planks. He's heavy as fuck." His voice carried over the night air in a whispered shout.

I grinned huge. "You heard the man. Help him."

Cash stalked toward his brother. "Who the fuck's that?" he demanded, pointin' at the man over Kit's shoulder.

"New friend." Kit laughed softly. "His patch said his name was Piston. Maybe we should change it to rat 'cause I reckon that if we get him down the *Cell,* we can persuade the fucker to tittle-tattle on the Sinners by tomorrow lunchtime."

Cash waited as Kit transferred the man onto his shoulder. "Jesus," he heaved. "This fucker's been eatin' his oatmeal."

Breaker fell into step next to me as we trudged back to the SUV behind Cash and the prisoner. I loved it when a plan came together. Nabbin' Piston was an unexpected bonus.

"I'll be glad when we can get our bikes out," Kit said thoughtfully. "The snow has to melt soon, right? It's been a fuckin' long winter."

My steps faltered. "Breaker. You just got into our enemy's camp and set up four devices ready to detonate, and you did it undetected. Then you neutralized an enemy *and* somehow managed to bring him back for questionin'." I barked out a laugh. "And you wanna talk about the goddamned weather?"

Kit's eyes danced. "All in a day's work, brother."

I shook my head disbelievingly. Kit had done more for the club in one night than the rest of us had done in six months. He thought tactically, and he had the talent to back it up. Suddenly I was seein' a very different man to the fuckboy he usually portrayed.

"Breaker." I lowered my voice so that Cash couldn't hear. "Why are you screwin' around? You could be so much more than just a good time. You've got fuckin' skills, man."

Kit looked at me pointedly and nodded toward Cash. "You got any older brothers, Atlas?"

I shook my head. "Just got Rosie. She's younger than me."

"Can you imagine bein' the younger Stone bro to that one?" He nodded toward Cash.

My brow wrinkled as I thought about his words. "Can't be easy," I admitted. "He can do no wrong in Dagger's eyes."

"And then throw Bowie into the mix," he added. "Let's just say it's cold as fuck bein' in the shadow of the two golden boys."

I let the meaning behind his words sink in.

Kit was right when he implied that his pop and brothers never took him seriously. The man was a decorated veteran. He'd given a lot for his country, but if you asked John, he'd say Kit was a dog dick. He'd be correct, but tonight had proven that he was much more than that.

Kit jogged toward the SUV. "I'll get in the back with him. He'll wake up soon, and I'll need to put him out again." He opened the door and gestured for Cash to transfer Piston into the back of the vehicle.

"It's cool," Cash replied. "I'll just knock him out."

"In the back of a cage? While Atlas is drivin'?" Kit deadpanned. "That'll work out well."

"What the fuck would you do differently?" Cash straightened to his full height and turned to his brother. "Sing him to sleep? A chorus of twinkle, twinkle, big bad Sinner?"

Kit side-eyed him. "No dickwad. I'll do what I did ten minutes ago. I'll cut off his airway until he passes out again."

Cash's brows snapped together. "You can do that shit?"

"Come on," Kit said tightly. "Let's get back to the clubhouse." He jogged around to the other side of the SUV and slipped into the seat next to Piston.

We all jumped in the vehicle and slammed the doors shut behind us. "Ready?" I asked, lookin' over my shoulder at Kit, who was fumblin' in his pockets.

"Take this to be on the safe side." He handed his Walther P99 to Cash. "Don't want this sneaky fucker gettin' hold of it and shootin' us all up."

Cash took hold'a the weapon and gave me a stunned look.

Xander was startin' to recognize Kit's exemplary trainin' and probably felt inferior. Honestly, he wasn't the only one. Kit had proven that you shouldn't judge a book by its cover, whatso-fuckin'-ever.

He was fly as fuck.

"We gotta jet," Kit ordered. "We need to be off these roads when I detonate. Don't want the fuzz seein' us here when that shithole goes up. They'll ID us straight away. We gotta time it right so I can be in close enough range for the signal to get through."

I caught Breaker's eyes in the rearview. "Boom and jet?"

He dipped his chin in agreement and held up a small, black device. "Are we all sure about this?" His stare slid from me to Cash. "If we do this, there's no going back. We're declaring outright war."

I started the engine, pressed down the gas, and slowly edged the SUV away from our hidin' spot. As I guided us over the icy terrain and toward the road, the vehicle rocked gently.

Breaker was correct in making us think about what we were about to do.

It was big, and it had consequences.

Life would change the second that he pressed down on that device.

Atlas

It struck me as crazy how one second in time could mean so much to so many people. We were at a fork in the road, and one direction was leadin' us to a dangerous club war.

Cash's stare went from me to Kit. "They hurt my woman. I stood there and watched as Bear butted a gun to her skull and threatened to squeeze the trigger. Can you imagine how that felt? I thought she'd be killed in an instant." His face hardened. "I want all those fuckers dead, and it starts now."

My jaw clenched. Cash was right.

"Press the button," he ordered.

"Do it," I rasped. "The entire club voted for it. We made the decision."

Kit jerked a solitary nod and pressed his thumb down on the detonator.

I counted, *One, two, three, four-*

An almighty explosion thundered through the air behind us, the force of the blast makin' the SUV rock.

"Jesus," Cash murmured, scramblin' to look back at what remained of the Sinners' clubhouse.

"It's done," Kit said, voice flat.

I glanced at both the men quickly, then turned back to concentrate on the road.

And as we sped toward Hambleton, one thought flashed through my mind.

It was official.

We were at war.

Chapter Six

Sophie

Whenever life kicked my ass, I went to the gym.
Marshal Arts training was the only thing that gave me any sense of control after what happened with Luke. My career was high-stress, so when I wasn't working, you could usually find me either at my house or the gym in town.

Krav Maga was my primary discipline. I'd practiced it on and off since Ned and I decided about seven years ago that we needed to exercise more. Back then, I didn't take it seriously, at least not until my ex-husband beat me. That was when I began to train hard, determined that nobody would ever do that to me again.

When I flew back from Europe, I stopped in New York, where my friend's husband owned a boxing gym. I spent hours there going over techniques and practicing every day.

That was when I began to take Krav Maga seriously. I trained so much that it eventually became muscle memory. I couldn't physically punch as hard as a man, so I learned *where* to punch instead for maximum effect—eyes, nose, throat, solar plexus, groin, and knees. I could easily escape from most holds. My groundwork was excellent, as were my strikes, take-downs, and throws.

Krav gave me back my confidence; it gave me back my life. I thought my self-esteem was pretty good and began to believe in myself again.

Until Atlas.

It had been a few weeks since he'd turned up at my house, and I was still furious. He'd got to me. At first, it touched me that he stormed in, ready to take down the person he thought was attacking me, but that gratitude only lasted until he started with his insults.

My mom always said there was a silver lining to every situation, and our mommas were usually right. She also said that when someone shows you who they are, believe them. That was a piece of advice I held close.

Atlas had cured me of my little crush. He'd shown me he was an asshole, and finally, I got the message. I'd managed to avoid him since our last encounter, though that wasn't difficult, seeing as I'd worked all over the holidays and into January. I had no family in Hambleton, so I volunteered to work doubles as my colleagues wanted to spend the holidays with their kids. I accumulated so many vacation days that HR made me take some time off.

Three whole weeks.

Today was day one, and my internal body clock jolted me awake at five a.m. I couldn't get back to sleep, so I got up, fed Vic, showered, and went straight to the gym.

It was early; therefore, I was surprised to see a few people there already.

I'd already dressed in my workout gear at home, so I locked my gym bag away and made my way straight to the ring where Callum O'Shea and his brother Donovan were already sparring.

Those two were what I called bruisers, meaning that they'd punch you so hard in the head that your ears would ring for days. All three O'Shea brothers had boxed for years. The youngest brother, Tadhg, was a decent kickboxer too.

The O'Shea boys were loud, proud, and funny as all hell. I liked them immensely.

Donny's eyes fell on me as I walked past the ring. One side of his mouth tipped up, and he flashed me a sexy lopsided grin. "Morning to ya, Sophie love. You're looking fresh as a fuckin' dais-" He let out a loud grunt as Callum's fist smashed into the side of his head.

"Eyes on the fuckin' prize, Donny boy," Cal crowed, bouncing on the balls of his feet.

Donovan's stare jerked toward me. "They already were you eejit."

Callum flashed me a grin. "Ignore my brother, Sophie. He can't help himself. The ugly feck's been without a woman for too long."

I let out a quiet snort.

Ugly was the last word I'd use for any of the O'Shea brothers. All of them were tall and muscled, with black hair and bright blue eyes. They were also funny and quite sweet when they turned on the charm. I'd bet my last dollar that none of them would be short of female company.

The two men began to throw punches while ducking and diving to avoid the flurry of hits thrown back.

I sat on the floor, back to the wall, and watched the fight.

Callum's form was looser than Donovan's. I knew Donny boxed for his military unit, so he'd had more formal training. Cal had the air of a street brawler, while Donny was much more controlled. They were surprisingly light on their feet. Even though they probably both weighed in at around two-hundred pounds plus, they made it seem effortless.

Cal's brute strength and Donovan's agile footwork had me transfixed.

Boxing, to me, was a lot like a dance. There was a kind of grace to it. One move flowed into another like they'd been choreographed.

Martial Arts had its own steps and formations too. Like a dancer, you had to have a good fitness level and train hard to be good at it.

Donny ducked left, then right, and threw a jab straight into Cal's ribs. Callum let out an 'oof' as Donovan's fist cut across his jaw.

He recovered quickly and jabbed at Donny's chin.

I winced as Donovan's head snapped back. That had to hurt.

Both brothers bounced around the ring, throwing punches at each other. After a minute of trading blows, they high-fived each other's gloves, laughing.

"Good job, bro," Donovan said teasingly. "I'll make a decent fighter out of you yet."

Cal pulled at his glove with his teeth, grinning at his brother. "Dream on, Jarhead. I went easy on ya. Da would kill me if I beat on the family simpleton."

I shook my head, smiling. "You two are hilarious."

Cal threw an arm around Donny's neck and pretended to punch his head. "The little feck doesn't stand a chance against his older and much bigger brother." He laughed.

Donovan pushed him off with a chuckle.

Callum turned to me. "Wanna spar, Sophie darlin'? You said you'd teach me how to get out of that chokehold."

"Yeah." I nodded. "But I need to warm up first."

Donny smirked. "I'll get you nice and hot."

Callum slapped him across the stomach. "Don't speak to her like that."

"I'm just funning," his brother retorted. "Stop fuckin' hitting me."

Atlas

I smiled as I went to the wall and grabbed a mat, listening to their bickering. I started some hip rotations and arm circles, releasing all the tension in my back.

The boys got their mats and joined me as I began some knee kicks, lunges, and full-leg rotations.

"Okay, boys, let's do some two-two-one palm strikes." I quickly pushed one palm out twice, then the other once, and repeated the action.

"Will you show me that hair pull move?" Donny asked. "Cal couldn't stop talkin' about it."

Callum grinned. "I showed Aislynn that one too. It's a great move."

"It's a good offense technique for women to learn. Your sister will agree when I say that women usually go for the hair." I moved toward Callum and braced. "Attack."

He immediately came at me.

His hand darted out and connected with the top of my head. I smacked mine down on top of his, then lurched forward and kneed him hard in the groin.

He let out a low groan and doubled over.

Donovan hooted and clapped. "Again," he demanded. "Show me again."

Callum looked up at me and quirked an eyebrow. "Hope you got some energy, Soph. It's gonna be a fuckin' long day."

An hour later, we were still going strong. "Sweep!" I shouted as Callum crouched down and swung his leg out. His foot moved right and connected with the back of Donovan's knees. Donny let out a grunt and hit the floor.

Loud cheers came from the direction of the door.

We'd acquired an audience. Some of the guys from the gym had been cheering and clapping us on. I saw that a couple of the Speed Demons were watching too, but I didn't know them personally.

Strong hands grabbed me from behind, and an arm slipped around the front of my neck.

Jules Ford

Without thinking, I lunged backward and kept running. I felt my assailant's feet falter, and he began to fall. I dropped deadweight on top of him, my back connecting with his front.

Another loud cheer went up.

I craned my neck to see Callum sprawled out on the ground underneath me, fighting for breath.

"You winded the fucker," Donovan called out, laughing.

Whoops, and hollers rang through the room.

I got up and peered down at Cal. "You okay?"

He punched hard at his chest and noisily sucked in a breath. "You got me there," he gasped. "Couldn't get my breath." He slowly got to his feet and held his hands up. "You're a fuckin' machine."

"Teach me," Donny called over. "I wanna go back to my unit and fuck 'em all up."

"You can't learn everything in a couple of hours," I replied. "I trained eight hours a day for a full year to get my black belt."

Cal made a gurgling noise. "Now she tells me she's a fuckin' black belt. You ever need a job, Soph? I'll hire you to work the door of the Shamrock."

"Bad idea," Donovan said smugly. "Put Sophie on the door, and it'll be wall-to-wall assholes tryin' to get chatty with her."

I felt my cheeks heat.

Donny had been throwing me side glances for the last hour. More than once, I'd caught him checking out my ass.

He was a good-looking guy; I was sure beautiful women always threw themselves at him.

I was short, and my body was compact. My tits were small, and my ass was high. I didn't think I'd appeal to someone like Donovan.

Atlas' voice floated through my mind.

She's got the body of a fifteen-year-old boy.

Atlas

My cheeks burned hotter at the memory.

What made me cringe was that he said it to John. It burned that he'd spoken badly about me to a man I respected, and it had knocked my confidence.

I wasn't a raving beauty, I knew that, but all my life, people had told me that I was pretty, even Luke.

Atlas made me second-guess myself, and I hated that I let him. He'd affected the way that I felt about myself. As much as I knew that I shouldn't let his words affect my state of mind, I couldn't help it. I didn't know if it was a woman thing, but when people, especially men, commented negatively on our looks, it stung.

Now Donny was looking at me like he wanted to eat me for dinner, and all I could do was wonder why. I was angry with myself for letting a dick like Atlas determine how I viewed myself.

"Do the gun thing," Callum suggested. "That'll get 'em all creamin' their tighty whities."

I rolled my eyes, smiling. "Boys and their toys. I'll never understand it."

He moved to the corner, crouched down, and rummaged inside his gym bag. Suddenly he sprung up and came at me, pointing something at my face.

My hands shot out, and grabbed hold of his. I kept moving forward, maneuvered sideways, and banged his hands off my knee until he dropped whatever he was holding. Then I struck out with my elbow, one two into Callum's stomach.

The room erupted in hoots and cheers as he groaned and fell to his knees. Whatever he was holding dropped to the floor with a clatter.

"Fuck!" he rasped, holding his stomach. "My cell."

"Shit." I bent down to pick it up, relieved that the screen was still intact. "Why the hell did you attack me with your cell phone?" I demanded, handing it to him.

He slipped it in the pocket of his baseball shorts "I was pretending it was a gun."

"And I believed it for a split second." I shook my head. "You scared the life out of me."

Donovan barked out a laugh from the floor. "Ya should've kicked his ass, Soph."

"I think she already did," a deep voice said from the door.

I spun around and saw John Stone standing at the entrance with Hendrix. They had another man with them, Iceman, I think his name was.

"Yo, Dagger," Callum called over.

"Is that young Donovan back from the wars?" John called over in his rich, deep voice.

Callum and Donny walked over to greet the men. After some manly hugs and fist bumps, they all moved back inside the room, talking and laughing.

Ice made his way toward me, a massive grin on his face. "That was some fuckin' cool kung-fu shit ya just did, Doc."

I picked up my drink bottle. "It's called Krav Maga."

"Is that the same discipline that the Israeli military use?" he asked cocking his head in question.

"Yeah. It mixes martial arts, kickboxing, wrestling, and good old street fighting." I leaned my back against the wall and took a sip of water. "How long were you watching?"

"We've been here since you first started sparring." He nodded toward the upstairs mezzanine area where the offices were. "Prez had a meet with the manager. Couldn't take my fuckin' eyes off ya." He placed his arm on the wall above my head, effectively caging me in. Not in a creepy way, though.

I took in his handsome face, light hair, and bright blue eyes. He looked a bit too 'boy next door' to be part of an MC, but then many of the men in the club weren't exactly your long-haired, beer-swilling, stereotypical bikers. Cash was probably one of the most handsome men I'd ever seen. Hendrix had long hair but also had

Atlas

muscles and was gorgeous. Even Atlas, with his asshole attitude, beard, and tattoos, looked more like a bodybuilder than a biker.

"Why do they call you Ice?" I asked.

"I'll tell ya another time." A slow smile spread over his face. "How 'bout over dinner?"

I looked up at him and blinked. "Dinner?"

"Yeah, dinner. You like Italian?" he asked, cobalt eyes darting between mine.

Oh my.

Shocked, I tried to think of a response.

Atlas was the first guy I'd been interested in for years, but that whole scenario went downhill fast. I swore off men after what happened at my house a couple of weeks ago.

Ice seemed like a great guy, but he didn't give me the same feeling as Atlas. I wondered, should I have held out for that with somebody else? Or should I give him a chance? A part of me wanted to accept, but at the same time, I didn't want to lead him on.

"Could we go out as friends?" I asked.

It was his turn to echo me. "Friends?"

I smiled to take the sting out of my words. "You seem great, but I'm not sure I want anything serious. I'd love to go out and get to know you better, but I doubt it will be more than a friend thing."

"You wound me, Doc." He held his hand over his heart and staggered back a step. "Okay. How 'bout we go out, eat, talk, and see what happens? No pressure."

I grimaced slightly. It was okay for Ice to say there was no pressure, but all I felt was pressure.

He seemed sweet and fun, though. Would it really be so bad to go somewhere that wasn't the hospital or my house? It'd be great to have a conversation that wasn't about a prognosis or treatment. The only time I chatted these days was with Queenie.

Jules Ford

Ned's voice echoed through my head. *Oh, for God's sake, just go out with him. It's a date, not a marriage proposal. Live a little, Soph; you'll be dead one day.*

My cheeks burned slightly as I smiled up at him. "I love Italian food."

He went into his pocket for his cell, tapped on it, and handed it to me. "Need ya digits, babe."

I took it from him. "Are you sure about this? I'm not like the girls I've seen you guys hang out with." I started to tap out my number.

"What type's that?" he asked. "Beautiful, smart, and strong? As far as I can tell, you fit that type perfectly."

My belly went warm. Jeez, he was smooth.

Ice gestured behind him. "Babe, Prez asked me to tell you he wants a word."

I looked over his shoulder to see John making his way toward us. His stare darted between Ice and me, a small smile playing around his mouth. He clapped Ice on the shoulder. "Get what you needed, brother?"

Ice took his cell from me with a grin. "Yup."

John nodded and looked at me. "You gotta minute?"

"I guess," I said, frowning. What did John want with me? Nothing good ever came from the President of a motorcycle club wanting to talk. If another one of his men needed a blood transfusion, he was out of luck.

"Let's go up to the office," he suggested. "There's more privacy up there."

I bit my lip nervously. "If it's about the other week, I'm good."

"No," he said quietly. "Look. We watched what you just did, and I gotta little proposition for ya, Doc." He nodded toward the stairs. "Probably best we do this in private."

Jesus. The Speed Demons had caught me in a spider's web made from leather. I'd done them one favor, and now it was open season. "I've already explained that it was a one-time thing. I'm not going to be your resident bullet extractor."

A big grin lit up his face. "Resident bullet extractor? Doc, we ain't livin' in the Wild West."

"Not what it looked like the other week," I snipped.

John held his hands up. "Look, I just wanna talk. Gimme five minutes. I promise if you don't like what I gotta say, I'll respect that."

"Five minutes," I agreed. "But John, I've already told you, the last time *was* the last time."

He grinned and held his arm out, gesturing for me to go ahead.

I walked past him and started up the stairs. My stomach gave a jolt when I glanced over my shoulder to see John, Ice, and Cash all following me.

What the hell did they want with me?

I was a small-town doctor with no affiliations and no experience dealing with the crap they likely did. My life partner was a cat. Paying my bills a day late kept me awake at night. I hardly lived life on the edge.

Now I had a meeting with an MC president and his men. More worryingly, I likely had a date with one of them too. Life had gone from zero to a hundred in the space of a few weeks.

My heart began to thump a little faster as a stab of worry hit me about the conversation I was about to have.

What the hell have you gotten yourself into now.

Chapter Seven

Atlas ~ Now

My chest puffed out slightly as I looked around the bar at the wall-to-wall black leather cuts. January was the start of a new year but also the beginning of combat and weapons training.

I couldn't help grinning at the stink of testosterone, leather, and cigarettes. It was the smell of brotherhood, and I fuckin' loved it.

Two of the Stone brothers were sittin' at a table together, lookin' like someone had shit in their coffee. I rested my back to the wall and rolled my eyes to the heavens, prayin' that the two fuck-ups would pull their heads out of their asses ready for trainin'.

Cash's face was set in a permanent scowl, probably because his woman had left his ass a few weeks ago. He'd had a session with his shrink yesterday, and the poor little golden boy was all butthurt because he had to talk about his delicate little feelin's.

Boo fuckin' hoo.

Breaker. Jeez, as much as he was a good man to have on his side, he was also a soft ass.

He'd been fuckin' the same club whore that had screwed up Cash's relationship with his woman. He'd suspected what I'd already known all along. She was up to no fuckin' good. She'd gotten pregnant and told Kit he was the daddy. We didn't know that she'd been workin' undercover for our rival club, the Burnin' Sinners, and the real daddy had turned out to be Bear, their Prez's son.

I was confused as to why he was bein' a crybaby about it, though. Anyone else would've been praisin' the Lord above that they were off the hook. The thought of wakin' up to April every mornin' made my balls run back up inside my gut.

The main doors swung open. I looked up expectantly, fully expectin' Maury to push his way through holdin' a lie detector test, but it was just Prez makin' his way into the room with the Veep, Abe, and Bowie trailin' after him.

I made my way to stand next to Prez and the boys, Cash, and Ice followin'.

Prez glanced at us all. "We ready?"

"Yup." Cash

I jerked a nod.

"Ready," Bowie muttered.

Dagger eyed the room, clearing his throat. "Brothers!" he called out.

The noise died down to silence.

Prez looked around. "You've all got your itineraries. Half of you begin fight trainin' this mornin'. the other half are out at the shootin' range, then we swap places this afternoon. The Veep's got bonfires made up outside, but best you wrap up warm. It's colder than a bitch in a barfight out there."

I looked at Bowie and grinned. "Come on, Barbie. Let's go party."

Atlas

"Keep ya fuckin' hands up, Reno. You're all offense and no defense." I grimaced as Shotgun's fist crashed into the brother's temple.

"Fuck," Reno muttered as he staggered back, losing his balance and landin' flat on his ass.

I looked to the heavens, shakin' my head. "Jesus fuckin' save me."

"It's okay," Bowie said quietly from beside me. "Look on the bright side. Reno's got a good aim. He'll end up on the sniper team with any luck, so we won't have to deal with his glass jaw." He looked toward the group of men sparrin'. "Take a ten-minute break, brothers. We've got a while before lunch, then we rotate."

Groans and mutters rose through the air as the men sank to their asses, swiggin' from their water bottles while they talked amongst themselves.

That mornin', we began training. Our rival club, the Burning Sinners, had been making some heinous moves. Piston had confirmed that Bear was runnin' a trafficking ring.

We'd already made a statement by blowing up their home. We needed to get the men ready in case they retaliated, which was why we were down at the gym.

Prez had put Bowie and me in charge of teachin' the men hand-to-hand combat. It was clear that some of the boys were outta shape and outta practice.

"It's like watching a Marx brothers movie." I unscrewed my water bottle and pointed it toward the men. "That's some slapstick shit right there."

Bowie shook his head. "I dunno what happened, brother. We used to have weekly sparring sessions back when I prospected. I remember fightin' in the ring most weekends."

I nodded as I thought back to those times. "Problem was, when we gave up our one percenter badges, we had to focus on the businesses. We let go of the gun runnin' and drug distribution, but the brothers still had to pay the bills. Plus, we were so used to havin' scratch in our pockets that we didn't have time to keep our fightin' skills fresh or spend all day in the gym. We didn't need to seein' as how our lives instantly became less dangerous. Years of peace made us complacent. The Sinners have started with their bullshit, and we're playin' catch-up." I nodded toward the boys. "Problem is we ain't got time to re-train everyone."

Bowie blanched slightly. "Maybe the Martial Arts expert that Pop's bringin' in will help."

I checked my watch. "Where is he anyway? Shouldn't his ass be here by now?"

"Pop said she's got some shit to deal with before she comes."

My eyes jerked to him. "She? What the fuck are you talkin' about?"

"Great." He winced. "I told Pop I'd let the cat outta the bag."

"Cat outta what fuckin' bag?" I felt a muscle tick in my jaw.

"Fuck." He grabbed the back of his neck. "You're not gonna like it."

My shoulders tensed; chest suddenly uneasy 'cause I hated bein' kept outta the loop.

Prez knew this, so why hadn't he pulled me into the office and had a powwow with me instead of leaving me standin' around like a fucknut, not knowin' what the hell was happenin'? How was I supposed to keep the club safe if I didn't know what shit was goin' down? Especially after we blew up the Sinners' goddamned clubhouse.

I narrowed my eyes at Bowie. "You'd better fuckin' tell me what's been goin' on, or I'll go see Prez myself."

A door banged in the distance, and voices floated down the stairs to the gym.

Atlas

Straight away, I recognized Prez's deep timbre, followed by Abe's chuckle. Then a girlish giggle registered, and my gut pitched. Heat throbbed through my veins as soft footsteps sounded from the stairs.

Bowie's hand clasped my shoulder before he leaned into me. "The guy who was supposed to train us canceled a few days ago. Dad was gonna tell you, but then he found someone else that could help. Thought it might be better if he kept it quiet."

A growl rumbled through my chest.

"Thing is Atlas. Dunno if you're gonna like the new guy, or should I say, the new chick."

My eyes slid back to the stairs as another sexy, throaty laugh sounded. Then Prez appeared, followed by Abe, then another figure.

A woman.

She was tiny, dressed in black yoga pants and a black tank top. Her frame was petite with understated curves. My eyes traveled over her glossy, dark hair that she'd tied up in one'a those bun things with strands fallin' down. The curve of her neck accentuated her porcelain skin, which had been covered in cat scratches just weeks ago.

I couldn't help but notice her elegance as she reached the bottom step and strutted toward me. My eyes were glued to her swayin' hips, accentuated by her skintight black workout pants.

Something about her affected me deeply, and it all began with that sexy little mole on her top lip that silently begged me to suck it.

Every time I saw her, she drew me further in. My body seemed to respond to hers. I couldn't understand how she kept pullin' me deeper into her orbit.

Fine whisky eyes locked on mine and widened slightly. Her perfect white teeth sunk nervously into her puffy bottom lip, and my cock came to life.

Jules Ford

I liked that I made her nervous. I fuckin' *loved* that I threw her just as off-balance as she did me. The hot little bitch could probably see the pissed-off expression that I knew was written all over my face because her cheeks flushed pink, and she began to play with a lock of her thick hair.

My hands went to my waist, and I sucked in a deep breath.

Why the fuck did this shit always happen to me? It was like the Universe took great pleasure in fuckin' me hard up the asshole.

"What's *she* doin' here?" I glared at Prez.

"Soph's come to help with trainin'," he explained with a grin.

My lip curled. "No fuckin' way is that ever gonna happen."

Prez rubbed at his beard. "Don't get all pissy, Atlas. I knew you'd have a bitch fit, so I kept it under my hat. Sophie's a black belt in Krav Maga. I've seen her in action, and I'm tellin' ya, she can help us."

"Black belt in stalkin' me more like." My stare swept from the doc's head down to her toes, then up again. "What's she gonna do?" I mocked. "Nag us to death?"

Her face twisted with hurt, and I suddenly felt like the biggest asshole on the planet. I ignored the ache in my chest and focused on Prez. "You can't bring a woman into an MC and expect everyone to jump on board." I flung my hand out toward the doc. "This is a man's world, Dagger. The brothers ain't gonna listen to her."

A muscle in Prez's jaw ticked, a surefire sign that he was about to pop off. "Watch your mouth, brother. I'm Prez of this club which means I can do whatever the fuck I want." He looked at Sophie, and his face softened. "I apologize for Atlas' attitude, Doc. Go to the men and do your thing while I have a word with my SAA here."

Atlas

Stitch shot me a glare, nodded, turned on her heel, and made her way over to the crowd of men openly watching our exchange with blatant interest.

"What the fuck's the matter with you?" Abe hissed. "Where do you get off sayin' that shit to her?" He took a step toward me and pointed at my chest. "What's goin' on with you? You're an asshole, but you're usually at least respectful. What've you got against the doc?"

I folded my arms across my chest, effectively battin' his finger away, and glowered at him.

Prez's eyes turned to slits. "I know what's goin' on. He's into her but has some outdated sense of chivalry, and he reckons he's not good enough. Or some bullshit like that."

Abe's face scrunched up with confusion. "Well, of course he's not good enough for her. The same as I'm not good enough for Iris or Bowie for Layla. And let's face it; Cash ain't good enough to lick Cara's boots after the shit he did to her." He let out a sarcastic snort. "But ain't that the point? We choose women who are way too good for our fucked-up asses and try our damned hardest to be better men for 'em."

Abe was right in what he said.

The club's ol' ladies were all good strong women who could hold their own in any dust-up. But they also had the kind of sweetness that made their men worship them. They were also loyal to a fault.

Sophie wasn't an ol' lady, but she'd already displayed the makings of a good one.

She'd gone over and above for the club, savin Bowie, then comin' in to treat me. She was tough and smart but also had that extra somethin' that I admitted had gotten under my thick skin from the first time I spoke to her.

But I had to weigh up all of the pros and cons.

Just by lookin' at her, I could tell she'd suffered some shit in her past. Bringin' her into the club when we were at war would only add to the nasty crap she was carryin'

91

around. The second that Bear held his gun to Cara's head, I knew that life was about to change drastically. And after setting those explosives, it was only a matter of time until shit hit the fan.

Two clubs goin' head-to-head was gonna result in some ugliness that we hadn't yet prepared for. How could I bring Stitch into a club war and not add to the sadness behind her eyes?

What kind of man would I be if I did that?

I had two choices. Hurt Sophie's feelings now or risk her suffering worse later.

The sound of whoops and hollers made my stare glide toward the ring. My palms grew clammy when I noticed that Shotgun was talkin' to Stitch.

She pointed to the top of her head and walked over to the corner of the ring.

Shot called somethin' down to Reno, and they laughed. He rolled his shoulders and called over to the doc, "Ya ready, little girl?"

"An attacker wouldn't ask that, but yeah, come at me." Stitch crouched into the same fightin' stance that I saw in her house.

"Here we go," Prez muttered. "Now you'll see what's what."

My gut jerked as I watched Shotgun lurch toward her. He pulled his fist back and took a swing at the tiny woman.

Everything inside me screamed to protect her. My body surged toward the ring, but Prez grabbed my arm. "Stop gettin' your balls twisted up," he said quietly. "Just watch."

Heart in mouth, I looked on helplessly as Shotgun bore down on the doc. Then my eyes widened as Stitch let out a war cry, leaped three feet, swept her foot up high, and kicked Shotgun in the face. His head cracked backward before he crashed down onto the floor of the ring.

A collective gasp grazed through the room.

Abe cackled.

I blinked. Doc had knocked the fucker out.

My cock kicked inside my gym shorts.

Damn.

I saw her crouched again in her fight stance, ready to spring into action. My eyes slid from her sexy hair and down to that seductive curve of her neck that I couldn't get outta my head. Slim shoulders, toned arms, and teeny tiny little titties, the entirety of which I could probably fit in my mouth.

It was like a single beam of sunshine shone down and lit her up. Suddenly, I was seein' Sophie 'I'll kick your ass' Green in a whole new light, and fuck me, I liked it.

I liked it a whole goddamned lot.

Silence filled the air for a few seconds. Then the men started shoutin'.

Reno jumped into the ring and knelt beside Shotgun, slappin' his face hard. "You okay, brother?" he shouted.

Shot didn't answer seein' as he was out fuckin' cold.

Bowie barked out a laugh. "He's knocked out ya stupid fuck. He's not deaf."

Abe pointed at Sophie, who was climbin' down from the ring by then. "If I could get my leg up that high, you'd be teachin' me that move later. It's a cryin' shame that I'm too fuckin' old and decrepit." A knowing grin snaked across his face. "But you can teach me that hair-pullin' shit that Callum O'Shea couldn't stop talkin' about."

Prez rubbed his hands together, grinnin'. "I saw that. It was a great move."

Sophie put her hands to her hips. "I'll teach you anything you want. That's why I'm here." Her eyes came to mine and locked. "There's no way I can teach your men the full discipline in the time I've got, but I can help. If somebody comes at you guys with a knife or a gun, I can teach them how to disable them. If someone gets you in a chokehold or comes from behind, I can show you all how to get out of it and turn it around on the assailant. But what I'm not here to do is waste my time, Atlas. I know you're SAA, and if you give me a hard time, everyone else will. So, you've got a choice to make. Either we draw a line under all the bullshit and start again, or I go and don't come back."

Prez looked at me and shrugged. "She can show us some useful shit, brother. Don't let your personal feelings get in the way of what's best for the club, yeah?"

It may have been a good thing for the club if Stitch helped out, but it likely wouldn't be good for her. If the Sinners ever got clued in that she was helpin' us train, she'd become an instant target. They'd mark her ass big time.

I gave Prez a knowin' look. "You know what could happen. The question is, can you live with the consequences? 'Cause I'm not sure that I can."

He nodded slowly. "I told Doc the pitfalls when I recruited her. She knows the score, and she says she can handle it."

"What about you, old man?" I asked, turning to Abe. "Your ol' lady's been on the receivin' end of some fucked-up shit. Can you live with yourself if history repeats?"

The club secretary thought for a moment. "The least we can do is protect her if she helps us. How 'bout we assign her a prospect? Like a twenty-four-seven bodyguard?"

A loud huff sounded from next to me.

I looked around to see Stitch glarin' between the three of us. "Excuse me. First, don't talk about me like I'm not standing right here. It's rude. Second, I don't need a bodyguard. What's the point of that when I could kick all your asses with one hand tied behind my back?"

I'd never been into sassy chicks before, but my cock didn't get the goddamned memo seein' as he raised his head to take a little ol' look around.

Atlas

Abe grinned. "I reckon you could give us all a run for our money." He nodded toward me. "Even that stupid fucker."

"Watch it, old man," I warned.

Stitch heaved out a sigh. "Look. Obviously, you don't want me here, so I'll go." She smiled sadly at Prez and Abe and went to turn away.

"Wait." The words leaped to my lips before I could stop them.

My mind scrambled for somethin' to say. The thought of Sophie leavin' like that made my gut twist, but the idea of her knowin' she'd got under my skin pissed me off. I had immense respect for the woman, but I couldn't let her know that if I wanted to keep her at arm's length.

I folded my arms across my chest. "I like that you came here for the club, so I'll give you a shot. You and me in the ring. We'll do a week's trial if I think you've got what it takes." I leaned down, so our faces were close. "You up for it? Or you scared?"

Her eyes narrowed. "You're such an asshole."

My cock jumped harder at her sweet strawberry scent. "You ain't seen nothin' yet, baby." I straightened and looked her up and down with a slight sneer.

Prez rubbed his beard thoughtfully.

Abe grinned from ear to ear. "Wait until I tell my Iris about this. She's gonna fuckin' love it. Dang, that there sexual chemistry makes me wanna go get me some mornin' delight."

I shot Stitch the death glare. "Don't start listenin' to him and gettin' any funny ideas, okay Doc? You ain't my type."

She shot me a smirk. "And you think you're mine?"

I jerked my thumb toward the ring, ignoring how my chest panged. "Bitch, we gonna rumble or what?"

Her eyes flashed with anger. "Yeah, *bitch*. We'll rumble." She turned on her heel and stomped toward the ring.

"Mark my words, brother," Prez crowed. "You're gonna regret that."

Bowie's eyes followed the doc before he glanced back at me, grinnin' huge.

"Come on," Stitch called from the ring. She lowered her voice to imitate me. "Ain't got all day, bitch."

Abe roared with laughter. "I fuckin' like her. She's got some balls."

"Anyone who gives him shit is okay with me," Prez gloated. "Good on her."

Ignorin' 'em, I made my way toward the ring, puttin' a little extra bounce in my step. I could almost feel the burn of Stitch's eyes watchin' my every move.

The sound of the men chattin' died down as they saw me approach. Shotgun was sittin' on his ass, clutchin' his head in his hands as I walked by. He must've come around while we were talkin'. I couldn't help flashin' him a grin. Bet he was rattled. Poor fucker did get his ass handed to him by a tiny woman. He wasn't gonna live that down anytime soon. I'd make sure of that.

I jumped into the ring, ducked under the ropes, and moved toward Stitch.

She was leanin' back against the far corner, her arms stretched out by the side of her, holdin' on to the thick ropes as she watched me stalk toward her.

"Ya ready, sweetheart?" I dropped my voice. "Don't you worry your pretty little head, Toots. I'll go easy on ya."

She ignored my brothers' roars of laughter. Instead, she stepped away from the ropes, crouched down, and lifted her fists to shield her face. "Show me what you got, Danny boy," she sang.

I couldn't help thinking that her defensive stance was better than Reno's was earlier.

Atlas

That should've been my first clue that there was more to her than met the eye. The second clue hit me in the face, literally when she leaped forward, let out a warrior's cry, and threw a punch at me.

A sickenin' crunch sounded with the force of her strike right before my nose exploded.

Pain radiated from my eyes to my ears. I couldn't see a thing through the involuntary tears that sprang up, a normal, physical reaction to a blow across the hooter.

A hard kick connected to the back of my calves, and suddenly I was fallin'. My knees crashed to the floor of the ring with a loud thud. Pain shot through me, and I let out a groan.

The room erupted in shouts as an arm snaked around my neck. Suddenly, I was in a chokehold.

"I'm sorry. Did I hurt your poor nosy wosey?" Humor laced the doc's tone.

My instincts kicked in. I cracked my head back hard, catchin' her face.

She let out a little yelp, and her grip loosened.

Takin' advantage of the fact she was caught off-guard, I leaped up and spun to face her. My heart dropped into the pit of my gut when I noticed the angry red mark slashed across her cheek, probably from when I'd just headbutted her.

Fuck!

She scrambled, and immediately moved into her defensive position, knees bent, fists up over her face. "More," she demanded, perfect white teeth clenched. "Come at me, asshole."

"Go on, girlie," Abe yelled. "Fuck his dick up with one'a them roundhouse kick things. "Make the fucker weep."

Prez threw his head back and laughed.

Roars rose through the room, along with shouts.

"Did you see that shit?" Reno asked, awestruck.

"How the fuck did she do that?" Tex demanded loudly.

"I put fifty bucks on the doc," Prez yelled.

I looked around, dazed, wondering what the fuck just happened.

I was a fighter growing up, but I still got my ass handed to me the same as everyone did when they were learnin'. But I could count on one hand how many men had brought me to my knees in the last ten years. I was a big guy, so not many could reach me, and I was a tough guy, so not many could even get close.

Stitch had done the impossible in a matter of seconds, and that was some goddamned impressive shit.

My hand lifted to my bloody nose.

I'd broken it fighting twice before, once when I was seventeen and again when I was twenty-one. Sophie had got me good. She hadn't busted it that time, but somethin' told me that if she wanted to, she could've fucked it up again.

I already had a grudging respect for her. She was a doctor, tough and ballsy. More than that, though, she had courage.

My hand lifted and pointed to her. "You!"

Silence fell over the room.

Sophie dropped her fists and stood to her full height, punchin' her hands to her hips. "What?"

I took a step toward her. "What you just did..."

Her eyes narrowed.

My voice lowered. "Show me." I turned to address the room. "You fuckers, watch closely. We're going through it slow mo. We're gonna do it once with the doc explainin' everything as we go along. I expect you to follow. You get me?"

Mutters of agreement went up.

Abe's hoot cracked through the air as I spread my legs, bent slightly, and held my fists over my face, copying Stitch's earlier stance. "Don't hold back, Stitch, gimme everythin' you got."

Her face morphed into an evil grin. "Don't worry, Toots," she said almost too sweetly. "I'll go easy on you."

Chapter Eight

Sophie

Sweat dripped down my face as I cracked my knee into Ice's kidneys, ducked low, then swiped his legs out from under him with my foot.

He fell to the floor and let out a loud groan.

I stood slowly, raising the fake gun I'd just taken from him, and glanced down at the men watching us in the ring. "You could all see by that demonstration that you don't need brute strength to disable someone armed. If you keep your head, you can maneuver your body to work with the gun's trajectory."

"What if they're about to shoot?" A voice called out. "That move you just did would work great if someone threatened us with a gun, but the Sinners won't think twice before puttin' a bullet in our brains."

My eyes veered over to Atlas, standing with his back against the wall, arms folded across his chest. His usual cocky smirk was plastered across his beautiful asshole face as he took in the conversation with interest.

My blood pressure spiked the same as it had been since I got here.

I'd been ignoring his side-eye and snide comments for days. He was looking for a reaction, and I was determined not to give him one. But it was getting to me.

Trying to teach these men how to fight was like banging my head against a wall. They met everything I did with grumbles and complaints. The Demons were rude and belligerent, and I was on the verge of giving up.

Atlas had probably told them to give me a hard time to test me.

I was trying my best to brush it off, but it was becoming clear that I was wasting my time. Ice, Breaker, and the officers were the only men who took me seriously, which was soul-destroying.

I held my hand out to Ice and helped him up. "Wanna do another demonstration?"

He dusted down his shorts. "Anytime. I mean, you keep kickin' my ass, but I gotta say, I can't find it in me to care."

Ice and I had become friendlier the last few days. He was one of the few men who were respectful toward me. He seemed to appreciate what I was trying to do for the club, unlike Atlas and his little asshole-in-training sidekick Shotgun, who was still butt hurt because I'd kicked his ass on my first day here. I assumed he was embarrassed about being taken down by a woman; he wouldn't be the first to feel that way. I even got it, but I didn't understand why they were turning their noses up at techniques that could help them one day. It didn't make sense.

Ice sent a grin my way and picked up the fake gun. "When are you gonna let me take you out?" he asked, tone low so the others wouldn't hear.

I held my fists up to protect my face. I regretted agreeing to a date. Iceman was great, but I didn't see him in a romantic light. However, I wasn't the type to go back on an agreement.

Atlas

"How about when we've finished training?" I offered.

"Ain't waiting that long." Quick as a flash, he pulled his arm up and pointed the weapon in my face.

I carried out the same move as I had with Callum a few weeks before.

My hands shot out and grabbed the gun, then I lurched forward, turning my body. I knocked his hands off my knee, and the fake gun dropped to the floor. One, two quick, hard jabs of my elbow smashed into Ice's hard stomach, and he fell to his knees.

"Jesus." He gasped as he lay with his back to the floor of the ring, trying to catch his breath, and he began to laugh.

It was infectious, and I couldn't help joining in before loud footsteps sounded from the hardwood floors.

I craned my neck to see Atlas stomping toward me.

My heart jerked at the sight of him in black gym shorts black tee straining across his massive pecs. He folded his arms across his chest and glared, his flexing biceps grabbing my attention.

"What the fuck was that?" he demanded.

Ice's head snapped to face him, and he got to his feet. "What the fuck was what?"

"That move." Atlas pointed to us. "Why haven't you shown us that before?"

I leaned on the ropes, facing him. "I've been working up to it. I went through the basics, and none of the men seemed particularly interested, so I kept going over them to ensure they'd sunk in. Only Ice and the other officers are ready for more at this point."

"That's the kinda shit we can use," Atlas insisted. "What good would that arm and leg rotatin' shit do in a fight?"

Barks of laughter rose from the men.

My face heated as I stared down at him.

Jules Ford

It was the first time that he'd addressed me properly in days. Mostly, he talked indirectly to me while he spoke to the men. He hadn't given me any instructions on what he wanted me to show them. He just smirked as I metaphorically fell flat on my ass.

At least now, we were getting somewhere.

"You've been here nearly a week and today's the first time I've seen you show us somethin' useful," he snapped. "We're bikers, not fuckin' choirboys. We don't need basics; we need shit that's gonna help us in a fistfight or when those assholes corner us. D'ya think this is some kinda game, woman?"

I dropped my hands, balling them into fists. "No, I don't," I retorted, ducking under the ropes and jumping down. Every muscle in my body was taut as I stalked toward him. "Why would I think it's a game, Atlas? Do you think I haven't been on the wrong side of a fistfight?" I let out a snort. "Honey, I was confined to a hospital bed for a week because I got beaten so badly, and believe me, I wouldn't wish that on my worst enemy. I'm trying to stop that from happening to you and your boys, but you think it's more important to prove a point than to learn something."

His black eyes narrowed.

I probably should've taken that as a cue to shut my mouth, but I was too mad. For days I'd been ignored and treated like I was a joke. Enough was enough.

"John asked me to come in because he thought maybe I could show you some tricks that could help," I continued angrily. "But what's the point when you and all the other assholes shoot me down? Don't worry, though. I've finally got the message. You're not goin-"

"-Who beat you," he interrupted. His voice was quiet, but that wasn't fooling anyone. The fury in his tone almost made an icy shiver prickle across my skin.

That's what he took away from my speech. "None of your business," I whispered.

Atlas

I didn't broadcast what happened to me, but at the same time, I usually wasn't embarrassed to tell people. I discovered over time that I could use it to make me a stronger person and to help others, so that's what I did. I worked with a women's shelter teaching self-defense, and after learning how to defend myself, I was more confident, at least when Atlas wasn't giving me shit.

But right then, looking at the rage on his face, I wished I'd never said anything.

His face was red, eyes flashing with anger. His lip curled into a snarl.

My stomach twisted until it was all knotted up inside. I was suddenly unable to speak.

"Session's over," Atlas bellowed in his deep, throaty voice. "Everyone back here tomorrow at eight a.m. Bring your fuckin' A game 'cause the doc here is gonna be teachin' us that gun move, and every single one'a you pricks are gonna pay attention. Do you fuckin' get me?"

The men shouted their agreement and started to file up the stairs, except for Ice, who came to stand next to me. His strong arm snaked across my shoulders. "You okay, babe?" he asked, although his bright blue eyes fixed on Atlas. "How 'bout we go upstairs for a coffee, and we'll arrange that date?"

Atlas glowered.

I went to tell Ice that I didn't think we should go out until I'd finished the club's training. "Well, I-" but Atlas cut me off. "-If you've got time for that, Iceman, then we ain't keepin' you busy enough. Have you looked into the March run yet?"

Ice barked out a laugh. "No, seein' as it's only fuckin' January."

"What about target practice?" Atlas demanded. "Drix told me your aim stinks worse than dogshit. Don't you think your time's better spent practicin'?"

My gaze bounced back and forth between the two men.

Ice's arm tightened over my shoulders.

Atlas' hands balled up into fists, his eyes spitting hot lava.

"You don't gotta tell me what to do, *brother*," Ice gritted out. "I'm an officer too, and you ain't the fuckin' boss of me. I know what you're doin', and I think you need to remember one small detail. I've got Prez's blessing." He smirked.

Atlas took a step toward us, his face twisting with anger. "Don't mean a goddamned thing."

"Yeah, it does," Ice retorted, not backing down. "You had your chance, remember? You fucked it up, and from what I've seen this week, you haven't stopped."

I looked between the two men.

It was like they were talking in riddles. So much anger charged the air that I could almost see electricity spark between them. Neither was going to back down.

"Hey." I looked up at Ice. "It's okay. We'll do it another time."

Ice glanced down at me, and his face softened.

"She can't anyway," Atlas muttered. "She's stayin' down here. Want her to teach me that gun disablin' move. Don't worry. I'll make sure she eats." His mouth quirked up.

Ice nodded, a knowing look on his face. "Right. So that's how it is, huh?"

Atlas folded his arms across his chest. "Yip."

Ice's lips pressed gently against the side of my head. "I'll catch ya later, Soph," he murmured into my hair. "How 'bout I come over to your place later? We can watch a movie and order in."

"Umm." I scrambled for something to say. I'd told him that I just wanted to be friends. I hardly knew him, and I didn't want a man I hardly knew in my house.

My discomfort must've been written all over my face because Atlas lifted a hand to cover his cocky grin. That

Atlas

one move majorly pissed me off. He wasn't only being an asshole to me but also to Ice, and that wasn't fair.

Mr. Cocky Ass needed a lesson.

"Is seven okay?" I asked, smiling sweetly at Ice.

A deep rumble escaped from Atlas' chest.

Ice looked down and me and grinned. "See ya then." He turned on his heel, walking across the room and up the steps. "I'll bring Chinese." He gave me a loose salute and disappeared.

Atlas glared at me. "You're not interested in him, so I dunno why you're leadin' him on?"

My mouth compressed into a hard line. "I'm not leading him on." I spun and headed toward the ring. "He's kind, he's respectful, and it's just one date. Why do you care anyway? You've made your feelings about me clear. It's none of your business."

He fell into step beside me. "Is that what this is? You tryin'a show me what I'm missin?"

"I can't do anything right as far as you're concerned, can I, Atlas?" I snapped. What was his problem? I'd done what he told me and left him alone.

"Not when you make a date with him, fuck no." He reached out and grabbed my waist, tugging me into him so hard that I stumbled into his chest.

Shocked, my eyes darted up to his. My stomach went heavy when I saw concern shining in his black orbs. "What are you doing?" I asked, confused.

"Who hurt you?" he demanded gently.

My heart thudded. "Mind your business."

He stared down at me, forehead furrowed.

I lowered my gaze as his thumb stroked across my hip precisely as he did when I removed the bullet from his shoulder. My eyes rested on his tee-covered chest. He was breathing heavily too.

My hip seemed to tingle from his touch. I almost let out a moan.

Jules Ford

What was his game? Why did he keep denying this thing between us? Every time we seemed to get closer, he pushed me away again. We were going around in circles so fast that my head spun.

"Eyes to me," he murmured. "Don't shut me out, Stitch baby." He bent down until our foreheads were touching.

My gaze lifted back to his.

"Don't go out with him." He said the words so quietly that I almost didn't catch them.

Dark eyes locked with mine, and he lifted his head slightly. Slowly, his face moved closer to mine.

My thoughts began to race, screaming at me to pull away. It was like groundhog day. We'd been here so often that I knew what he'd do next.

Humiliate me.

The door opened as if on cue, and voices floated down the stairs.

Atlas jumped away from me as if I'd burned him. Swiftly, he made his way toward the ring, pulled himself up, and ducked under the ropes.

My throat immediately heated because it was evident he was trying to put as much distance between us as possible. It was so confusing. He was making all the moves, not me, and now he'd reverted to asshole mode.

The door slammed again, and a child's high-pitched little voice filled the air.

"Aaassleeess."

Huh?

Little feet began to pitter-patter, and another sweet voice rang out. "Uncle Dan. Are you here 'cauth me and Thunny are ready?"

"Down here, Gabby," he called out just as two little girls came into view, followed by the ugliest dog I'd ever seen.

I smiled as they ran to the bottom of the stairs and skipped toward us, holding hands.

Atlas

One girl had reddish brown hair and huge grey eyes. I recognized her immediately as Layla's daughter, Sunshine.

I'd met her at the hospital last summer when someone shot Bowie. She wore a cute pink workout outfit with a matching sweatband holding her hair back.

Her friend was dressed identically. She had long, dark hair and huge, dark eyes.

I covered my laugh with my hand.

Both little girls had drawn on black eyes. They looked so cute but hilarious at the same time.

"Assless, we've come to do boxings with you," Sunny sang. "Mama and Iris said that we can as long as we don't annoys you." She let go of Gabby's hand and began to twirl, calling out. "Look at my outfits."

The other little girl pointed to her face. "We've got black eyes, Uncle Dan. Tho if we get hit it won't matter."

The door banged again, and women's voices began to carry down the stairs toward us.

"Can't believe they've kept her away from us."

"Abe said she's been here all week."

I looked toward the stairs, recognizing Freya's voice. "We'll work out session times with Sophie," she said quietly. "Do you think Cara would work on Cash for shooting lessons?"

Four women came into view on the stairs.

I recognized Layla and Freya and I'd met Iris the morning after I took Atlas' bullet out. I didn't recognize the other woman.

"Cara won't speak to him. We've got more chance of getting around Boner," Layla muttered.

"Easy. I can do that, no problem." Freya laughed.

"Fuck," Atlas muttered, shaking his head.

"My Abe will help us with shooting practice," Iris said.

Jules Ford

Atlas cleared his throat and rumbled, "I'll fuckin' help you. If you women are gonna pick up guns, I wanna make sure you don't shoot my dick off by mistake."

"Five dollars, please, Assless," Sunny yelled.

"Yeah, Uncle Dan," Gabby called out. "Five dollarth pleathe."

Atlas looked down at the girls with narrowed eyes. "Christmas day's over. Bank's closed."

Laughter filled the air as the women reached the bottom of the stairs.

"Gabby. Uncle Dan's already paid lots of money into the college fund," the dark-haired woman said. "You don't want to bankrupt him. Who'd give you your allowance then?"

Atlas looked up at the heavens, muttering under his breath.

I grinned at his obvious embarrassment. God only knew what they were talking about, but anything that made Atlas pissed was okay with me.

The ugly dog bounded to the ring and jumped at the side, whimpering to get up.

"JB needs a walk," Atlas rasped, looking down at the two girls.

"I already did, Assless," Sunny punched her hands to her little hips, obviously offended. "Jolly Batman dids a pee in the yard, but then he wanted hugs, and Iris was cooking bacon, and it's his favorite, so he cames in. He loves you, Assless. Look how happy he is."

Jolly Batman sat and looked up pleadingly at Atlas, his tongue lolling out of the side of his mouth.

"Fuckin' dog's spoiled rotten," he bit out. "Needs a kennel and to be kept outside."

"He'd be sad in the yard," Sunny insisted. "And it's too cold. Anyway, you're just a meanie."

"Meanie. Meanie. Uncle Dan's a meanie," Gabby chanted.

Atlas

Sunny grabbed her hands, and they began to skip around. "Meanie. Meanie." They sang at the top of their voices. "Assless is a meanie."

Atlas scrubbed a hand down his face. "Fuck me." He bent under the ropes and jumped down from the ring.

Layla's lips twitched. "Stop it, girls. We're here to ask Sophie if she'll train us, not torture Atlas."

"But Mama," Sunny said. "I's already a good fighter. My daddy teached me. Look!" She bent forward, stuck her little fist out, and sprinted fast toward Atlas.

"Sunshine! No!" Layla shouted, but it was too late.

Sunny ran smack into Atlas' groin.

He let out a loud 'oof' and bent over double. All color drained from his face, and he turned a weird shade of green.

"See, it worked," Sunny shouted and started jumping around. Gabby joined her. "It worked. It worked," they sang loudly.

The dark-haired woman and Iris busted out laughing.

Atlas fell to his knees, groaning loudly with his hands clutching his penis.

I winced.

"I'm so sorry," Layla said, rushing toward Atlas, her face bright red. "Are you okay?" Her hands flew up to her mouth. "Oh, my God."

He let out a strangled moan.

"I won. I won," Sunny chanted, still jumping around with Gabby.

My heart went out to him. He was in pain. It didn't matter that he'd been an asshole for the last week. I wouldn't let anyone suffer if I could help it. Sometimes I wished I could control the healer in me, especially when the person who needed help was a prick like Atlas.

"Let me take a look?" I suggested.

"Fuck no," he rasped. "I'm not gettin' my schlong out in front'a the girls." His familiar deep voice was almost a squeak.

"We'll go." Layla bit her lip, attention still on Atlas. "But we'll come back later when you've finished the afternoon training. John told us about that hair-pulling move. We'd love to see it."

I leaned down toward Atlas and helped him up. "Come on. Lucky for you, there's a doctor in the house."

"You'll be okay, Atlas," Iris called over as they all made their way to the stairs. "Sophie will take you in hand."

Jesus!

Layla started to giggle.

The other woman snorted. "He'd love that."

"Fuck off, Ro," Atlas barked.

God only knew why my cheeks burned.

I was a doctor. I'd seen men's genitalia before, but if I was honest, the thought of seeing Atlas' penis made my skin grow warm and uncomfortable.

The sound of footsteps faded as the women exited the gym. My lips pursed as I took Atlas' elbow and led him toward a big wooden bench on the far side of the room. "I know it's sensitive down there, but they're more robust than you think."

"Bet Bowie told her to fuckin' get me in the schlong," he grumbled. "Wouldn't put anythin' past that smartass fucker." He limped, obviously in pain.

"Stop being a baby," I scolded. A memory pinged in my head of the night Atlas got shot, when Cash hauled him onto his side like a sack of potatoes so I could look at his back. "You've probably done worse to them. Take your shorts and underwear down, please, so I can look."

"It'll be okay," he muttered

I rolled my eyes. "There's no need to be embarrassed. I've seen one before, you know. I'm sure yours is nothing to get excited about."

He smirked. "Ain't embarrassed, Stitch, and I bet ya fifty it is."

Atlas

I shook my head exasperatedly. "It's a penis. All men have one. I need to check you out in case Sunny gave you a hernia. Now, stop being a baby, and let me see…." My voice trailed off as he dropped his shorts.

I looked down, and my body locked.

His penis had swollen to almost the width of a soda can. My eyes nearly popped out of my head, and I winced. He must've been in agony. "Umm… Okay, so you've got some swelling going on down there. It's probably a good idea if I drive you to the ED. I think you need to get it X-rayed."

He bent forward slightly and peered down at it. His fingers grabbed hold, and he shifted it left, then right, examining it closely. His eyes came to mine, slightly bewildered. "Looks normal to me."

My mouth fell open.

Oh, my God!

"That's normal?" I asked, disbelief lacing my tone. Surely that wasn't its regular size?

He shrugged. "Yip."

I looked down at it again, almost reeling. Even soft, it was probably the biggest penis I'd ever seen, not that I'd seen many.

In the early days of our marriage, I'd watched some porn with Luke to experiment. I remembered a guy with a giant dick in the movie, but even that was smaller than Atlas'.

It must have been seven or eight inches, *soft*. Long and thick with a slight curve and protruding veins. The head was like a giant mushroom. It wasn't ugly, though, and he took care of himself because the dark hair at the base was neatly trimmed.

It was a handsome penis.

Flabbergasted, my eyes met his again. "What size does it go to when you're… you know?"

"Hard?" he asked.

I jerked a nod.

Jules Ford

He grinned. "Twelve on a good day, eleven on a bad."

Jesus.

I gaped. "How can you?... How do you?"

"Fuck?" He smirked.

I nodded again, lost for words.

His eyes went half-mast. "Lots of prep."

My pussy flooded at the thought of what lots of prep with Atlas might entail. A prickle of awareness flickered over my skin, making the tiny hairs on my arms stand up.

"You're blushin'," he said gently. He raised his finger and traced a line across my throat. "Or is that a sex flush?" A wide smile spread across his face. "Does my big dick make you hot, Stitch baby?"

Yes!

"No!" I squeaked.

He leaned forward, so our faces were close. "So, you're sayin' that if I slipped my hand down your sexy, tight little pants right this second, your pussy wouldn't gush all over my fingers?"

Goosebumps trailed down my arms. I tried desperately not to rub my thighs together, even though I needed to ease the ache that pulsed through my clit.

I'd never gotten this turned on by just looking at a dick before. No man had ever had that effect on me, not even Luke, back in our honeymoon period.

Everything about Atlas appealed to me, which was ridiculous because he wasn't even the kind of man I usually found attractive. He just had something about him that I couldn't explain. It was like he had an inner quality that pulled me into his riptide and wouldn't let me go.

But riptides were unpredictable and volatile. I needed peace of mind.

His eyes shone with interest, exactly as they did at the hospital the first time he ever kissed me and then pulled the rug out from under me minutes later.

Atlas

I was naïve then, and I fell for it, hook, line, and sinker, but I'd learned my lesson. I may have been hopeful that Atlas was a decent man once, but he'd shown me countless times that he wasn't, at least not to me.

I took a step back and pulled my spine straight. "No damage done." Forcing my gaze away, I moved to the opposite side of the room to grab my gym bag.

"Where you goin'?"

The anger in his voice made me glance back to see him reach down and quickly pull up his shorts. Heavy footsteps echoed around the gym as he stomped after me. "Get your ass back here, Stitch. Things were just getting interestin'."

I hauled the strap of my bag over my shoulder and headed for the stairs. The air in the room suddenly seemed hot and oppressive, even though it was snowing outside and the air-con was on low.

I was desperate to get out of there, to get away from him before he made me vulnerable and humiliated me just like he did every other time.

"Stitch!" he called after me as I swept up the stairs. I kept my eyes ahead and ignored him. He wasn't going to make a fool of me again. No way would I let him.

"You can run, baby, but I'll catch you. I'll always catch you."

I kept going, and I let out a snort. Maybe I was naïve when it came to Atlas, but stupid?

Never.

Chapter Nine

Atlas

Whisky eyes swam through my mind for the hundredth time that mornin'.

I had to reach under the table and push my burgeoning cock down. I'd been gettin' massive chubs on and off for the last three days since Stitch's eyes were glued to my dick down in the gym.

"What the fuck are you doin' under there?" Prez demanded, nodding down at my schlong.

Ice let out a snort.

"Probably tryin' to find it," Cash muttered.

I smirked. "Haven't you got a shrink to go and whine to?"

Cash looked down and shut his big mouth.

Good choice.

I glanced at Prez. "How long are they gonna be? I got shit to sort. Ain't it law that nobody can be late to Church?"

"What you gotta sort?" Drix demanded. "Nobody's got work while we're organizin' the trainin'. All you gotta do is turn up at the gym and learn some Krav Maga."

I sat forward. "When's Colt due back? Need him to look into somethin' for me."

"What the fuck do you want with Colt?" Prez asked. "It's not like you to use his services."

My eyes darted to Ice, and I shot him a cocky wink. "Need a background sweep done on Stitch. Wanna know everything there is to know about her."

A soft gurgle escaped his throat, not that I gave a fuck.

For the last few days, I'd been touchin' Stitch in training as much as humanly possible. Every time Ice the fucker went to do a demo with her, I called him off and took his place.

I'd had my hands glidin' over every inch of her tight little body, all in the name of Krav Maga, and I made sure he saw every touch. I'd fuckin' loved watchin' him get more and more frustrated.

Me bein' handsy also worked in my favor 'cause I had a point to prove to the doc.

My attitude toward her up to then had been sketchy. I knew that. But before I saw her train, I had no clue that she could take care of herself. I'd heard through the grapevine that she was a tough broad, but nobody told me she was such an accomplished fighter.

Watchin' her did two things to me.

One. It gave me hope.

She was a talented fighter. If any woman out there could hold her own, it was her. That suited me 'cause I didn't doubt that the Sinners' bullshit would blow back on the women. If anyone went after her, I knew she'd be able to defend herself, and that made me feel a whole lot fuckin' better about bringin' her into the club.

Two. The way she fought was sexy as fuck, and that made me crazy for her.

Her body was toned and strong, and she moved gracefully. I couldn't drag my eyes away, and the more I watched her, the more I wanted to sink my cock into her little pussy.

Atlas

Stitch's particular body type had never appealed to me before. She always tied her hair up and didn't wear make-up much, unlike the women I usually ran with. But the closer I looked, the more I realized she didn't need it.

She was naturally beautiful. I couldn't stop obsessing over her.

"What's going on between you and Sophie?" Abe asked, eyes twinkling. The smartass knew what he was doin'. Every man at the table sat forward to listen to what I had to say.

Sometimes sayin' nothin' was more meaningful, so I just quirked an eyebrow and kept my mouth shut for a change.

"He's bein' a dick," Ice gestured toward me, face hard. "The minute I asked Sophie out, he started chancing his hand. In training, he's all over her like a rash. He's doin' it to try to get to me, the fucker."

"Thought you weren't gonna bother with the pretty little doctor?" Abe looked between Ice and me, smirkin'.

I rested my elbows on the table. "Ain't no shame in a man changin' his mind."

The entire room went silent.

I smirked as I took in my brothers' shocked faces, except Abe, who was grinnin' from ear to ear.

"No fuckin' way!" Cash's voice held a thread of surprise.

"What?" I fixed him with a stare. "I'm allowed to rethink my decision."

Prez looked at me knowingly. "You know the doc ain't the type to let you fuck her and chuck her, right?"

I let out a chuckle. "You think I haven't worked that out?"

"What about your harem?" Ice asked angrily. "You gonna put Soph on rotation? Visit her when you can fit her in around all your other women?"

My body tensed. "Are you for real? You've got some nerve, Iceman."

He looked down at his hands.

"People in glass houses shouldn't throw stones, brother. Tell 'em what you were doin', or should I say *who* you were doin' last night." I looked him up and down. "You talk to me about harems."

Abe glared at Iceman. "Now you gotta tell us. What've you been up to?"

"Fuck off, Atlas," Ice muttered under his breath.

"Okay dickwad, I'll tell 'em." My eyes scanned all my brothers' faces. "After my meetin' with Prez last night, I went straight to bed. Just as I got to my door, I turned, and lo and behold, Stella strolled out of Ice's room smilin' like a kid who ate all the candy."

Iceman's eyes hit his boots.

"Ya stupid prick," Abe muttered, his lips thinning in disgust. "How d'ya think you're gonna get a good woman like Sophie if you're still takin' up with the club girls?"

"I had a little think about that too," I went on. "If Iceman had all these feelin's for the doc, why's he fuckin' other women?" My lips flattened as I shook my head at him. "Seems to me he doesn't give a shit about her."

"Jesus." Ice glowered at me. "It's not like she's my ol' lady. We've not even gone on a fuckin' date."

Prez held his hand up. "Whoa. Hold up a minute. You told me you were goin' over to her place with Chinese food the other night. You wouldn't stop talkin' about it. It was like Hannah Montana met a Jonas brother with all the excitement and date talk. I thought you was gonna have a fuckin' period any minute."

I let out a roar of laughter. Didn't know who the fuck Prez was talking about, but that period shit was funny as hell.

"Who the fuck's Hannah Montana?" Drix demanded.

"Billy Ray Cyrus' kid," Cash muttered.

Atlas

"What, the achy breaky heart dude with the crazy mullet?" He looked confused. "He's got a kid called Hannah Montana?"

Bowie began to laugh. "No. His girl Miley played a chick on TV called Hannah Montana."

"Miley Cyrus?" Drix asked, face scrunched with confusion.

Cash snorted.

Hendrix grinned. "She can wreck my balls all day long."

Chuckles went up.

"Okay. I'll take the bait." Abe pointed at Ice again. "What's that gotta do with his date."

"Just sayin'." Prez chuckled. "He was excited about it. Reminded me of a giggly fuckin' schoolgirl."

I laughed so hard that I had to hold my stomach. The other guys joined in.

"For fuck's sake," Ice snapped. "The truck wouldn't start. Okay?"

Cash's chuckles died, and his eyes slashed to me questioningly.

My lips twitched 'cause I knew Cash would keep his mouth shut. It was the first lesson a man earned in the slammer.

He shook his head at me slowly.

"Why didn't you take your bike? Or one'a the club's SUVs?" Prez asked Ice.

"It was snowing," he explained. "And the SUVs were all inside the garage. There was a party that night, and all the guys blocked them in with their cages."

Prez's face scrunched up in confusion. "So, what did you do? Fly to her?"

Ice looked down. He couldn't meet Prez's stare. "Nah. I stayed here and partied."

Abe's eyes went massive. "You dick. Did you at least call her and cancel?"

"Yeah!" the Road Captain looked offended. "Course I did. I'm not a fuckin' idiot."

"That's a matter of opinion," Abe mumbled.

I barked out another laugh. I fuckin' loved seein' Ice get his dues.

Prez shook his head in exasperation. "Let me get this straight. You had a chance with a sweet, pretty doctor, and instead of runnin' with it, you decide to stand her up and party at the club instead?"

"Well. When you put it like that…." Ice grimaced.

"You were all for it last week." Abe scratched his head as he thought back. "You thought she was the best thing since crotchless panties. What the fuck happened?"

Ice sat back in his chair and scrubbed a hand down his face. "Yeah, I know. And now I've fucked it."

"Ice," Prez barked. "Talk!"

"She won't agree to another date," Ice scraped out. "She just wants to be friends. I've fucked up big time."

Cash let out a chuckle.

Prez brought a hand up to his mouth to cover his smile.

I threw my head back and roared with laughter at the fuckin' idiot. A part of me was proud of Stitch for standin' her ground. She didn't take shit, and neither did I. We had that in common at least.

If Ice wanted her, he would've moved heaven and earth to get to their date, but he fell at the first hurdle. Then, days later, he's screwin' a club girl – that's even if he waited days. If I knew Ice, and I did, he probably fucked a club girl at the party the night he arranged to see Stitch.

If Ice *had* gone out of his way and made it to her place that night, I might have backed off. On second thoughts, I wouldn't have backed off what so-fuckin'-ever. I knew I wasn't the best bet for her, but I was a better bet than him.

Sucked to be Ice 'cause I'd decided that I was gonna make my move after all.

He didn't stand a chance.

A knock came from the door. All eyes turned to see Bowie stalkin' into the room with Boner behind him.

"'Bout fuckin' time," Prez muttered. "Told ya to go fetch Boner. Where was he? Tokyo?" He glanced at the Prospect. "Wanted you here to talk about training, but before that, tell me, how's ya bullet wound?"

The Sinners had shot Boner a few weeks back while he was operating the gates. Luckily, they didn't hit anything vital. Freya had managed to stitch him up without much trouble.

Boner tapped his waist. "Can't feel a thing, Boss."

Dagger's lips curved up. "This is your first time at the big table. All Church virgins have to complete a ritual or get the fuck out."

Boner's eyes grew wide.

"Nobody's gonna ask you to do anythin' crazy," Hendrix added. "This is tradition, and the Speed Demons are all about that. Your Prez has asked you to complete a club ritual. No ritual, no cut. Do you feel me?"

The prospect didn't seem any happier.

Cash and I exchanged a look, lips twitchin'.

Dad nodded at Boner's jeans. "Drop ya breeches."

Chuckles rose through the air.

"But Boss. I ain't wearin' no underwear." Boner's face turned pink. He looked around the table with a shocked expression. "Why I gotta show you my dick?"

Abe let out a snort.

"Why you runnin' around my clubhouse without undershorts?" Prez demanded. "We gotta ritual to carry out, Prospect. Now we all gotta look at your meat and two veggies. Jesus, save us."

I roared out a laugh.

"Come on, Prospect," Drix barked. "Do as Prez says. Drop ya pants. You're among men. We've all got dicks."

Boner's belt gave a chink as his jeans fell to the floor. He quickly pulled the hem of his tee down to cover his schlong.

"Now ya gotta jump on one leg," Prez ordered.

Boner's eyes went huge, but he obeyed and started jumpin' up and down on his right foot.

I swear I heard his dick slap against his thighs. I bent forwards in my seat, tears formin'.

"Now pat ya head," Prez ordered.

Boner kept hoppin' and raised a hand to his noggin, his other still coverin' his junk. The poor fucker looked mortified. His face was scarlet, his expression pained.

"Turn around and face the wall, but don't stop what you're doin'." Dagger bit back a smile.

Boner kept hoppin' but turned his body until his lily-white ass was starin' us in the face, his glutes wobbling as he jumped.

The floodgates opened, and every man at the table began silently busting a gut.

Prez was coverin' his mouth with his hand, hidin' his chuckles.

Tears streamed down Abe's face as he held his stomach.

Everybody's shoulders shook as they tried to keep their hoots and hollers contained.

We knew Prez's game. He did the same shit to all the members when they were about to get patched in. Ritual? Nope. It was just Prez hazin' Boner the same as he did to every other brother when they were about to patch in. Every member had to go through it, or they'd never get their cut.

Abe busted out laughin', unable to keep his chuckles under wraps anymore. The rest of us followed suit, fillin' the room with roars and catcalls.

Boner stopped jumpin' and froze on the spot.

Atlas

Prez held his hand up, gesturing to us all to shut up. "S'okay, Boner. Pull your jeans back up your ass. Seen all we needed to see there."

Everybody laughed harder.

Boner pulled his jeans up and fastened his belt before looking at us unflinchingly. Brave when you considered that the first time in Church was as intimidating as fuck. Plus, he'd just been jumpin' around like a lunatic with his dick in his hand.

Boner winced. "There is no ritual, is there, Boss?"

We all busted out laughin' again.

"No, Boner, there's not a ritual," Dagger replied through his guffaws. "So next time a man asks you to drop your pants and start jumpin' around, think twice. You need to wise up."

Bone shrugged. "If he's hot, I'll jump around with my dick out all day long."

Another laugh escaped me.

I liked the Prospect. He was down to earth.

Hendrix leaned forward, arms on the table. "Didn't know you liked men, Boner. Usually, that shit sweeps around the clubhouse like wildfire."

Cash shrugged. "The boys probably don't give a fuck. Boner's not the first gay brother we've had."

"I'm not gay, Cash," Boner corrected. "I'm bi. I like men and women."

Abe let out a hoot. "Good on ya, boy."

"How does that work out for ya, Bone?" Ice asked, leanin' forward. "Tell me, brother. Do you have threesomes or just alternate?"

A pink stain appeared on Boner's cheeks. "Both."

"Lucky little fuck," the Road Captain muttered.

"No difference in you fuckin' two women, Ice," Boner muttered. "Only the woman shares me with the other guy instead of another chick. And you can't tell me that none of you've shared a woman before. Remember,

I've seen you guys at club parties. I've picked up your wraps."

"Well, hot damn," Prez muttered, rubbin' his beard. "We'll have to look into gettin' club boys in soon." He looked at me. "Any men ever apply to be a club whore?"

I thought back to the constant flow of applications we received. Many women asked to join the club, but I couldn't recall any men. "Nope. But if Boner wants a guy to come in, I can ask around. Know a gay MC in Vegas and Oregon. I can enquire with them. He ain't patched in, so if we find someone, it'll have to wait until he passes probation." I turned to the Prospect and gave him the death glare. "*If* he passes probation."

Boner shrugged. "No need to look on my account. I'm fussy about where I stick my dick."

That was true enough.

I'd never seen Boner go with one'a the club girls. He talked to them and was always respectful. He played taxi driver when they needed to go somewhere and helped them out, but it was more of a friend thing.

Prez rubbed his beard, keeping his stare on Boner. "Right. How's the target practice goin'?"

"Good. We've got the sniper team picked out," Cash informed Prez while he nodded at Boner.

The Prospect went to the inside pocket of his cut, pulled out a folded piece of paper, and handed it to Dagger.

Prez took a glance and passed it to me.

I looked at the names and smiled when I saw Reno's name scrawled on the list. Bowie would be pleased. "Looks okay to me, boss." I passed the piece of paper to Bo.

"What did you think of target practice trainin' Bone?" Prez asked. "You reckon it went well?"

The prospect jerked a nod. "I liked Cash's process of elimination. How we arranged it made certain that we'd get the best shooters. We got a good team of men."

Atlas

Prez sat back in his chair. "Good. You can go. Get Sparky in for a break, and you take over the gate for a while. You think you're up to it?"

I watched as Boner gave another nod, turned, and disappeared through the door, closin' it quietly behind him.

Abe looked around. "Does he know anythin' yet?"

"Nah," I told him. "Nothin'. We still doin' it in a couple'a weeks?"

"Yup," Drix confirmed. "But we still need to decide on his road name. Gotta get the patch ready for Iris to sew onto his new cut."

Prez got up from his chair and went to the desk. "We got it down to two names, right."

We all made noises of agreement.

"Okay," Prez walked back to the table with post-its and pens, then handed them to us. "Think about the names. All of you write down the one that you think suits him best. Pick the name that represents him the most. Got it?"

I thought about the suggestions we came up with and scrawled the one I liked best for Boner. After folding it in half, I handed it to Prez.

As soon as Prez had a hold of 'em all, he unfolded them and read through the names.

"Looks like Boner's got a road name." He held up a post-it for us to see.

"Lucky fucker," Ice muttered. "That's a cool as hell name."

"What's the matter with Iceman?" Prez demanded. "That's cool too."

Ice curled his lip slightly. "I was named after someone else."

"Wait," Drix said, lookin' confused. "Did you fly fighter jets in the Navy?"

Ice shrugged.

125

"And you look like that actor from Top Gun." He snapped his fingers a few times as he thought. "Val Kilmer. That's the dude you look like."

"So they say," Ice agreed. "But now I've grown my hair and beard, so it's a moot point."

Bowie leaned forward to address Drix. "Val Kilmer was cool as fuck in Top Gun."

"Didn't chicks go crazy for that guy?" Abe asked.

Ice grinned.

"So, what's the fuckin' problem?" I asked him.

"Didn't say there was one," he replied. "Just think Boner's road name is cooler."

"Give me fuckin' strength." Prez looked heavenward, muttering before his eyes snapped back toward Ice. "We should'a called ya fuckin' Goose seein' as ya squawk like one."

We all started laughing at Ice while he shook his head, smilin'.

"Okay," Prez continued. "Next on the agenda. Have we had any Sinner sightin's?"

"Nope." Cash nodded to me. "Atlas and me have been questionin' Piston. He told us they've only got half their men there. Bear's gone, and he took April with him. Right now, Thrash's SAA's runnin' the show.

My mind went back to the night we blew up their compound. They hadn't retaliated yet, but it was only a matter of time. Kit had been workin' with me on tactics. We were as ready as we'd ever be.

"Breaker did well the other night, Prez. He's a good tactician." I looked at each man in turn. "We should be usin' him in all the plannin'."

Kit's military unit didn't take losers. The problem was when he came home, he partied too much and was labeled a fuck-up. Since then, the brothers pigeonholed him as the good-time brother. Nobody had given him a chance to prove himself.

Atlas

Now Breaker didn't even bother trying. It stood to reason that if you told a man he was a waste of space for long enough, he'd start to believe it.

I quirked an eyebrow at Bo. "You all underestimate him, but you're wrong. Breaker's tactically minded and an expert in blowing shit up."

Prez dropped his head into his hands. "Fuck me. Hugh Heffner and Vin Diesel doin' recon together. God help us all." He looked up. "I'm not sure Kit's the right choice. He's goin' through the wringer right now, and his head's outta the game."

Dagger was right, but the only way to get Breaker's noggin back in the game was to make him play it, but his pop had written him off.

"I've got faith in him," I reiterated. "And I'll happily have him workin' on my team. He'll do good, and he's got that crazy streak you sad old fucks haven't." I grinned to take the sting outta my words.

"Okay," Prez said quietly. "Use him. But try not to get into any trouble, brother. We got enough goin' on. We don't need you and Kit makin' shit worse." He looked around. "Any other business?"

Silence.

He grabbed the gavel and banged it into the sound block. "Church is out."

Chairs scraped as we got to our feet and headed for the door.

Cash clapped me on the back. "Wanna word, brother."

I knew exactly what he wanted to talk about, but I thought he'd at least give it a day before he called me out on my shit.

"See you out there," Cash called to the brothers filing through the door. "Just wanna quick chat with Atlas about the trainin'."

When their footsteps had faded away, Cash turned to me. "You're a sneaky fuck. Now I get what you were up to."

I played dumb. "Huh?"

"The night Ice said he was takin' Sophie out, you were in the garage with your head under the hood of his truck. What did you do?"

I pressed my lips together, tryin' not to laugh.

"Did you, or did you not sabotage their date?" Cash asked.

I held my hands up defensively. "I just disconnected the battery. If Ice wanted to take Sophie out, he would've found a way. All I did was test his mettle."

Cash scratched his chin and thought for a minute. "Yeah," he murmured. "Guess he wasn't that interested in her if he gave up at the first hurdle."

"Yip," I agreed. "He could'a called a cab if he was that desperate, right? Now she won't give him another chance, so I'm gonna slide in there."

He leveled me with a look. "Brother. Are you sure about this? Have you ever had a steady woman before? You know that Sophie ain't the type to be okay with bein' a one and done."

I folded my arms across my chest and glared. "D'ya think I'm as stupid as you?"

"Atlas, come on," he cajoled. "Do you even really want her, or are you just tryin'a get at Ice?"

My blood began to heat, but as much as Cash's thought process pissed me off, I could understand his way of thinking.

I'd only ever fucked women before, never had anyone special in my life. I was a biker through and through, and I liked living free. Rules didn't interest me. I was all for men makin' their own rules as long as they didn't hurt anyone. I'd always put the club's needs before my own, no questions asked, and that fulfilled me, but since I'd met Sophie, I'd begun to think that maybe it was time to take life a bit more seriously.

The doc was the first woman in a long time to seize my interest and hold it. I knew I'd fought it at first, purely 'cause we lived in different worlds. But I'd seen the sassy, kickass, take no shit side of her, and I liked it a lot.

"I'm willing to give it a go," I said with a jerk of my head. "She's a good woman. I could do worse."

"Good luck with that." Cash grinned. "The boys told me about you givin' her a hard time in trainin'. You think she's gonna go for it after you acted the asshole?"

I went to reply, 'hell yeah,' but the words got stuck in my throat. Cash didn't know half of it. Bein' an asshole to her was nothin' compared to the rest of my bullshit.

Stitch had been standoffish with me over the last few days, which worried me. I was just startin' to feel some genuine interest, but now *she* wasn't on the same page.

A thought hit me like a juggernaut.

The pretty doc had dug herself deep under my skin; surprisingly, I liked her there more than I probably should.

My heart gave a kick as the memories of me bein' a dick flashed through my mind. I recalled how I spoke to her when I stormed her house over a cat attack, and I fuckin' cringed.

Every interaction up to then had consisted of me givin' her a hard time. If I was bein' honest with myself, I couldn't remember one kind word.

My gut sank to my boots.

Fuck.

I raised my hand and rubbed at the sudden tightness in my chest while my thoughts scrambled.

I'd been a total dick toward Stitch, and that behavior had come back to bite me in the ass. If I wanted to get to know the doc better, I had to pull out all the stops and show her there was more to me than just an asshole.

Unfortunately, I was startin' to realize that I'd burned many bridges.

Last Summer, I gave Bowie a piece of advice. Maybe I should've been takin' that same advice and applyin' it to my current situation.

A wave of sickness washed through me, and I scraped a hand down my face.

I'd been a bona fide cunt, and now looked like a big ol' grovel was in my future.

Atlas

Chapter Ten

Sophie

My skin tingled as Atlas trailed his fingertips across my back.

I sucked in a breath, my stomach fluttering.

The utter confusion that had been prevalent for days reared its head again, and I looked up at him questioningly. I didn't get it. One minute he laughed at my body. Then his hands were all over me.

He grinned at me, eyes soft. As much as I hated myself for it, I couldn't help thinking how beautiful that was. When he smiled, really smiled, his face was stunning.

It was my second week at the clubhouse, and we were flying through the training.

Things were going much better than I thought they would when I first came here. Lately, there'd been a change in him. That meant there'd been a change in all the men because they took their cues from him.

It was hard to believe that the complex, unyielding man who'd frustrated me to no end mere days ago had done such a complete U-turn. The abrasiveness that used to lace his tone with every interaction had turned into courtesy and respect. The hard attitude and dismissive looks from a week ago morphed into honest conversations, thoughtful questions, and a wicked sense of humor.

A sense of camaraderie had grown between us. The glower that had been a permanent fixture on Atlas' face was long gone. In its place was an openness I'd never seen from him before.

I should've been heaving a sigh of relief and enjoying the relaxed atmosphere, but instead, it made me more agitated.

I was waiting for the moment he pulled the rug out from under me, the same way he always did. I was so suspicious of his motives that I jumped like a cat on a hot tin roof every time he touched me. It was exhausting because I was highly aware that leopards didn't change their spots.

"You okay, Stitch?" His mouth was so close to my throat that I felt his warm breath skate over my skin. "Ready gorgeous?" he murmured.

I shivered. "Yeah. Try and take me down, big man."

Two strong hands grabbed my shoulders, and a thick, muscled arm snaked around the front of my neck.

Muscle memory took over, thank God, because he made me lose my focus. I lurched backward, causing his arm to loosen. Taking advantage of that, I ducked and spun around to escape his hold.

"See that, brothers?" Atlas boomed to the men watching. "Simple, but effective. Look at the size of Sophie and then me. It ain't about brute strength. It's about thinkin' on your feet and gettin' scrappy. Now, give it a go."

Calls of acquiescence sounded as the guys got into pairs and began practicing.

My back warmed, and I knew Atlas was there because I could feel his body heat. I couldn't help but shiver.

"You okay there, Stitch?" he rasped. "You look a little warm."

Atlas

I closed my eyes. "I'm fine," I said with a soft sigh.

"I can see you're fine, baby," he mumbled. "You're more than fine. You're fuckin' perfect."

His words penetrated my brain, and my back stiffened.

Was he making me the butt of the joke again? Did he think I was going to keep falling for his games? I'd given him countless chances, but he'd only thrown them back in my face. Did he think I was gullible enough to fall for his shit again?

I whipped around to face him.

For days he'd been getting me worked up. He needed to stop. It was driving me crazy, and it was very confusing.

"What are you doing?" I hissed. "You keep touching me and making little innuendos, and it's very unsettling, Atlas. One minute you call me a stalker, and then you're all touchy-feely."

He gave me a cocky grin. "We're just trainin'." He took a step toward me and dropped his voice. "Stands to reason we're gonna have some close contact. What's the problem? You pissed 'cause you like it?"

My hands clenched into fists. "A week ago, you didn't want to be in the same room as me."

"So." His lazy stare swept down my body and up again. "A lot can change in a week."

I went to reply, to tell him he was an asshole, but my throat had gone dry.

"Stitch, look, I-" He went to take my arm, but I brushed him away.

"No," I grated out. "I don't get it. One minute you're asking me out. The next, you're openly getting a woman to give you a blow job in front of me. I'm on a never-ending merry-go-round ride with you and can't get off. Can't you see how crazy all this back and forth is? You've made it clear that you don't see me romantically, and that's fine. But don't then turn around and think it's okay to flirt with me because that's not fair." I stared at him pleadingly. "It has to stop."

Atlas' dark eyes softened, and his hand reached out and grabbed mine. My heart squeezed at the tingle of electricity that flowed through my fingers.

"Stitch baby," he began, then he jerked his gaze away from me and stared over my shoulder in the direction of the men.

That's when I realized that the sound of chatter had all but disappeared.

I winced and slowly craned my neck to see every male in the room watching us with undisguised interest.

I closed my eyes.

Perfect.

I turned back to Atlas, pulled my fingers from his, and raised my hands to my burning cheeks.

My breath hitched as black eyes bored into me.

It was like he could see inside my mind, see my brokenness. I didn't know if I was coming or going. I wanted him, but I didn't *want* to want him. It was all getting to be too much.

Atlas' soft black eyes finally left mine and swept around the room as he bellowed at the men. "Trainin's over for today, everyone. Get the fuck out."

The men muttered amongst themselves as they gathered their gym bags and filed toward the door. A few gave us cursory glances as they made their way out.

I looked away, cheeks still heated.

Shotgun came lumbering up to the ring, sending me a furtive glance before his stare went to Atlas. "You sure you want me to go, boss?" he asked.

"Fuck off, Shot." Atlas's eyes turned back to me. "You've been given an order. Don't make me goddamned repeat myself. Get the fuck out!"

Shotgun's mouth twisted. "But-"

Atlas

"-But nothin'," Atlas bellowed. "Don't you fuckin' question me. Go!" His eyes remained on me as he snapped at his club brother.

I held his stare, determined not to let him know how jittery he made me feel inside. I couldn't let him see what he did to me. I had to remain calm on the surface even though it felt like I was paddling like mad to keep afloat.

As soon as the door slammed closed, Atlas grabbed my hand and tugged me into him. His other hand came up and gently tucked my hair behind my ear. "Sorry for bein' a dick, Stitch."

I caught his eyes and stared incredulously. Was he crazy?

I'd buried every romantic thought after that day at my house, and now he was playing games *again*. I'd come to terms with the fact that he didn't want me. Hoping would be stupid because hope didn't get me anywhere last time.

All he ever did was let me down.

His entire body coiled like a spring. "What's goin' on?" he demanded. "Why you bein' bitchy? I thought you liked me?"

"Me? Bitchy?" I retorted. "You've been a disrespectful jerk since that first day I met you at the hospital." I poked him hard in the chest. "You've yanked my chain since day one, Atlas, and then you wonder why I'm suspicious? You're unbelievable."

His eyes surveyed me. "I thought that we got along well that day. We were gonna go out, and then you did a disappearin' act. You'd leave the room whenever I tried to speak to you. Or you were busy with a patient or a surgery." He jerked his thumb toward me. "*You* fuckin' ghosted *my* ass, not the other way around."

A strangled sound escaped my throat. "Oh. I'm sorry, was that your identical twin that I saw in Mag's place all over another woman?"

I tried hard to keep it together, to show him that he didn't affect me. But maybe I was going about it all wrong. Perhaps he needed to understand that there were consequences to his words and actions.

I took a deep breath, trying to calm my racing heart. If I couldn't control my emotions, the already heated conversation would blow up.

I pressed a hand to my chest, suddenly defeated. "You never wanted to take me out. It was only ever about what you could get from me."

A frown covered his face. "What are you gabbin' about, woman? If I didn't wanna go out, I wouldn't have asked. Do you think I go around asking random chicks out on dates? You're talkin' in fuckin' riddles."

Something twisted inside my chest.

Why was I so embarrassed about *his* actions? He was the one who should've been ashamed, seeing as he was the asshole who spoke badly about me to John that day. "You're an asshole," I ground out. "Do you get off on gaslighting me?"

"Fuck this," he snarled and stomped to the side of the ring. "You're one'a them bitches who fucks with a man's head, ain't ya?" He ducked under the ropes and jumped down to the floor. "This is why I don't need a goddamned woman. It's like dealin' with a fuckin' crazy person." He walked to the side of the room, picked up his belongings, and began toward the stairs. He had no clue that I'd overheard him that day, and now he was twisting everything and making me out to be the crazy one.

Hell to the fucking no.

That was not the way I wanted it to go.

I was the one who was supposed to call *him* crazy and rude. I should have been flouncing from the room while he looked on and regretted every word that came from his bitch mouth.

Atlas

My hands trembled because I knew I couldn't let him storm off, not without throwing every hurtful word he said about me right back at him.

"I heard you," I cried out.

His steps faltered, and he looked over his shoulder. "What do you mean, you heard me?"

I took a deep breath to steady my voice. "If I get close, charm her. She'll go out of her way to look after him and not fuck off and leave him like she just did." My tone was flat, like the bitterness that had taken up residence in my heart was suddenly reflected in my voice.

He stilled, and the satisfaction of seeing that encouraged me to continue.

"I'll take one for the team," I croaked. "You told John I'm easy on the eye, but I haven't got enough ass for your taste. Though I think my favorite part was when you laughed at me and said that I had the body of a fifteen-year-old boy." I blinked back the tears that burned the back of my eyes.

He froze in place for a full minute before his body slowly turned toward me.

Even twenty feet away, I could see the shock emanating from his eyes, though his face was blank.

"Never stuck it to a prissy man-bitch before." I retorted. "I'll let you know how that shit goes."

His large chest expanded, and his eyes swept heavenward.

He was well aware that there was no way out of this one. I had him.

"Is it just me that you're an asshole toward?" I asked softly. "It's just that I overheard people talking about you when Bowie was sick. I caught snippets about how great you are. They said that you're a hard man but protective. They talked about how everyone looked up to you and how grateful they were that you looked out for them. But that's not my experience of you at all. What did I ever do to you that made you say things like that?"

"Stitch baby." He rubbed at his temple frustratedly. "Let me explain."

"It is what it is." I shrugged, suddenly sick of the conversation. "Stop playing your stupid games. You plainly said that you don't see me like that."

"I didn't mean it, baby," he said quietly. "I felt guilty that Bowie got hurt and took it out on you. I watched you give him CPR, then leave him, and it fucked my head up. I was lettin' off steam though I get that it sounded terrible. I thought it was the wrong time to get involved with someone."

"So why ask me out?" I demanded. "Why kiss me and then act as if I'm nothing?"

"You were never nothin', Stitch," he said wistfully. "That's the fuckin' problem. You were always somethin', babe, but not somethin' I can ever have, not really."

I swallowed thickly, emotion burning my throat.

Danny 'Atlas' Woods was the embodiment of everything that every mother had ever warned their daughters about. He was rough and not just around the edges. If you made him bleed, you'd see the word 'biker' flow out of his veins.

But I'd learned over my time at the club that there was way more to him than that.

He was smart. He had a quick wit and laughed so heartily that it was impossible not to giggle with him. He cared about people, and that caring streak came with so much warmth that being around him was like sitting around an open fire.

He exuded such a sense of safety that nobody could hurt me if I were in his presence.

Except for him, of course. He reveled in hurting me.

"Leave me alone," I pleaded. "Walk away, and please just leave me alone."

"I tried," he retorted. "No can do."

I sighed audibly. "Try harder."

"Stitch," he began, but the door at the top of the stairs banged, and a voice called out. "Coooooeeeeee!"

Female voices and laughter floated down to us.

Atlas didn't take his eyes off me. "We'll continue this powwow later."

I ducked under the ropes and jumped down to the floor. "Nothing to continue. You know where you stand, and so do I. I've promised the ladies that I'll give them some self-defense tips. It's probably best if you leave us to it."

His eyes held mine as the sound of shoes clattered down the wooden steps. "Don't gimme the brush-off Stitch," he clipped. "Meet up with me later and clear the air."

I almost laughed. "No, I won't meet up with you. As I said, we both know where we stand now."

A throat cleared from the direction of the stairs. "What's going on?"

Layla, Iris, and Rosie exchanged curious looks. Tristan, who I knew from the salon, was with them. His gaze slid between Atlas and me.

"Have we caught you at a bad time?" Rosie asked with sass.

"No." I smiled brightly. "Your timing couldn't have been better. Your brother was just leaving. Come on in. I'm ready for you."

Atlas began to stomp up the stairs, his eyes still glued to me. "We'll catch up later, Stitch," he promised before disappearing from view.

Tristan stared at the staircase for a few seconds, then turned back to me. "What the hell's going on between you two?" He fanned his cheeks with his hand. "In the words of the great Nelly, it's gettin' hot in here."

"Nothing's going on." I bent down and grabbed my bottle. "All water under the bridge." I unscrewed the top and took a sip.

"Right." Rosie waggled her eyebrows. "So, you admit something *was* going on if it's water under the bridge. Gotcha."

I sighed softly. She had me there.

The last person I wanted to discuss Atlas with was his sister. I couldn't think of anything worse. Imagine the conversation.

Hey Rosie, I saw your brother's cock. He's got nothing to be ashamed of there.

"Leave her alone, Ro," Layla chastised. "Why would she talk to you about Atlas?" Her lips tipped up in a knowing smile. "Don't worry. I'll get everything out of her later."

"Seems to me that our SAA doesn't know up from down these days." Iris looked at Layla with a wide grin. "Funny how he only started losing his head when Sophie showed up."

"Meredith, honey." Tristan made his way over to me and tidied the strands of hair that had escaped my ponytail. "Come on. You can tell Uncle Trissy all about it. Have you and big boy been doing the horizontal mambo?" He lowered his voice. "Bet he's a monster in bed, right?"

"Wait." Layla's perfectly shaped eyebrows drew together. "Who's Meredith?"

"The doc," Tristan replied, nodding to me.

I rolled my eyes heavenward. "He calls me Meredith Grey."

"You're nothing like her." Iris laughed.

"Not in looks, no, but their lives may as well be the same," Tristan explained. "Meredith Grey's head of general surgery, and so's our Sophie. Meredith's beautiful, and our girl here's a beauty too." He raised a hand to his forehead dramatically. "Meredith needs

Atlas

Trissy to work his magic on her tresses, and so does our pretty doc." He whipped my tie out and fluffed up my hair.

"Hey-" I began to protest, but he cut me off.

"-I'd take it up a few inches to show off that gorgeous jawline. Then I'd hack some choppy layers into it." He pulled away from me, clapped his hands together, and squealed. "The volume would be to die for."

"You should let him do it, Sophie," Layla agreed. "Tristan's a hair genius."

I bit my lip. "I don't bother with my hair much these days. I'm always either working or training, so I only ever get it trimmed."

"I know." Tristan's lips pursed. "I keep telling Anna to give it some oomph, but she ignores me." He clasped his hands together in a begging motion, looking at me imploringly. "Let's go do your hair, Meredith. Please?"

I looked around for help, but all I got were nods and smiles.

"Have you got your kit with you?" Layla asked him. "We can use mine and Bowie's room. It's got an attached bathroom, and the lighting's great."

"Have I got my kit with me," he repeated with a roll of his eyes. "Doe girl. I'm a professional. Where I go, my kit goes."

Layla smiled at me brightly. "It'll look great. What do you think?"

I gestured around the gym. "What about training?"

Layla shrugged.

My eyes darted from one expectant face to the next. *Should I?*

Before Luke, I'd always made the most of my looks. How could I not when Kennedy was my best friend? Anyone standing next to her was in danger of fading into the background.

It wasn't a competition; Ned was so beautiful that competing against her would've been pointless. It was more of a 'trying to keep up' thing. We'd always shopped together and gone to the salon together. I had great clothes, and I always styled my hair. I wore make-up and went to bars and concerts. I socialized.

Then I met Luke.

Everything was good at first. We went out a lot; he loved it when I dressed up for him. But eventually, he began to criticize and accuse me of dressing up to meet other men. It became easier to stop making an effort.

After the divorce, I didn't want to stand out. If anything, I wanted to hide away. Maybe that was why I traveled. Nobody knew me, bothered me, or even saw me half the time. Kennedy always complained that I wasn't living. I'd always denied it, but maybe she was right.

Things had changed since I'd moved to Hambleton.

I'd changed.

People said good morning to me on the street. The coffee shop owner knew my name. I was making friends, albeit slowly. Even being at the clubhouse helped me gain confidence by forcing me to interact with new people. I'd slowly crept out of my shell because being in Hambleton made me a part of something.

Atlas had wounded my pride, but I didn't want to hide anymore.

Why should I?

A bubble of excitement bounced around my stomach. My eyes lifted to Tristan's.

"Let's do it."

"Voila!" Tristan let out a hoot as he whipped the protective sheet from my shoulders. "You look even more beautiful if I say so myself. Uncle Trissy's worked his magic again."

Atlas

I looked in the mirror and smiled. The genius had made me look five years younger.

Tristan had taken a few inches off my hair until it rested below my shoulders. The light brown of my eyes popped brighter. Even my lips seemed bigger.

Iris gave a stiff nod. "Yep. Looks good."

"You're so pretty!" Layla exclaimed.

Rosie smirked. "Bet my brother will love it."

Bees swarmed inside my stomach as her comment sunk in.

"Ro." Iris' tone held a note of warning.

"Well, he's obviously into her," Rosie argued. "I bet you twenty bucks that when he sees her, he throws her over his shoulder and ties her to his bed."

Iris nodded. "Agreed."

My gaze shifted down.

"Sophie, you should come to Boner's patch-in party," Layla exclaimed.

My eyes shot back up, and I stared at her.

I'd heard about those parties. Kennedy was invited to one when she defended one of the Three Kings MC members on gun-running charges a few years ago. She said it was wild.

"Boner's what the what?" Tristan squealed.

"You can't say anything because Boner doesn't even know yet, but he's getting patched in," Layla said quietly. "He passed probation with flying colors."

"Yes!" Rosie exclaimed. "Patch-in parties are the best. Booze, music, debauchery." She did a little happy dance. "You'll all love it."

"Can I come?" Tristan asked, eyes pleading. "I need debauchery in my life. Please!"

Layla laughed. "Of course. We'll all go. I'll ask Cara and Anna too."

"We haven't had a night out for ages." Tristan pouted. "Even when we met for drinks before the holidays, Brett Stafford appeared and ruined our fun."

Layla and Iris exchanged a look.

"What do you think, Sophie?" Rosie asked. "Are you craving a night of flowing booze, music, and debauchery?"

Good question.

A year ago, hell, a month ago, I would've run a mile, but this was a new beginning, right? I looked at my fabulous new hairstyle. Tristan was right when he said it would bring my features out. He'd made me look and feel better than I had for years. I was goddamned fantastic. Why not show off?

My eyes lifted to Rosie's, and I smiled brighter than I had in years. "I think it's a great idea."

Chapter Eleven

Atlas

One solitary light shone inside the *Cell*.
My eyes slashed straight ahead to the man whose hands were zip tied to the back'a the chair. I took in his dirty clothes, long, grey, lank, greasy hair, and unkempt salt and pepper-beard. His shoulders slumped, head hangin' forward. His face was relatively unmarked, apart from a black eye and a small cut on his jaw. But then he'd sung like Mariah at the Grammys, so we'd gone easy on him.

"Come on, Piston," I coaxed. "You can do better than that. Where does he keep the women?"

The Sinner lifted his head slowly. "Told you. I never got involved in that shit. I'm with Thrash, not Bear."

I glanced at Breaker, who lifted an eyebrow. That was the second time that Piston had said somethin' to that effect. It seemed that it wasn't all kumbaya in the Sinners' camp.

"Tell me about that," I ordered. "What's the difference with bein' with Thrash or Bear? You're all Sinners." I looked him up and down with a sneer. "Sick fucks, every one'a ya."

Piston's head shot up, and he glared. "No! I don't do what Bear does. I'm part of Thrash's crew. We're old school. We don't deal in the same shit."

"You mean women and little girls?" Kit demanded. "Fuck you, Piston. You stand by and let it happen. You don't have a moral between ya. If you allow it then you're as bad as him, worse even 'cause it makes you weak too, seein' as you say you know better. Everybody knows that if you don't stand up to bully boys and sick cunts it makes you just as complicit."

"You don't know what you're talkin' about," he rasped defensively. "It's not as easy as you think."

I leaned forward on my chair, starin' hard into his eyes. "Seems easy enough to me. Your Prez takes the little fucker in hand and makes an example of him. Job done."

Defeat washed over his face. "Thrash can't do anythin'." He closed his eyes. "He's dyin'."

A bad feelin' crawled through my chest, and I shifted in my seat.

"Thrash has got lung cancer," Piston continued. "The forty a day finally caught up with him. He's confined to bed at the clubhouse, got weeks, maybe a couple of months. Hell, he may be already gone for all I know, the time I've been here." His eyes lifted to meet mine again. "Thrash is the only one who's been able to keep Bear reigned in. For all the good it's done. Bear's gonna take over by force, if necessary. God help us all." His thin lips set in a hard line. "If you know what's good for ya, you'll find him and take him out before it's too late."

My eyes narrowed at the dark shadow that crossed his face.

How fucked up was that? The Sinners had two factions in the same camp. Old versus young. The problem was that the older boys were on their way out, startin' with Thrash, so it didn't take Einstein to work out which way it was goin'.

Breaker glanced at me, his eyes conveying the same thing that mine probably did.

Hell was about to break loose.

Atlas

"Any idea where Bear's gone?" I leaned forward, restin' my elbows on my knees, hands danglin' down. My stance seemed relaxed to everyone else, but underneath the mask, my heart was pumpin' hard.

Piston shook his head.

I rose from my seat and bent down until I was in his face. "Where's he gone?" I snarled.

Piston's eyebrows pulled together. "You think I wouldn't tell ya? The fucker's gonna bring the club down. Believe me, if I knew where he was, I'd take him out myself."

Burnin' heat stabbed my gut. Without a thought, I made a fist, pulled my arm back, and punched Piston across his face.

Piston's head snapped back, and he let out a low groan. "You can come at me all day long, asshole, but I've got nothin' else for ya. Bear don't share his hangouts with the likes of me. You'd do better nabbin' one of his crew."

Kit stepped forward. "You gotta woman? Kids? Daughters?"

Piston jerked a nod. "Yeah. Gotta wife and two daughters. You gonna go kidnap 'em? Bring 'em here and abuse 'em in front of me? Get me to talk that way?" He let out a snort. "Fuckin' pricks."

"We don't do that shit," Breaker retorted. "But if you turn full rat, we can get 'em out. Move 'em to a different state for their safety. You're as good as dead. there ain't no way out for you, but you can still save them."

Piston smiled so widely that I could see the blood that coated his back teeth. "Don't worry about my family. They'll be gone by now. My ol' lady knows what to do when I don't check in with her. As soon as they heard about the blast, she would'a taken the girls and disappeared."

He was tellin' the truth. I could see it in his eyes.

Piston's jaw ticked. "It's a funny old life. When you join an MC, you think it's gonna be long rides, parties, women, and glory. Live free. That's all I wanted. It's only when you get older that you realize you're not free. All men are bound by a set of rules, just different ones." His stare flicked to me. "I've broken the biggest one by tellin' you what I know. I ratted, and I'm ready to die for it."

Kit looked perplexed. "It seems like you've got honor, Piston. I'm surprised you opened your mouth at all. Makes me suspect that you've been tellin' us bullshit."

"I ain't lyin', Demon." He gave a slight shake of his head. "As I said, I got daughters. Pretty girls, good, decent. Could'a been them he sold." His eyes came back to mine, full of resolve. "I don't condone that shit."

My phone buzzed from my pocket. I grabbed it and read the text.

Techno Boy *Prez says we got what we need for now. I got smthn for u 2.*

I stood, glanced at Kit, and nodded toward the door. "I'll send a couple'a guys down with some food and a beer, Piston. You need the bathroom?"

He hung his head again and nodded.

Kit made his way across the room, and I stepped beside him, deep in thought.

Piston had told us the truth; I could feel it in my bones.

We needed to find Bear, and soon. Thrash was the only one standin' between him and the presidency of the Sinners. As soon as he passed, there was gonna be a power struggle. If Bear won and got the big chair, there'd be out-and-out anarchy. The only ones who could stop him were the old timers, and somethin' told me they'd be

Atlas

no match. Bear didn't give a fuck. He was a lunatic, which didn't bode well for them or us.

We stepped out into the corridor. I turned to Tex, who was guarding the door. "I'll send two brothers to feed him and take him to the bathroom. Keep your weapon trained on him at all times, yeah?"

"Gotcha," Tex muttered.

We made our way up the stairs. "What do you think?" I asked quietly.

"I think we need to find Bear and put a bullet in his head. He's the key player. If we put him down, there won't be a club war, and it'll also put a stop to this traffickin' business. Two birds, one stone."

"Atlas!"

I turned to see Colt comin' toward us holdin' a big plastic file in his hand. "Prez and Veep saw it all on the live feed. Said they're gonna hole up for a meet." He raised the black file. "Let's go to the bar. I think you'll need to sit down for this.

"Ex-husband? Let me get this straight. You're sayin' that her ex beat her so badly that her skull got cracked open?" I scraped a hand down my face. "Goddamned motherfucker."

"He hit her, she fell and whacked her head off a dresser." Colt looked around the bar, makin' sure that nobody else had picked up on our convo. "The buck stops with him whichever way you look at it, so yeah, brother, that's what I'm sayin'."

It felt like someone had shoved a red-hot poker through my chest at the thought of any man takin' his fists to a woman's face.

I knew that shit happened on the daily. I believed it was the most cowardly thing a man could do.

Jules Ford

But the thought of Stitch's prick of an ex doin' it to her made me think hard about how I could get her some payback.

"Here's the police report," Colt continued. "Also got the report that the detective who works for her girlfriend's law firm wrote up. It fills in the gaps that the cops missed."

I grabbed it off him and flicked through. My chest burned as I read it.

"Fuckin' cops are useless," Kit muttered from the seat next to me.

"Yeah," Colt agreed. "But it gets worse, Breaker. He was a detective. The PI thinks that his buddies in blue did some sneaky shit to the crime scene to try and protect him."

My jaw clenched.

Me and the pigs were like oil and water at the best of times for exactly that reason. They abused their power. That made 'em corrupt, end of goddamned story.

I let out a low growl as I flicked the page over.

"I see you've got to the photograph section," Colt said quietly. "Sophie's friend got them taken at the hospital in front of another lawyer and a doctor. She used 'em to get the divorce rushed through. Stitch is a big earner, but she doesn't pay a dime in alimony. Her girl used 'em in case the ex demanded her hard-earned scratch."

I breathed deeply and concentrated on keeping my shit together.

"Jesus," Kit muttered. "Why did you have to show him them?"

"Right," Colt retorted. "And risk Atlas cracking' *my* skull off a dresser? Don't gotta fuckin' death wish, Breaker." He took his cell out and pressed some buttons.

My cell phone suddenly pinged from my pocket.

Atlas

"Just sent the report and pics to your phone. Gonna see what else I can uncover. I'm guessing you want me to confirm his current whereabouts?"

Colt was no slouch. Anyone who knew me also knew that I'd already be plannin' my retribution. I had zero tolerance for this kinda shit, especially when it involved my woman.

"Yip," I confirmed, holding out the file. "Thanks, brother."

"Anytime." He took the file from me and stalked away.

Kit glanced at me before takin' a sip of coffee. "What a shit show. Did you know she was divorced?"

"Nope." I popped the 'p' casually like I didn't have a care in the world, but I wasn't fooling Breaker. He could see my hands clenchin' into fists just from thinkin' about the horrors she went through. A wave of sickness rolled through my gut as I thought about what she'd suffered. All the pieces began to slot together. Sophie trainin' hard so she could make herself strong and uniquely capable. Makin' it so that nobody could hurt her again.

What a fuckin' woman.

She was magnificent.

And she was all mine.

I knew it now, just like I knew it the first time I saw her at the hospital when I ran scared like a little bitch. The effect she had on me was so fuckin' mind-blowin' that I didn't know how to handle it or her.

She was perfect and perfect for me, but instead of nurturing our connection, I went and did the very thing I warned Bowie and Cash about and royally fucked everything up. I was thirty-eight, but I'd acted like a fuckin' schoolboy.

Now I had work to do.

"Fuck!" I spat, lookin' upward and shakin' my head at my own fuckin' idiocy.

Kit grinned, watchin' me freak the fuck out. "I know what you assholes are like when you meet your women."

"What the fuck are you yapping about?" I snapped. "Still drunk?"

He let out a humorless laugh. "So, your stomach's not eating itself from the inside out 'cause your woman's already been married? Your brain's not chanting kill, kill, kill, 'cause you wanna go beat some retribution outta the asshole who dared put his hands on her?"

Kit had it in a nutshell. My guts *were* burnin', and the kill switch in my brain *was* activated. However, there wasn't much I could do about it right then. What I had in mind would take some careful plannin'. If I went off half-cocked, I'd probably catch myself a life sentence.

Kit rested his elbows on the table, holding his coffee cup to his mouth. "Funny that. You'd burn down the world for your woman, but you'd have put a bullet in April's head without a second thought not so long ago, even though I said she was mine."

I sat back and studied him closely. "Hurtin' April wasn't somethin' I would've enjoyed, brother. She was a traitor to the club, and she knew all along what the consequences for that would be. You were away in the military when she screwed shit up for Cash. Believe me when I tell you it was a bad time. Your dad was just about holdin' it together, and your brothers were a mess, Cash 'cause of Cara, Bowie 'cause of Sam. Then Xander got sent to stir, Cara left, and nothin' was the same. April did that for no other reason except pure, unadulterated hate, not just for your club family, but your blood family too."

"I get that," he agreed. "But I think there was more to April betrayin' the club than any of us know." He put his cup down carefully. "When I pulled her outside that day, she was frightened. Bitch was shaking all over. Said she'd do anythin' to stay at the club. I think that fucker made her snitch on us." He slumped in his chair. "Now, after what Piston just told us, I think she would've been better off dead."

Trust Kit to try and see the good parts of her. I'd probably forgotten what a decent man he was because he usually hid it so well.

He got high, fucked anythin' with a pulse, and partied for days, but that wasn't all there was to him. He had a good heart. Kit would never hurt anyone unless he felt it'd make the world better. He'd seen humanity's best and worst, which brought me to my next question.

"How you sleepin'?"

"Okay on the nights that I drink and fuck," he replied automatically, "It's when I don't that I have the nightmares. I relive it all, the explosions, the cries, the smell of burnin' flesh. It fucks with my head..." His voice trailed off as his eyes glazed over. "Lately, April's been in the dreams. She looks at me and begs for help while she burns. Her screams are fuckin' terrifying, Atlas."

My heart went out to Breaker for the shit he went through on the daily.

I'd walked past his room early one mornin' and heard screams and shouts. He'd been out of the military for a few months, and it was clear he was strugglin'. When I listened to the commotion, I'd let myself into his room to see that he was in the grip of a nightmare.

I'd never seen somebody in so much emotional pain. He was reliving somethin' traumatic, somethin' that would screw with a man's mind.

When Breaker woke, he broke down and told me everythin' that had happened to him and his unit. He talked about the good friends that he lost.

Like many brave soldiers, Kit's mind was wracked with survivor's guilt. I could'a wept for him.

"Have you been in touch with the Vet Centre recently? Didn't you have a couple of buds there that you used to talk to?"

Kit nodded slowly. "Jones got married and moved away. Renz went off the grid. Nobody knows where he is."

"What do you think happened to him?"

"Dunno." He shrugged. "If he killed himself, they'd have found the body by now. Knowing Renz, he probably got sick of people's bullshit and went to a cabin in the woods to escape it all." He seemed to get lost in his memories for a minute before he turned to me. "You goin' to Vegas?"

A grin stretched across my face. "Do bears shit in the woods?"

He smiled back at me. "Want me to go with ya? I'm a regular there. I know the players. You'll need to get a meet with Tote if you're gonna kill a cop in their territory."

Kit loved Vegas. He visited a couple of times a year. It didn't surprise me that he knew some members of one of the biggest MCs in the area. I'd met Tote, Prez of the Three Kings MC, when the Demons used to run guns. Good times.

"How's Locke doin'?" I asked.

"Should've known you'd be buds with their SAA," Kit grumbled.

"We go way back," I said with a laugh. "Fucker got himself into some shit at Sturgis one year. I backed him up, not that he needed my help."

"I miss the long rides and the rallies," Kit muttered. "Winter's been a fucker this year. Can't wait to get back on my bike."

"Yeah," I grinned. "Iceman's settin' up the first run of the year. March first. It can't come around fast-e-fuckin-nough."

"You may have a backpack this year," Kit teased. "You'll be wifed-up the rate you're goin'."

Atlas

Usually, the thought of havin' an ol' lady made horror punch through my stomach, but that time, a blanket of warmth settled over me.

That stung seein' as the woman I was into hated my guts.

After our argument, I'd taken a step back. She needed time to calm down, and I needed time to think about how the fuck I was gonna make everythin' up to her.

I cringed at the bullshit words that came outta my mouth that day at the hospital. When I spouted that bullshit, it was a bad day for me.

I blamed myself for Bowie gettin' shot and was overcompensating with the need to get him looked after. I remember talkin' shit to Prez, but I didn't mean a word of it. Maybe I was tryin' to save face. I'd always given the boys shit when they took an ol' lady. If I'd made them believe I had ulterior motives in takin' Sophie out, I would've avoided the same treatment.

Could'a kicked myself, 'cause even then, I could see that she'd suffered. I should've handled her with more care.

I never once suspected that her ex-husband abused her.

That fucktard had let her down badly. Not only had that prick broken her spirit by beatin' on her, but he'd also broken her trust in all us other males.

That meant the next man in her life - namely me - had some work to do. I needed to rebuild Sophie's confidence, and I could've kicked my own ass because after the bullshit I said about her, I'd fallen at the first goddamned hurdle.

Instead of buildin' her up, I knocked her down, which made me angry with myself. She deserved a man who took her insecurities away, not some prick who made 'em worse.

Kit suddenly tensed. "Incoming," he said under his breath.

I glanced furtively over my shoulder to see Layla, Ro, and Iris strut into the bar. Tristan and Sophie trailed behind 'em.

I did a double-take when I saw that Sophie's hair was different. It was shorter but fuller. My eyes slipped over her face and the elegant curve of her neck. "Fuck," I turned back to Breaker and reached under the table to adjust the crotch of my pants.

"She's a pretty thing." Kit eyed her appreciatively. "Can't believe her ex did that shit to her. She's healed well."

"Yip," I grated out. "But we both know that the outside heals faster than the inside. Who damned well knows what shit's swirlin' inside her head?"

"So, it's your job to quieten the demons, right?" Kit nodded toward the girls who had sat down with their drinks and were laughing and talking amongst themselves.

Sophie looked around the room, and our eyes locked.

Somethin' passed between us, a current of electricity. It was almost tangible like I could reach out and get a shock from it. Pretty typical seein' as she'd been a shock to the system since the first time I saw her. Then, all the weeks that followed in trainin' had forced me to get to know her on a deeper level.

I was done with fuckin' around. My chat with Piston had proved that life could turn to shit with a snap of the fingers. Who knew how long we'd be on the earth? I'd been lookin' at it all wrong. War didn't mean pushin' her away. War meant grabbin' hold of her and keepin' her safe.

How had the mighty had fallen, huh?

A plan began to form in my mind.

Atlas

Words were easy, but I needed actions. Sophie had seen the worst of me. It was time to show her the best parts.

If I took on this mission, it would be the most important one of my life.

I had to tread carefully, slide in there, let her see the real me, and make it so she'd never wanna let me go.

Sophie was the doctor, but she was gonna have to step aside 'cause I was gonna turn shit on its head by healing her.

It was time to commence with 'Operation Charm Stitch.'

Chapter Twelve

Sophie

I checked my hair in the mirror and applied some clear lip gloss.

It was my last week training the Speed Demons. Weirdly, I was sad that I wouldn't see them every day. Soon I'd swap their basement gym for hospital corridors.

It was a bit of a blow.

The sullen looks, mocking smiles, and rude digs had transformed into laughter, good-natured joking, and a sense of camaraderie that I'd never experienced before, except with Kennedy. In the last week, I'd really enjoyed being there, especially since I'd gotten closer to the women.

My new friendships had put a spring in my step. It was beginning to feel like I was part of something for the first time in years.

But the most surprising friendship was the one that had grown between Atlas and me.

After our argument, he'd changed.

He brought me coffee in the mornings. He made sure I ate. He laughed, joked, and smiled to the point where I couldn't help staring at his face in wonder.

Atlas wasn't traditionally handsome. He was rugged with a few faint scars and a nose that in my professional opinion, had been broken several times. But his smile lit up a room, and my heart beat faster every time he smiled at me.

I knew that it was stupid to feel that way. I also knew it would never go any further than friendship, and I was content with that. I'd resigned myself to the fact that being his friend was better than being his enemy.

The words I'd heard him say about me at the hospital weren't cool. Neither was his behavior after that. Since then, I'd gotten to know him better, and I could see that it wasn't the norm for him. I'd never forget those words, but I could forgive them. It wasn't like he was my boyfriend, and he wouldn't ever be. I liked him and probably still carried a teensy crush, but we weren't a good fit.

I was a doctor in my early thirties, I wasn't a teenager, and I was too old to bear grudges. It all seemed a bit pointless, especially now that we'd gotten to know each other more and were in a better place.

Shit happened, right?

The loud rumble of an engine began to roar through the air, getting louder as it drew closer to my house.

Bending down, I gave Vic a stroke before making my way to the front door. I saw a big black SUV pulling up outside through the peephole.

I fastened my coat, grabbed my purse and gloves from the kitchen table, and opened the front door. After locking it behind me, I picked my way up the path toward the SUV.

Sparky had been picking me up every morning and taking me home every evening. Abe had insisted that my car wasn't seen in the compound because it would look suspicious. Everyone in town knew that I practiced Krav, and he didn't want people putting two and two together.

Of course, I'd argued at first, but he was right. Why court danger? Plus, gas was expensive, and a girl had to eat.

Atlas

I grabbed the handle and tugged the car door open. "Morning Spark," I sang. "Cold one today, right?" I turned to smile at the young guy and froze.

Atlas was sitting in the driver's seat, grinning at me in a way only he could. My eyes swept down his body. He wore black jeans with a hoodie.

My heart skipped a beat. Jesus, he looked hot.

"Mornin' Stitch baby," he rumbled. "Spark had shit to do, so you're stuck with me bein' your Uber today."

"Hey," I greeted him, sliding into the car. I pulled my seat belt across my body, snapping it into place with a slight tremor in my fingers. Seeing Atlas out of the club had thrown me a curve ball.

"All set?" He looked down at the clip and shook his head. "It's not clicked in right, babe. Gotta sort it; I'm carryin' precious cargo."

I held my breath as he undid the belt and snapped it back into the slot, his fingers brushing over mine.

My heart leaped at the contact.

We grappled all day in the gym, so his hands were on me a lot. That almost gave me a conniption, but skin-to-skin contact like we just had made my fingers sizzle.

I looked at him and blinked.

He grinned, giving me his sexy wink, then we pulled away from my house.

My eyes went like saucers as I fixed them to the windscreen.

Is he flirting with me?

I wound the window down slightly, suddenly needing air. My skin felt stretched too tight across my bones.

"You okay, baby," Atlas enquired in his deep voice. "Hot?"

I swallowed the lump in my throat "Just a bit car sick," I squeaked.

He frowned. "You eaten?"

Jules Ford

I tugged at the neckline of my jacket, skin suddenly prickling. "No. I've got a protein bar in my purse. That will tide me over until lunchti-" Atlas suddenly brought the car to a screeching halt, did a turn in the road, and began to drive us in the opposite direction.

"-Hey." I whipped my head around to face him. "What are you doing?"

"Goin' to Mag's," he replied, keeping his eyes on the road. "You need a decent coffee and one of her lemon from heaven bars. Can't train thirty bikers on an empty stomach, baby. You'll fuckin' pass out, and I'm not havin' it."

My mouth hung open, and I stared at his face. "I can't eat a lemon from heaven bar for breakfast. I'll put weight on."

"You can fuckin' eat two," he muttered. "Goddamned protein bar. You're a doctor. You know better than that. How the fuck are you meant to train effectively when you haven't eaten a morsel?" He pursed his lips angrily. "A few fuckin' calories won't kill ya, woman."

My eyes scanned his face. "That's right, I forgot. I haven't got enough ass for your tastes."

He muttered something to himself and then glanced at me before his eyes returned to the road. "Don't take what I say to heart, Stitch. I haven't got a fuckin' clue about anythin'. Half the time, I'm talkin' outta my asshole. The other half, I'm biggin' myself up. You're a beautiful, smart woman, and your ass is goddamned perfect, just like the rest of ya."

Wait. What?

My entire body went taut. How did I go from having the body of a fifteen-year-old boy to being perfect?

A sick feeling washed through me.

Was this some kind of joke?

The truck screeched to a halt. Atlas snaked his arm across the back of my seat and looked behind as he parallel-parked the SUV like a pro. "Since when do I know anything about anythin'. I'm a man, so it stands to reason that I'm a fuckin' idiot ninety-nine percent of the time." He swung his door open. "Don't move," he ordered before jumping out and closing the door with a thud.

I watched, stunned, as he jogged around the front of the SUV, hauled my door open, and held his hand out for mine. "Don't got all day, Stitch baby."

My gaze locked on his outstretched hand.

Even his fingers were thick and long, his nails neatly trimmed. There was no sign of dirt or car grease under them, even though he sometimes worked in the club's auto shop. He'd cleaned up, and I couldn't help but wonder what the hell was going on?

"Why are you being so nice to me?" I asked quietly. "Did you bet the others that you could charm me or something?"

He jerked his hands to his hips. "It's breakfast, Stitch. We're here 'cause we need to eat. Now, get your ass outta the car. It's goddamned freezing."

My bottom lip poked out. "You're not the boss of me." I pouted playfully.

His lips twitched then his face broke out into a grin. Within seconds he was roaring with laughter. As usual, it was infectious.

A smile stole over my face. "Shut up, you tool."

He roared with laughter again.

I let out an involuntary chuckle. "Stop it."

He bent over and hooted, wiping his eyes. Smiling, he held his hand out again. "Ain't a bet, Stitch. I was an asshole to you before, and I apologize. It's like I said. I'm the last person you should listen to seein' as I'm not too bright sometimes." He did a come-hither sign with his fingers. "Don't got all day."

Jules Ford

I looked at his face, trying to find the slightest sign of deception, but all I could see were soft, dark eyes and a sexy smile.

My hand snaked to his. He squeezed my fingers, and goosebumps skated down my arms.

I couldn't help thinking that it felt right.

"Come on, Stitch," he urged, pulling me gently out of the SUV. "Let's eat." He closed the door behind me and held my hand tight as we made our way down the sidewalk. We were silent, but it wasn't uncomfortable.

The bell above the door jingled as Atlas pushed it open and motioned for me to go before him. "Age before beauty," he joked as I walked through.

I slapped his chest playfully. "You're so bad."

He threw his head back and laughed. "Oh, baby. You have no idea how bad I can be." A soft look overtook his features. "Table at the back. Go. Sit."

I smiled at Magnolia and weaved through the tables full of chatting customers. My chair made a scraping noise as I pulled it out and sat. Atlas stood at the counter, pointing to the glass display holding cakes and cookies.

He was gorgeous.

Through his hoodie, I could see the cords of his muscles rippling as he moved. He was a big guy, towering above everyone else in the coffeehouse.

I tilted my head to one side, admiring how his jeans hugged his rock-hard ass.

In a way, I was glad that he'd friend-zoned me. I was happy that our friendship wouldn't be complicated by sex. It was much less pressure.

I suddenly recalled how big he was everywhere, and a blush stole through my cheeks.

He handed cash over the counter to pay the bill, lifted the tray crammed with food and two big takeaway coffee cups, and began walking toward me.

Our eyes locked, and I swear my belly swooned.

Atlas

He must have caught my not-so-subtle way of checking him out because he grinned as he placed the tray on the table. "Get that down ya, Stitch."

"Jesus." My eyes widened. "I can't eat all that."

He'd bought four bars of lemon heaven cake, four cookies, two croissants, and two coffees.

"It's not all for you." He patted his stomach as he took the seat opposite me. "I'm a growing boy."

I let out a laugh and nodded to the tray. "If you eat all that, your gut will grow."

He grinned. "You callin' me fat?"

"Well, you called me skinny," I shrugged one shoulder. "It's only fair."

His grin lingered as he emptied some sugar sachets into his coffee. "I like you, Stitch. You give as good as you get. Apart from the other officers, my ma, Rosie, and the ol' ladies, you're probably the only one who dares."

"What about your dad?" I asked, lifting my cup.

"Died when I was fourteen," he stated. "Heart attack. He was out mowin' the lawn one mornin' full'a the joys of spring, and then he was gone. Didn't suffer, thankfully."

I studied him closely, thinking about how hard that must have been.

When I first met Atlas, I thought we had nothing in common, but the more I got to know him, the more I realized that wasn't true. Both our fathers died when we were young. Maybe, we were both products of that in our own ways.

"I'm sorry, Dan." I smiled sadly, reached out, and covered his hand with mine. "It must have been hard on you all."

"Yeah," he replied. "Emotionally and financially. Can you imagine a fourteen-year-old boy tryin'a keep everyone's shit together? Ma was a mess; Rosie was confused, and on top of that, we were flat broke." He sat back in his chair, deep in thought. "We lived-in small-town Oregon at the time, a place called Unity Creek. It was beautiful, but it didn't have much in the way of work. I ended up doin' odd jobs for the local MC just so we could put food on the table." He took another swig of his coffee. "Nothin' illegal mind. Thinkin' back, I reckon they knew my situation and created little jobs for me."

My heart wept for him.

I was right. There was much more to Atlas than a big mouth and muscles. I couldn't imagine a young boy with all that grown-up responsibility weighing down his shoulders.

"Still check in with the Hell Dwellers." He smiled to himself. "Great club. Gotta lotta respect for their prez, Grizz. He helped me build my first bike." He let out a chuckle. "My bud Hunter will cream his pants when he finds out about you. Fucker's like a magpie the way he collects medical equipment."

My brow furrowed. "What do you mean when he finds out about me?"

Atlas sat forward and placed a cookie and a lemon heaven bar on a plate. "Eat," he ordered, putting it in front of me. "Please, Stitch baby. You'll get sick."

Smiling, I took a bite of cake and moaned as it melted in my mouth.

Atlas grinned indulgently and watched me chew. "All Freya talks about is how talented you are and how lucky the town is. How did you end up in Hambleton? Surely the big city hospitals are more your speed?"

"Not at all. I was looking for a slower pace of life, and I was born here, so it seemed like the right move." I took a sip of coffee and watched while a look of surprise took over his face.

Nobody in town knew about my past. I hadn't told anyone, and I didn't understand why I confided in Atlas.

"My mom and dad adopted me," I explained. "Can you believe I was born in the same hospital I work in

Atlas

now? I was given to them days before Mom took a new nursing position in Las Vegas."

He nodded, deep in thought. "Where did you go to med school?" he asked.

I shrugged. "Duke."

He rolled his eyes, smiling. "Should'a fuckin' known you'd be an over-achiever."

When I spoke, my voice was hesitant. "I found academics easy. It was the social aspect that I struggled with. I was shy and found it difficult to make friends because I was homesick for my mom and Ned."

Atlas' massive shoulders tensed. "Ned?"

"My best friend." I couldn't stop myself from smiling. "She's great. She's got twins, a boy and a girl. They're eight now. She's a single mom. The kid's dad was in the military. He died not long after they were born." I sipped my coffee. "They're the only family I've got since my mom passed a while ago."

His dark eyes met mine.

I braced because I knew what was coming. I could feel it.

"If they're your only family, why did ya leave Sin City?"

I slowly chewed on the lemon heaven bar, giving myself time to scramble for an answer.

It was hard to talk about Luke with him, especially after he'd let me down in the past. Letting myself be vulnerable was all very well, but allowing it with a man I didn't fully trust filled me with dread.

So, I played it safe.

"Bad divorce." I kept my tone purposely light. "I needed to get away from everything, and they say a change is as good as a rest. Plus, I was lucky to get the head of department position. That wouldn't happen at a well-known hospital for a surgeon my age. It was a no-brainer, really."

He nodded thoughtfully. "Ever thought about lookin' for your birth mom?"

I circled the rim of my coffee cup with my fingertip and let out a small sigh. "I don't know. I've made inquiries in the past, but nobody couldn't find my records. I left Vegas and traveled for a while, then moved here. I let sleeping dogs lie after that."

His hand reached across the table and began to play with my fingers. "You got us now, Stitch. No better family than the Demons."

Dark eyes fixed on mine, and my heart gave a tug. "Thank you," I whispered.

Our gazes anchored together, and time seemed to stop.

I couldn't look away, even though I could feel myself getting pulled into his riptide again.

My mouth twisted into a wry grin.

It was typical that the first man I'd been interested in since Luke didn't like me in the same way. It was good that we were friends, though; I didn't want to jeopardize that.

"Shouldn't we get back?" I asked.

"Yeah, babe." He dropped my hand. "Guess we *should* get back. Gonna leave ya to train the boys today. Got things to do and people to see. Should be back in time to catch the afternoon sesh."

I wondered for a second what things he had to do and what people he had to see. Weirdly, in my mind, the words all jumbled to; he had people to do and things to see.

My heart dropped at the thought of him seeing a woman, but I swallowed my disappointment and went to stand. He could do what he wanted; we were just friends.

Picking up my purse, I started for the door. As I stepped forward, a strong hand grabbed my arm, pulling me back.

I looked up to see Atlas' stare boring into me.

Atlas

"Hand, babe," he said.

My nose scrunched up. "Huh?"

He held his palm out upwards. "Hand, babe."

My breath hitched when his fingers caught mine, and we were on the move.

The occupied tables went by in what seemed like a flash as we headed toward the door.

"They're ready for you," Magnolia called out to us.

Atlas grabbed a box as we swept past. "Much obliged." He let go of my hand to push the door open and wave me through but caught it again as we headed toward the SUV.

Letting go, he placed the box on the car's roof while he opened my door, settling me inside gently.

The day was getting weirder by the second.

I didn't take my eyes off Atlas as he jogged around the front of the car, swung the door open, and jumped behind the steering wheel. He twisted around and dumped the box on the back seat.

One thought kept going over and over in my mind, and my belly fluttered like crazy.

He held my hand.
He held my hand.
He held my freaking hand.

"You held my hand," I breathed.

He started the car and checked for oncoming traffic before pulling into the road. Then he did that sexy one-handed steering wheel rotation before glancing at me. "Yip."

Skin suddenly hot, I skewered him with a look. "Why?"

He settled back in his seat with one hand relaxed on the steering wheel. "See. It's like this Stitch. When you're out with me, you're out with me. Did you see Carl fuckin' Tucker sittin' to the right of us?"

"Who's Carl Tucker?" I asked, eyebrows furrowing.

Jules Ford

He let out a grunt. "Carl Tucker's a little scrotum who sits on the town council. One of the many around here who thinks his shit don't stink. Then there was young Harrison Bell at the counter."

A memory pinged. "I know Harrison. He had a sports injury and came into the hospital. Sully dealt with him." My voice reflected my confusion. "What's he got to do with it?"

"When you're out *with me*, you're out *with me*," he repeated. "Don't expect assholes to give you the eye or keep lookin' at ya hopin' you'll look back. Don't like pricks disrespecting me. Fuckers needed a reminder that when you're out *with me*, you're out *with me*."

Folding my hands in my lap, I looked through my side window. "So, you held my hand because you felt disrespected by other men who looked at me."

Eyes still ahead, he jerked one stern nod. "Yip."

"Right," I muttered, leaning back into the seat and sighing.

It was his pride talking. He didn't hold my hand for me. He held it for everyone else's benefit. Why did I keep reading more into every little thing he did?

My emotions were up and down and round and round, and my nerves couldn't take it anymore.

It's fine. I'm fine, I kept telling myself repeatedly, but the sinking feeling in my stomach said a different story. Everything was far from fine. All the hand-holding, smiling, and intimacy had sparked hope again, but it wasn't the same for him.

A lump clogged my throat as I recalled how he seemed so intent on learning more about me and my life back when we were at the coffeehouse.

He seemed to care, and I guessed he probably did generally, but not in the way I wanted. What was the matter with me?

The lump in my throat began to heat, and my pulse throbbed as a thought hit me.

Atlas

Did he know what he was doing? Was it on purpose?
My shoulders slumped.

He was still playing games with me. Shame on him for doing it again, and shame on me for letting him.

My lips pursed.

When you're out with me, you're out with me.

I rolled my eyes heavenward.

"Why you quiet?" he demanded, maneuvering the car left to turn into the Demon's compound. He waved at Sparky and waited for the gates to open.

"I'm not quiet," I snipped. "I'm just thinking about how I can't wait to go back to work." *You game playing asshole.*

His eyes narrowed on me. "Right." He cursed quietly under his breath as he swung the SUV into the parking lot.

I folded my arms across my chest and let out a little huff. My mind was still racing with horrible thoughts.

Instead of stopping outside the main door, he drove around the side of the building to the club's auto shop. It was a fifty-by-fifty single-story structure with a corrugated roof. It looked a bit like the main clubhouse but smaller. I assumed it was used as storage for the main business back in the day.

The men had rolled up the metal doors, allowing me to see inside the building where brothers in overalls worked on cars situated half in, half out the doors.

He turned to face me. "Just need a word with Bowie." His seatbelt clicked and whooshed up above his shoulder. The cold air hit me for a few seconds before his door slammed shut, and he stalked toward the auto shop.

I remained in my seat. My teeth sunk into my lip as I looked around, not knowing whether I should stay put, or get out, make my way into the main clubhouse, and get my ass down the gym.

Awkward.

Voices floated toward me from outside.

I looked around and saw Layla and Sunny walking hand in hand toward the auto shop. Ice came out wearing navy overalls and a black tank. The top part hung down, and he'd tied the arms around his waist.

Y*ummy*.

My eyes traced down his muscled, tattooed arms before I noticed that Layla had turned and started waving at me. Great, now I had to get out and say hi, or she'd think I was rude.

Throwing the door open, I got out of the car and lifted a hand in greeting. "Hey!"

Layla started toward me. "Is that one of the club's SUVs?" she asked, gesturing toward the vehicle.

I looked around. "Oh. Yeah. I went for breakfast with Atlas." I kept my voice bright and breezy, like going for breakfast with a six-foot-five'ish, two-hundred-and-sixty pound'ish biker was an everyday occurrence.

Her mouth fell open. "Atlas took you for breakfast?" Her already huge eyes went more enormous, and shock flickered over her face.

Just as I went to answer, a deep voice called out, "Sophie!"

I saw Ice strutting toward us, overalls still around his waist. "Mornin' babe." He looked me up and down, and a grin spread across his face. "Ain't you a sight for sore eyes."

Layla jabbed a hand to her hip and popped it. "Atlas took Sophie for breakfast."

Ice's mouth fell open that time. "Huh?"

"Yeah," Layla replied. "I was just going to take her into the clubhouse and ask her all about it."

Shit.

They were getting the wrong idea. I had to put them straight, or it would get back to Atlas. I almost balked at the thought of all the crap he'd give me if he assumed I was starting rumors about us going out to eat.

Atlas

"It was just breakfast." I held my hand up. "It's not what you're thinking."

Ice's eyes fell over my shoulder, and he stood straighter.

"Really?" Layla smiled as she looked behind me toward the auto shop.

"Yeah. Atlas is just being friendl-" I let out a squeak as someone tagged my waist from behind and spun me around.

Atlas's angry stare went from me to Ice, then back to me again. "Yo, baby." he rumbled. "I gotta get these lemon heavens to my bud. Catch ya later, yeah?"

His neck bent, and the world stopped turning as he touched his mouth to mine.

My heart exploded in my chest. Then my clit exploded as Atlas grabbed my ass and pulled me into his groin, circling his hips against my pussy with a grinding motion.

My brain short-circuited because suddenly, I couldn't think straight. It wasn't a deep kiss, but it was still one of the best ones of my life.

He lifted his head and smirked down at me.

I stared up at him, shocked. My lips felt swollen.

"Catch ya later, Stitch." He touched his mouth to mine again and turned for the car.

My eyes locked onto him as he got inside the SUV and fired it up. He smirked at Ice, giving him a loose salute. Then he shot me a sexy wink, turned the car around, and peeled out of the parking lot.

Ice fixed his stare on the retreating vehicle as the taillights disappeared around the corner. The car went out of sight, and he turned back to me, his face heated. "Fuck!" he bit out, pulling his overalls up and angrily punching his arms back through the sleeves. "He's such as fuckin' asshole." He turned around and stomped back toward the auto shop.

My eyes caught movement.

John and Bowie stared in my direction.

Bowie had Sunny perched on his hip as she chatted away with him. He grinned and said something to John, who gave me the thumbs up.

"Oh my God," I cried softly. "What the hell's happening? He said he didn't like me that way, but then he held my hand and said, 'when you're out *with me*, you're out *with me*'." My heart gave a hard thud, and I clutched my chest. "Oh my God, I'm having palpitations. What's going on?"

Layla let out a laugh and shook her head. "Babe. Welcome to my world." She glanced at Bowie, turned back to me, and took my hands.

"Sophie." Her eyes held mine, and she let out a tinkling laugh. "It happens to the best of us, sweetie. I think you've just been Atlas'd."

Chapter Thirteen

Atlas

My head was fucked, and not just a little bit, either.
The other day, lookin' at that fuckin' file that Colt gave me. Seein' the giant cut on Stitch's head, the bruises, and the welts. Even the X-ray of her cracked skull. I knew I wanted to take that shit away and make everything better.

Then earlier that day, sittin' in the coffee house, being so comfortable around her that I spoke about stuff I never usually shared, I knew she was special.

No woman had ever made me feel so at ease. Usually, I looked at chicks as fuck vessels to let off steam with, but since I met Stitch, I'd done a complete one-eighty.

Fleeting fucks with hardened chicks that knew the score didn't appeal to me anymore. I wanted sweet. I wanted to cuddle. I wanted to curl up on the sofa and watch movies. When I grabbed Sophie's hand at the coffee shop, I had to inhale a deep breath and calm my shit 'cause I knew I never wanted to let it go.

The issue was, I didn't know how to court a chick.
I wasn't that man.

My previous efforts consisted of crookin' my finger and waitin' for them to come runnin'. My inexperience came into play in the car on the way back when her mood

Jules Ford

completely changed. Fuck knows what I said or did wrong, but she went from soft to hard. All I knew at that point was that I was outta my goddamned depth.

When we got back, I had a quick word with Prez, then came back outside to see Iceman sniffin' around her again. At that moment, I could've happily punched his fuckin' smarmy face. Every time I turned around, he was there suckin' up, and it was startin' to irritate the fuck outta me.

Without a thought, I made my move and claimed her in front of the brothers. Now, everybody knew my intentions, but I still didn't know how to make Sophie receptive to 'em. Rather than stick to the plan and allow her to get to know me, I'd jumped ten steps ahead.

I was out on a limb and needed help, but there was only one person I could trust to keep their mouth shut.

Monument Street had no parkin', so I found a space at the top of Main Street and walked over. Hambleton was a beautiful small town. Quaint family stores, town square, war monument, and park. Quintessential small-town America.

It was the ideal place to settle down and have kids, or at least it would be when we got shot of the Sinners problem.

Box in hand, I crossed the street and tapped lightly on the vast window of the old fire station buildin'. I looked up, mentally calculatin' how much scratch it would take to sort the place out. The amount made my eyes water.

I caught movement from inside and watched as Cara made her way to the door, turned the key, and opened it. "Morning!" she said, her eyes fallin' on the box and lightin' up. "Did you bring me lemon from heaven bars?"

"What the pregnant chick wants, the pregnant chick gets," I assured her. "Wouldn't fuckin' dare argue with you at the best of times, never mind when you're hormonal." I handed her the box, moved inside the massive room, and locked the door behind me.

My eyes went around the place, and I made more mental calculations. "It's certainly big enough, Wildcat, but it's gonna take some green to get it the way you want it." I started to walk around, inspecting the place closer. "You need scratch. You come to me. Got it?"

Cara bit into a lemon heaven bar and groaned. "Oh, my God. These things are better than sex."

I let out a snort. "Then Cashy boy ain't doin' it right."

She popped a hip, full of attitude. "Right enough to knock me up, so it turns out."

My eyes went to her still-flat belly. "How ya feelin'?"

"I'm okay. Nauseous, so I bet the morning sickness will kick in soon. But Layla tells me that's a good sign."

"I know you're okay physically, woman." I tapped the side'a my head with my index finger. "Wanna know how you are in there."

Cara paused for a second, then nodded toward a small, round garden table set up at the side of the room. "Come on. If you're going to psycho-analyze me, we may as well be comfortable."

I followed her over. After I sat, I studied her closely, lookin' for signs of trauma. She was tired, but I expected that seein' as she'd been through an ordeal recently.

I didn't doubt she wasn't sleepin' well. PTSD will do that to a person. What Bear did probably only added to the bullshit that Cash pulled years before.

"I'm okay," she said softly. "Better now than I was a few weeks ago. My therapist has been great, though I think he was shocked when I told him what happened."

I shrugged. "I get that. Anyone outside the club would'a gone to the pigs."

"Yeah," she agreed. "They would, but it's not like that for us."

"You sleepin'?" I asked, takin' in the shadows under her eyes.

"Now I am." She smiled sadly. "It wasn't just the Bear stuff. It was everything. A lot happened in the space of a few weeks. It was bound to take its toll."

I nodded gently. "Are your baby hormones goin' wild, too?"

She let out a little laugh. "It's weird, but I feel calmer than I have in years." She patted her belly. "This little one made me realize how toxic my relationship with Cash had become, not just together, but singularly too. I don't want to give my kid any hang-ups, Atlas. It's time to grow up."

I sat forward, restin' my arms on my knees. "And that's why you're gonna be a cool mom, Wildcat. You're puttin' the kid first already."

Cara smiled big at me. "What's been happening with you? Layla tells me that a certain pretty doctor has turned your head."

I scraped a hand down my face. "Yeah."

"Well, tell your face that you're happy, for God's sake. This time's supposed to be the honeymoon period where your smile resembles the Joker. You look like a bulldog chewing a wasp."

My stare hit my boots. I'd never felt so fuckin' needy in my life. "Dunno if I'm what she needs, Wildcat," I told her quietly. "I'm into her and the idea of makin' a go of it, but I'm a hard man to love."

Her head reared back, eyebrows knittin' together. "You're a what the what?"

"I ain't exactly marriage material. I'm a dirty biker who's screwed around but never even had a steady fuck buddy. Got a mom and a sister who depend on me. Got a shit ton of fuckin' enemies, and to top it all, we're about to pop off with a one percenter MC who dabbles in the skin trade. Why would she wanna be with me?"

Atlas

Cara pretended to stick her fingers down her throat in a fake gaggin' motion. "Boo fucking hoo. Cry me a river, Atlas. Why are you making excuses?"

My eyes narrowed. "What the fuck, bitch?"

"Don't bitch me, asshole. It's simple, do you like Sophie enough to see a future with her?"

My insides balked at her no-nonsense tone. "Yeah," I agreed. "She's cute and tough and has a heart of gold. She went through some nasty shit in her past, but I think I could be good for her. I dunno how to go about it, though. How do I romance her? What shoes and purses do I buy? What fancy restaurant do I take her to? I'm clueless about all that shit."

Cara held her hand up to stop me. "Atlas. If that's what it takes to impress Sophie, she's not for you. You need an independent woman who can buy her own purses. You already look after your mom and Rosie. You need someone who can support you, not someone who's going to pile on the pressure." Cara cocked her head questioningly. "I'm confused. Did Sophie ask you for all that? She doesn't seem the type to give a crap about all that stuff."

My gut churned 'cause she hadn't. She'd never asked me for anythin'.

Cara gave me a death glare. "Atlas, you're a fucking idiot. You've got it so wrong. Shoes and fancy dinners are nice, but Sophie's independent. She needs a partner, not a sugar daddy."

"Fuck." I looked up, breathin' hard. "Can't work women out. Everythin' Cash and Bowie told me's fuckin' bullshit."

Cara looked like she was gonna hit me. "Why are you listening to those two twats? Cash isn't exactly a role model when it comes to relationships. And Layla's only recently started speaking to Bowie again after his last fuck-up." She leaned forward and patted my arm. "And Sophie isn't Layla or me. She's her."

Jules Ford

My head pounded with all this new information. Hand to God, I didn't have a fuckin' clue how to treat a woman. "What the fuck do I do then?" I demanded.

Cara relaxed back in her chair again. "You've been looking after your mom and Rosie for so long that you stopped looking after yourself. You've given so much to everybody else that you're running on empty. You've got nothing left to give. A woman like Sophie Green will fill up your love tank. You won't have to give her anything because she'll give it to you first."

I snorted at the 'love tank' comment to hide my confusion.

So many people had given me their opinions, but they all told me different shit. My head was spinnin'. Sophie made me feel like I was out at sea without a fuckin' lifejacket.

I clasped my hands together in a beggin' motion. "Wildcat, help me. I don't know how to do this shit. I only know how to be a biker. I could kill a man twenty ways with my eyes closed but put a decent woman in front of me, and I'm lost."

"Men are so stupid." She deadpanned. "Honestly, it's so fucking simple, asshole."

My eyebrows drew together.

"It's not rocket science. Men think women are complicated, and we've evolved into these hormone-ridden bitches that are hard to please. Making a woman happy isn't difficult. Get your phone out, Atlas. I'm about to give you the best advice you'll get in your life. Feel free to pass it around because if more men knew these tricks, the world would be much better."

I pulled my cell outta my cut and went to my notes.

"One," she began. "Feed us."

My eyes snapped up to hers. "Feed you?"

Cara nodded. "Yep. Feed us. If we order a salad and want some of your fries, go with it. While we're on the subject, at *that* time of the month, bring chocolate."

Atlas

I began to type, puffin' my chest out. I could do that easily.

"Two. Call us back. If you *really* can't, text."

My eyes veered up again. "Simple as that?"

Her lips quirked. "Three. Tell us we look pretty. If we've spent an hour getting ready, we need someone to reassure us that it's all been worth it."

I shook my head and kept clickin' on the tiny keyboard. This wasn't hard at all.

"Four. You're the big spoon, always. No fucking about, no excuses."

I grinned at that one because I already knew the score. It was pretty universal. No man wanted to be the little spoon, especially if he was a big fucker like me.

She smiled sadly. "And the most important one, don't stick your dick in anyone else."

My eyes lifted to hers again, and I caught her raw pain. My heart dropped. Cara could be such a fuckin' banshee that people forgot she had feelings too.

"Sorry, Wildcat," I murmured. "If it's any consolation, he's hurtin' more than you. He's a fuckin' mess."

Tears sprung to her eyes, but she kept smilin'. "He's an asshole, so yeah, that does help a lot. Thanks."

I roared with laughter.

It seemed that our Wildcat was startin' to get her mojo back. She was hilarious. She could make a grown man cry with her banter. I'd seen many a brother tear up when she got on a roll and let rip. I almost felt sorry for Cash. His woman was gonna give him a run for his money.

My eyes took in the expansive space.

It would turn out well if Cara kept it simple. White walls, wooden floorin', and a fuck load of art. "Who's doin' the work in here? You gotta good six months' worth of buildin' work ahead."

"Yeah," she agreed, lookin' around. "I'm going to take my time and find the right contractor. There's no rush. I want to do it right. Plus, I have to put more funds aside, sell some shares and see how big the cash pot is."

I smiled to myself.

There was no doubt that as soon as Cash got clued into this place, he'd move heaven and earth to get it sorted for her. The Demons had a construction company, and we could get all her materials at a cost price. Add on that Cash was fuckin' loaded and could afford to pay a couple of men's paychecks without even makin' a dent in his fortune. This place would be rockin' and rollin' in no time.

"You'll get there." An idea pinged, and I jerked up straight. "We're throwin' Boner a patch-in party on Friday. You comin'?"

She glanced back at me enquiringly. "Layla mentioned it, but I'm staying away from Xander, remember?"

A wide grin spread across my face. "What if I can get rid of the whiny fucknut?"

"You think you can?" Her brown eyes glittered with humor. "You'd never have torn him away from a patch-in party back in the day. He used to love them."

Cara was right, but recently, he was a changed man.

Cash did used to love patch-in parties, we all did. but since Cara left him he didn't find joy in many things. He'd be better off out patrolling and would probably prefer it. Cash was in therapy and working through a lotta shit, so he wasn't in the right frame of mind to party.

"He was drinkin' back then," I mused. "Won't be much fun for him, stone-cold sober without you there." I waggled my eyebrows.

Cara's lips curved up. "Atlas. You're bad."

I threw my head back and barked out a laugh. "You know Wildcat. It seems that you're not the only person to think that."

Chapter Fourteen

Sophie

'Give it Away Now' by the Red Hot Chili Peppers thumped through the speakers of the Speed Demons clubhouse. My eyes went to the stage where two strippers were doing their best to entertain the crowd by bumping and grinding in time to the bass.

I turned to Tristan. "These guys will love Ned." I nodded toward the makeshift stage. "If they're the best strippers in the area, she may give up law for a while and go back to dancing. She'd make a fortune."

Tristan's face lit up. "Lawyer girl's a secret stripper? Oh my." He clapped his hands together quickly.

"She stripped her way through college." I laughed. "She's very proud of it and didn't have a cent of student debt." My eyes turned back toward the dancers. "She was an amazing dancer back in the day."

"I can't wait to meet her," Tristan crowed. "She's my kinda gal."

I smiled, looking around the table. Layla was opposite me, with Cara on one side and Anna on the other. Rosie was on my left, and Tristan on my right was next to Anna. We all wanted to sit at this table to get a clear view of the bar.

The sound of a loud whoop cut through the air.

Jules Ford

I looked around and caught sight of the club girl who went with Atlas on the night I extracted the bullet from his shoulder. Cherry was bumping and grinding on a table, surrounded by men yelling encouragement. All she wore was a pair of red panties and a smile.

I quickly turned my face away while a blush heated my cheeks.

I was from Vegas, a town well known for crazy parties and even crazier behavior, but this place could give Sin City a run for its money. Boner's patch in-party was already wild.

He still didn't know what was about to happen. Prez told the club that the party was a way to let off steam after the training they'd done. I'd finished my Krav lessons a couple of days earlier. I was due back at work after the weekend.

To say that I was going to miss everyone would be an understatement.

My last few days of training had been excellent, except for one elephant stomping around the room.

Atlas hadn't left me alone since the morning of our breakfast.

I'd been more skittish than ever since he'd kissed me in the Demon's compound. It had sent me into a complete brain fart.

I'd tried to keep my distance; he was a player, and I didn't want that. He'd already pulled me in and spat me out twice. He was so confusing.

Every time he put his hands on me in training, his touch seemed to burn. My blood was on fire, and a lump had stuck in my throat for days.

Pressure weighed on my chest. Sometimes it seemed like I was suffocating.

Lemon heaven cake, coffee, and a chat about our lives had stoked the fire again. Add in his touches and eyes that seemed to soften every time they traveled over me, and I was still like a cat on a hot tin roof.

Atlas

I'd replaced the batteries in my mechanical boyfriend so often that I'd been praising the Lord above that he'd given me the foresight to get the rechargeable ones, or I would've gone bankrupt.

He'd been making all the right moves but not following through, so I was more confused than ever.

My skin felt hot and tight. It was the same feeling I got every time Atlas walked into the room lately, so I knew he'd arrived. It was like I could feel him.

I picked up my drink with trembling fingers and took a huge gulp of wine, trying to calm my nerves.

"The officers just walked in," Layla said, nodding toward the crowd of men. "Here we go."

We all stretched our necks up to see what was happening.

"This is exciting," Tristan murmured.

"It is," Cara agreed. "It's huge when the prospects become members. They work their asses off."

"There's a lot of horrible shit they have to do." Rosie let out a giggle. "But I knew the minute Boner prospected that he'd get through. I can always tell who'll make it and who won't."

"How many don't make it?" I asked, turning to her.

"Some get through." She shrugged a delicate shoulder. "More men either leave or get kicked out, though."

"Wow," I said under my breath, glancing over my shoulder as John stepped onto a chair and jumped up onto the bar. "You'd think it would be easy."

Rosie laughed again. "I couldn't clean up after these slobs." She shuddered. "Imagine their rooms, though my brother is a clean freak. He hates stuff out of place. Forget to put a cup in the dishwasher, and he'll put you on his shit list."

I rolled my eyes and turned on my chair to look around the bar.

Jules Ford

The tension in the air was palpable, like its own entity, making the atmosphere crackle with electricity. I loved how charged everything was. It felt scary, exciting, and memorable. The low lights and thumping music just added to the air of excitement.

Goosebumps erupted down my arms, and I held my breath as I waited for John to open his mouth and speak.

A piercing whistle cut through the air. Somebody turned the music off, leaving the sound of men laughing and chatting.

"Brothers!" Atlas bellowed. "Shut your fuckin' holes. Your Prez is about to speak."

John's face was stern, almost mean. Hendrix and Atlas stood in front of the bar, arms folded across their chests like sentries guarding their king. Their faces were blank, giving nothing away.

People still muttered softly, finishing up their conversations.

"Shut the fuck up, assholes," Atlas bellowed.

The sound of voices died down, and silence reigned. The room went so deathly quiet you could almost hear a pin drop.

"Boner!" John yelled. "Get your ass over here."

Every eye turned toward the door to see the prospect's head snap up. "Me, Prez?" His voice was thick with confusion.

"No other Boners around here, Prospect." Hendrix's voice was hard. "Did your prez fuckin' stutter? Get your ass here now."

I caught Cara and Layla exchanging a knowing look. Anna's eyes were glued somewhere toward the bar. I followed their direction and was surprised to see that she was staring at Hendrix.

I couldn't blame her. The VP was a sight to behold, with his long hair and tattoos, but my attention was drawn to the tall, muscled Sargeant at Arms standing beside him.

Atlas

Atlas' chest was bare, apart from his leather cut that did nothing to hide the myriad of tattoos that ran down his arms. The black crow's wings etched onto his pecs seemed to point down, drawing your eye to his chiseled six-pack.

Something hit me deep in my core. Atlas was so gorgeous. My heart fluttered, and my pussy clenched so hard that I squirmed a little in my seat.

Our eyes locked, and he sent me a sexy grin. Of course, he knew exactly what he was doing to me. He'd had a lot of practice, after all.

"Boner," John barked, pulling me away from my thoughts. The prospect was already at the bar. The men lifted him to stand next to his president.

"Hand over your cut." John held his hand out, glaring at Boner. "You don't fuckin' deserve the privilege of being a Demon's Prospect no more."

Bewilderment flashed across Boner's face, swiftly followed by a touch of hurt, then anger. "No!" he rasped. "Sorry, Prez, I don't mean to disrespect you, but whatever you think I've done, I promise I haven't. I've tried to be a decent prospect for the club and worked hard. I won't let you take it away from me for nothin'."

John ducked his head, glaring at the other man. "Give me your cut." His voice was like death.

Boner's back snapped ramrod straight like he was standing to attention. "Sorry, Sir. No, Sir." He barked the words like a soldier addressing his commanding officer.

The poor guy was distraught. Anxiety came off him in waves, face was almost purple with frustration. I almost felt bad for him, but I knew what was to come, and I think the other guys in the room were beginning to understand too.

John's arm suddenly shot out and grabbed the prospect's shoulder. "Boner, you gotta give me your cut, *brother*. You'd look like an asshole wearin' two." He leaned down and grabbed the new leather cut someone passed him from under the bar.

Boner went stock still; not even a breath passed his lips as blue eyes locked onto his prez,

unblinking. I could almost see his brain working overtime.

After a minute, his entire face lit up. He whipped off his prospect cut and flung it into the crowd, letting out a loud whoop.

Men began to laugh. Shouts of congratulations cut through the air.

John held up Boner's new leather. "Speed Demons, want ya to welcome our new brother." He slipped the cut over Boner's shoulders and turned him around so everyone could see his new road name. "Our new Speed Demon... Arrow!"

"Why Arrow, Prez?" someone called out.

John gave Arrow a clap on the back. "'Cause the fucker's a straight shooter, not just with a gun, but from there." He tapped his heart. "He shoots as straight as an arrow."

The room erupted in roars. Heavy boots stamped, and a chant began to rise through the room.

"Arrow! Arrow! Arrow!"

The noise was deafening and touching because every brother was ecstatic as they welcomed their new brother into the club.

Describing the emotions that gripped me seemed impossible. I was choked up with happiness because Arrow had found his place in the world.

He was part of a whole new family.

You could say many things about the Speed Demons, but at the top of the list would be that they were tight-knit and looked after each other.

My chest tightened. I bit back the sudden tears that stabbed behind my eyes.

I wanted that so badly for myself.

Atlas

I'd been missing Ned more than ever in the last few days. She always knew what to say to make me feel better. She'd know exactly what to do to take my mind off Atlas and the kiss that had screwed with my head.

"Go drink, Arrow. Tomorrow we're putting you to work." John ducked down, swiping a beer bottle from the bar and raised it high in the air. "Mess with a demon?" he bellowed.

Every man and woman in the room lifted their glassed and yelled in unison, "And we'll raise hell."

A shiver ran down my spine as another loud cheer almost raised the roof.

Somebody turned the music back up, and my foot began to tap along to the opening bars of 'Insomnia' by Faithless. I smiled as I watched people start dancing and singing along with the words.

Tristan jumped up and pulled Rosie to her feet. "It's our song," he yelled, tugging her into the middle of the crowd of dancers.

I felt a stab of envy as I watched them having fun. Something tugged inside my chest, and I wished that I could let loose like Tristan. That was another reason I missed Ned. She would've dragged my ass up there and made me enjoy myself. She'd put on a show and force me to lose my inhibitions.

I was still thinking of Kennedy when my eyes traveled across the room to see Atlas stomping toward me. He flashed a smile, and my heart bounced. Movement caught my eye. I noticed a woman sashaying toward him. She was topless with fire engine red hair.

Cherry stepped in front of him and suddenly leaped into his arms. His hands clamped onto her ass, and she bent forward and kissed his lips hard. Her back was to me, so she covered Atlas. I couldn't see exactly what was happening, but it was pretty obvious.

The pain that rushed through my chest took my breath away. I watched them make out, suddenly numb.

It's fine. It's fine. But as much as I kept repeating the words in my head, nothing felt fine. It felt like somebody had cut off my airway, and I struggled to breathe.

Why would he do that? Why would he kiss me and then kiss her? But I already knew the answer, and as much as I felt gutted, I wasn't altogether surprised.

More games.

Suddenly, I needed to get out of there. I was out of my depth and hated how my fingers tremored, and how my heart thudded against my ribs.

I yearned for the safety and comfort of my little house. There was no conflict there, no confusion, and no beautiful bikers who kissed me so deeply that I felt it down to my soul. All I wanted was for my life to return to the way it used to be.

Ordered and easy.

Reaching under the table, I grabbed my purse. "I'm going to head out," I shouted over the music so that Layla and Cara –deep in conversation – could hear me.

"It's early yet," Layla shouted back.

"Yeah," Cara yelled. "Please stay."

I held my hands up. "I'm sorry. I've got an awful headache. I want to go home, curl up and sleep."

Layla looked around at the festivities. Her eyes must've rested on Atlas and Cherry because she winced and looked at me sympathetically. "Let me find Bowie. He'll get a hang around to drive you."

"It's okay. I've only had one drink. My car's here. I'll drive myself." I lifted my hand in a wave, turned, and made my way through the main doors to the parking lot.

I didn't look back.

The night air was icy cold. We were already into February, but the temperatures hadn't risen. Although it hadn't snowed recently, it went well below zero at night. I hardly noticed though as I picked my way over the icy ground toward the colossal garage where I'd parked my car earlier.

Atlas

The images of Cherry and Atlas together ran through my mind.

My belly churned.

I knew they had a history. Cherry was the woman he called for a blowjob after I'd taken that bullet out of his shoulder. Even then, I could tell that they were comfortable with each other.

I'd been such an idiot. He was a slutty biker, and I was just a girl he'd toyed with. I should've known better. I was nothing like her, unlike the women he was used to being around.

I looked down at the white pinstriped tuxedo dress that skimmed my thighs and the black gladiator high-heeled sandals that I thought were so risqué when I'd looked in the mirror earlier. I smiled ruefully.

Compared to some of the women in that clubhouse, I looked like a nun. Ned would say I acted like one too.

My eyes veered up again, and my steps faltered. Ice was leaning back against the garage's metal walls, one leg bent, foot flat against the wall. His arm lifted, and he took a pull of his cigarette, the tiny red light from the lit end glowing in the dark.

"Those things will kill you," I joked as I approached him.

He gave a little start, and his head jerked toward me. "Hey, beautiful," he almost crooned.

"Party not to your liking?" I asked, coming to a stop and leaning back against the garage directly next to him. I hooked the strap of my purse over my shoulder.

"It gets a bit much sometimes," he replied thoughtfully. "The noise, the music and everyone shoutin' over each other scrambles my brain. I just needed some peace, ya know?"

"I know exactly what you mean," I confirmed.

He looked directly at me. "You leavin' already?"

"Yeah." I rubbed my arms, trying to warm them. "It was a bit much for me too."

He took another pull of his cigarette, blowing smoke rings as he exhaled. "What did Atlas say about you takin' off?"

"Nothing." I closed my eyes to block out the flood of tears that rushed up my throat. "He was too busy with Cherry to notice."

Ice cocked an eyebrow. "You sure?"

"Yeah." I worried my lip with my teeth. "When I left, his hands were grabbing her ass. I think they were kissing."

Ice let out a low whistle. "Well, I'll be damned. Who'd have thunk it? Good ol' Atlas fuckin' it up before he even got it off the ground." He shook his head slowly, muttering under his breath. "And he calls me a fuckwit."

The night had been a total disaster, Jesus, the last few weeks had.

Why couldn't Atlas just let me get on with my life and stop toying with me? First Luke, now him. I let out an audible sigh. Suddenly I was so exhausted by all the games and heightened emotions. It all hit me, along with the wracking ache in my chest.

I couldn't stop a solitary tear from sliding down my cheek.

"Babe," Ice exclaimed softly. "Why are you crying?" He flicked his cigarette away before snaking an arm across my shoulder, pulling me into his chest. I let out a tiny sob when he kissed my head. "Don't let it get to you, Soph. He's not fuckin' worth it."

It was like I'd opened the floodgates. Weeks of push and pull had finally tipped me over the edge. I rested my forehead on his chest and just cried. I wasn't usually emotional, not really. The build-up of all the feelings had messed with my head and heart for weeks. Or I was just plain hurt by the kiss I'd just witnessed.

It seemed like everything was falling apart.

Atlas

Where were the walls that I'd carefully constructed around my heart? Why did I keep letting bastards inside just so they could hurt it?

Ice pulled back slightly and tilted my chin up with his finger. "I'm sorry, babe. I'll kick his ass for ya. Feel me?"

"Okay," I whispered. "But if Atlas needs a hospital, please don't send him to mine. I may just finish him off." I giggled through my tears.

"That's my girl." He gathered me into his arms again, giving me a tight squeeze. "Ain't one of us assholes worth cryin' over. Believe me, babe. You're too good for him."

I felt cold inside and out, freezing. My warm, cozy house called to me. I was desperate to get out of there.

"I'm gonna go home, run a bath, and sleep all weekend." I pulled back and looked up into Ice's handsome face. My smile faded because a thought hit me hard.

It didn't matter that there were nice guys in the world. If there were an asshole within a five-mile radius, I'd sniff him out like a bloodhound in heat. I must have had 'come and get me, fuckboys' tattooed across my forehead.

My throat was still clogged when Ice grabbed my hand and led me to my car. "Keys," he demanded.

Sniffing, I fished inside my bag and handed them over.

The locks beeped and flashed. Ice opened the door and gestured for me to get in with a flourish of his hand. "Your carriage awaits."

I turned back, leaned up, and kissed his cheek. "Thank you," I whispered. "Why don't we meet up soon and go for that dinner?"

"No, babe," he rasped, taking my hand and stroking his thumb over mine. "As much as I want to – and believe me, I do want to - I can't. You're not mine. You belong to somebody else."

My heart began to thump wildly at the meaning behind his words.

Did he mean Atlas? He was mistaken. But even so, I knew he'd done the right thing by saying no. As I said the words, I wanted to take them back.

If I went out with Ice, I'd use him to boost my ego and make myself feel better. That would make me a game player, and in hindsight, it would make me no better than Atlas.

I squeezed his arm. "You're right. I'm sorry." I smiled sadly as another tear rolled down my cheek.

Ice brought a hand up and gently wiped it away with his thumb. "So am I, Doc." He jerked his head toward the car. "If you don't jet soon, we'll both freeze to death."

My chest tore in two at the wistful edge of his tone. I hoped like hell that I hadn't bruised his heart. He deserved someone who was all about him, not a broken woman who crushed on somebody else, a woman trapped so far in her past that she couldn't live in the present. He deserved someone who looked at him like no other man in the world existed.

"Thanks, Iceman." I turned, got into the driver's seat, and pulled my seatbelt across, snapping it into place. "Take care."

You too, babe." He swung my door closed and watched as I started the engine and pulled out toward the gates.

And as I looked in the rearview and saw that he was watching me drive away, I silently asked God why it couldn't have been him.

Chapter Fifteen

Atlas

My head twisted as I watched Sophie's brake lights glow in the darkness. They dimmed again as she put her foot on the gas pedal and pulled outta the compound.

"You may as well step forward. I know you're there." Ice's voice sounded as flat as my fuckin' heart felt after seein' Sophie break down like that.

The second I threw Cherry off and bitched her out, I turned to look for Stitch, only to see her slipping out through the main doors. After askin' Layla and Cara where she was runnin' off to, I followed her outside. I didn't mean to eavesdrop on their convo, but I wanted to know what was nigglin' at her enough to make her wanna walk out on me.

"Cherry busy?" Ice's voice was so sharp it almost cut the air like a blade.

I let out a humorless laugh. "You know me better than that, Iceman. You fuckin' love gettin' in between us, but I'm tellin' ya now, you need to stand down."

Ice cursed under his breath, lookin' up at the stars. "Stand down? Brother, I stood down the night I was supposed to go to her crib. Remember? When you fucked with my truck?"

Shit. Fuck. Shit. What could I say to that? Fuckin' busted.

"I stood down by walkin' back in that clubhouse and not gettin' a prospect to take me," he continued. "There were a hundred trucks that I could'a borrowed, but I didn't because *I stood down.* Ya think I didn't want to be inside her instead of club gash that night?" He shook his head disbelievingly. "I would've loved to get to know her better, but you know why I didn't, *brother?*" He almost spat the word. "'Cause six hours earlier, I watched her look at you like you'd hung the goddamned moon. You think I wanted to get in there and screw up her head more than you'd already fuckin' done?"

My shoulders tensed.

I should've known that Ice was onto me for the truck business. He flew fighter jets back in the day, so I knew he was no fuckin' idiot. Asshole probably saw everythin'. Didn't mean I'd take him speakin' to me like an asshole, though.

"So, what did I just witness?" My lip curled. "You tryin' to *not* get into her pants? 'Cause from what I just saw, you couldn't wait to give her a shoulder to cry on. Arms around her, heads together, whisperin' like the both of you got secrets."

Ice pulled a packet of smokes out of his jacket pocket and tapped one out. "I'll give ya two weeks." He put the cigarette between his teeth and lit it. His eyes never left mine as he inhaled deeply and blew the grey smoke into the night air. "Fourteen fuckin' days, and if you don't sort it by then, I'm goin' after her, and I'll gladly do the work that you should've already been doin'. And I'm warnin' ya, brother, next time around, she won't pick you."

My chest went tight like it was caught in a vice.

Thinking about Ice and my woman together made me want to rip his head off. "Don't even say it. I'm warnin' ya. If you or anyone else goes near her in that way, I'll meet you in the ring, and we'll slug it out." The urge to wrap my hands around his neck was so strong that I had to force them to stay down.

Ice took another drag of his smoke. "If just sayin' it makes you that fuckin' crazy, you better get yourself over to her crib. Apologize for allowing Cherry to jump all over y-"

"-I didn't allow fuck all," I interrupted. "Cherry jumped up, and I caught her without even thinkin'. When I realized what the fuck was happenin', I threw her off and told her never to touch me again. When I looked around, Stitch was already through the door."

Ice threw his head back and bellowed out a laugh. "Jesus. You're gone for her. Love seein' ya all tied up in knots." He clapped me on the shoulder. "Go to her, brother. Show her you mean business."

Ice was right. It was time to man the fuck up.

I needed to throw my hat in the ring and show Stitch that I was going to start taking her seriously. The only problem was, I'd fucked around so much she may've had enough. And after the Cherry incident, I wouldn't blame her if she wanted to boot my ass to the curb.

I rolled my shoulders, tryin' to loosen the tension that gripped my neck.

It was time to pay Stitch a visit.

"There comes a time in a man's life when he has to hold his hands up and admit he's wrong. Stitch, today's that time for me...' Fuck! Umm. Okay. Stitch, about Cherry. Well, I haven't fucked her for months. In fact I-"

Kit's laughter came through my truck's speakers. "You can't talk about bitches you've fucked. Are you goddamned touched in the head?"

Jules Ford

My brain almost exploded. "Well, I don't fuckin' know, do I? Never apologized to a chick in my entire fuckin' life."

"Not even Rosie?"

I barked out a short laugh. "Especially not fuckin' Rosie. The minute you let her think she's got one over on ya, your fuckin' life wouldn't be worth livin'."

I'd been thinkin' on what to say for the full drive to Stitch's place. Not a fuckin' clue entered my head. In fact, my mind blanked. In the end, I called Breaker for some help. He'd fucked enough women to fill a goddamned football stadium. If he didn't know how to sweet talk a female, then I may as well have given up, turned the truck around, and fucked off home.

"Look," Kit said reassuringly. "Apologize and tell her how you feel. How hard can it be?"

"Surely it can't be that fuckin' easy, Kit. Jesus, where's the Wildcat when you need her? Are you sure Cara's not there? I'm up shit creek without a paddle, and you're as useful as a chocolate fireguard."

"She went home just after you disappeared," he explained. "She was exhausted. Said it just hit her. Layla's gone too. I can get Tristan for ya. He's cuttin' a rug on the dancefloor as we speak." He hooted out another laugh. "That little hottie, Julianne Hough's got nothin' on him. He's doin' the fuckin' caterpillar and gettin' cheered on by a gaggle of rowdy bikers."

"Nah." I turned my truck onto Stitch's street. "He'll tell Ro. Fuck that."

"Atlas, say sorry. Sophie doesn't seem the type of chick who'll make you beg. She's not a crazy bitch. She's a fine fuckin' woman, and I reckon she'll want you to speak from the heart."

"Speak from the heart?" I chuckled. "Apologies, Breaker. Did I interrupt you washin' your vagina?"

A click sounded, and the line went dead.

Fuck. He's hung up on me.

Atlas

"Touchy prick," I murmured to no one. "Was only fuckin' jokin'."

After a few more minutes of goin' over all the shit in my head, I pulled up outside Sophie's place and turned off the truck. My eyes took in the house. It was in complete darkness except for the porch light.

"Here goes nothin'," I said under my breath as I jumped out and slammed the door shut. Ass nippin', I made my way through her front garden and onto her porch.

Raisin' my fist, I banged three times on the door and waited.

Nothin'.

I lifted my hand again and thumped hard. "Sophie!" I yelled. "Open up, babe. My ass is freezin' up out here. It's so icy it could sink the goddamned Titanic."

Silence.

"Sophie!" I bellowed again.

My heart leaped as a light flicked on inside the house. Light footsteps padded through the hallway toward the door.

I stood straight and plastered a smile on my face, even though my heart was beating outta my chest so fast I was starting to go light-headed.

The door cracked open, and fine-whisky eyes peeked through the gap. "Atlas," she said in a sleepy voice. "What are you doing here at this time?"

My voice stuck in my throat, and my mind went blank.

What the fuck *was* I doin' there? I didn't have a speech planned. Didn't know what I was doin', or what to say. Kit's words pinged in my brain. *Speak from the heart.*

I must've been havin' a mini-stroke 'cause 'speakin' from the heart' suddenly didn't seem like such a bad idea.

So, I spoke from the heart.

"I'm sorry about Cherry," I said softly. "She jumped at me, and my brain seized up. Next thing I knew, she planted a smooch, and I was so fuckin' shocked that I froze. I know I've been an asshole to ya, but give me another chance, Stitch baby?"

She opened the door a little wider, and her body came into view.

My stare went from her head to her sexy toes.

I nearly groaned out loud.

She was wearin' a silver grey silky, slinky, lacy thing that lovingly cupped her pert little tits. My mouth began to water as her hard, pointy little nipples popped out to greet me. You could've hung a ring off the sexy little fuckers.

My eyes traveled down, and my cock kicked when I saw that the lace skimmed just under her pussy. I decided there and then that one day I was gonna fuck her into the headboard while she wore that fuckin' cock stiffenin' contraption. Then I was gonna fuck her all over again and rip the thing clean off her.

"You're one sexy bitch," I muttered. "Hand to fuckin' God, my cocks weepin' for ya, Stitch. Feel like a college kid in a brothel."

Her whisky eyes went huge. "I am?" Her eyes dropped to my thickening dick, and a slow smile took over her face. "But I thought you didn't like me in that way?"

I adjusted my cock in my jeans. "Jesus, Stitch. You're so hot that sometimes I feel like I'm burnin' up just from bein' close to ya."

Still beamin', she looked up into my face. "Thank you for the apology."

I took a step closer. "No problem, baby." One hand slid into her hair. I tipped her chin up, and bent down, touching my mouth to hers hard before pullin' away.

She looked up at me with a dazed expression and murmured, "Wow!"

Atlas

I bent my neck again, tugged her into me, and kissed the goddamned bejesus out of her.

A tiny hand slid around my ass, pullin' me closer.

I groaned into her mouth, and my cock stiffened. The heat of her silk-covered pussy engulfed my dick, and I almost came right there and then.

Her lips were soft and pillowy. Nobody made me feel the way that she did and suddenly I couldn't get enough of it. She set me alight.

I groaned again and kissed her harder, my mouth diggin' into hers. Hard little nipples poked into my chest, and my cock turned hard as fuckin' iron.

My mind blanked. All I could feel was Sophie's soft little tongue pressin' against mine. She smelled like strawberries, her shampoo, maybe. The sweet scent was all around us as I pressed our mouths together.

"Baby," I growled. "I have to go, or else I'll take you in that bedroom and fuckin' ruin ya."

Jesus, I was so fuckin' hard it was almost painful. But I knew I had to tread carefully with Stitch. She'd been through a lot, and I didn't wanna bamboozle her.

When we fucked it'd be 'cause she felt comfortable enough to do it.

She pulled away slightly. "I can't… I'm not. I mean-"

"-Sshh. It's okay," I murmured, my eyes dartin' between hers. "I'm not gonna fuck you yet, Sophie. Wanna take my time so we can get to know each other properly. Get me?"

I almost moaned again as I watched her straight, white teeth sink into her bottom lip.

She looked up at me wide-eyed and innocent. "Thank you," she whispered. "It's been nice getting to know you all. I've enjoyed training the boys."

I grinned at her cockily 'cause I knew I had it in the bag.

Jules Ford

Sexy little bitch was eatin' outta the palm of my hand.

Fuckin' knew the old Atlas charm would razzle-dazzle her.

Just as I was about to ask her if she wanted to go on a date, she reached up.

"Take care, asshole." She gave my face two hard pats. "I'll see you around, not." The door slammed in my face, and I was left standin' alone on her porch.

I blinked.

Huh?

The interior light went out, and the house was bathed in darkness again.

She'd left me standin' out on the porch in the freezin' cold, not that I noticed it seein' as my blood was starting to boil.

"Open the door, Stitch," I bellowed.

All I heard in reply was a tinklin' little laugh, then she called out, "Goodnight. You better get back to the party. Cherry's probably waiting for you with her legs open."

My chest began to burn. I rolled my neck from side to side and bellowed, "Open the goddamned door. Now!"

"Fuck off," she called out. "I'm not playing your pathetic games anymore. Get off my porch, or I'll call the cops."

The burn rose through my throat. "Open the door, Sophie, or I'll goddamned open it for ya."

That was when I heard her voice again, but she wasn't talkin' to me, she was on her cellphone. "Oh, hi. Is that the Sheriff's office? Yeah. I'm Doctor Sophie Green. I work over at Baines Memorial." Silence. "Hi, Marge. Yeah, I remember your grandson, Harrison. How is he?" More silence. "Yeah. Sorry to bother you, but some guy is shouting and banging on my door. He's making a nuisance of himself. I think he's drunk. Can you send a squad car to move him on?"

Atlas

My body locked.

Crazy bitch called the fuckin' cops on me.

Jesus.

I scraped a hand down my face, thoughts scramblin'.

Okay, so maybe things were way worse than I realized. Had I gotten Sophie that pissed? I thought back to our breakfast a few days ago. She was okay on the whole. I'd been getting closer to her since, playin' around, touchin' her in trainin'. Nothin' too full on, but she must've understood that I was making my play.

Couldn't give a fuck about the pigs. I'd tell the little pissants to go fuck 'emselves, but standin' around and shoutin' like a lunatic wasn't impressing her. I had to go back to the drawin' board.

"All-fuckin'-right," I yelled. "I'm goin'. But this ain't over, Sophie. I'm gonna come back and sort this shit out. You can run, baby, but you can't hide."

"Bye, asshole," she yelled.

My shoulders slumped, all anger leakin' outta my chest. I leaned my head against the door and sighed. "Baby. Whatever I did, I'm sorry."

"It's what you didn't do, Atlas." Her voice sounded closer as if she was behind the door. "You've had weeks to make your move, but all you've done is toy with me. And that's not even the worst thing. You called me names. You acted like a dick. You even accused me of stalking you. And okay, I get that Cherry took you by surprise earlier, but that was the last straw on top of everything else." She paused, then murmured, "I'm scared to trust you."

My stomach clenched hard.

"Stitch, I'm fuckin' crazy about you, baby," I stated. "I'm just a stupid idiot. I've never felt like this before I met you, so I'm fuckin' everything up."

"Why are you playing these games, then? You say you're crazy about me, but you had Cherry's ass in your hands earlier. Giving another woman any attention when you say that you're into me is an asshole move. You have your hands all over me in training, but then you back off. You kiss me, but then you back off. Why can't you just be straight with me? I feel scared, Atlas. You're not showing me that you're worth taking a risk for."

Shot to the fuckin' heart.

She was right, I had fucked around, but it wasn't 'cause I didn't wanna make a move. It just took me a while to come around. By the time I did, I'd already screwed everything up.

I leaned against the door. "D'ya think I'm not scared too, Soph? I've never done this before. I'm fuckin' terrified, baby."

"Then why did you come?" she asked.

I dropped my head, restin' it on the door. "'Cause, Stitch baby, I've realized that I'd rather be scared with you than without you. I swear you can trust me."

Another sigh. Then Sophie asked a question that made me go cold. "What if that was me kissing someone tonight? How would you have felt?"

A flash of pain shot through my chest at the mere thought of some asshole's mouth on my Stitch. I brought my hand up to rub away the ache. "It ain't over, baby," I said through the door. "Gimme a chance to make it up to ya. I'll show you that I can be a steady guy."

There was a long pause before she spoke again, her voice full of pain. "I want someone who wants me, Atlas. I want a man who'll fight for me. All you've ever done is push me away." She let out a little sob.

My heart crashed into my gut.

I'd gone and fucked up, and it felt like I had a noose around my neck. "I'll show ya, Stitch baby. If it's the last thing I do."

I listened for her voice. Must've stood there for a full two minutes waitin' for her to say somethin', anythin'. Even if she opened the door, slapped my face, and bitched me out, I would've accepted it, even welcomed it.

But she didn't. The silence was deafening.

Head still bowed, my hand went to the door and rested on it for a few seconds before I turned and walked to my truck. I could feel her eyes burnin' into me.

I turned and walked backward, holding my hands out to my sides. "I'm gonna show ya, Stitch baby," I called into the night. "I feel your eyes on me 'cause you warm me like the sun. Sometimes I can't look in your face 'cause it shines so fuckin' bright."

Silence.

I jumped in my truck, clicked my seat belt on, and screeched outta there.

My jaw set. I wasn't giving up. I'd waited so goddamned long for a woman like Stitch to shine her light on me. There was no way I was gonna let her go.

Chapter Sixteen

Sophie

"Look," I told Kennedy, flipping my cellphone screen to pan around the room. Flowers covered every surface. "It's like Proflowers and 1800flowers had a love child, and it's shit all over my house."

A soft laugh came from the cell's speaker. "He's certainly gone all out, that's for sure. But I thought you said that he friend-zoned you?"

"He did," I confirmed.

Ned let out a frustrated sigh. "Okay. Start from the beginning, Soph, because what you're showing me and what you're telling me don't mesh."

I went through the entire story. From the day we met to ten days ago when he turned up at my door after midnight and told me he wasn't giving up.

"Sophie," she screeched. "You're such a dork. Men don't take you out for breakfast and tell you all about their family and deceased fathers if they just want to be friends. What's the fucking matter with you?"

My brain cells began to ping. "But Atlas said I had the body of a fifteen-year-old boy."

"Talking big in front of his boss," she said decisively. "Men are like little boys; they hate losing face."

"That's what *he* said," I mused.

"Whoa, hold up. Did Atlas tell you that already? Why the hell didn't you believe him? Especially since you've said yourself that it was out of character."

"I don't know," I whispered. "I thought he was just trying to get around me."

"Well, duh," she yelled. "He's doing more than that. He's trying to get into your chastity belt." She began to mutter, "Jesus Christ, Sophie. What the fuck's wrong with you? Didn't I teach you anything? A man doesn't go to all that trouble if he doesn't want you. He's been subtly chasing you for weeks."

"Oh," I breathed.

A lump formed in the pit of my stomach. "Why didn't he say something instead of sending stupid signals?" I cried. "Admittedly, I'm not very good at picking up signs like that. I'm a busy woman, Ned. If a man feels a certain way, he has to spell it out. Plus, it's not like I'm the most confident person in the world, so it's easy for me to downplay stuff like that." I raised a hand and rubbed my aching forehead. "Shit."

Ned must have cracked up laughing for a full minute. "You're dangerous without me, hon. How do you feel now? Are you going to give him a chance?"

I looked around at the myriad of white and pink peonies, roses, and lilies. Even though I hated pink, Atlas was certainly persistent. I was secretly impressed by that. All I ever wanted was for him to do something to show me that he cared. It was a shame that he was subtle to the point of non-existence because if I had noticed him making an effort before, it would've gone a long way.

But was it too late? I'd resigned myself to the fact that 'we' weren't going to happen, and I'd accepted it. Did I want to open that particular can of worms back up and let him in?

There were pros and cons to both sides of the argument.

Atlas

I missed the girls. I'd been working long shifts and hadn't had time to speak to them. I also missed the boys, even Shotgun. The way things were at the moment, it wasn't like I could walk into the compound and go and say hi to everyone. It would've been nice if Atlas and I could've gotten along.

Also, if I was being honest, I missed him too.

For weeks we'd been working together, joking around and having fun. It was like having a whole new life suddenly ripped away from you. I hadn't stopped thinking about him. Even when I was on shift, he was always in the back of my mind shouting 'Stitch, baby' and giving me shit.

"I don't know, Ned. It's hard for me to trust people. Add in all the crap he gave me, and it's almost ridiculous that I want to go there again. But…" My voice trailed off.

"But what?" Ned prompted.

I sighed, still rubbing my aching temple. "I don't know. There's just something about Atlas that makes me feel safe."

"Soph, if a man told me that I warmed him like the sun, I'd have his pants down his ankles in five seconds flat, and my mouth would warm something like the sun." She let out a cackle. "I think he really likes you. Men like him don't turn all romantic if they don't give a shit. Why don't you go and talk to him?"

My stomach churned at the mere thought.

How could I threaten to call the cops on a biker, then turn up to talk to him without a care in the world? Not for the first time in the last week, I regretted that call. After he left, I called back and told them I was mistaken.

"I'll think about it," I reassured her. "You don't have to worry about me. Now, tell me, how are the kids? I miss you all so much."

"We all miss you too," she murmured. "Kady made you a vase in pottery. It's the weirdest-looking thing I've ever seen. I don't think Fulpers have much to worry about quite yet."

I let out a giggle. Kadence was so gorgeous. She was all Kennedy in looks, but unlike her mom, she was a perfect little lady. She loved art and always made me cool stuff. When she was younger, she used to paint me a picture every week because she said every refrigerator needs magnets and paintings.

She was right.

"The boy's okay," she continued. "The coach picked him for the baseball, and football teams, so he's walking on air." She paused. "Shit, that reminds me. I have to go and pick them up from guitar lessons. We need to go to the sports stores. They both need new sneakers. They're growing like weeds."

"You go," I told her. "I have to finish some paperwork anyway."

"Cool," she replied. "Remember what I said, though."

I played dumb. "Huh?"

"Go and talk to him, Soph. I know what you're thinking, but remember, if he didn't want you, he wouldn't send you flowers daily for a week."

I closed my eyes. "I know you're right. But it's hard for me, Ned. I wish I were more like you sometimes. I wish it were easy for me."

"Babe," she said gently. "You're amazing the way you are. I wouldn't change you for the world. Go to him. If he says he wants to be friends, then that's okay. At least you'll know. Isn't it better to regret something you have done than something you haven't?"

She was right.

Sage advice at the end of a telephone from a smart woman was something that every girl needed. We could obliterate wars and world hunger in one fell swoop if Kennedy Carmichael could be available to take calls.

"Love you, Ned," I told her.

Atlas

"Love you too. Now, I gotta get mini-Slash and mini-Taylor from guitar lessons. I'll call you next week."

We said our goodbyes, and the line went dead. My heart ached the same way it did every time we hung up the phone.

God, I missed her. It was so hard not seeing her or the kids. They were coming for a visit in the Summer, so at least I had that to look forward to. And it gave me some time to sort my awful love life out and get back on track.

I glanced at my watch, checking to see if I had time to make a pit-stop at the clubhouse on my way to the hospital. As much as I hated the thought of the confrontation to come, I knew I couldn't carry on the way I was. Living on your nerves was the recipe for a heart attack.

Ned was right.

It was time to get things worked out with Atlas, one way or another.

Chapter Seventeen

Atlas

Prez banged his fist down hard on the table. "So, you're tellin' me that three assholes, who may or may not have been Sinners, broke into *our* lumberyard and took the materials we need for the job on that new mall? How the fuck did this happen?"

Colt tapped on his tablet. "We've got 'em on camera. They dressed in black balaclavas, jackets, jeans, the lot. They weren't wearin' cuts so they could've been kids. Or assholes thinkin' they can steal from us."

"It don't make sense," I butted in. "Every person in a hundred-mile radius knows not to fuckin' steal from us. We may not officially be one-percenters, but word gets around when we have to make an example out of somebody."

Cash leaned to the side to see the tablet's images. "They ain't built like kids. I think we all know who it is, brothers. The question is, what are we gonna do about it?"

The officers around the table went quiet as they thought.

Ice broke the silence. "What we can't do is fuck up their clubhouse." He chuckled. "It's already on its last legs."

Snickers sounded through the room.

Ice was right. Their clubhouse had a hole in one side which they were rebuildin'. A thought pinged in the back of my mind. That was it! Rebuilding. That was the key.

"Just thought of somethin'." I looked at the expectant faces of the men around the table. "We blew their clubhouse to high heaven, meaning they have to rebuild it. What better way to get one over on us than stealin' our goddamned materials?"

"Fuck!" Prez barked. "He's right."

Abe shook his head, almost smilin'. "Wiley little fuckers."

Bowie lifted his shoulder in a nonchalant shrug. "Gotta give it to 'em. I would've done the same."

Cash laughed. "We all would've. It's the best way they could've said 'fuck you' without drawin' attention to 'emselves." He rolled his eyes. "And there was me thinkin' they'd shoot up the clubhouse."

Prez rubbed his beard, deep in thought. "I think we can safely say that Thrash is still alive. If Bear was in charge, I reckon the payback would've been much worse."

"Maybe we should thank our lucky stars that stealin' materials was the worst thing they've done," Colt suggested.

Hendrix sat forward. "You mean what they've done so far." He let that sit for a minute. "This is war. Thrash hasn't got the stomach for killin' seein' as he's at death's door, but that won't last forever. Once his boy takes over, we all know that shit's gonna hit the fan. I say we should try to disable 'em before Bear even sits his ass in the big chair."

Bowie's forehead creased. "Disable 'em how? You want us to start takin' pot shots at 'em as they're ridin' around?"

"Why not?" Drix shrugged. "At least if they know that we're looking for 'em, they'll stay on their turf."

Atlas

Prez nodded his agreement. "I agree—the time's right to take it up a notch. Order every brother to carry their weapons at all times. First sign of trouble, they shoot." He turned to me. "Have you spoken to the Kings about your visit?"

"Yeah. Locke's on it." I sat back and looked around the table. It would be the most important mission of my life. "Colt's lookin' into Price as we speak, and the Kings are diggin' their end too. When we've got everythin', I'll take a trip, do what I gotta do, and get out."

Prez grinned. "You sure about this?"

I gave one jerk of my head.

"We should put extra men on the women and the businesses," Abe commented. "The best way to get to us is through our scratch or hearts. Don't think for one minute either's safe 'cause they ain't."

My senses pinged louder and louder as Abe's words sunk in.

How the fuck could I keep Stitch safe when she wouldn't even talk to me? Freya was back safe at school in Colorado. Bowie was on Layla, Cash on Cara, and Abe on Iris. All the men with wives and kids were lookin' out for 'em, but I knew that if I showed up and told Stitch that I was gonna be her shadow, she'd kick me in the nuts.

Fuck. I looked to the ceiling and prayed, asking if my gonads could still do the job after I approached my woman.

"Anyone on the pretty doc?" Ice asked as if he'd just read my goddamned mind.

My head jerked in his direction. "You don't need to worry 'bout *my* woman. I've got her, brother." I paused. "Get it? Got it? Good."

"Just sayin'." He held his hands up, smilin' at me all cocksure of himself. "You're busy with your important as fuck SAA duties. I wouldn't mind keepin' an eye on her. It'd be my pleasure."

Every stare sliced toward me, and the men silently waited.

Black spots danced behind my eyes. My hands curled into fists as a sound escaped from deep inside my chest. "Shut the fuck up," I scraped out.

Ice laughed.

Ice fuckin' laughed.

"Stand the fuck down, Iceman," Prez warned. "He'll pop off at ya, and I ain't gonna fight for your honor. Think about your words, Ice."

"Already stood down." The Road Captain's face hardened. "You had fourteen fuckin' days to sort your shit. It seems to me that your time's nearly up."

My jaw clenched. The asshole actually went there.

I'd called Stitch a hundred times; she wouldn't pick up. I'd gone to her place to hash it out; she wouldn't answer the door. I'd even gone to the goddamned hospital only to be told that she had back-to-back surgeries and wouldn't be available for hours.

I'd spent nearly a grand on goddamned flower deliveries to her house. If she wasn't there, I'd instructed Lucy from *Blooms* to redirect them to the hospital.

I knew all that effort was only step one, but I needed an in. I needed to do one thing that would get through. One thing that would make Sophie pick up the phone and call me fuckin' back.

For the first time in my life, I was a desperate man. However, if Ice thought he'd slide in there and take my place, he'd be goddamned, loop the loop crazy. It would be over my cold, dead, decaying body.

Nostrils flarin', I stared him in the face, silently darin' him to say another word about my girl.

He stared back for a minute, bold as fuck before leaning back on his chair, not a care in the world.

Ice better beware. You're on my shit list now, motherfucker. Strike one.

I relaxed my hands and dropped 'em on the table.

"How about we get Sparky on her again?" Hendrix suggested. "They get on okay, and he's harmless as fuck." He nodded toward Colt. "While she's at work, techno boy here can patch into the security feed and keep watch."

Colt looked up from his tablet. "It's a big hospital. Can't have eyes on her all the time. The back stairs don't have cameras, as far as I know, unless they're hidden. I can patch into their security feed and find out, though it would be more sensible to give her a shadow. At least that way, there'd be no blind spots."

Veep turned to the boss. "Anyone else we can spare, Dagger?"

Prez's head dipped in a nod. "Now trainin's done, yeah. I'll do it myself if I have to."

My eyes rolled so far in my head that I could almost see the back of my skull. I'd sort my woman out. I didn't need help to wrangle what belonged to me.

Cash checked the list in front of him. "Next on the agenda is our first run of the season." He looked toward Iceman. "You sorted it?"

"Yup," he replied. "Meet here, nine. Iris'll cook up a storm, helped by the lovely Layla and the little pocket rocket Rosie."

My jaw clenched.

Fucker had a death wish.

Ice grinned at the look on my face before continuing. "We'll fill our bellies, go potty and ride out by ten thirty." He leaned forward, elbows on the table. "I've marked out the route. With all the shit goin' on, I reckon we should stick within Hambleton town limits. Our last stop will be the same place we've gone to for the last couple of years. Magnolia's."

Cheers went up around the room.

It had been a hard winter. We'd put our bikes away after the night the Sinners hunted Cara. It had been far too dangerous to ride, especially in a rural area like Hambleton, where the roads went untreated.

The first run of the season was a big deal. Time to fuckin' ride at last.

"Can't wait to get back on my bike." Bowie rubbed his hands together, smilin'. "Sparky's out there now, linin' 'em up and washin' 'em down."

"He'll have 'em gleamin' by the time he's finished." Abe grinned. "He's a good'un, but we need another prospect. Everyone keep an eye out, yeah?"

Sounds of agreement filled the room.

"Roads are nearly clear of snow now," I pondered. "Fuck waitin' for the run. We can get back on the road when the mornings warm up. If Sparky's sorted her in time, I may get Lana out and go for a little test ride later."

"Good idea," Ice agreed. "My Marilyn could do with her pipe's warmin' too." He stroked his chin in thought, glancing slyly at me. "Wonder if Doctor Sophie wants to ride behind me."

My brain exploded.

Strike fuckin two.

The thought of my woman ridin' bitch behind Ice made me boil over. If the asshole wanted a reaction? I'd give him a fuckin' reaction.

Slowly, I got up from my chair, body tight as a drum. I bent over the table and put my face in Ice's. "Ya think?"

Cash jumped up and grasped my shoulder, attempting to pull me away. "Don't pay no mind to him, Atlas. He's just bein' a smart ass."

I put my finger in Iceman's face. "One more fuckin' word, I'll make you wish you'd stayed in bed this mornin'."

Ice smirked. "I think she'd like it on the back'a my bike."

My body locked.

Strike, fuckin' three.

"Here we go," Prez muttered.

Atlas

"Sheeeet." Abe snorted.

"Fuck me," Drix grumbled.

Cash gripped harder onto my shoulder. "Fall back, Atlas," he ordered.

"Get ya hand off me, Cash," I gritted out. "*Brother*, there needs a lesson in keepin' his mouth shut."

Prez leaned toward me. "Cash told you to fall back, Atlas. You gonna listen, or you gonna pop off?"

Tension cracked the air.

I turned my head, glarin' at Cash's hand. "You ain't my prez yet."

He shrugged 'cause he knew what had been goin' on in the last week.

Ice had been diggin' at me ever since the night of Arrow's party. I'd shrugged it off, taken everythin', but this time he'd gone way too far. Talkin' about my woman and my sister was disrespectful and not somethin' I'd do to a brother, not ever. Disrespect me, and I disrespect you more. Like for like. Eye for an eye.

If Ice wanted to hit me where it hurt, namely, my woman, I'd hit on the only woman he had in his life.

Time to school a motherfucker.

I pointed at Ice. "Outside!" I moved so fast that my chair scraped back and hit the wall with a crash. Rage filled my lungs, so I didn't even notice my brothers all jump up with me. I was so focused on my goal, so blinkered. It was like I had tunnel vision.

"Jesus fuck," Abe muttered.

Six pairs of biker boots stomped after me as I stalked through the door and down the hallway toward the bar.

Chest burnin', I headed straight over to the long bespoke wooden countertop, put one hand on it, and hauled myself over to the other side, landin' with a thud. I reached underneath and pulled out the Louisville slugger we kept under the bar in case of trouble.

"Whoa!" Hendrix shouted. "Atlas. You need to chill."

Jules Ford

Abe cackled out a laugh. "Like fuck he does."

I ignored 'em and jumped back to the other side, heading for the main doors.

Every man trailin' behind started to shout at me to calm down. I didn't give a rat's ass, though. There was only one thing on my mind.

Disrespect.

My teeth gnashed as I threw the main doors open and sauntered outside to the parkin' lot with the heavy baseball bat slung over my shoulder.

My body may have seemed relaxed, but I was firin' on all cylinders.

The boys in the bar must've seen my face twisted with fury. I didn't often lose my shit, but the set of my jaw and the stiffness in my stance signaled that I was about to flip.

Every brother in the bar rose from their chair and followed us outside.

For an SAA, I was pretty easygoin', but anyone who knew me also knew one thing, don't fuckin' diss me. Ice was about to find out that pushin' me too far was gonna cost him big.

Sparky was kneelin' on the ground, scrubbin' an electric blue Harley Cruiser. He looked up at me stormin' toward him and gulped. "E-Everythin' okay, Atlas?" He got to his feet. "Gonna do your gal next. Just need to finish Ice's ride first."

"Move aside, Prospect," I demanded.

Cash appeared beside me, mutterin', "Goddamn it. No, brother."

"Go on At," Abe crowed. "Show the fucker who he's messin' with."

"Abe," Cash barked. "You're not fuckin' helpin'."

I heard Abe cackle. "If that little twat talked about my Iris like that, I'd have knocked him on his ass. What if he told you that he'd put your Cara on the back of his bike? Would ya be so fuckin' soft on him then?"

217

Atlas

Cash's body stiffened. "Fair enough," he muttered, walking away.

My body twisted toward the horde of men watchin' me

Shouts went up from the crowd, but I didn't hear the words, didn't fuckin' care. The only thing on my mind was teachin' Ice a lesson in keepin' his mouth fuckin' closed.

Pullin' the bat down off my shoulder, I twisted my body, aimed, and swung it full force into his headlight, shattering it with a loud crash.

Satisfaction coursed through me.

Ice yelled, "You prick! Fuck you, Atlas."

Bellows and hisses went up from the crowd.

"Jesus!"

"He's lost it."

I turned, swung my arm out, and pointed the slugger at Ice. "Good luck puttin' my girl on the back of your bike now, Iceman."

His face was red as he spluttered and cursed. "You crazy fucker!"

I threw my head back, let out a roar, and walked around to the back of his shiny cruiser. "You keep strikin' out with me, Iceman," I yelled, aimin' the bat at his back fender. I swung hard and smashed it against the metal with a loud crunch, "My turn to strike out with you."

"Get the fuck away from my bike!" He shook his head, shock bleedin' out of his eyes.

I grinned.

The fucker hadn't seen nothin' yet. I hadn't finished.

My eyes scanned the parkin' lot. It was full of trucks and cages, but there was only one I was lookin' for. I grinned as my stare rested on a gunmetal grey Ford F150, and I began to stalk toward it. "Show's not over yet, folks."

Jules Ford

"No, Atlas," Ice screamed. "Stop. I won't have a ride."

I turned to face him and lifted my arms out at my sides. "That's the fuckin' point!" I walked backward, still grippin' the Louisville slugger. "Can't take my woman out if you got no vehicle, eh, fucknut?"

I spun around, swung the baseball bat, and slammed it into one of the headlights.

The crowd roared.

"Jesus!" Ice bellowed from behind me. "You're fuckin' payin' for that!"

"Ain't payin' a dime." I pulled the slugger all the way back and swung it into the other headlight. The sound of it smashing into tiny shards reverberated through the air.

My ears pricked up as Ice let up another bellow among the shouts. 'Oohs' and curses came from the crowd witnessin' my every move.

"Ain't payin' for that bastard one either." I laughed and hauled myself up with my free hand, landin' on the hood of Ice's truck.

"No," he roared. "You asshole. Get the fuck down from there. You'll dent her."

I turned to face him, pointin' at him with the bat again. "Dents are the last thing you should be worried about, you fuckin' dick." I turned to his windshield, swung out, and roared, "Home run," as I smashed the bat right into the middle with every bit of strength I had left.

The sound of shattering glass cut through the ether just as tiny cracks began to run through the toughened windshield.

"Fuck!" Ice roared.

I twisted my body to see him fall to his knees, hands behind his head, eyes pained as he stared at the mess of his truck. "What the fuck did you do?" he yelled.

I jumped down to the ground, landin' solidly on two feet. "I warned you not to fuckin' test me, *brother*. Now

Atlas

I'm tellin' you again." I sauntered toward him, swingin' the baseball bat back over my shoulder. "Keep my woman's name outta your goddamned mouth. Not only did you disrespect me, but you disrespected her too. My girl doesn't hop from one biker to the next, so you sayin' shit like that doesn't fuckin' fly with me, asshole. Be warned, next time you talk about what's mine like that, I'll crack your fuckin' skull open."

Ice had the good grace to look guilty.

"Jesus fuck." Prez's hands went to his hips, and he looked toward the heavens, shakin' his head. "Crazy fuckin' fuckers. Bandit'll be rollin' over in his grave." His eyes sliced toward the truck. "It's like dealin' with fuckin' lunatics."

Bowie stared at my face as if he'd never seen me before.

Drix's jaw ticked, his eyes slidin' between Iceman and me.

Abe clapped me on the shoulder. "Good on ya, son." He stared down at the Road Captain, who was still on his knees in the dirt. "Maybe now you'll shut that pissy little mouth of yours."

The men laughed, hooted, and hollered.

Cash's lips twitched. His hard stare fell on somethin' over my shoulder. A huge smile took over his face, and he nodded behind me. "Incomin', brother."

The sound of a car approachin' registered through my angry haze. I craned my neck to see who it was. My heart jerked when I saw Stitch's silver Explorer pull into the parkin' lot.

The adrenaline from smashin' up Ice's shit pumped hard through my veins.

I grinned 'cause I knew my baby had finally come for me. It was like no feelin' in the world. Nothin' could touch me, and I'd make sure nothin' else could touch us.

She parked up and watched as her gaze fell straight upon me.

Something tugged me in her direction. A feelin' took over like you get when you can't resist somethin', and you don't give a flyin' fuck about the consequences of touchin' it. All I needed to feel complete was to have her close.

My feet moved like they had a life of their own. I sauntered toward Stitch's car, and our eyes met through the windshield.

Shouts and laughter still filled the air behind me. My brothers' encouragement made my chest feel like it was growin' to double its size.

I hauled her door open and got down on my haunches until we were eye to eye.

"Hey, baby." I reached out and stroked her cheek. "Missed ya beautiful face."

Her eyes went huge as I leaned forward, grabbed her arms, and tossed her over my shoulder. "Come on, darlin', it's time we made up." I stood tall, Stitch takin' the place of the Louisville slugger that just five minutes ago adorned the same position, slung over my back.

She let out a piercin' screech from my back. "Let me down!"

Wolf whistles filled the parkin' lot as I gave her ass a light slap and headed for the clubhouse. "Settle, Stitch baby," I rumbled. "Don't wanna drop ya."

She let out a frustrated shriek. "You're incorrigible."

"I dunno what that means, but you're probably right, woman." I barked out another laugh as tiny hands beat against my back.

"Atlas, you're crazy!" Stitch yelled as I swept through the double doors and hit the corridor leadin' to my room. Suddenly, she laughed, and my heart bloomed.

I grinned to myself, gut leapin', 'cause the time had come for me to lay it all out on the line.

Very soon, Stitch would know exactly who she belonged to.

Chapter Eighteen

Sophie

You know that feeling when you drive too fast over the top of a hill, and your gut leaps? That was the sensation I had in my stomach as Atlas gently dropped me onto the bed.

I looked around the room, wide eyes blinking hard and fast.

Grey blinds, a black lamp, and a black-and-white patterned comforter were the first things I noticed. There was a massive TV on the wall facing the bed. A nightstand and a dresser stood next to a single wardrobe that rested against the opposite wall.

Weeks of uncertainty began to unravel. I let out a laugh, shaking my head incredulously. "You kidnapped me." I couldn't help smiling as I said the words because I wasn't scared. I knew he didn't force me into his room to hurt me. I got it. It was just his way.

He sat on the edge of the bed, snaked his arms around my back, and lifted me.

I let out a squeal as I landed on his lap. My breath hitched as his hard cock dug into my ass. Heart beating out of my chest, I turned to him. "Jesus," I whispered.

"No, Sophie, darlin'." His eyes turned liquid soft. "Just a man." He leaned forward and nuzzled into my

Jules Ford

neck. "A man who's made so many goddamned mistakes with you that I've been layin' awake at night regretting so much shit that it's impossible to sleep."

My eyes closed, and my heart fluttered because, finally, he was being real with me.

I settled into the feeling of safety that swirled around me whenever I was in his presence.

"A lot's happened, Atlas. Maybe we should forget the whole thing." But I knew I didn't want that even as I said the words.

He lifted his head, and immediately, I missed his warmth. "Can't, babe. Tried."

"Okay," I replied softly. "In that case, we need to talk. I first want to say thanks for the flowers, but stop now. It's too much."

His shoulders slumped like he was relieved. "Had to get your attention, Stitch baby. You wouldn't talk to me. Had to do somethin'." His head hit the pillow as he lay down, looking up at me. "Sorry about Cherry. Hand to God, it won't happen again."

My mind returned to that night and the image of him standing outside my door, begging me to talk to him. "Maybe I overreacted a little." I winced slightly.

"Nah," he corrected. "You were right. I would've flipped my lid if it had been the other way around. The thought of someone else's hands on you makes me wanna lose my shit." His fingers curled into fists as he spoke. I could see his words weren't fake.

Oh, the irony. It seemed that taking notice wasn't so difficult. The signs had always been there. Ned was right.

After my phone conversation with her, I thought long and hard about what he said on my doorstep the night of Arrow's party. My mind kept going over the last few weeks. The sensual touches. Our deep conversations. The way he teased me in training as he tried to build rapport and make me comfortable.

Atlas

After mulling it over, I realized that he *had* been making moves all along. I'd just missed it. So why was that? How did I not see the signs?

It didn't take me long to figure it out. The truth was, I was insecure. I'd been that way ever since that awful day with Luke. The instant he punched me, my world changed in a moment, and I started to lose my belief in the world and myself.

Kennedy called it perfectly. I got scared, so I wrapped myself up in a safe little bubble and stopped living. If I'd overheard Atlas saying those things to John about me five years before, I wouldn't have cared, but because my self-esteem was so low, I allowed it to affect me.

Kennedy had always told me that people could think anything they wanted about you; you couldn't control it. But what you could control was the way you felt about yourself.

When I left Vegas, I traveled with the intent of healing, but what I did was create distance. When I went to New York, I thought I was strengthening my mind and body, and yes, Krav did that for me to a point, but it didn't help me recover my confidence.

I had to do that myself.

My heart leaped as Atlas' big hand grabbed me and pulled me down onto the bed. I sighed contentedly when I felt him snake an arm around my waist and kiss the back of my neck.

My pussy clenched as he molded his huge body to my back, tucked me into him, and spooned me. For the first time in a long time, my mind wasn't looking for an ulterior motive. I felt at peace.

"I know you need time, Stitch baby," he rasped into my neck. "And I'll give you as much as you need, just don't shut me out. Let me show you who I am. Let me prove that I'm not the asshole who treated you like shit all those times before."

Jules Ford

I'd been thinking about that for days.

Atlas wasn't a dick at heart; he was kind and protective, but why say and do all that shit in the first place? What was it about me that brought the asshole to the surface?

"Why did you do it?" I asked. "I know you well enough to understand that you don't usually behave like that."

I felt him stiffen. After a minute, he relaxed. "Straight up?"

"Yeah," I whispered. "Straight up."

"I'd seen you in town before we met properly at the hospital. You always looked down at the floor, never lifted your head. I knew that you'd been through somethin'."

It was my turn to go stiff. We were having an honest moment, but the last thing I wanted was to ruin it with the mention of Luke.

"You're right," I confirmed. "But I don't want to talk about it now."

His fingers rubbed my hip soothingly, and I relaxed again. "It's okay, baby. You'll tell me when you're ready. Gotta lot to prove to ya first." He squeezed my hand. "So, like I was sayin', I thought it would be better if you hated me. The club's got all this shit with the Sinners. Didn't wanna leave you vulnerable…" His voice trailed off.

"Go on," I encouraged.

He kissed my neck again. I knew he was stalling, but I stayed quiet and waited.

"You're outta my league, Soph," he croaked. "You're beautiful and so fuckin' smart. I don't even got my GED. Bet you know a shit load of rich doctors, men who probably suit you way better than me. I'm just a dirty biker. Don't even own a suit, babe." His fingers stroked my skin. "Was worried the novelty of me would

Atlas

wear off after a while. Thought you'd come to your senses and leave my ass."

I went to tell him that he was being stupid, but then I remembered having the same reservations at first.

On the surface, it didn't seem like we had much in common, and we didn't. But that wasn't important because when Atlas wasn't being a dick, he was protective, generous, and funny. And he might not have had his GED, but even that was beautiful because he sacrificed his education to look after his family financially.

He was far from stupid.

It was plain as day that Atlas was a good man. When you'd seen the worst of humanity, it was easy to recognize the best of it.

Pushing up on the bed, I turned my body so we faced each other. I gently traced the dark shadows under his dark eyes with my finger. "What happens next?"

He nuzzled my neck with his nose. "First, I'm gonna woo you. Gonna prove that I see and understand what you need. I'll make it so you don't want anyone but me. I want you on the back of my bike. We'll get to know each other properly. You gotta remember that people have seen us out. The Sinners will target you, so we need to be careful. I reckon word will have gotten out that I was hammerin' on your door and shouting shit."

I let out a giggle. "Yeah. I know." I made my voice deeper. "You warm me like the sun."

He chuckled so hard that his shoulders shook. As usual, I joined in. It was infectious.

After a minute, our laughter died. "Can't give you romance, baby. Dunno how. I'm gonna say and do the wrong things all the goddamned time. Probably make you pissed every day. But I'll do right by ya. I'll give you all of me if you gimme all of you."

My eyes narrowed. "Are you quoting songs at me?"

His eyebrows snapped together. "Huh?"

Jules Ford

I smiled because he really was clueless.

Danny 'Atlas' Woods wasn't such a complicated man. His vocabulary was limited to cuss words, and he was probably the most frustrating person I'd ever met. He was rude, crude, and honestly didn't give a shit about many things.

But he treated the things he cared about - namely his family and his club - like gold. The thought of being on the list of things Atlas loved made me gooey inside. He was worth the risk of caring for.

But I still wanted him to work for it. I wanted him to fight for me.

I lifted, resting on my elbow. "I'll give you one more chance to get to know me, Atlas. Any more shit and you're out."

His eyes got a faraway look in them, and he grinned widely. "Won't fuck it up, Toots. Trust me, gonna make you my girl if it's the last thing I do." He leaned up and pecked my lips with his.

Ignoring the flutter in my belly, I gave him a severe look. "I mean it. Last chance."

"Got it." He jerked his head in one nod. "There's shit goin' down, so I want you to stick with Sparky. He's weapons trained, and he picked up Krav like a pro. Anythin' happens, or you see anythin' weird, even a feelin', you call. You got Prez's number, too, right?"

"Yeah." I couldn't help smiling at how beautifully he was caring for me already. He was so worth the risk.

"I'll give you Cash's number. I'm going on a run, probably in about six weeks. I asked him to do a drive-by or two at your place while I'm away. What shifts you workin' this week?"

"I've got surgeries booked seven a.m. to nine p.m. every day except Friday. I finish at seven. Then it's my weekend off."

"Don't make any plans," he ordered gruffly. "You're on the back'a my bike. Gotta toughen up that peachy

Atlas

little ass of yours ready for the club runs. All day on a bike won't be pretty if you're not used to it."

My heart soared.

Riding a motorcycle was on my bucket list, weird seeing as most doctors hated them, but I trusted Atlas to keep me safe.

"Can't wait. I'll cook for us at night at my place. We'll need to chill out if we go out during the day." I patted his rock-hard abs. "It's like you said, you're a growing man."

He reached up, cuffed the back of my neck, and tugged me down for a kiss. "Sounds good, baby."

The urge to explore his mouth with mine was strong. I pressed my lips to his mouth, his tongue gently touching mine. He groaned, and the next thing I knew, he'd pulled me down and flipped me.

"Wow," I breathed, throat hitching with need.

His huge body moved over mine, caging me in. "Fuck!" The word came out strangled. "I can't, baby. It's too much. I want you so bad that even makin' out like teenagers makes wanna fuck you into the mattress."

I knew exactly what he meant.

It had been so long for me that even kissing him got me hotter than the July sunshine. I wouldn't sleep with him yet. It wasn't that I didn't want to, he was gorgeous, and I knew he'd look after me that way. I guess it all came back to the same old need of wanting him to work for it.

He rolled off me, crawled across the bed, and stood. "Come on." He held out his hand. "You gotta go. I got shit to do. Gotta sort that away job with Breaker. If you keep lookin' at me the way you are now, I'll tie you to the goddamned bed."

"Your run. It's nothing dangerous, is it?" I held my breath.

He grabbed my hand and pulled me to my feet. A strong hand cupped my chin, and he stroked my face with his thumb. "No, baby. Ain't a thing. Just biker relations at that club in Oregon that I told you about. We're makin' nice with our allies in case anarchy breaks out. We gotta think of all eventualities. If the Sinners play dirty or get outside help, we'll need to do the same. Decent allies equate to back-up and numbers."

"So, you're just meeting with allies?" My shoulders relaxed, and I let out the breath I'd held while he spoke. "Thank God."

"Hey," he rumbled, tipping my chin up. "I'm not gonna take any chances. I know what I'm doin'. So does Breaker. Gotta say, though, I like that you're worried. Like it even better that I've got you to come home to. Never had someone waitin' for me before 'cause I was waitin' too, baby, for you."

My heart flipped over.

"You do alright for a man who says he can't give me romance." I leaned up, slid my hand around his nape, and pulled him down for a kiss.

He bent, grabbed my thighs, and hauled me up. Muscled arms caught me around my back, and my legs went around his hips. He walked us to his door, opened it, and headed down the corridor toward the bar. "Like you in my arms, Sophie."

My heart bounced, and I was suddenly euphoric. I threw my head back and laughed. "But you don't have to carry me."

His eyes caught mine, and they softened. "Fuckin' love havin' you close like this. Could fit you in my pocket." He kissed my nose again.

The moment we hit the bar; I heard the conversations start to die down. I held my breath because I could feel every eye on me.

Claps began to sound out. Within seconds, the roof seemed to lift as an enormous cheer went up, and the air filled with wolf whistles, hoots, and shouts.

Atlas

I giggled like a schoolgirl and buried my flaming cheeks into Atlas' chest. The beat of his heart thudded against my face. Deep inside, I could feel his rumble of laughter as he headed for the main doors.

It was joyous.

The cold air hit my skin when he walked us outside, but it didn't bother me. I couldn't feel it even though it was the end of February, and I'd left my coat in the car.

It seemed that I always felt warm when I was with Atlas. It had been that way since the day I met him.

"Gonna call you later," he muttered. "I know you can't answer when you're at work, but whenever you see that I tried, know that I was thinking of you. Don't want you to call me, baby. Always wait for me to call you." We reached my car, and he gently placed me back on the ground.

I tipped my head back so I could see his face. "Why?"

"'Cause I only want you to call my number if there's a problem. That's gonna be our code. I call you, but you don't call me unless you really need to. Got it?"

"That's not fair-" I began to protest, but he cut me off.

"-Give me that, please. Ain't gonna ask you for much, Stitch baby." He waved his hand between us. "As long as I got this, don't need nothin' else except to know if you've *got* that. So, tell me, do you *got* that?"

"Yeah," I agreed. "I've got that."

He smiled, and that made me smile.

Something caught the corner of my eye.

My head twisted to see Ice over the other side of the parking lot, close to the auto shop, bending over the front of his truck, doing something to the headlights.

He saw us and straightened to his full height. After taking us in for a few seconds, his mouth stretched into a huge grin, and he gave us a loose salute with his index finger.

Atlas shoot him one of his badass chin lifts, before looking back down at me. "Ready to jet, baby?"

I nodded, and he helped me into my car. Reaching up, he pulled my seatbelt across my lap and fastened it securely. "Call ya later?"

"Yeah," I replied, starting the engine.

Atlas took a step away and banged lightly on the roof.

Pulling away, I turned my car around and headed toward the gates. My eyes went to the rearview to see Atlas standing there, arms folded across his chest, watching me leave.

My heart exploded, and my veins filled with something that I hadn't felt for years, something that made me smile while pure joy coursed through my blood.

Something like love.

Chapter Nineteen

Atlas

Arrow lifted the tray and knocked it against the SUV's trunk.

"Be fuckin' careful with that, brother," I ordered sharply. "No point doin' all this if you're gonna make a fuckin' mess of it all."

He grinned and shook his head good-naturedly as he walked toward the main doors to Baines Memorial hospital. Breaker and Bowie followed him as they carried bags and trays of food.

My stare went to the long line of trucks and SUVs the boys had parked. Then my eyes snapped to the queue of Demons that were carryin' pasta, pizzas, salads, and such like through the doors.

"Start at the top floor. I'll deal with the ER," I called over to 'em.

"If this don't impress her, nothin' will," Cash muttered as he lifted the last bag outta the trunk. "Can't believe how much dough you've spent. You could give me some lessons in romance."

My ass nipped when he reminded me of the small fortune I handed over to Giovanni a half hour ago, but I shrugged nonchalantly for Cash's benefit and lied through my fuckin' teeth. "Don't give a fuck about the scratch. You and Colt can make it up for me on the stock market, right?"

"I guess." He shrugged as he fell into step beside me and we made our way toward the hospital.

"Anyway, asshole, I gave you that list, didn't I? Use that, and ya can't go wrong."

Cash barked out a laugh. "Already broke the 'not stickin' your dick in someone else rule, brother, but I'm workin' on it."

The list that Cara gave me was workin' like a fuckin' dream.

I'd already called Sophie ten times a day and left countless messages lettin' her know I was thinkin' of her. True to her word, she never called me back, and I liked that 'cause I wanted her to see me makin' the effort. My feelin's were growing stronger for her every day, and it wasn't a chore to spoil her.

The night before, we'd talked on the phone until she fell asleep, and I could honestly say I'd never felt closer to another person before in my life.

We laughed, then she cried as she said how much she missed her friend from LV. We told each other our life stories, though she still didn't tell me about her ex- prick. What she did mention in passin' was how she didn't eat much while at work. My girl liked food that was fresh and cooked well. Baines Memorial didn't quite cut it.

I got it, she was a doctor and wanted to be healthy, but some days she worked for sixteen hours straight and only ate a sandwich that she'd made the night before, and that was only if she hadn't fallen straight into bed after a double shift.

No wonder she was so slim.

I wasn't havin' it, so I made a plan which kind of escalated seein' as I thought about how doctors, nurses, orderlies, surgeons, secretaries, even the cleaners all looked after us. On a fuckin' mission, I decided I would treat everyone to lunch.

Atlas

We walked through the main doors and turned for the ER department that took up half of the ground floor. People stared as we walked on by, but then we were convoy of bikers carryin' bags of Italian food through a hospital, not a sight you'd see every goddamned day.

Freya had messaged Sully. He told her that Sophie was seein' to an emergency in the ER. Sure enough, when I strutted in, she was lookin' at X-rays with the man himself.

Her mouth fell open, her shocked eyes followin' the men who loaded the surfaces with food. She spied me, and her eyes bugged out. "What's going on?" She put down the X-ray and made her way toward me.

I stomped toward her, heart thumpin' at the sight of her in scrubs and sexy secretary glasses. I decided I'd make her wear those fuckers in the near future when I got into her pussy. An image of my woman with her hair loose, wearin' nothin' but those glasses and a pair of lacy stockings pinged through my mind, and I had to fight against the ragin' hard-on that pressed against my jeans.

"Lunch," I announced, ignorin' my chub. "Don't like the idea of you not eating all day, baby, so I brought the food to you. There's enough comin' in to feed all the staff." I grabbed her hand. "Eat for me, please."

A collective sigh went through the room. I looked over Soph's shoulder to see a group of women smilin' at us with dreamy eyes.

"Did you pay for all this?" Stitch asked as she watched a nurse pull the lid from a tray of lasagna. "I can't believe it."

"Wanted to feed ya." I cupped her cheek. "Don't like the thought of you goin' hungry." I leaned down and kissed the top of her head.

She looked around again and her cheeks stained scarlet. "Did you do all this because I told you I didn't like hospital food?"

Jules Ford

The same collective sigh breezed through the room again.

"Oh my God," some woman whispered.

"That's the most romantic thing I've ever seen," another lady breathed.

"Screw the food," a different female voice sassed. "And screw his motorcycle too. I volunteer as tribute to ride that man all day." Giggles and more sighs cut through the air.

Sophie brought up her hand to hide her grin. Her eyes shone with happiness as she gazed up at me. "I'm going to have to pull them all off you at this rate. All my colleagues want my man." Her cheeks blushed an even brighter pink.

"I'm a one-woman kinda guy." I tugged her into me and touched my mouth to hers. "Gonna leave ya to it, baby. Make sure you eat."

I waved my hand and turned to leave, but she stopped me. Liftin' on her tiptoes, soft hands tugged me down so that she could whisper in my ear. "Some of these people aren't paid well, Danny. You may have just given them their best meal of the month. I'm proud to be with a man like you."

My throat thickened.

Jesus fuck. Nobody called me Danny, and nobody had ever said shit like that to me before. She was a fuckin' catch, beautiful and intelligent, but her heart was the best thing about her.

She made me feel good about myself.

Christ, I was gonna start blubbin' like a bitch if I didn't get outta there soon.

Jutting my chin up, I turned and stomped toward the doors while shouts of thanks cut through the air.

The staff seemed happy.

My chest puffed out.

The emotions that warmed my insides were new. The only people I did shit for were my brothers, Mom, and

Atlas

Rosie. It was okay, but it didn't make me feel any particular kind of way.

In total contrast, doin' that for Sophie and seein' her so happy made me feel like the king of the world.

At that moment, I swore I'd spend the rest of my life makin' that woman proud of me.

It was true what they said. Behind every great man, there was an even greater woman.

"Do I even know you?" Prez snapped up at me. "What happened to the asshole SAA who yanked every fucker's chain and laughed at people's misfortune?"

"Dunno what you mean, Prez." I leaned back against the ropes and grinned. "I'm a ray of fuckin' sunshine."

Cash removed his mouthguard and let out a laugh. "Don't get it twisted, Atlas. You're a mean fucker who's met a good woman. Just like the rest of us, you've fallen flat on your goddamned ass." He held his boxing gloves up in a defensive stance and jabbed my arm. "She's way outta your league. Lucky for you, lightnin' struck, and against all odds, she seems to like your fat, raggedy old ass."

"Heard that your feedin' of the five thousand routine went down well with her," Drix called up to the ring. "Been seein' a hot little nurse. She told me that half the female medical staff are prayin' for the doc to dump your ass so that they can make you feel better."

"No fuckin' way," I replied with a laugh. "I'm a one-woman man. If it ain't my Sophie, then it won't be anyone."

"Can you fuckin' believe this?" Cash demanded, reachin' down for his water bottle. "Suddenly, the brother who never wanted a woman is not only wifed-up to the hilt, but he's also bein' lusted over by half the chicks in town. You couldn't make it up." He lifted the bottle and took a swig.

Bowie let out a laugh. "Atlas is more married than I am at this point. Layla's been askin' me why I don't do all these romantic things for her like our SAA does. Fucker's making us all look bad." He turned to Cash. "Seems you need to take a leaf outta his book if you're gonna get Cara back."

"Just read the list I gave ya." A wide grin slid over my features. "That's all you need."

"Can't believe he got a woman before me," Hendrix mused. "He's always been an asshole to women. I take them out, wine 'em, dine 'em, and I'm still single. I can't fuckin' believe it."

Veep was right. Three months ago, if someone had said I'd be wifed up by Easter, I'd have had 'em committed. Should've known she'd wriggle her way even deeper inside.

She'd changed me. Suddenly my moody ass had become chill, mellow, and lovin' life. My nuts were also double their normal size 'cause they hadn't blown inside a chick since last summer when Bowie got shot. I needed Stitch to jump my bones, and knew exactly how to do it.

I grew up watchin' eighties and nineties flicks with Ro, all the classics. I watched the nerd get the jock and vice versa, so I knew exactly how I was gonna work my ticket.

It would be fuckin' epic.

The door at the top of the stairs banged open. I looked up to see Breaker clattering his way down toward us.

"Yo, motherfucker," Cash shouted over to him. "We're just talkin' about our SAA all loved up with a woman."

"Take that jealousy down a notch, Cashy boy. Cara wouldn't piss on ya if you were on fire." I turned and looked closer at his face. "What's that?" I asked pointin' at his cheek.

Atlas

"What the fuck?" he muttered swipin' at his face.

My eyes peered closer. "Thought I saw your face turn green."

"Fuck off, asshole." He reared back and walked to the ropes, mutterin' what a dick I was under his breath.

Kit walked over to us in the ring. "He's doin' well." He nodded toward me. "Yesterday Sophie was an asshair away from weepin' 'cause she was so goddamned happy."

"What the fuck do you know about makin' women happy ya little dog's dick?" Prez barked.

Kit grinned. "Nothin' little about my dick, Pop." He grabbed his crotch over his gym shorts. "Never had any complaints. The chicks come back for more, so I can't be doin' too bad. I've always remembered what you've told me since I was knee-high to a grasshopper."

Dagger looked on confusedly. "What?"

Kit waggled his eyebrows. "Ladies come first."

Abe grinned. "You've come a long way from the kid who used to follow Bowie and Cash around. You used to do everything they told ya. Remember the time they made you climb that old tree with the dead branches? Still remember that yell and the thump when you hit the deck. That was some funny shit."

I busted out laughin'.

Cash side-eyed Bowie. "Yeah. You did use to do everythin' we said. I remember."

"Yeah, remember that time he...?" Bo's voice trailed off.

Breaker looked between his brothers. "Don't you fuckin' dare."

Bo grinned from ear to ear. "They'll love the story."

"Bowie," Kit warned.

Cash laughed. "Come on, Kit. We kept your secret for years. You're a man now. Who the fuck cares?"

Breaker's eyes narrowed.

Jules Ford

I bit down my bubble of laughter. "Tell us then." I could see by the gloatin' looks on Cash and Bo's faces that this was gonna be a good one.

"Well," Cash began. "I was about thirteen, Bowie twelve, so Kitty here must've been what, ten or eleven?" He looked at Bowie.

Bo nodded. "Eleven and a mouthy little fuck. He thought he was the big man."

Kit heaved out a breath and looked up to the ceilin'.

"We pinky swore after it happened that the tale would never pass our lips." Bowie laughed. "But it was coming up twenty years ago, so I think we've passed the statute of limitations on it by now."

"Fuck me," Breaker muttered. "I'll never hear the end of this."

Me and Abe looked at each other, grinnin'. He was my partner in crime with this shit. We gave the boys as much crap as we could throw at 'em.

"Well, it's like I said," Bowie began. "Cash was about thirteen. I was twelve, Kit was eleven."

I leaned forward on the ropes and looked down at him.

"Mom and Dad had just got separate rooms," he continued. "Mom said that Pop snored. Though I suspected all along that they were 'consciously uncoupling,'" he did quotation marks with his fingers, "but everyone else knew zilch."

Abe had already started laughin'.

I grinned. "Go on."

"Well," Cash interrupted. "We were lookin' through Mom's room. Fuck knows why, but we were little shits who thought it was a good idea at the time."

"Probably lookin' for smokes, ya little fucks." Dagger pursed his lips.

Cash shrugged. "Maybe. But anyway, I digress. So, we ended up in Mom's bathroom and started going through her shit."

Atlas

Me, Drix, Dagger, and Abe leaned forward.

Kit scrubbed a hand down his face and blew out another hard breath.

"Me and Cash had already done sex-ed, so when we came across a little pot with a rubber thing in it, we knew what it was." Bowie's shoulders started to shake.

"Kit grabbed it," Cash interrupted, "and said, 'oh, it's a condom.' Then he started screwin' around and put it on his head to be funny. Then he pulled it over his mouth with both hands, tryin'a blow it up."

"Well, we've all done that, boy." Abe turned to Kit and clapped him on the shoulder. "Don't worry about it. Condom blowin' is some funny shit."

"Haven't finished." Cash grinned from ear to ear.

"There was somethin' we didn't tell him," Bowie added.

We all leaned further in. "What?" I demanded.

Cash burst out laughin'. "It wasn't a condom."

Kit covered his face with his hands.

Cash's shoulders began to shake. "It was Mom's fuckin' diaphragm."

"Oh fuck!" I yelled before busting a gut in the middle of the boxin' ring. I fell flat on my ass 'cause I was laughin' so goddamned hard.

"Jesus fuckin' Christ." Abe hooted and bent double as he roared. His finger went to Kit, whose face was burnin' red. "You had your m-m-mother's p-pussy innards all over your f-f-face." He couldn't get his words out for laughin'.

Drix was fuckin' cryin'. He swiped at his eyes and barked out another loud laugh. "Fuck, it explains a lot. He was addicted to cunt by the age of ten. Pity it was his mother's."

We all roared again.

Cash was on the floor with me laughin' so hard he had to hold his stomach.

Prez sniffed and looked down his nose at Breaker. "Dirty little fucker. Whatcha do that for?" His hands went to his waist, and he looked to the heavens. "Little cunts. Where the fuck did I go wrong with these little shits? Thank God for Freya."

Cash and me laughed harder.

Abe's hand went to his crotch. "I can't – I'm gonna piss myself. I-I can't." He began to hobble to the door that led to the bathroom and showers that serviced the gym, still holding his dick in his hands while his shoulders shook and tears ran down his face.

Kit looked at Bowie and Cash, and his eyes turned to slits. "Fuckin' assholes," he gritted out while all of us except for Prez busted a gut again.

I looked around through my tears, and my heart grew big as the sky when a single thought went through my mind.

Fuckin' love these boys.

Chapter Twenty

Sophie

I swung my car door open, planted my feet on the ground, and stood tall.

Flicking a hand out behind me, I clicked my key fob, and the locks beeped. I smiled like the cat that got the cream and began to walk – actually, no – I *strutted* toward the hospital like a dancer slash bartender from Coyote Ugly.

Cheryl Lynn's 'It's Got to be Real' was the soundtrack in my head that day. I sauntered across the parking lot in time to the pounding beat playing on a loop through my mind. I stopped myself from doing a funky head strut and sashayed into the hospital with a confident smile playing around my lips.

For once, I had a lot to be confident about.

Life was good.

I loved my job, loved my friends, and was absolutely starting to fall in love with the tall, muscled, gorgeous man in my life. It had been a long time coming with Atlas and me, but we were finally getting there, and I had no regrets about giving him a pass.

Within weeks, he had busted through every wall I'd carefully built. My Atlas was thoughtful and cared about the little things. He made sure I ate and made sure I was comfortable and happy. He went out of his way for me.

So far, I hadn't regretted giving him a chance. I was a woman in my thirties. I didn't need flowers and sweet nothings. It wasn't about getting over a miscommunication with a grand gesture. He was an asshole to me, and if he wanted me to give us a real chance, I needed him to show me that his asshole behavior was worth putting up with to get to the good stuff.

I mean, we could all be assholes, right? As long as his dickishness only reared its head when it was appropriate, I was good. I took his explanation at face value, but if he thought he could treat me badly again in the future, he'd be history.

Only time would tell, but so far, so good, better than good, in fact.

It was perfect.

Nettie at the main reception greeted me as I walked through the main doors. "Morning, Doctor Green. How's that man of yours?"

I sent her a smile and called out, "Good thanks, hon. Lovely day isn't it?" I floated toward the elevators and pressed the button for the third floor.

Everyone seemed to smile and greet me since the day that Atlas brought in all that food. People who'd never spoken before suddenly had time for me. I didn't think it was a mean thing. I suspected that one act of kindness had brought out the best in people.

It was nice, though. For the first time in a long time, I felt seen.

The surgical floor was quiet when I walked out of the elevators. My colleagues must have been in the staff lounge. The entire surgical team usually congregated there before we got started.

"Morning," I said breezily as I swept through the doors and headed toward my locker. Their greetings met

Atlas

me as I dug my key out of my purse and opened the small metal door.

I froze.

My surgical caps and blue scrubs were all folded neatly, exactly how I left them the day before, but on top of them sat a square CD case.

I took it out and turned it over, examining it. "Has someone been in my locker?" I asked confusedly.

The room went quiet for a few seconds before a chorus of denials rang through the lounge.

There was faint printed writing on the CD.

I peered closer and froze as I saw the words.

Yo Stitch did you a mixtape
The songs remind me of your sweet ass

Atlas
Spotify – Atlas' Mix Tape

As I looked at the CD, I first thought that his grammar was shitty. Then the meaning behind what he'd done penetrated my brain, and my heart began to fill with delight. I almost swooned.

He did me a mix tape.
He did me a mix tape.

At that moment, I wished I hadn't agreed never to call him unless it was an emergency. All I yearned for was to pick up my cell and squeal down it. It was probably one of the sweetest things anyone had done for me, as well as being romantic.

I fished my cell phone from my purse and texted Iris asking her to tell Atlas that I got it and to thank him.

Grabbing my scrubs, I put my belongings away in my locker, secured them, and went to get ready for surgery number one.

I was in a love haze.
He did me a mix tape.

Jules Ford

My stomach pitched hard.

We'd spoken for hours last night and messaged each other a few times earlier that morning. He hadn't mentioned a thing. I wondered how he got into my locker, but that train of thought lasted about eight seconds because I didn't care. He'd gone out of his way and done something sweet, and I was starting to feel a certain way for him.

Head over heels.

My day had started out fabulous and was only getting better. My chest was warm and swirly, and I was in a fantastic mood. Suddenly, I felt very smug that I'd given Atlas one last chance because he was turning out to be the absolute bomb. The perfect boyfriend.

Plus, Atlas was hot.

And he had a big dick.

Yasss.

My colleagues already waited in the OR when I walked into the bathroom annex, where we washed our hands. I gave the CD to one of the nurses and asked her to load it.

I always played music when I did routine surgeries. They could become mundane after a while. Music helped me relax and also lifted the atmosphere in the OR.

Smiling dreamily, I scrubbed my hands with soap and water and held my arms out to the nurse, who snapped my gloves on. She tied my mask and secured my surgical cap before holding the door open for me to walk through to the waiting patient.

I stood at the operating bed and looked down at the patient. "Ladies and gentlemen. Mr. Leverson needs his gallbladder removed, and I've decided that Doctor Sullivan will be the lead surgeon today."

Sully's back snapped straight.

I grinned. "Have you done a gallbladder removal before, Doctor Sullivan?"

Atlas

"No, Doctor Green," he replied. "But I've assisted in many."

"It looks like you'll be writing all about today in your diary later, seeing as it's such a milestone. The floor's yours." I stepped away from the patient and allowed Sully to take position. My eyes swept to one of the nurses. "Music, please, Lois."

She nodded and went over to the controls.

The opening bars of Van Morrison's 'Brown Eyed Girl' filled the room, and my heart flipped into my throat.

My mom sang that song to me when I was a girl.

Whenever I heard the words, I was transported to happier times, back when everything was easy and simple. I closed my eyes and let the intro sink into my soul for a minute. Then Van began to sing the lyrics, and the sweetest memories of my momma appeared in my mind.

Hey, where did we go? Days when the rains came.

Down in the hollow... Playing a new game.

Laughing and a runnin', hey, hey... Skipping and a jumping.

In the misty morning fog with our, our heart's a thumping, and you... My brown-eyed girl.

The warm glow inside my chest spread outward to warm my organs. Atlas couldn't have picked a better song.

An old movie reel played in my head.

My momma brushing my hair out at the kitchen table.

Movie nights when she used to drizzle homemade caramel sauce all over shop-bought popcorn, making it taste like the most fantastic thing in the world before we snuggled up together on the sofa.

Watching while she danced around the house with the vacuum cleaner, singing at the top of her voice.

I bit back tears, but they weren't sad. My heart was bursting open with joy. In one simple gesture, Atlas made me remember the good stuff. I thought back for the first time in years, and it wasn't all about Luke and violence.

Instead, it was about love and nurturing and my gorgeous momma.

Beautiful.

Beaming, I looked at Sully. "Are you ready for your first-ever cholecystectomy, Doctor Sullivan?"

His eyes lingered on the patient. I could almost see him going through the procedure in his head. "Ready, Doctor Green."

Still smiling behind my mask, I looked around the room at the staff. "Let's go."

After work, I went straight to my car and made a call.

The mix tape Atlas did for me was epic.

By the end of Mr. Leverson's surgery, we were all bobbing our shoulders and singing along to the tracks, all of them classics.

One of them was a song I hadn't heard until I went to London. The band who wrote it was huge there in the nineties. When it started playing, I almost screamed out loud with excitement.

Did I already mention it was epic? Because it was *totally* epic.

I clicked a few buttons on my cell and started my engine while I waited for it to connect.

"Hey beautiful," Ned's voice sang down the line. "You just finished work?"

"Yeah." I laughed. "I've had one of the best days ever. Guess what Atlas did for me?"

"Multiple orgasms?" she asked, quick as a flash.

I laughed again. "No. We still haven't slept together. He wants to wait."

Atlas

"It's not normal," she argued. "Babe. It's been years. Has it closed back up? Don't you need to give it a workout now and then so you don't get re-virginized?"

I rolled my eyes. "How many times do I have to tell you, Kennedy? Your hymen doesn't grow back."

She burst out laughing. "Okay, so tell me, what's the tall, dark drink of water done to make you smile now?"

I paused for a second for effect. "Atlas made me a mix tape."

The line went dead. Crickets.

I frowned. "Ned. Are you there?"

Silence.

I checked the connection and frowned harder when I saw it looked fine. "Kennedy?"

The line crackled. "Sorry, babe. Every teen movie made in the nineties called me and asked for their idea back." She burst out laughing.

I bristled a little, suddenly feeling overtly protective of Atlas and the cool thing he did for me. I loved my mix tape; it was the shit. "Track one was 'Brown Eyed Girl,'" I told her.

The line went quiet again. I knew that would have an impact, and I was right because Ned breathed out a soft "Wow," before asking, "what was track two?"

I smiled smugly. "'Free Falling.'"

"Tom Petty?" she screeched.

I laughed. "Ned. 'Dr. Feelgood' was track six."

"Oh my God," she squealed. "I used to strip to that."

"I know!" I shouted, a la Monica Geller from Friends.

"People used to come for miles to watch my 'Dr. Feelgood' routine," she continued. "It was my biggest money maker. That song paid for at least a year of law school. I used to bump and grind my ass like a belly dancer on very strong caffiene. It was like a money cloud appeared in the middle of Crimson Velvet and rained notes down on my barely covered ass." She let out a soft sigh. "Those were the days."

"Ned," I murmured. "Guess what?"

"What?"

"He put 'Tender' by Blur on it."

"Oh my God!" she screeched. "How did he know it's your favorite song from London?"

"I dunno," I laughed joyously. "It's uncanny. It's like Atlas knows me better than anyone except you. We've only been seeing each other a little while."

"It's crazy," she agreed. "Jesus, I'll have to come and see you soon. I could do with one of those hot bikers in my bed."

I winced. "Ned. They couldn't handle you."

"I'll take two, then." She giggled.

I laughed because she probably would.

"We don't all have to be frigid tits like you, Soph. You may as well get a habit and declare that you're going to marry Jesus." She paused. "Wait. I may have one you can have from an old routine."

We chatted as I drove home. Kennedy told me about the pro bono case she was working on.

Ned dedicated one day every week to carrying out free legal work for a women's shelter in Vegas. She represented women in court and helped them claim the right benefits if needed. She even dealt with restraining orders and represented the victims in court.

I turned the car into my street, and my eyes widened when I saw Atlas' truck parked outside my house. "Oh my God, Ned. He's at my house."

My belly went all tingly.

She let out a hoot. "Go on, girl. Thank your man for your mix tape, and tell him I said congratulations. He played it perfectly." She paused. "Remember, Sophie. This is a new start. Forget the past. It's got no bearing on the present—new leaf. You've got nothing but good going on. Let it wash away the bad shit, and always

Atlas

remember that whatever happens, you've got the twins and me."

My heart panged.

"You are everything, Sophie," she continued. "And if Atlas is as clued in as I think he is, he'll show you that. You've just got to let him."

I teared up at her words. Kennedy Carmicheal was beautiful and tough. She had a big mouth on her, but she also had a huge heart. I wished she and the kids could be here with me every day. "Love you." I smiled.

"Love you too. Call me tomorrow. I need all the gossip." A click sounded, and the line went dead.

My eyes went to Atlas' truck before they veered to my house. The lights were on.

I'd given Atlas a key because he said he'd send Mason and Sera to feed Vic when I was on a double shift. It seemed he had an ulterior motive too.

I got out of my car and beeped my locks on. It was dark, but the air had warmed up over the last week. We were shooting fast toward April, and spring was definitely in the air.

I made my way over to my porch and climbed the steps. My stomach prickled with burning anticipation of seeing Atlas.

That mix tape said everything I needed to know.

He was amazing.

I mean, a mix tape? Who did that? Usually, you'd meet someone, and he'd be great until he reeled you in. That was when the asshole would come out. It was the opposite with Atlas, thank God.

I turned my key in the lock and immediately heard him talking.

"Come on, tiger. Your momma will be home soon. I need to get gone."

My mouth dropped open at the loud meow that sounded out.

Was he talking to my cat? My hand came up to my mouth to stifle a giggle.

Vic was an asshole, she didn't even like me most of the time, but it seemed that the slutty little flirt was all about big, bad Atlas.

"Hey," I greeted him as I walked into the kitchen. I stopped when I saw him putting a dish in the oven. "What's all this?" I asked, watching Vic weave in between his legs.

His black eyes went soft as he looked up at me. "You're early, baby." He stood straight and shut the oven door. "Come 'ere." He gave me the Patrick Swayze Dirty Dancing one finger beckon, and my pussy fired up on the spot.

As I walked toward him, I saw fresh chicken in Vic's bowl.

My heart jerked, and I stopped dead. "Did you feed my cat?" I breathed, looking up at him wide-eyed.

He ducked his eyes, and a pink spot appeared on his cheek.

"You made me a mix tape, and you fed my cat," I blurted out.

"Well, yeah." He shrugged.

I began to ramble. "You put 'Tender' by Blur on the mix tape and 'Brown Eyed Girl.' My mom used to sing that song to me. I felt really and truly happy for the first time in years. And then Ned said you were good and to let you wash away all the bad shit, and she's right. That's exactly what you do."

He grinned. "Babe-"

I held my hand up to quieten him. "I know you're a big ol' asshole, but I also know you're not. You fed the rest of the hospital and me. You say I look pretty like *all* the time, *and* you made me a mix tape. A*nd* you fed my cat."

Atlas

"You already said that, baby." He nodded toward the stove. "That'll take about an hour on low. I've run you a bath and-"

Wait - He ran me a bath?

"You ran me a bath?" I squeaked.

He made a 'meh' face. "It was nothin'."

The tingles in my belly spread to my lady bits. "Stay there!" I ordered.

"Stitch. It's okay. I-"

"-Stay right there while I go make use of that bath. I'll be ten minutes. Do not leave this house."

Without waiting for a reply, I swept out of the kitchen and ran up the stairs to the bathroom, taking off my clothes as I went.

Danny 'Atlas' Woods was going to get lucky tonight, but I'd had my hands in people's insides all day. I needed a fucking bath first.

Within ten minutes, I'd bathed, shaved my legs, and brushed my teeth. I ran out of the bathroom and into my bedroom like my ass was on fire. Tipping my head upside down, I grabbed my hairdryer and scrunched that shit until my hair was out to there.

I didn't wear makeup to work, so I slicked on some gloss and a sweep of mascara. Grabbing my lotion, I sat on the bed and went to work on making my skin feel smooth.

Excitement stirred in the pit of my stomach.

We'd already had 'the talk.' We'd both been tested, and I'd been taking contraceptive pills since college. I'd been ready for a while. Add on the mixtape, the looking after Vic, and the bath; Atlas had tipped the scales considerably. A dreamy smile tipped my lips because I knew that there'd be no going back for me after we did this.

I'd be his.

I went to the drawer, picked out a pair of black lace hooker panties, and pulled them up my ass. My black,

Jules Ford

silky robe hung behind the door, so I shrugged it across my shoulders.

A quick spritz of my best perfume later, and I was gliding out of my bedroom and sashaying down the stairs, though I wasn't a 'sashay' kind of gal, so it probably looked more like I had a bum leg.

The enormity of what was about to happen hit me then. I breathed in through my nose and out through my mouth until my fingers stopped tremoring and my heart beat normally again.

This was it.

Atlas had his back to me when I walked into the kitchen. He swung around. "Baby, loo-" His voice stopped dead as his eyes roamed over my body. "Jesus, fuck."

I ran at him.

He went on the back foot and braced as I leaped into his arms.

I pressed my mouth to his in a bruising kiss, and my legs snaked around his hips. My pussy clenched as I felt his cock harden against the thin, silky material of my robe, digging into my core.

Jesus, help me. I'm about to get some of that big dick.

"You got lube, baby?" he asked against my lips.

I froze, pulling back slightly. "Will we need it?"

He made another 'meh' face. "You know I'm hung like a pony, Stitch baby, and you're just a tiny little thing. D'ya wanna be able to walk tomorrow?"

Okay, so yeah, he had a point. My mind went straight to my 'special box of tricks' hidden in my closet. "I may have, but it'll be old."

Atlas grinned. "As long as the lube lubes, we'll be golden." He started to walk us through the hallway and up the stairs. "You sure about this?" he asked. "'Cause I can wait. I've waited all my life for you. We can take our time."

Atlas

I pressed my forehead against his, looking into his eyes. My heart felt like it was melting at his beautiful words. "I've never been surer of anything," I whispered.

"I'll take care'a ya," he whispered back as he stared deep into my eyes.

"I know you will," I murmured, touching my lips to his. I pointed him in the direction of my room, and before I knew it, the door was open, and he'd tossed me onto the bed.

My hair fell everywhere, so I lifted onto my elbows, blew it out of my face, and watched Atlas be a fucking sex god. Even observing him strip gave me an out-of-body experience.

He dragged his tee off his head by the back of the neck – that sexy as all hell way men do. Then he flicked the button of his jeans open, and I almost came on the spot.

I'd seen a lot of naked men through my job, but I'd never seen one as beautiful as Atlas. His massive pecs were adorned with those fantastic, tattooed crow's wings that led my eye down to his muscled abs and tapered waist. His skin was so golden and smooth that my mouth watered with the need to taste it.

He stalked toward me, chest heaving, muscles rippling, and the buttons of his jeans undone. The look on his face conveyed quite clearly that he was going to eat me all the way up.

My pussy flooded.

Yasss.

My robe had gone a bit skewed, but it still covered my tits. I smiled seductively – or at least I tried – and made a big show of pulling at the black sash before letting the robe fall open to expose my black hooker panties and bare breasts.

His eyes greedily roamed my body, and he let out a strangled moan before dropping his jeans and stepping out of them.

My mouth watered at his huge, swinging dick.

It was long, thick, and beautiful. It jutted up past his navel, defying every law of gravity that existed because it appeared way too goddamned heavy to be pointing north like that.

Lord Jesus, save me from big fat dicks, or maybe don't.

He prowled toward the bed, put one knee on it, and grabbed hold of me. Strong hands dragged me up until I was on my knees, and we were face to face. He slipped the robe off my shoulders until it pooled on the bed.

"Oh my god," I whispered. "This is so hot."

His eyes flicked over me, and he let out another strangled moan. A hand reached out to my hip, and he tugged me toward him, making me fall forward onto his chest. "Hot little bitch," he rasped before his mouth took mine in a heated kiss.

He turned me on so much that I almost came on the spot.

His lips worked mine. Then they gently nipped my skin as he kissed his way down to my throat.

"Gonna ruin ya," Atlas murmured. "Gonna make that cunt burn with my big cock, baby."

My pussy fluttered because that *really* got me worked up. I gasped at the sensation of his hand moving underneath my hooker panties and stroking confidently over my clit.

I squirmed as I felt myself get wetter with every touch. It was my turn to let out a guttural moan as he stroked me with expert fingers. My skin felt like it was burning up. Suddenly dizzy, I reached out to hold on to anything to ground me, but all I came into contact with were rock-hard abs.

He rubbed my clit before his hand moved lower, and he began to gently fuck me with his thick fingers. I squirmed, encouraging him to go deeper.

Atlas

"Touch my cock, baby," he ordered. "Give it to me hard."

My hand gripped him roughly, and he let out a hiss.

I couldn't fit my fingers all the way around his massive dick, so I used two hands. One to work the thick shaft, the other to tug the huge head. A drop of pre cum appeared at the tip, and I smeared it around, using it for lubrication. I gripped him harder, moving both hands up and down his entire length.

He let me play for a few minutes while I explored him. He seemed to like it when I was rough with him because he moaned every time I gripped harder.

"Gotta stop that, baby," he murmured. "Ready to fuck you now, but you need some prep. He grabbed my hips and threw me onto my back, yanking my legs apart.

My hips rocked up as he lowered his mouth to my pussy, latched onto my clit, and sucked hard. I let out a loud moan as I felt his lips tug my clit into his hot mouth. His tongue lashed against it, and I almost went blind.

"Oh fuck. Oh fuck. Ohhh fuuuuck." Black spots danced behind my eyes. I moaned over and over, thighs trembling as every nerve ending began to tingle. I could feel the build already. Sixty seconds he'd had his mouth on me. In one minute, Atlas gave me more pleasure than I'd ever known.

Ever.

"I'm gonna come," I cried.

Still licking me, he looked up, and our eyes locked. "Fuck yeah. Come in my mouth, hot little bitch." His eyes slid back to my pussy, and he went back to work, sucking and pulling on my clit.

It was all too much, his mouth on me, his thick fingers still fucking me deep. Pressure began to build in my belly, and I cried out as a blazing orgasm ripped through my body.

Jules Ford

Strong fingers dug into my ass, pulling me closer like he was feeding from me. He hummed across my clit, and my eyes rolled in the back of my head.

My hips jerked into the air uncontrollably. I let out a squeal as I kept coming. I felt a strong arm fall across my stomach, pinning me in place as Atlas ate me through my climax.

I whined with the intensity caused by his growl as he sucked my pulsing clit into his mouth, prolonging the pinnacle of my orgasm for what seemed like hours.

Jesus.

My eyes swept down to look at him, my thighs trembling like I'd run a three-minute mile.

I had never come like that, ever. And it took Atlas minutes.

Ned was going to pee her lingerie laughing. She was right. It *had* been too long.

I began to come down, and he lifted his eyes to mine. "Where's that lube, babe?"

My arm fell across my eyes, and I let out a contented sigh. "White box. The top shelf of the closet."

He hauled ass off the bed and stalked over to the door.

My eyes followed his butt as he walked, and I couldn't help smiling lazily. My head was still in the clouds, my body still pulsing from the earth-shattering climax he'd just given me. It was probably why I wasn't thinking straight. It was only when I heard rustling coming from the closet and Atlas suddenly appeared with the box that I panicked.

His eyes flashed at me as he rummaged through the contents. "Quite the collection you've got here, Stitch baby. Gotta say it's not what I expected." He reached into the stash and pulled out a pink mini vibrator that Ned had gotten me for a joke present and examined it.

My cheeks set alight. "Oh, my God!" Mortified, I jumped off the bed and tried to grab it from him, but I wasn't very effective, seeing as my legs weren't working as they should.

Atlas held it up, so I couldn't reach it. "Now, Stitch, let me see what's in the love box." He let out a laugh. "It's okay, baby. I think it's hot." He peered inside again and took out an unopened packet holding a butt plug with a fake pink diamond at one end. "Fuck me," he rumbled, holding it in the air. A slow smile spread across his face. "And there's me thinkin' you're a good girl."

I buried my face in his hands and peered at him through my fingers.

He threw the box on my dresser, grabbed the bottle of lube, and began to stalk toward me, smirking. "Don't feel so bad about dirtying you up now, sexy little bitch."

Face still red, I collapsed on the edge of the bed and almost drooled at the sight of his abs as he stalked toward me. His still-hard cock jutted up his stomach, and I couldn't help licking my lips. My pussy clenched hard at the sight of him. He didn't hold an ounce of fat. Muscles rippled every time he moved.

Beautiful.

Stopping directly in front of me, he took hold of his cock and tapped it twice against my lips. "Open up for me," he ordered.

My mouth opened, and my wide eyes slid up to his.

He eased himself inside my mouth. I almost gagged even though I couldn't have been taking more than a third of it. He was just so goddamned huge.

"Jesus," he rasped. "Suck it hard, baby."

I looked up into his face and obeyed. My cheeks hollowed, and I breathed through my nose. My fingers trailed up his thigh, and I cupped his balls with one hand and tugged lightly.

"Fuck me," he rasped.

His hand grabbed the back of my hair, making a ponytail. He watched me suck his length with burning eyes, pulling my mouth up and down his cock. "Love the feel of your lips on me, baby," he crooned. "It's hot as fuck." He eased himself out of my mouth, and I released him with a loud pop.

He pushed me back on the bed before grabbing the bottle of lube off the nightstand and crawling up beside me. "How d'ya wanna do this?" he asked. "Don't wanna hurt ya."

"Well, I think that goes in there." I pointed between his groin and mine.

He grinned as he snapped the lid of the lube open, squeezed some in his hand, then stroked it over his dick.

I tried to breathe, not quite believing that it was finally happening.

Atlas and me were about to have sex.

No nerves assailed me, no doubts, no regrets. I was all in.

I thought I was in love with Luke, but even then, subconsciously, I think I recognized that it wasn't quite right. Inexperience made me not understand it at the time, but now I did because this *was* right. This was everything.

It wasn't about sweet words, hospital food deliveries, or even mix tapes.

It was all about that thing between us, that feeling he invoked in me. He made me feel safe and protected. I trusted him, and having experienced the opposite, I could recognize his integrity and kindness.

Atlas moved over me again, his eyes burning into mine. "Ready, baby?"

My heart swelled in my chest. "Yeah."

His gaze flickered over my face. I could see the emotions swirling in his eyes. "You're mine—me and you together givin' it a real shot. No goin' back. This is it."

My eyes welled up. "I was yours the day you stormed my house to save me from my cat."

Atlas

He gently pressed his forehead to mine. "For me, it was six months before that when you tried to stab me with a letter opener in your office. Knew then that I'd never meet another you."

Warmth flooded my belly.

That was the day we met.

Wow.

"Ready?" Atlas asked.

I replied with one nod.

His fingers dug into the back of my legs, and he pulled them up around his hips before easing his cock inside me.

My back arched off the bed, and I moaned as my pussy burned.

"Jesus," he rasped. "So fuckin' tight." He lifted his head, neck straining with the effort of holding back.

I winced. It felt good, but the deeper he drove, the more it burned like hell.

"You okay?" he asked.

I nodded, trying to hide my wince.

"Liar," he muttered and eased back out. "Ain't gonna work if it hurts, baby."

I suddenly felt cold and empty. "No," I whined. "It's fine. Don't stop."

"Shh." He snaked a hand down, took hold of his cock, and began slowly stroking himself. Then his huge hand gripped the base, and he started jacking.

My eyebrows shot up. "Atlas. Don't waste it." I groaned. "That's a perfectly good hard-on, and it's been a long damned time. Just keep trying."

"Trust me, Stitch. Know what I'm doin'." His hand stroked harder, and the veins in his neck popped out. "Won't leave ya stranded," he rasped. "We just need a bit more lubrication."

I looked down and watched him stroke his cock harder and faster. My pussy pulsed with need. "Jeez," I said breathlessly. "That's so hot."

"Gonna come just inside you. Then I'm gonna... Jesus, fuck." He moaned. "Get ready." He moved his cock to my opening. "Fuck. Fuck. Fuck," he chanted as his hand stroked faster. He let out a groan, and his cum began to spurt out. His eyes darted down, and he aimed the tip of his cock just inside my pussy. He let out a long, deep groan as he pumped his fist harder.

My pussy warmed from Atlas' cum. "Oh, my God." I squirmed. "That's the hottest thing I've seen in my life." His heat seeped into me, and my hips gyrated, seeking friction.

He rolled back on top and slid inside me, that time meeting less resistance. "Jesus, fuck." He moaned. "Tightest little pussy I've ever had." His hips snapped against mine, and he seated himself deep inside me with a jerk.

My pussy clenched around him, and our eyes locked. "You're still hard?" I breathed.

"Can go twice, no problem, baby. Wear your glasses and a pair of lacy stockings for me, and I'll squeeze in round three, no trouble." He pulled his hips back and eased into me again.

I arched off the bed and moaned.

The sensations at first were weird, not painful, but I could definitely feel every inch of him.

He thrust slowly at first, taking care and being gentle with me. That made me relax even more.

Carefully, I began to move with him.

My hips rose to meet his strokes. Eventually, we began to fuck harder.

At that precise moment, I understood the term 'hurts so good.' It pinched for sure, but it didn't negate the pleasure. If anything, the slight pain made me even hotter and wetter.

"That feels really, really good." I gyrated harder, meeting him thrust for thrust.

Atlas

Atlas' eyes rolled before his neck bent, and he kissed my lips. I felt his hot mouth travel down my throat, and he groaned a loud curse.

His strokes got harder, and it felt really, really good.

Dark eyes slid down to where our bodies joined. "Love watchin' you take me, ya fuckin' tight-pussied little bitch." He began to pound me harder. "Fuck, yeah."

His hands came to my hips, pulling my legs up around his back. "You're takin' me so good, Stitch baby." He groaned and rotated his hips in a circular motion so that he put pressure on my clit every time he slammed into me.

The pleasure was intense. I was still pulsing from my last orgasm, so my eyes rolled when Atlas went even deeper and hit that pleasure spot. It almost felt too much, but at the same time, not enough. Pressure began to build inside the pit of my stomach for the second time. "Don't stop, Danny." I moaned.

He buried his face in my neck and began to thrust harder, grunting every time he pushed into me.

I could feel him everywhere, inside me, on my skin, in my pussy, and in my heart. He'd somehow dug his way in, and I loved the feelings of intimacy between us.

I moaned again as he bucked his hips, frantically fucking me into the mattress. The pressure in my stomach began to spread through my body.

A cry escaped my throat. Every nerve ending was on fire, and my toes curled with all the sensations Atlas was invoking. My climax began to ebb and flow, and I knew it would be immense.

My pulse thrummed with everything that was Atlas. He was in my blood.

His face burrowed deeper into my neck, and he groaned again as he fucked me savagely. It was seeing him so uncontrolled that set me off. There was no warning. My stomach muscles tightened as I came again with a loud cry. Every cell in my body rushed to my core and exploded as I bucked against him.

I felt a sting in my neck, and I knew he'd marked me, but I didn't care. The bite just added to the sensations that pulsed through me. My back bowed off the bed.

Atlas let out a shout and planted deep inside me. I felt him shudder as his cum burned my insides. He groaned and pumped harder as he rutted against me. "Fuck yeah." He cursed again, over and over. His hips jerked uncontrollably for a full minute until, eventually, his movements began to slow. He gently slid his cock in and out while he kissed my shoulder.

His head lifted from the crook of my throat, and our eyes locked.

I smiled lazily when I saw that he looked as dazed as I felt.

"You okay, baby?" he rasped. "Did I hurt ya? I tried to be careful, but you felt so goddamned good that I lost my head." He rested his forehead against mine.

"I'm good, honey," I breathed. "That was amazing."

"Yeah." He lifted up and onto his hands and pulled out of me with a groan.

I winced as I lost his weight, his warmth, and what seemed like a liter of cum.

He snaked an arm underneath my shoulders and moved me until I curved into his side.

I sighed contentedly and trailed my fingers across his chest.

His hand slid into my hair. "You're one sexy little bitch," he muttered. "Honest to God thought you were gonna slice my cock off at the root. Your pussy was so tight."

I belly laughed.

The action made me lose a little more of Atlas, and I grimaced as I wriggled my ass into the biggest wet patch known to man. "It's a mess down here," I murmured. "I'm going to have to change the sheets."

Atlas

I watched, fascinated, as he laughed. Not for the first time, I marveled at how young he looked when he wasn't being SAA.

"Babe," he grated out, voice thick with humor. "If the bed sheets don't resemble a Midas shop floor after I've fucked you, then I ain't doing it right." A huge smile spread across his face. "You know you gotta trust the Midas touch."

I giggled and laid my head on his shaking shoulder. "After what we did, I'd have thought you were more of a jiffy lube kinda guy."

He laughed again and pulled me closer into his chest. "You fuckin' kill me, baby. I've met my match in you, Sophie, and I think I kinda like it."

My eyes lifted to his, and I beamed.

He made my heart so full of love that tears welled up again. My joy was overflowing.

Dark eyes filled with emotion. Atlas bent his neck and touched his mouth to mine. "That's it, baby. That's what I meant when I said you warm me like the sun. That look, that smile, it's fuckin' blindin'."

I sighed and burrowed further into him, and it dawned on me that I understood what he meant.

After everything that had happened in my life, after all the loss and trauma, Danny 'Atlas' Woods finally warmed me like the sun too.

Chapter Twenty-One

Atlas

The clubhouse bar buzzed with excitement.
The first Saturday in May dawned clear and bright, and it was going to get even warmer later. It was like the Gods had heard our prayers and gave us the perfect spring day for the first run of the year with our women.

The last few weeks had been the best of my life.

Sophie had taken to ridin' like a pro.

I'd taken her out whenever we could get away. One time we even got as far as Colorado before we turned back. Now it'd turned warmer, and she was always on the back'a my bike. Sophie was the only woman to have ever been there, and she'd be the only woman who *would* ever be there.

We'd been together a couple of months, but I already knew that she was it for me.

I wanted to be around her all the time. We talked, we fucked, then we fucked a bit more. We laughed like kids. We trained together. The only time she wasn't in my company was when we were workin'.

She was funny, sweet, kind, and sexy as all hell.

I'd looked after everyone all my life, and now her too. The difference was, Sophie looked after me right back. She fed my soul in ways that sometimes overwhelmed me. Cara would say that my love tank was brimmin' over, and it was, all because of Stitch. I never realized that I'd been livin' in darkness before, not until she shone her light on me.

We'd gotten closer than close, but she still hadn't told me about what her ex did to her. That didn't offend me. There was good reason to be glad about it.

The Kings and Colt had gotten everything we needed, and we'd organized the trip.

Everyone except the officers thought we were goin' to Unity Creek, Oregon, to gather allies for the comin' war. Video footage of us there already existed, courtesy of Colt. Some witnesses were gonna say they'd seen us in town, courtesy of the Hell Dwellers MC.

But Oregon wasn't our destination.

Sophie wouldn't suspect me if anythin' happened to her ex because, far as she knew, I had no motive.

That was important in a court of law. Not that I thought I'd ever stand before a judge. Colt, Breaker, and I had planned everything down to the last tiny detail, plus I'd also roped in some old friends for backup.

Arrow's shout jerked my mind away from my thoughts, "Yo, Atlas. The Doc's just pulled into the lot."

My heart bounced.

I twisted on the bar stool and got to my feet. A small smile played around my mouth at the mere thought of seein' my girl.

I'd never been this man, excited to see a woman, lookin' forward to havin' her arms wrapped around me on the back of my bike, tits pressed against me, my hand claspin' her knee.

"Jesus," Cash drawled, eyes snappin' to Bowie. "Love's young dream."

Bo laughed. "Never seen him so fuckin' giddy. He'll be carryin' her picture around next."

I almost winced as I thought about all the images I had of Sophie on my phone. "Least I gotta woman hangin' off my back for the run." My lips twitched. "Unlike some."

Bowie let out an amused snort. "Layla won't come, she's gotta feed Willow, and she's not goin' on the back'a my bike until she's completely healed." He nodded to his brother. "And Cash won't have Cara on his bike while she's pregnant."

"Yeah." I deadpanned. "Cause if Cara weren't expectin' she'd be here, right? Wonder why she's not come to see her man off?"

Cash's eyes narrowed on me. "Fuck off, asshole. I'm workin' on it."

Grinnin' like the proverbial cat that got the cream, I gave him a hard clap on the back and made my way outside to meet my girl. I stepped out in the lot and looked up at the morning sun that warmed my face. I basked in it for a few seconds before my eyes fell on Stitch, and excitement stirred in the pit of my stomach.

She glided toward me, smilin' dreamily.

I strolled toward her grinnin' happily.

I stopped midway and crooked my finger. Sophie kept on comin' and walked straight into my chest. I bent my knees, slid my hands around her thighs, and hauled her into my arms. Her legs immediately locked around my waist, soft arms snakin' around the back of my neck.

"Hey, big man." She thrust her face into my throat. "Missed you."

My heart filled with contentment.

I couldn't say I ever wanted to fall for a woman. Never thought there was one out there that was right for me, but instantly my soul fuckin' bloomed for her. My heart kept growing bigger, like it was burstin' so full of emotion for this tiny woman that it needed to expand to contain it all.

I walked us over to my bike and sat her ass on the seat, then I stood between her legs and touched my forehead to hers. "You okay, Stitch baby?"

Her sigh was one of satisfaction. Soft hands stroked my back. "I am now. You?"

I drew back slightly to look her full in the face and grinned. "You eaten?"

"Of course." Her eyes danced as she smiled at me. "You're such a feeder. I've eaten more in the last six weeks than the whole of last year."

"You gotta keep your strength up," I chastised gently. "You got a demandin' job, and you train. Plus, you gotta man to keep happy in the bedroom now, so you need to eat more than a fuckin' lettuce leaf for lunch."

Her hand curled around my nape and pulled my head down, touchin' her lips to mine. As we kissed, Ice's voice yelled across the parkin' lot. "Ten-minute warnin' pricks and chicks. Then we're gonna jet."

Fuck, I still had shit to sort before we set off, somethin' that Sophie wasn't gonna like one fuckin' bit.

I looked deep into her eyes. "Got somethin' I want you to wear out on the run, baby." Without givin' her a chance to question me, I hauled her into my arms again and headed into the clubhouse.

Her head pulled back slightly as I walked us through the bar toward the corridor that led to my room. The look on her face was one of confusion as she cocked her head to one side. "Is what I'm wearing not okay?"

"It's not that baby…" My words faltered.

Her eyebrows drew together.

I paused for a second, tryin' a think of the best way to explain to an innocent like Soph that we were gonna be exposed.

The Sinners hadn't made any moves since they robbed us of those buildin' materials, but we still needed to watch our backs. For the last two weeks, my senses had been high on alert. Thrash wasn't doin' well. That was the only reason we'd been able to fit a few runs in since the weather had turned warmer. We knew when he

Atlas

died that we'd have to be more careful. It was only a matter of time until shit got real.

I made my way into my room and placed Stitch gently on the bed. "Thing is, baby, ya know the Sinners are bein' pains in our asses?"

"What's that got to do with what I wear?" she asked, voice tinged with concern.

I went to the wardrobe, pulled out a box, and placed it on the bed next to her. "You gotta wear that for me today, baby. Need to know that you're protected from any bullshit. If anythin' happened to you, I couldn't live with it."

Brow furrowed, she went onto the box and pulled out a sleeveless padded waistcoat with Velcro straps hangin' off it. Soft hands held it up, and her confused expression turned to one of horror. "Is this a bulletproof vest?" Her wide eyes darted to me, then back toward the vest. "What the hell, Atlas? If it's that dangerous, why are we even going?"

"No. It's not like that." I knelt next to the bed and took her hand reassuringly. "Baby. It's just a precaution. I don't want your back exposed today. You'll always have all my brothers at it, but wearin' that would make me feel better about you ridin' out with us."

Her lips pressed together, and her eyes flicked over the vest. "On second thoughts, maybe it's a good thing I'm going. Is there any way we can take my medical bag with us just in case there's any trouble?"

My gut jolted.

"If anythin' happens, you'll be outta there, babe. You're not stayin' behind to tend to the wounded. That's askin' for trouble. First sign'a danger, you get outta there."

She rolled her eyes. "Is an SUV still going to follow us?"

"Yeah," I confirmed. "But if there's any trouble, you have to take cover with the other women. I mean it, Soph.

Jules Ford

You're the obvious choice to protect the other ol' ladies. Christ, you could probably do a better job than half the men."

She pulled the BPV over her shoulders. "Show me how to do this thing up. I'm a doctor, not an engineer."

My chest rumbled with laughter. "Come here, Stitch baby. I'll sort ya."

Within minutes, I'd fitted the vest and helped Soph shrug her leather jacket on over the top of it. We walked hand in hand down the hallway and back through the bar toward the doors.

"I just need to run to my car," she murmured as we made our way outside. "Got my medical bag in there."

"Jesus, woman," I scolded. "Already told ya. No medical bag. If shit happens, you're outta there." My girl didn't listen to me. No shocker there.

"Be back in a second." She released my hand and ran over to her Explorer.

Hands-on hips, I stared at the sky. "Fuckin' woman's a pain in my ass," I muttered frustratedly.

"Got your hands full there, Atlas."

I looked down to see Abe helping Iris onto the back of his bike. She had her 'property of Abe' leather jacket on and a silver chrome helmet that matched her ol' man's bike.

He looked over at me and grinned. "They're worth every bit of trouble. You'll see."

"Watch it, old man," Iris warned. "Or I'll put laxatives in your dinner."

Abe twisted his torso and gave Iris a huge smacker. He pulled back and cackled while she giggled like a schoolgirl.

I couldn't help smilin' at the two of 'em.

Their story spanned years. At times it wasn't pretty; some would call it downright ugly, but they'd made it. They were as much into each other now as the day they met.

Atlas

Iris had become Mason and Sera's surrogate mother, and she'd bloomed.

That woman was a born carer; at last, she had two people on which to shower all her love and attention. Because of her and Abe, the two teens were thrivin'.

It was a beautiful thing.

I mounted my bike and twisted around, lookin' for Soph. I shook my head when I saw that she was at the doors of one'a the club SUVs handin' Sparky her medical bag. He took it off her with a smile.

Sophie waved at him before turnin' to jog across the lot toward me.

The corners of my mouth hitched as I watched her gorgeous hair fly out. My woman was stunning in her black jeans, biker boots, and leather jacket.

Who'd of thought the doc could turn into such a hot little biker babe?

My mind returned to the first day I met her, particularly our first kiss.

She'd stirred somethin' inside me even then, though I didn't understand it at the time.

It was why I was so adamant about pushin' her away. A voice in the back'a my head told me she was special, but I ignored it. I wasn't ready, and honestly, she scared the shit outta me.

Now though, she'd weaved her spell, and I was fucked. She'd drawn me in, not that I cared. I loved bein' around her because she made me happy.

She got me, I got her, and it was easy.

"You okay?" she asked as she approached me. "You're deep in thought there."

I took her hand and helped her on behind me. "Just thinkin' about how goddamned hot you look in them jeans." I handed her one'a the helmets that were hangin' off my ape bars. "That peachy ass is gonna get a spankin' later for not doin' as you're told."

"Promises, promises." She burrowed her head into my back and giggled. "Remember when you said I had no ass? We've come a long way, baby."

My neck craned, and I grinned back at her. "Told ya not to listen to anythin' I say. I dunno what the fuck I'm talkin' about."

She pulled her chin strap tight and reached into her jacket pocket for her gloves. "It's okay big man." She leaned forward, snaked her arms around my waist, and rested her cheek on my back. "You've more than made up for it."

Her words hit me straight in the heart 'cause she was right. I had, but only 'cause she made it so simple.

Sophie was a sweetheart and the very definition of low maintenance. She said it like it was and never nagged or grumbled. What I'd fallen for was her zest for life. Through her, I was experiencing everythin' for the first time again. She made everythin' so fuckin' joyful, from her maiden ride on the back of my bike to eatin' somethin' from a roadside truck when we'd ridden to Colorado. She did everythin' with delight and enthusiasm.

Other women would have made me buy 'em shit and make grand gestures, but Soph didn't care about all that. Just like me, she preferred the simple things in life.

Big respect to Cara. She called it.

The roar of engines rose through the parkin' lot with the pop-pop-poppin' noise that only a Harley could produce.

I closed my eyes and breathed it all in for a few seconds.

I came alive when I was on my bike. It was what I was born for. Ridin' made me happy, and I was at peace with Sophie wrapped around me.

Ice had decided that we should ride in double formation with him at the front with Prez, me, and Drix

Atlas

behind them, Cash and Abe behind us, then Bowie and Arrow.

Patched members took the back in two's, makin' the line about thirty-five bikes long and around seventy men strong. The growl of our revs got louder, the men's way of lettin' their Road Captain know that they were ready to roll.

Ice looked back down the line, smilin' huge. His arm went up in the air, and his finger twirled. A loud cheer went up, and we slowly rode through the gates and onto the one main road that took us through town.

Soft hands gripped me from behind. My heart bounced as I felt Stitch lean away and yell out an excited whoop.

I couldn't stop the huge grin from spreadin' across my face.

My head swiveled to the left.

Hendrix's eyes slashed to Sophie. He grinned at the sight of my woman so goddamned euphoric.

The sun shone high in the sky. I knew it would heat up pretty quickly. Spring was in full force, as evidenced by the abundance of tree blossoms and colorful flowers that sprouted on the walkways along the side of the road.

Hambleton was a beautiful place. Rural, classy small-town USA where people still lived by conservative American values. I loved the town as much as I hated it. The way of life suited me, but there was a downside too.

You only had to look at how Hambleton's elite treated Bowie's ol' lady to recognize that some of the townsfolk were assholes. The club had it under control. We'd already driven Richard Allen outta town. Next, we'd set our sights on the Barringtons.

It was Saturday, and Main Street was busy. Word would've gotten around about the run. The townsfolk were already sittin' on the patio chairs and benches that took up the sidewalk outside Magnolia's, The Shamrock, and Giovanni's.

Jules Ford

People looked up expectantly, starin' as our convoy rode slowly by. Kids ran beside our bikes, shoutin' and wavin', their parents, smilin' and raisin' their hands in greetin'.

As we rode past Giovanni's, the door opened, and Mayor Henderson and his wife walked out.

Elise glanced up at us and froze. I'd heard she was in her late forties, but she looked ten years younger. Her gaze caught on the head of the convoy, and she beamed at Prez, who sent her a one-finger salute in greetin'. Her eyes sparkled.

The Mayor's stare veered between his wife and John, and his face twisted. He said somethin' to Elise before grabbin' her arm tightly and pullin' her away down the street.

She tried to snatch her arm back, but he clutched tighter, and her face twisted with pain. He pulled her close, mutterin' somethin' in her ear, and her features suddenly blanked.

My eyes narrowed. Stitch's body locked at my back, and her fingers dug into my stomach. She saw it too.

My hands gripped the handlebars tightly, and I glanced at Prez, waitin' for him to make a move.

He'd looked straight at the couple, so he must've seen what Henderson did. I thought he'd have a big reaction, but his face swiveled forward, and he kept on riding.

A bad feelin' prickled through my gut.

My girl was spooked, and who could blame her after what she'd been through? I couldn't react or comfort her because she didn't know I'd discovered what her ex did. I needed to keep my head, especially in light of what Breaker and me planned to do.

I stroked her knee as we got to Main Street's edge and hit the road that would eventually lead us to the town limits.

Atlas

The stores and restaurants fell away until nature surrounded us again. There were fields to our left and a few acres of forest to our right. I couldn't take it in, though. Henderson's behavior was still on my mind.

Maybe that was why I didn't immediately notice anything amiss. I felt it, though. Darkness crawled through my gut.

Somethin' made me turn toward the trees, and I caught a flash of light.

No sound penetrated my helmet or the roar of our bikes, but I knew what it was. The realization hit me like a brick.

It was the discharge from a gun.

Everyone moved at the same time. Hendrix sped forward to Prez, and Abe rode up by my side to take Drix's place. He stared into the cluster of trees on our right.

Somethin' big was happenin'. I could feel it in my bones.

I glanced behind me and saw Cash, Bowie, and Arrow crowdin' our backs, protectin' Iris and Sophie. I'd never been more grateful for my brothers at that moment.

My stare slid forward again. Hendrix, Prez, and Ice were in the process of pullin' to the side of the road.

My mind raced, senses on high alert because I knew somethin' was very fuckin' wrong. I pointed to where Prez was talkin' to Drix to indicate that we should also park up. That was when I saw Prez and Veep look toward the trees to our right.

Hendrix began to shout just as Prez ran for us, and all hell broke loose.

Somethin' whizzed past my ear, and my wing mirror suddenly shattered. A searin' pain shot through my leg, and I struggled to control my bike for a split second. My ape bars wobbled, but I managed to keep my shit together, even though my leg was burnin' with pain.

Jules Ford

Shotgun rode up to my right, and together, we pulled over to the side of the road, a few yards further up from Prez.

Abe stopped behind me, then Cash and Bowie. The men started getting in position, making a shield of bikes along the roadside.

"Woman. Go!" Abe yelled to Iris.

She jumped off and ran behind the bikes, crouchin' low.

"Go, Sophie. Please, baby," I shouted.

She jumped off my bike, looked down, and her face lost all color. "Your leg, Danny," she screeched. "You're bleeding."

"Cash," I bellowed. "I'm hit. Get her safe."

Bullets pinged again, and Sophie let out a squeal. My heart hammered at the thought of her bein' hit. I whipped around and saw Cash dragging her behind the bikes toward Iris.

My shoulders slumped.

"Can you walk?" Drix shouted as he got back on his ride.

"Dunno, Veep, but I can ride." I nodded toward the direction of the shooters. "I'm gonna go catch me a Sinner."

Drix jerked a nod and mounted his ride. "Weapons out. Shoot to kill."

"I'm comin'," Arrow shouted. "I can ride a bike and still shoot a fucker between the eyes."

"Wait!" Bowie went to get on his ride.

"No!" I shouted. "You gotta new baby. Protect Prez and the women." I revved my engine and shot off down the road, the sound of Arrow and Hendrix's bikes roarin' behind me.

Bullets stopped flyin' as we got further away from the scene. I craned my neck to see my brothers crouched behind a long line of bikes, weapons out, firin' back at the trees on the opposite side of the road. It reminded me of an old Western movie. I couldn't believe that a goddamned gunfight would pop off a mile outta Main Street.

The pigs were likely to show up any minute. We needed to move in quickly to catch the shooters before the cops pissed on our parade.

I saw a grass verge by the road. My hand went inside my jacket, and I slipped my weapon outta my body holster before pointin' my wheel toward the small incline. My leg felt like it was on fire, but I could still maneuver, probably because the adrenaline was doin' its job. I rode up the verge, Drix and Arrow on my tail, and headed through the trees toward where the gunfire was comin' from.

Luckily it hadn't rained for a few days, so we could ride easily over the hard terrain, though we had to slow down somewhat 'cause of the uneven ground.

Goin' in hard was our only option 'cause they'd hear our bikes comin'; they probably already knew we were on their tail from the roar of our engines. I prayed that one of 'em would make an error as they tried to escape.

We rode into a clearing, and I noticed two bikes parked next to a tree stump.

My chest tightened. We had the fuckers trapped. They couldn't get away without comin' face to face with us. My veins thrummed with the force of the blood pumping through 'em. My heart seemed to pound in my ears instead of my chest.

The sound of gunfire cracked through the air. My head jerked to see two guys runnin' outta the trees toward us, haphazardly firin' their weapons. They were so panicked that they weren't even aimin' properly. Most of the shots were either fired wide or way over our heads.

I turned my wheel toward 'em and rode like a bat outta hell.

One of 'em let off a round, and a bullet whizzed past my ear.

My chest contracted as I heard a cry behind me, but I didn't stop and look. I sped up and rode straight into the fucker.

I braced as my wheel hit him hard. He flew up, soared through the air, and crashed face down in the dirt. He slid for a few inches until comin' to stop, not movin' a muscle.

My chest lit up as the roar of motorbikes cut through the air. Drix flew past me, following the other guy who was running in direction of the trees, while I slowed to see the bastard who'd just shot at me.

Dismounting slowly, I pulled my helmet off and glanced down. My chest twisted when I noticed that blood saturated the leg of my jeans. It burned like a motherfucker, but that didn't stop me from limpin' toward the piece of shit who was lyin' motionless, face down in the dirt.

As I walked closer, I could read the word sewn into the rocker on the back of his cut.

Enforcer.

I kept goin' until I was standin' next to him.

My jaw ticked. Those cunts had shot at us when we were out on a social run with our women. I bared my teeth, pulled my good leg back, and slammed it into his torso so hard that it jerked up from the ground. With a snarl, I shoved his body with my boot, roughly turning him over.

I glared down at his face. He couldn't've been more than twenty-five. I sniffed back and hocked a glob of spit onto the patch of his cut—a skull with flames comin' from the top.

His face was fucked-up, big time. There was blood and flesh everywhere. His ugly mouth hung open to show missin' teeth that he no doubt lost as he crashed into the floor. The fucker was motionless, maybe knocked out, perhaps even dead. What the fuck ever.

A rustlin' sound came from behind me.

Atlas

I glanced over my shoulder to see Arrow staggerin' toward me. Blood seeped through his fingers clutched to his shoulder.

My back snapped straight. "You okay?" I took a step toward him, but he waved me off impatiently.

"I'm good. Fucker got the top of my shoulder. A GSW there won't kill me." He looked down at the Sinner, lip curlin' in disgust. "What we doin' with him?"

"What do *you* wanna do?" I asked. "Kill or capture?"

Arrow's reply would be an indication of his character. There was no wrong answer; either worked for me, but what Arrow said next would tell me if he thought tactically

"My heart's tellin' me to shoot him in the head," he bit out. "But my head's tellin' me to sling him across my bike, ride him back to the compound, and take him down the Cell."

"Your choice." I folded my arms across his chest, starin' between him and the Sinner. "I'll happily put a bullet in his head."

Arrow kicked him gently and drew in a deep, audible breath when a trickle of blood ran outta the Sinners' ear. "Think God made the choice for us." He gestured to the blood. "He's fucked."

Blood from the ear usually indicated brain damage. "He probably scrambled his noggin when he cracked his skull on the floor." I shook my head and huffed out a breath of frustration, watchin' as more blood trickled. "Reckon he's braindead already."

The sound of an engine roared through the trees. I jerked my head up to see Hendrix ridin' toward us.

He pulled up beside me. "They got away," he said. "There was eight of 'em altogether. I saw their cuts. Definitely Sinners."

I nodded to the man on the ground and muttered, "There's one less of 'em now."

Drix's eyebrows snapped together as he looked down. "Jesus."

"He ain't gonna help him." I ran a hand down my face. "He'll be in the devil's playground soon."

"Ain't worth puttin' a bullet in him." Hendrix shrugged nonchalantly. "He's as good as dead already. Cops'll be all over this. No point leavin' evidence that'll put one of us in the big house." He looked up as the sound of tailpipes roared, gettin' closer by the second. "Sounds like our boys."

A flash of blue shone through the foliage. A second later, Ice rode into the clearing, followed by Tex. They pulled up next to us and idled their engines. "Sophie's fine," he assured me. "She's down there seein' to the wounded."

I ducked my head and grinned. Not many women could pull it together after being used as target practice. I was an asshole for holdin' off so long when it was evident to me now that she was the perfect ol' lady.

Ice's eyes fell on Drix, then darted to me. "Prez needs you all back." His angry stare fell on the Sinner, and he sneered. "At least it's one for one."

His words registered, and my heart froze.

Drix thrust a hand through his hair and looked up to the sky. "Fuck!" he bellowed.

I bent down to retrieve my helmet and limped over to my bike, mind goin' crazy. No flicker of pain registered as I threw my bad leg over my bike and fired it up. After what Ice just told us, I was numb to it.

We set off through the trees, lookin' for the small verge that would lead us back down to the road. Dark thoughts paralyzed my brain.

The second I hit the asphalt, I glanced toward my brothers and saw that the majority had crowded around the SUV.

Heart in mouth, I slowly rode toward 'em.

Atlas

Stitch was kneelin' down, seein' to Shotgun. He'd also gotten shot in the leg. My eyes swept over her, makin' sure she looked no worse for wear.

She looked up at me and shook her head sadly.

Prez stood apart from the men, shoutin' into his cell with a hand grippin' his salt and pepper hair. He closed his eyes, suddenly lookin' every one of his fifty-five years. I pulled up beside him, cut my engine, and waited.

"When did it pop up?" Prez barked down the phone. "How could it have happened last night, and we only just found out?" Prez looked at me, shaking his head. "Right," he muttered. "We'll wait for the cops. Then we'll head back."

A noise registered behind me as I dismounted and pulled my helmet off. I craned my neck to see Abe standin' by the line of bikes comfortin' Iris, who was sobbin' into his chest. She was heartbroken.

I watched her cry, and my gut went cold.

Prez stabbed at his cell and heaved out a breath. "Thrash died last night. Bear turned up with his crew an hour after the event. He and his boys took out every man who questioned his presidency, five in total. Colt said it's all over the dark web. It popped up thirty minutes ago."

"And Bear's first act as president was to ambush us?" My throat burned so hot that my molars gnashed together. "Who copped it?" I demanded, glarin' toward the SUV.

"Come on," Dagger ordered. "Wanna see for myself."

Prez began to walk toward the SUV. I fell into step behind him, Abe and Iris trailin' behind me.

Cash and Bowie were tellin' everyone to step back from the vehicle, shoutin' that there was nothing anyone could do.

"Fuckin' Sinners!" Reno bellowed. "He's just a fuckin' kid."

The brothers roared and cursed their agreement.

That first hint penetrated my brain, and a dark shadow slithered through my chest. Clarity hit me, and a face flashed behind my eyes. My lungs burned. I sucked in some air to try and cool down my insides, but every breath I took was heated.

I knew.

Fuck.

"Sophie!" I croaked. "Here, baby. I need you."

Within seconds she was by my side.

I looked down at my woman's face.

My gut clenched when I noticed tears and blood were steaked over it. I snaked an arm around my woman's shoulders and pulled her body close to mine, tryin'a to give her some comfort, or maybe the comfort was for me; who knew?

"It's not fair, Danny," she whispered. "It's just not fair. He was so young."

Heaviness seemed to weigh me down. Somehow it was worse when it was the young ones. They hadn't lived.

I guided Sophie toward the SUV. I had to look upon his face and vow that his murder wouldn't go unavenged. Even in death, he'd always be a Demon, and I wouldn't rest until I'd taken down his killer.

Cash leaned back against the driver's door with his head in his hands. He must've heard our approach because his stare flew up to meet mine, and he shook his head sadly.

"Poor kid never stood a chance," Bowie murmured as he walked to us from the passenger side.

"At least he didn't suffer," Abe grunted from behind me. "He wouldn't've known a thing about it." He turned into Iris, givin' her words of love as she let out another quiet sob.

Cash stepped away from the vehicle to allow me, Prez, and Sophie to pass. Blood ran down my leg, but I hardly noticed. My mind was whirring with pain and disappointment because I knew who'd been drivin'.

Dagger swung the door open and glanced inside. His usually tanned face paled, and his hand went to the top of his head, obviously distressed.

Dazed, he stepped away, allowing me through to the SUV. I held my breath as my gaze snapped to the driver's seat. I forced myself to commit to memory the spark of light Bear's actions had taken from my MC.

Hazel eyes, usually full'a life stared up, unseein'. The mouth that always had a smile across it now hung slack. I couldn't understand how one side of his head was perfect with no hair outta place, but in total contrast, the other side was half missin'.

Fragments of skull, brains, and blood had splattered over the back of the seat, but I didn't look away. Instead, I took in every detail of the man who looked back at me with dead eyes and took a mental snapshot. I wanted to remember so that when I next saw a Sinner, I could do the same to them.

They'd taken one of our own from us, left a hole in our hearts.

At that moment, I swore to my dead brother that I'd get him retribution and wouldn't rest until I saw Bear buried in the ground.

Those fuckers had murdered our Sparky.

Atlas

Chapter Twenty-Two

Sophie

Even though the drinks flowed and the music thumped, Sparky's funeral was a sad affair. It was weird because Iris told me about biker wakes and that they celebrated the lives of the men who had passed. Because of that, they always turned into wild parties.

Sparky's wasn't like that at all.

Sadness filled the clubhouse that a well-loved and well-thought-of young man had gone out in such a way.

John had stood up at his funeral and talked about him in depth.

His real name was Tyler Marsden. John had named him Sparky because he was so bright. He was twenty-one, just. The only saving grace about the whole affair was that he'd at least be with his beloved mom, who'd passed a couple of years before from a long-term illness.

It was like John said in his speech, now they were together.

The club had become Spark's family. The entire MC had been in mourning in the week since the run. Sparky had touched every man's heart in one way or another, and they felt his absence.

Atlas took it all on his shoulders, of course.

I told him over and over that there was nothing he could've done. The shot was fatal. Whoever had been driving that SUV would've met the same fate.

Jules Ford

It was brutal, but poor Sparky was in the wrong place at the wrong time.

After a week, the connotations were finally beginning to sink in. The only people to blame for the death of that promising young man were Bear and the Burning Sinners.

The police had gone to the scene and taken statements from everybody.

Warrants were out for Bear, and his new VP, Knuckles. We didn't even know if Bear was at the shootout, though it was evident he was behind it.

The two clubs were playing tit for tat, but with Sparky's death, the stakes were suddenly a lot higher. Those stakes were why we were at a wake, saying goodbye to a young man who hadn't deserved the premature ending that he got.

Layla and Bowie sat opposite us, Cash next to them. Rosie was burrowed into one side of Atlas, me into the other. We'd talked and laughed about when Spark first came to prospect at the club, and he'd flirted shamelessly with Rosie. He'd discovered later that she was Atlas' sister and had run away every time Atlas walked into the same room.

The funeral had been at eleven that morning. It was seven p.m. now, and the party was finally warming up.

Atlas was staring at our clasped hands, deep in thought.

He'd kept me close to him since the day of the club run, but he hadn't been himself.

I squeezed his hand. "Are you okay, honey?"

"Yeah." He squeezed me back. "Just thinkin' about that day, wonderin' if I could've done somethin' more."

I twisted my body to face him and cupped his cheek. "Don't take that on, honey. It's not yours to keep. There was nothing that anyone could have done."

Atlas' face twisted.

"No, Dan," I whispered. "It's not your cross to bear. You didn't point a gun at him, honey. Let it go, please. Sparky loved and respected you. He wouldn't want you to take that shit on." I looked deep into his eyes so he could see that I meant every word.

One side of his mouth tipped up. "I don't know what I did to deserve you, baby, but I'm glad I stopped screwin' around and locked you down. You're ol' lady goals, baby, in every fuckin' way. You're the best thing I ever did."

I smiled cheekily. "And I love it when you do me."

He barked out a laugh. "Proves that good things come to those who wait." His neck bent, and he kissed my forehead before turning to say something to Bowie.

I snuggled into his side and looked up. Layla was watching the dancefloor, smiling softly.

My eyes followed hers to see Mason teaching Sunshine and Gabby how to body-pop and break dance. I laughed softly at their little arms sticking out at weird angles while they tried to throw some shapes.

Seraphina had her head thrown back in laughter, and I smiled wider at her happy expression. It was a far cry from the sad, frightened girl I'd examined a few months before.

The teens were blooming under Iris, Abe, and the club's care.

Abe and Mason spent time at the auto shop every night working on an old Harley Super Glide for the teen boy - a mini-biker in the making. But how could he not be when there were so many men in the club that he hero-worshipped? It had to be that way. It was the natural order of things.

Sera and Iris were best friends. Where you found one, you could usually find the other. The shy teen girl was coming out of her shell and watching her blossom under the older lady's love and devotion was amazing. It turned out that Sera was a gifted baker. The Demons wolfed down everything she cooked and praised her to the heavens, usually making her cheeks bright red.

Layla and Bowie were parents to two beautiful girls, and he wouldn't leave her side. Maybe it was because he wanted to soak everything up about being a dad. Or perhaps it was because of the dark cloud that continuously hovered over us.

Cash and Cara were at least speaking.

He'd arranged for a couple of the brothers to go down to her budding art gallery and complete some building work for her. But I think it was Cash's only way to protect her. He fussed around Cara like a bee around pollen. She glowed with health and vitality now that her morning sickness had passed.

John and Hendrix were stoic. They didn't talk much about losing Sparky, but they were always there for the brothers if *they* wanted to.

Atlas worried me.

He was still amazing but always seemed quiet and preoccupied.

Two days after the disastrous club run, he asked me if I wanted to be involved with him in light of the war.

I told him I did, and I meant it. Pulling away from him wasn't an option for me. After the slow burn of the last eight months, we were finally together; although we were in danger, I'd never felt safer. The constant threat meant I looked over my shoulder a lot, but I saw Atlas and the club at my back every time I did.

Why would I ever walk away from that?

Somebody laughed, making me focus back on the conversation around the table. Atlas' fingers squeezed my hand. He knew I'd zoned out because he noticed everything.

"What are we gonna do with his bike?" Bowie asked.

Pain slashed through Cash's eyes. "I think he would've liked us to keep it for a prospect like him. Someone who's lookin' for somethin'. Maybe a kid that

Atlas

hasn't got much in the way of material things. Someone who needs it, you know?"

Layla rubbed Cash's shoulder soothingly. "He'd have loved that."

I looked up as a shout came from the main doors. We all turned to see a very harassed-looking Cara rushing through the bar with Arrow hot on her heels.

"What the fuck's happened now?" Cash grumbled, rising from his seat and striding toward her.

Atlas stroked my fingers absentmindedly. "Somethin's goin' on," he muttered. "What's Cashy boy done this time?"

"Look again." Bo nodded toward Cara. "Wildcat, don't look pissed to me."

She was pointing to the door, talking animatedly to Cash. Her eyes were huge, and her face pale as she bit nervously on her thumbnail.

"She only does that when she's worried." Layla jumped up. "Somethings happened."

A look passed between Atlas and Bowie, and they both got up from their chairs.

Cash turned and made his way back, pulling Cara with him. A shadow fell across his face. "Tell 'em, babe," he ordered.

Cara ran a hand through her hair. "I'm sure I saw a couple of SUVs full of men driving down Memorial Street about a half hour ago." She flinched. "I think one of the drivers was Bear. I tried to call, but none of you picked up."

"Fuck!" Bowie patted his pockets, trying to locate his cell. "We went dark mode for the service, and the music's been loud. Didn't hear a thing."

Atlas cursed under his breath. "Where's Prez?" he demanded angrily.

Bowie dug his cell out of his pocket, stabbed at it with his thumb, and held it to his ear. "Pop!" he barked. "We gotta problem. About a half hour ago, Cara got a bead on a crowd of Sinners driving down Monument Street in cages." He paused for a minute. "Cool." He hung up, and his stare went to Atlas. "They're comin' back through."

"Gotta bad feelin'," Cash muttered. "Had it all day."

"I've had it since the club run." Atlas scraped a hand down his face. "The Sinners are in our town again. Word must've gotten out that we were layin' Spark to rest today. I'm thinkin' that the only time you're gonna get a club full of Demons is a church meet, a weddin'-"

"-Or a funeral," Cash bit out through gritted teeth. "Fuck!"

"Oh my God," Layla breathed. "Bowie?"

"Where's Willow?" he demanded. "You all need to get down the *Cell*."

Layla's hand flew to her mouth. "Iris took her into the kitchen for a feed."

A cold shiver trailed down my spine. After the ambush, I wouldn't have put anything past the Sinners. Bear was a level of crazy that bordered on psychotic. But would they take on an entire club?

A commotion came from the corridor as John and Hendrix came stomping through. Drix weaved his way to us while John went to the bar and hauled himself up to address the brothers. He put two fingers in his mouth and let out an ear-splitting whistle to get everyone's attention.

Someone turned the music off, and the men turned to face John.

"Brothers!" he bellowed. "The camera on the road leading to town malfunctioned earlier today." He pointed to Cara. "Wildcat sighted the Sinners 'bout ten minutes after it went out. We need to get into position."

"Do we know for sure they're comin' here?" someone called out.

"Nope," John replied. "But when there are three cages full of 'em drivin' through town, I'm thinkin' it's a good bet."

Atlas

Hendrix stepped forward. "Snipers! Get your weapons and move up to the roof. If you're a fighter, stay put but sort your weapons too. Shout out what ammo you need. We're goin' downstairs to bring firepower up, and we'll grab it while we're there."

The kids came running over to us just as Iris appeared in the doorway with Abe carrying Willow. "Girls," he barked. "Get the kids and take your asses downstairs, now. Be careful. We got someone down there. Stay away from him. Nobody's to go within ten feet." His glare came to me. "Sophie, make sure nobody gets close, right."

Atlas's hand curled around my nape, and he positioned my face to look up at his. All the chatter disappeared until it was only us in the room.

"Take the girls, baby," he ordered gently. "Follow Abe. He'll let you all in the Cell. There's water down there. It's a big room, no need for you to be close to the prisoner. Keep an eye ou-"

An earsplitting crack thundered through the air. A loud smash rang out as one of the windows shattered, and glass ricocheted through the room.

Yells and screams echoed as the men bellowed for everyone to get down.

A hand grabbed me and pulled me down. Deafening loud pops cut through the room.

I let out a scream. My hands flew to my ears, and a sick feeling roiled through my stomach because I recognized the sound of gunfire exploding through the clubhouse.

It was the Sinners.

Chapter Twenty-Three

Atlas

The pepper of gunshots flew through the bar, and we all hit the deck. Within seconds it was utter chaos. Men jumped to their feet and jostled into position. Hollers and shouts cut through the air, drownin' out the women's screams as the brothers yelled instructions to each other. Then the pounding booms of gunshots got louder as the Demons started to return fire.

Immediately I could tell which men had military training. Luckily, it was most of the club. Even Kit, who had crippling PTSD, seemed to morph straight into soldier mode as he reached into his hip holster and drew his gun.

My gut jerked as an explosion cracked through the room. My head whipped around to see one of the windows shatter. Bullets began to ping off metal, the ricochets bouncing off the walls. Shouts went up as people ran for cover.

"Atlas," Sophie cried, voice filled with terror.

My fingers squeezed hers before I got up on my hands and knees. "Stay down, baby. Keep the other women low too. Get 'em all together, crawl to the corridor, and get down the Cell."

A baby's cry filled the air. Layla began to scream for Willow hysterically.

I looked around the room, tryin'a concentrate. I needed to block the noise out and think straight.

Bowie crawled over to Iris, who clutched the baby to her chest. "Come on," he demanded. "Get the baby to the Cell." He looked back at Layla. "Doe. Move it. Get the kids safe. Now!"

I helped Sophie get onto her haunches and pointed toward Layla. "Go, baby, please. Need ya to get safe. The girls know where they're goin'. Follow, protect them."

"I don't want to leave you," she cried.

My heart fuckin' swelled because I'd found a woman who had my back. I knew without a doubt that she'd stay and fight with me if I asked her to. There was no way I'd let her, but knowin' what was in her heart made my protective instincts go crazy.

"I can't be effective if I'm distracted by you, Stitch." I kissed her hair. "We're gonna need a doctor after this. Get down The Cell with the women. Let me do what I need to do."

Her eyes welled up as she stared into mine. "I love you, Danny. Please be careful, honey."

Something kicked inside my gut, and I quickly touched my mouth to hers. "Ditto, baby. Now, go."

She nodded and got to her feet, calling out to the other women among the sound of booming gunfire. They all crouched low and followed her toward the hallway.

My hand reached into my body holster, and I took out my weapon. I couldn't help shootin' a quick glance toward the corridor to ensure Stitch was clear.

"I've got 'em, Atlas," Abe shouted over. "I'll get 'em safe and grab ammo and weapons while I'm down below."

"Comin' with ya," Ice yelled as he bent low, runnin' toward Abe. "I'm already out."

Atlas

More bullets careened through the ether and another window shattered.

My chest felt like it was gonna explode from my breaths which were sawing in and out.

There was broken glass everywhere.

Upturned chairs littered the floor, and the air was hazy with gun smoke. The bar was destroyed.

I checked each man's position, taking stock of the situation.

Demons crouched around the windows. They took shots when they could, then pulled back to take cover behind the walls as gunfire peppered back through. I looked around to make sure nobody was injured

"I'm out," somebody yelled.

"Me too," another man shouted.

Fuck. The only firepower we had handy were our personal weapons. We would have to make do with those until Abe and Ice came back up with more. We didn't have a choice.

I kept low and ran toward Cash, who was already firin' shots out of another broken window.

I glanced outside to see what was goin' on, then ducked under the ledge.

There was a large group of men in masks standin' outside the fence. They couldn't get through our new gate, so they were firin' at the clubhouse from their positions thirty feet away.

Blood pounded through my ears as men rushed around shoutin' instructions to each other. Not one man had lost his head. Everyone knew their role. Their military trainin' and our recent drills had prepared them for the Sinners' bullshit attack.

"You're late," Cash nodded toward the gun I'd cocked a few seconds ago. "I'm almost outta bullets."

"Had to get Sophie safe," I shouted. "Abe and Ice are getting' ammo and weapons. Keep shootin' and don't let them close to the buildin', or they'll try and storm it."

"Gotcha." He fired a shot and dived back behind the wall. "The boys need to hurry the fuck up; we'll be sittin' targets soon. I've only got fourteen rounds in this. I'm tryin' a make every shot count, but it's hard to pick them out since it's gettin' dark out there."

Prez's voice bellowed through the room. "When the weapons come up, I want the Snipers to grab what they need and head straight up to the roof. Stay low. Take a shot but remember to move around so they can't get a bead on your positions."

Barks of agreement rang out.

"Any injuries?" Prez shouted. "If you need help, speak now."

"A bullet graze, and a few cuts from the glass is all," someone called out.

"My ol' lady was bleedin' from her head," Fender confirmed. "But she's conscious, and she's with the doc."

"Sophie'll sort her, brother," I assured him, darting in front of the window. I fired a shot before throwin' myself behind the wall next to Cash. I almost jumped five feet in the air as a loud boom punctured through the room at my back.

I craned my neck, and my body froze, eyes buggin' out at the scene before me.

A young guy I didn't recognize was behind the bar loadin' the shotgun we kept underneath the counter. He stood tall, cocked the barrel, and aimed it toward the window. Lining up his shot, he fired that baby like he was Billy the fuckin' Kid.

Boom. Boom. Boom.

My brain rattled from the noise. I looked at Cash, nodding toward the bar. "Who the fuck's that?" I demanded.

He looked over his shoulder and watched as the guy reloaded and took another shot. "Dunno. Someone said

Atlas

that Fender's blood brother was gonna work the bar tonight for the funeral. Maybe it's him."

"Ain't he a Ranger?" I couldn't help grinnin' as I watched him aim and shoot again. The kid had no fear. He looked like he was havin' the time of his goddamned life.

"Fuck if I know." Cash shrugged, then jerked his head as a bullet whizzed past his ear. "Shit. Where's that ammo? That was too fuckin' close."

I looked up to see Colt runnin' toward us, bent forward.

"What's goin' on, brother?" I demanded. "Have you got eyes on 'em?"

He shoved a tablet under my nose. "There's about thirty men out there. Our cameras are hidden, so they haven't shot them out." He tapped on the iPad. "I'm controlling the gates electronically. If they get them open, we're fucked."

Cash looked at me, grinnin'. "Wanna play shoot the Sinner? The first man to five wins a goodie bag."

I laughed, despite myself. "You're one crazy fuck."

"They tried to take my woman, At," he retorted. "I won't rest until we've wiped their entire fuckin' club out." He pointed his gun out the window, aimed, and fired.

Drix let out a loud whoop. "Good shot, Cash. You got that fucker in the chest."

"One down, twenty-nine to go," Cash bellowed as a loud clang banged from the direction of the hallway.

I glanced back and saw Abe and Ice haulin' ass into the room, pushin' a giant plastic container on wheels.

"Sorry, brothers," Ice yelled. "We had to get this bumped up the stairs, and it's heavy as all fuck. Thought it'd be better if we could get everythin' up at once instead of goin' back and forth." He went into the container and started throwing ammo boxes at the men.

"What d'ya need, Atlas?" Abe shouted.

I aimed out the window and fired off a shot. "I gotta Glock-17. Need a pack of twenty-four if we've got 'em?"

"I gotta Glock-18 here and five packs of thirty-three rounds. Any good for ya?"

"Load her up." I took a minute and fired off my remaining bullets before turnin' to take the other Glock Abe passed to me. Lookin' back through the window, I closed one eye, took aim, and fired.

A grin stole across my face when a man wearing a black balaclava hit the ground.

"You got him, Atlas," Prez boomed. "Nice. There's a few of 'em down now, which is good considerin' we can't get many clear shots."

I threw myself behind the wall just as a bullet whizzed through the window.

My heart hammered out of my chest.

That was too close for comfort. I looked to the heavens, did the sign of the cross over my chest, silently thanking my guardian angel.

"Arrow, Cash, Colt, Reno, Fender," Drix bellowed. "You're all with me."

Cash moved toward the Veep. "Gotta go and snipe," he called back. "You gonna be okay?"

Another boom echoed through the bar as Billy the Kid took another shot through the window.

"Fuck me," Kit rasped as he ran over to me. "That one's like a kid in a candy store." He aimed and fired a shot. "I've got him, bro," he called to Cash. "Go and snipe."

Concern for Breaker stabbed through my chest.

No doubt this scenario was his worst nightmare. Poor fucker should've been shakin' in a heap on the floor, beggin' for his momma. Instead, he'd shaken it off, dug in, and did what he had to do.

My jaw set determinedly. If Breaker could function like a commando after everythin' he'd been through. I could fuckin' deal too.

Atlas

"Got one." He let out a whoop and turned to me. "You ready to rumble?"

Blood coursed through my veins, and my lip curled into a snarl. "Let's fuckin' party, Breaker boy."

"Bear's there," Prez shouted. "He's wearin' a balaclava, but I'd recognize his shitty tattoos anywhere."

I glanced out the window. Sure enough, Bear's loud rasp floated through the night air.

Aimin' my gun, I popped off another round.

"Another one just went down," Kit shouted as he peered outside.

A plethora of gunfire sounded from what seemed like above the clubhouse. "Snipers must be takin' their shots already." Prez let out a hoot. "They're startin' to drop like fuckin' flies out there."

Sure enough, the booms were dying down. Instead of a constant spray of bullets peppering' the walls, singular gunshots popped.

My entire body vibrated with satisfaction. We were getting the upper hand.

I peered outside. For the first time since everything went to hell, I could clearly see what was happening.

Three black SUVs lined up behind the gate. A row of men stood by the fence, shooting toward us. A few men sprawled out on the floor, obviously wounded. A couple dragged their legs as they staggered back to the vehicles. Men started to haul open the cage doors, bellowing shouts of 'retreat.'

I heaved out a breath.

Thank fuck.

My jaw clenched so hard it ached.

Those fuckers had caught us when we were vulnerable, but we'd still beaten their cowardly asses without much effort. They may have jumped on us, but we mobilized immediately, outshot, and outwitted 'em.

Booms fractured the air again, but they came from above. The sniper team was gunnin' for 'em now.

Shouts rang out as the masked men ushered their injured into their SUVs. After a minute, their tires squealed, and they finally sped away.

"They're standin' down," I hollered. "They got a shock when the snipers retaliated. They're runnin' for their fuckin' lives. Nice shootin', brothers."

Whoops, and cheers went up.

Dagger made his way over to me, rubbin' his forehead. "What the fuck just happened?" His back slumped. I could almost see the tension drain outta his body. "The assholes take out our boy, and then they come at us durin' his fuckin' wake?" He shook his head disbelievingly.

Prez was old school with old school values. The Sinners didn't have a moral between 'em.

"They ain't like us, Prez." I clasped his shoulder. "They fight dirty. It's like I keep sayin', we gotta stop thinkin' like soldiers and start thinkin' like one percenters."

Prez's eyes jerked around the room, and he started to shout orders. "Load up your weapons. We need to get into the lot, survey the damage and start fixin'. We got window panes and wood in the sheds out back. Won't fix bullet holes, but at least we can secure the compound for tonight." He raised a hand to rub his beard, grimacing as he looked at the damage.

Cash and Hendrix stalked into the room, rifles hangin' across their backs, and another cheer went up.

"Good work, brothers," Abe called out. "They shit their shorts when the boys above open fired."

"I didn't even have to reload." Cash let out a laugh. "They scrambled within minutes. I was almost disappointed in 'em."

Hendrix nodded his agreement. "They didn't expect us to mobilize like that. Not sayin' they got no vets in their crew, but the Demons are mostly ex-military." He jerked his head to Cash. "Talented soldiers have trained even the non-military boys, so we had 'em on the back foot as soon as we got into position."

Drix was right. That was the reason we recruited only the best. It seemed that decision had been a good one. What just happened proved that quality won out every time. The Sinners were scramblin' because we had the know-how and battle experience.

Cash looked around at the men who were sortin' out the bar. "We doin' clean-up?"

"Don't gotta choice," Prez replied. "We gotta get the place secured."

"Left Arrow on the roof in charge of the Snipers," Drix informed him. "They're gonna cover us in case those Sinner fucks left stragglers behind." He glanced at me, smilin' big. "You did well securing that infra-red equipment. My sniper boys are up on the roof playin' with it as we speak. They'll see the enemy comin' from a mile away."

Prez laughed. "Where did ya get that shit?"

My lips twitched. "Our friends in Oregon and Vegas can get anythin' we need."

"It's not what ya know-" Cash said knowingly.

"-It's certainly a case of who you know," Prez finished with a nod of his head. "Let's get into teams, and we'll start fixin' shit." He craned his neck, lookin' for someone. "Yo. Bowie!" he yelled.

Bowie looked around at Prez and gave him a chin lift.

"Get the women up from the Cell. We need Doc to examine the wounded and Iris to work her magic in the kitchen. It's gonna be a long night. We'll need coffee and food to keep us going." He shrugged. "Hell, the ladies can give out kisses and cuddles if needed."

My body locked.

Abe's shoulders stiffened.

A strangled sound escaped Cash's throat.

Bowie shot Dagger a death stare.

Prez threw back his head and laughed, eyes twinkling with humor. "Only jokin' boys."

My eyes fell on the bar. "Before we start clean up, brothers, there's somethin' that's happened tonight, and it's confused the fuck outta me."

"What the hell are you gabbin' about?" Prez asked.

I jerked my thumb in the direction of the bar where Billy the Kid was knockin' back a Jack and runnin' his finger down the cleavage of the one'a the club girls, cocky as you like.

"Can someone please tell me... Who the fuck is that?"

Chapter Twenty-Four

Sophie

Bang! Bang! Bang!
"Hold still, Ashley." I injected some local anesthetic into Fender's ol' lady's forehead. "Sorry, I know it's loud, but I need to glue this now if I want to stop it from scarring too badly."

She winced. "I'm more concerned about the kids. They'll be running wild."

"Sera's all over it, don't worry." I smiled.

"Can't believe they did this." Her eyes jerked to mine. "I'm glad you're here. Nicky says you're the shit. After today, I get why he thinks that."

"Thanks." I let out a short laugh. "I think Fender's the shit too."

"You must think we're all crazy gun-toting criminals, and I couldn't blame you. We've been with the club for years, and nothing like this has ever happened before."

I finished the job and took a step back to admire my work. "There. You're all done."

She stood up and nodded toward the window. "Can you believe how quickly they've got their shit together? The place was a wreck an hour ago."

I turned toward the loud banging. The room was a hive of activity. Men in groups were hammering and nailing new windows back into the panes. "They certainly work fast," I observed.

She shook her head, smiling. "Seventy men are doing the work, and the club owns a construction company. They do this stuff all the time."

"True." I returned her smile.

A loud bang punctured the air outside, and I almost jumped out of my skin. Jesus, I was a wreck. My nerves were in pieces after the shootout.

I shook my head disbelievingly. "They're laughing and joking around like they're at a party."

Ashley cocked a pretty blonde eyebrow. "A lot of them are ex-military. Their first instincts are to protect their own. They've been in wars, Sophie. I guess it comes naturally when you've lived and breathed that for most of your life. While we were downstairs worried sick, they were up here probably having the time of their lives." She rolled her eyes.

I watched as a young guy behind the bar flicked on the stereo system.

Old-school R&B began to thump through the speakers. Atlas had been calling the bartender 'Billy the Kid' for the last hour.

My eyes automatically darted to my man, who was laughing as he nailed wood with Cash.

You wouldn't think that an hour ago, the bar resembled a battle scene from an old western movie. They must've had nerves of steel, unlike me, whose fingers still tremored slightly. Not for the first time in the last hour, I wondered how they could be so unaffected by it all.

One day, maybe I'd get used to it.
Yeah, right.

I jumped again as a crash went up behind me, and a string of curses turned the air blue. "Fuck! Cash barked.

Atlas

"Slippery motherfucker." He looked up and jerked his chin toward the bar. "Yo. Billy. Go in that drawer behind ya and bring me the needle and nylon thread."

The guy went into the drawer, hauled himself over the bar top, and stalked toward Cash.

He was a good-looking guy.

I would've put him in his mid-twenties. He had lighter hair which he'd styled in a quiff at the front. He wore ripped jeans and a wifebeater. Silver jewelry adorned his neck and wrists, rings covering most of his tattooed fingers. He looked like a rock star.

Cash took the needle from him and stared. "Kid, can you sew?"

He eyed Cash like he was crazy. "Do I look like your mother?"

Atlas laughed and pointed to Billy the Kid. "I like him. He's got gumption."

"Who says that? Gumption?" Cash grumbled.

Atlas's head reared back. "Well, me. Stupid cunt."

I rolled my eyes at their bickering before focusing on Cash's hand. He'd threaded some black cotton on the needle. It looked like he was prepping to sew.

"What are you doing?" I called over.

His eyes lifted to me, and he held an arm up. Blood trickled down it. "Didn't think you, of all people, would have to ask." He grinned at his joke.

"What am I? Chopped liver?" I demanded.

He shrugged. "You see to the real wounded. Ain't the first time I've sewed myself up. It's just a fuckin' scratch." He stuck himself with the needle and began to sew.

My mouth dropped open. Just a scratch? His arm was pissing blood. "You'll get an infection."

He just laughed and carried on.

Ashley nudged my arm with hers. "They're all crazy."

Jules Ford

I watched, still open-mouthed, as blood trickled down Cash's arm.

Ashley clamped her hand to her mouth. "Ugh. I can't deal with that when I'm pregnant." She moved quickly toward the kitchen corridor where the bathroom was.

The main doors crashed open, and John stomped in, Bowie following. "They've left one'a their fuckin' dead out there." His hands went to his hips, and he blew a hard breath. "Now I gotta deal with goddamned decomposing Sinners stinkin' up the place. Like the trigger-happy cuntbags haven't stressed my ass out enough already today."

"Douse the fucker in whisky and burn him, Prez," Shotgun suggested.

My eyes snapped wide.

"Don't waste good whisky, boys," Billy the Kid called out. "Lighter fluid will do the job. Just saw some in that drawer. It's cheap, cheerful, and it'll do the job."

Prez grinned.

My eyes snapped wider, and I headed for the corridor. "I'm going to the kitchen. I need to be around sane people. Jeez, is it a full moon?"

Atlas grabbed my hand as I walked past. "Be in soon, baby." He landed a kiss on the top of my head.

I squeezed his fingers and made my way up the corridor to see what the girls were doing. I shuddered. All that talk of burning bodies had given me the heebie-jeebies.

The kitchen was buzzing when I walked in. Iris and Layla giggled and chatted as they cut sandwiches. Cara looked up at me. "Hey. Wanna coffee?"

"God, yes," I muttered. "They're all crazy out there. It's like biker's fun day out. I just left Cash sewing his own arm up."

Cara rolled her eyes. "I've told him not to do that. He's shitty at sewing. His scars always look worse when he's sewed himself."

Atlas

I cocked my head at her. "Plus, there's a small fact that he could get an infection and *die*."

Cara's eyes went far away. "Oh yeah. Never thought of that." She shrugged. "It'd serve the cheating fucker right."

Iris, Layla, and Rosie began to laugh.

Jesus, I thought. *The women are as crazy as the men.*

Iris started to line pastries up on a tray. "At least the food we made won't go to waste. There's nothing like a good shootout to give the men an appetite."

I dropped my head in my hands as Layla placed a mug of coffee in front of me. "You'll get used to it, Sophie. Moping around won't help the situation. It's best to try and make light of everything. And you've got to remember that nobody died. The men are saying it was a win for them."

Iris grinned. "Hold on to your panties, girls. You know how horny our ol' men get after a shootout."

My ears pricked up.

Layla cackled.

Cara rolled her eyes again.

Rosie punched her hands to her hips. "Yeah, go on, Iris, rub a bit more salt in my wounds."

Iris laughed and arranged more pastries.

My ears pricked up as deep voices sounded from the hallway.

"Wildcat?" Cash called.

"In here, asshole." She rolled her eyes for a third time that minute.

A few seconds later, Cash stomped through the door, followed by Atlas, Bowie, Abe, and John.

Immediately Cash went to the sink to wash his arm.

"You filthy pig." Iris slapped his side. "You'll get blood on the food."

"Sorry, Ris." He laughed and then made his way over to Cara. "We've been talkin', baby. Maybe you should move into the clubhouse for a while."

Jules Ford

Atlas came straight to my back, snaked his arms around my neck, and pulled me into him. "You too, Stitch baby."

I looked up until I met his eyes.

My heart fluttered when I saw the emotion conveyed in them.

Atlas slipped his arms around my shoulders and cuddled me from behind. "I'm gonna need to arrange an escort to and from work for you as well." His deep voice rumbled from inside his chest, making me shiver in delight.

Abe bit into a pastry and looked at Iris. "We're movin' in for a while too, woman."

She nodded. "Right. If the families are gonna be here, I need to organize the kitchen."

"I'll help," Layla offered.

Cara and I looked at each other, making an 'eek' face.

I was a basic cook, and even if I was great at it, I couldn't think of anything worse than standing over a stove all day.

Cash busted out laughing and shook his head at the expressions on our faces.

I shrugged. "I can't help. I work long hours, sometimes up to sixteen a day."

Cara nodded her agreement. "I'm working long hours getting the gallery ready, and you know I can't cook, though if you're desperate, I'll throw together some picky plates."

"Love your picky plates, baby." Cash grinned.

Layla squealed. "Me too."

"Picky plates isn't dinner." Iris sniffed. "It's rolled-up sandwich meat, pickles, and olives arranged on a board."

"And wine," Cara corrected. "Don't forget the best part." She glanced down at her belly, letting out a sigh as her shoulders slumped. "Shit. I can't even drink the

Atlas

wine." Her eyes slashed toward Cash, and she narrowed them angrily.

His stare hit his boots.

"C'mon," Atlas whispered in my ear.

I shivered again as he pulled me off my stool and out of the kitchen.

"Where are we going?" I asked curiously.

He tugged me forward, bent at the knees, grabbed the back of my thighs, and hauled me up. My legs snaked around his hips simultaneously as my arms banded around his neck. I kissed his nose gently. "Are you okay, honey?"

He walked us down the corridor to the bar and hit the hall for the bedrooms. "We need to talk, Stitch," he said against my lips.

I sighed. "If you're going to ask me if I want to stay around, don't bother, Danny. I'm not going to run off and leave you to face this shit alone. You need me, and I need you. We're here to support each other. I'm not going to turn tail every time the going gets tough. Got it?"

He nuzzled his nose with mine. "Wasn't gonna say that."

"Good." I sniffed haughtily.

He pushed open the door to his room and walked over to the bed, dropping me, so my body bounced a couple of times. I lifted until I was leaning back on my elbows and blew the hair out of my face while he walked back to shut the door. "What is it then?" I asked.

His weight hit the bed, and he laid down, pulling me on top of him. "Did you mean what you said to me when it popped off earlier, Stitch baby?" His hand swept my hair back and he leaned to kiss me softly.

My heart flip-flopped in my chest, and I smiled. "You mean when I told you that I love you?"

He jerked a nod, his dark eyes locking with mine. "It's okay if you said it in the heat of the moment. Mayhem tends to make people spout things that they wouldn't normally say. It's okay if you didn't mean it. I'll keep earnin' it until you do."

My body melted into his.

I loved it when he showed me his vulnerability. A man like Atlas wouldn't show me that side of him unless he trusted me with it. He was everything that I'd ever dreamed of. He'd given me the family that I'd never had. I knew things with the club weren't perfect, but for me, it was the imperfections that made it real.

My hand came up to stroke his cheek. "I love you." My eyes welled up. "I loved you when I didn't even know it, Dan. I don't care about club wars, shootouts, or even Sinners. As long as I've got you, I've got everything. You make me feel safe."

It was true.

I knew things were dangerous, but my man protected me so beautifully that I hardly felt it. I could look after myself, but I loved how much he cherished me.

I loved him more every day. He was the best man I knew, and I was in it for the long haul.

His finger came up to wipe my tear, and he smiled. "Gonna marry you one day soon, Stitch. Gonna plant my boy in your belly, then plant my princess. You okay with that?"

My heart fluttered wildly, and I nodded.

Then he said the words that made the world seem right again for the first time since my momma died. "Love you too, Stitch baby. I waited all my life to have you and make you mine; you *are* mine, and I'm yours. Want us to get wed asap, but until I can sort it, I need to ask you a question."

My belly went all swirly and warm. "What? I whispered.

His fingers slid into my hair, and he touched his mouth to mine. "Stitch," he said, voice low. "Be my ol' lady?"

Atlas

Chapter Twenty-Five

John

My eyes jerked from one brothers' face to the next before restin' on Bowie's pissed-off expression.

Yesterday's shootout bothered him the most. He had Sunny and Willow to worry about now, as well as Layla. Though I had to admit, my goddaughter had some balls. All the men, women, and club brats had proven their worth durin' the attack the day before.

The clubhouse was still gettin' fixed up. Abe had already looked into getting bulletproof glass fitted, but for the interim, we needed to make our home as safe and secure as possible.

The men had worked non-stop. I still hadn't slept. Neither had Cash, Atlas, or Drix. We were still too hyped up.

"Gotta say, boys, we kicked Sinner ass. They had casualties, but we didn't. We got 'em on the back foot, and I'm takin' that as a big ol' win." My stare slid back to my middle son. "How's Layla doin'?"

"Good." His hand clasped the back of his neck. "Doe's all for kickin' Sinner ass, and Sunny wants me to ask Sophie if she can teach her," he did quotation marks with his fingers, "kravvy magic."

The men all let out barkin' laughs while my chest puffed out with pride.

Trust my little Sunshine to make us all smile after the day from hell. But then, what did I expect? She was the sunshine in my life.

My stare went to Cash. "What about Cara? She bein' stubborn as usual?"

Cash shrugged. "It's not about bein' stubborn, Pop. She's always gonna do what she wants to do. I spoke to Seth. He's gonna keep an eye out for now, but if she gets any shit from those cunts she promised me that she'd move into the clubhouse."

My hand came up, and I rubbed my beard. "I'd feel better if she came straight in, Son."

"So would I, but Seth's dead against it. After the bullshit I pulled, I can't blame him. He's just tryin'a protect her from me-" His voice broke.

I stood up, bent across the table, and curled my hand around my boy's neck. He was feelin' it deep in his soul. He yearned for Cara and his kid. Xander was missin' out on so much, but he did the crime, so he had to do the time.

"I'm proud of you, Son," I rasped, suddenly choked up. "You're doin' everythin' you can to make it right, and it's not gone unnoticed by me, your brothers, or Cara. Your ol' lady's smart. She can see that you're sortin' your shit and you're growin' up." I released him and sat back down in my chair. "The only thing you can do that would ever let me down is give up."

Cash's eyes caught mine, and he smiled sadly.

I wished that I could take his demons away. But the man he was destined to be depended on him doin' it himself. I did not doubt that he'd succeed.

My eldest's eyes reddened, but he kept his shit together. "Thanks, Dad."

I gave him a chin lift before my eyes slid to my SAA.

Atlas

Atlas was the happiest I'd ever known him to be. Bizarre seein' as we'd been officially embroiled in a club war. He felt every hit deep down in his gut, which meant that a pretty little doctor must've been supportin' him just like a perfect ol' lady should.

I dipped my chin. "Your plans sorted, Atlas?"

A grin spread across his face. "Yip. Breaker and me are hittin' Sin City next week. Tote's sortin' our rides and then makin' 'em disappear when we leave. Spoke to 'em about sendin' a truck full of weapons and ammo to the club. It'll be here in two weeks. We've got plenty to last us until then if shit hits the fan again."

"What about Oregon?" I asked.

"Same," he replied. "Grizz also said they can swing down to us if we need more men."

"Interestin'," I mused. "Tell him I send my kindest regards." I leaned back in my seat and looked him dead in the eye. "Your woman's been good for this club. Was she freaked about the shootout?"

He studied his hands while he thought for a minute, then his eyes slid up to mine. "Stitch gets it. For a chick who's not used to our ways, she's a fuckin' trouper." He let out a snort. "I mean, she thinks we're all fuckin' nutso, but lucky for me, she seems to like it." He looked around at the men, smilin' huge. "Asked her to be my ol' lady, and she said yeah. Got the ring already. After I get back from LV I'm gonna make it official. It looks like I'm wifed up, boys."

The men let out whoops and shouts of congratulations.

My SAA ducked his head, lookin' bashful, but contentment radiated from him.

I was over the moon for him. Out of all the ol' ladies, I understood Sophie the most.

She was one of life's warriors. When the goin' got tough, she went out, trained, and kicked life's ass. She was exactly the woman he needed. She was all the sweet in the world, kind, carin', but she kept him on his toes.

I was always happy for any of my men when they locked down their women, but I also couldn't help the pang of regret stabbing through my gut.

Even after more than thirty years, I still missed the other half of me. Green eyes flashed through my mind, and suddenly my chest got tight.

"You okay, boss?" Drix asked.

"Yep." I breathed through the ache, turnin' to my number two. "How's your team doin', Veep?"

"Good." He glanced at Cash. "They're on a high from last night. Don't think the boys realized how effective they'd be."

"They were the icin' on our cake, Veep. We had the Sinners on the run, then you guys got on the roof, and they didn't know what hit 'em." I looked at Cash again. "You've got one'a the best aims I've seen, Son. Most of your shots were on target. When you're getting peppered with bullets, and you only have a small gap to aim through, I know from experience that shit ain't easy."

Cash jerked his chin at me.

I turned to Ice and Abe, who were seated beside each other. "Love your idea about bringin' that crate of guns and ammo up. In the long run, it saved us a lotta time."

"Thanks, Prez," Ice replied. "It took a bit longer than I'd have liked, though. Those steps were a bitch." He and Abe glanced at each other. "We had an idea. Could we put in a ramp? It'll be easier to get the weapons up and down and help with moving incapacitated prisoners."

I nodded slowly. It certainly had its merits. "I'll leave it to you. Get one'a the guys on the construction crew to see how complicated it'd be. If they can do it in a day, I'm happy for it to go ahead." I leaned forward, restin' my arms on the table. "Talkin' of prisoners, how's ours doin'?"

Atlas

Atlas rubbed his chin, deep in thought. "It's bizarre that I'm even thinkin' it, boss, but it's gonna sting when we kill him. Piston's like us, old school, and it's obvious from the way he talks that he despises what Bear's doin'. There are two factions in the Sinners' camp. The crew he ran with wasn't much different from us. He was great when the women went down the Cell durin' the shootout. Handcuffed to a fuckin' chair and singin' nursery rhymes with the kids, apparently."

I almost laughed at that crazy mental image.

Atlas was a tough man. I recognized that because I was a tough man, too, and I wouldn't wanna mess with him. But underneath his asshole disposition, he had a good heart.

"Will ya be able to kill him if needed?" I asked, more as a test than a request.

"Boss. If you order me to kill him, I'll do it. I don't have to like my orders, but I'll still follow 'em 'cause I know we're fightin' on the right side."

And that was it.

I knew he meant every word. He'd killed on my say before, and I was certain he would again. It was the one thing the Sinners lacked, the one thing that made us who we were and gave us so much success over the years.

Total trust. That belief in each other gave us the edge in the gunfight the night before.

Atlas knew I wouldn't kill a good man. I'd only order a kill on fucknuts who came after the family and assholes who hurt innocents.

My hand came up to rub my beard. Maybe it was time to pay our prisoner a little visit, get to know him and test his mettle.

A knock on the door pulled me outta my thoughts. "Come in," I ordered.

Colt popped his read around. "Got what you asked for, Prez."

I gestured for him to come inside.

He made his way into Church and went straight to the TV cabinet. "I went through all the footage on the camera's like you asked." He pulled the doors open so we could see the screen. "No Sinners came into town in the last week. I've run every plate on every vehicle driven in and out of Hambleton. There ain't a Sinner among them."

"I don't get what you're tryin'a say, Colt." Bowie's face twisted with confusion.

"Prez came to me last night, Bo," Colt explained. "The cameras we put up on the road to town somehow malfunctioned just before they rode in, but no Sinners were in Hambleton at the time." He began to play the video footage from the camera. The picture was grainy, but the entire area was deserted. Suddenly the screen was full of static and the image went black.

"See?" Colt pointed to the screen. "If a Sinner had come in and fucked with the camera, we would've seen 'em approach."

"Fuck!" Drix muttered.

"I've had my suspicions for a while, brothers," I stated. "We've had countless sightin's of 'em in town. Cash and Atlas pulled that van with Sera and Mason on the road to Hambleton, which didn't lead anywhere but here. They must've been bringin' her to someone who lives in town."

Colt clicked the video footage off and turned to face the table. "Someone in Hambleton must've disabled those cameras. They went up from behind and fucked with them. The Sinners must have an ally in our town."

"Who the fuck in Hambleton's got 'emselves mixed up with those fuckers?" Drix shook his head disgustedly.

I got how he felt.

Everyone in town knew the Sinners were evil. Workin' with 'em, and backin' 'em was askin' for trouble. They reminded me of a rat infestation. Once they got in, it was almost impossible to get shot of 'em.

Atlas

"Also," I continued. "We've been involved in two shootouts in the space of a week. The first time, we had to call the fuzz out. The second time, they didn't rear their heads. Usually, wherever there's gunfire, there are cops."

The men looked at each other, the ramifications slowly sinking in.

Two and two were startin' to make five.

Whoever was scratchin' the Sinners' backs must've somehow been gettin' their backs scratched too. The Sheriff's office was turnin' a blind eye.

Atlas's lips flattened. "Bet the pigs are in the Sinners' pockets."

"Make you wonder, huh?" I smiled wryly. "There's another question we have to ask ourselves, brothers." I sat forward and clasped my hands together. "We need to know who the Sinners are workin' with in Hambleton and why?"

Chapter Twenty- Six

Atlas ~ Ten Days Later

"You're sure they're unmarked?" I looked down at the two rides that were on their kickstands.

Locke clapped me hard on the back. Any other fucker would've winced with the force of it, but for me, it was like water off a duck's back.

"They're clean, Atlas," he assured me, noddin' toward the bikes. "You'll be ghosts on them."

"And you'll make 'em disappear when we bring 'em back?" I checked.

Locke shot me a venomous look. "You yanking my chain?"

"Just makin' sure," I muttered. "No need to eyeball me."

The SAA of the Three Kings MC knew what he was doin' without a doubt, but this had to go to plan, or it would be game over for Kit and me.

"Sure you don't wanna come to Kings Bar for a drink before you head out?" Locke asked. "It's a good time. Might relax you before you do the deed."

I took my sunglasses out of my shirt pocket and pulled my baseball cap across my eyes. "I'll take a raincheck. Gonna get it done and get back to my woman."

"I get it. Next time, yeah?"

We bumped fists, and I grabbed the bigger of the two bikes. "Breaker," I yelled. "Move it."

Kit came stalkin' outta the clubhouse with the King's prez by his side.

Tote gave me a chin lift as he sauntered toward me. "Any sign of trouble, you get your asses back here. We can hide you no problem."

"Hopefully, we can get it done and get the fuck outta dodge." I stuck out my hand and fist-bumped him. "Much obliged to you, Prez. You've all been very accommodating." I shoved my shades over my eyes.

"He's been on our radar for a while, Atlas. You're doin' us a favor. When it's all done with, we'll all have alibis. The cops won't be able to pin it on us. Are you boys covered too?"

"Yeah." I turned to see Kit mountin' up. "There's video footage of Breaker and me up at an MC in Unity Creek, Oregon. That's where we've been these past days. Been seen ridin' around town, doncha know?"

Tote and Locke watched us put our helmets on, grinnin'. "Watch your back, brothers," Locke called out as the bikes roared to life.

I gave him a chin lift, and we set off, tailpipes roarin'. But my mind wasn't on the engine's rumble or the warm sunshine. It was on the reason that Breaker and I had come here.

Retribution.

Kit sped ahead of me. After a few minutes of ridin' he pointed to a turnin' on the right. I followed his finger and saw that he was takin' us toward a rinky-dink buildin' about a half-mile up the road.

As we drew closer, I saw it was an old diner. We pulled into the half-full parkin' lot and pulled to a stop at the far end, switchin' off our engines.

Atlas

I took off my helmet and slapped on my baseball cap, pullin' it low over my face. Turnin' to Kit, I saw he was doin' the same. "This place clean, Breaker?"

"Yeah." He looked up at the buildin'. "No cameras, and it's outta the way. The Kings told me that the owner doesn't ask questions and forgets a man's face as soon as he walks out the door. Tip well, and they'll forget that you were ever here at all."

"Cool." I dismounted and leaned the motorcycle on its kickstand. "Could do with a cold beverage."

"Keep your gloves on, brother," Kit called from behind as I made my way to the glass door. I looked back at him, cocking an eyebrow.

"Prints." He grinned.

The bell over the door tinkled as we pushed it open and walked inside. The place had ten customers—three young guys on one table. Four men spread throughout, eatin' alone. Two women with a couple'a kids were just gettin' ready to leave.

The place reminded me of an old-school fifties establishment. In its heyday, it would've been a cool place to eat. It had dark wooden floors, red and white checked tablecloths, and a vintage jukebox sittin' in one corner.

Over time it had lost its shine. Everything looked a bit dated, though it smelled good and was obviously clean, which was good enough for me. We picked a booth that gave us a view of the door and took our seats.

Within seconds, footsteps clacked off the floor, and a waitress appeared next to the table. "Hiya, boys. What can I get ya?" She took out a pen and notepad and held them ready. She had bleached hair, red lips and smiled big. Was probably a knockout in her day.

I looked at her name badge. "Yo, Gina. Our buds over at the Three Kings said this is the place to come for a coffee on the lowdown."

She popped a hip. "Gotcha, darlin'." Her lips smacked as she chewed her gum. "Never saw ya."

Kit closed the menu he'd been perusin' and flashed Gina a killer grin. "I'll have the special, please, beautiful. And a diet coke."

She scribbled Kit's order down on her notepad. "What about you, sweetheart." She glanced at me, waitin'.

"Same for me," I told her. "But none'a that diet shit. Thanks."

"Gotcha." Gina put our cutlery and napkins down and took our menus from us. "Be back in ten," she said before headin' off toward the kitchen.

"Jesus," I muttered, lookin' around. "This diner's like every goddamned cliché in the book. "Didn't know places like this actually existed."

The corner of Breaker's mouth tipped up. "Welcome to Vegas, baby. The city of dreams and the home of cheesy clichés."

I stifled my laughter. "You come here a lot, doncha?"

"Yeah." He spread his arms out across the seat and leaned back. "At least a couple of times a year."

"It's a cool place," I mused. "Not sure I could visit much, though. It all seems over the top to me. This many people in one place make my teeth itch."

Breaker shrugged one shoulder. "The Strip's a lot, yeah. But there are better places to go, less touristy. A lot of cool clubs and underground poker games. I meet up with some military buds now and again, and we go crazy wild."

"Can't imagine my Sophie livin' here." I pulled my phone outta my pocket and laid it on the table. "Don't seem like her kinda place. She's the least flashy chick I know."

"You gotta remember the burbs here are like anywhere else. Lots of families, good schools. Some

Atlas

residential areas reek of money, and it ain't from gamblin'."

"Guess not." I checked my phone. "She fits into Hambleton so well that it's hard to imagine her anywhere else, is all."

Gina appeared with two glasses of coke and set 'em on the table. "Food will be ready in five." She turned on her heel and walked away.

Kit gulped his soda. "You gonna tell Sophie?"

My reply was automatic. "Fuck no. Won't ever put my woman in the position of knowin'. Her rules are different from ours. She values life, even the lives of scumbags like him. Do no harm, that's what she lives by, and she'll die by it too. It's why she's mine. She's everythin' that's good in the world."

A shadow crossed Kit's face. "Happy for ya, brother."

I cocked my head to one side and studied him.

Kit's eyes had gone glassy like he was deep in thought. He'd insisted on comin', even though he knew my endgame. Maybe he was gettin' cold feet. The man had seen enough death and destruction to last him a lifetime. In some ways, he valued life as much as Sophie did.

"You don't have to go through with it, Breaker." I leaned forward, restin' my arms on the table. "It's okay to back out if you haven't got the stomach for it. I can meet up with you after."

His eyes veered up. "No fuckin' way, brother. I'm not backing out. That piece of shit deserves everythin' that's comin' to him." He blew out a hard breath. "Can't believe the info that Colt and the Kings dug up."

"Not a word to Sophie," I ordered. "Remember, what happens in Vegas stays the fuck here."

Breaker leaned forward. "He did it again, Atlas, and they covered it up. Can't fuckin' believe shit like that really goes on."

I fuckin' believed it.

Cover-ups happened a lot more than people knew.

What we'd found out was particularly vile, though, seein' as it involved a cop's widow and kids. Sophie's ex-fucknut had somehow slid into a new relationship with the wife of one of his old colleagues who died in a jewelry store robbery a few years back, a woman called Maggie Hobbs.

Six months after Sophie left Vegas, he moved into her home with her kids. It all seemed promising initially, but as time passed, he slowly terrorized her.

The hospital photographs weren't pretty. Price worked her over good. He didn't give his new woman brain damage like he did mine, but he broke her arm twice and messed her face up repeatedly.

She tried to get shot of him and even reported him to his boss, but again, it got covered up. The Cop's good ol' boys club enabled him to continue abusing women.

"It's why I don't trust the pigs, Kit. Twenty-five percent are corrupt, and twenty-five percent are stupid. Granted, the rest do a stand-up job, but they're fightin' a losing battle half the time."

Kit's face flushed. He'd taken the information Colt sent particularly hard. I guessed that Military men who kept our country safe had respect for the cops seein' as they were all workin' to do the same job. When I factored that a couple of men Kit served with ended up in the force, I could see how his bubble burst.

"Well, after tonight, there'll be one less dirty cop to deal with, right?" His jaw clenched.

My face twisted into a satisfied smile. "Abso-fuckin'-lutely. If that fucker had gotten help, changed his ways, it would just be a case of workin' him over, but Price hasn't learned a thing. He's a fuckin' oxygen thief, and the sooner he's wiped off the Earth, the safer the world will be."

Kit's jaw had a determined set to it. "Agreed."

Atlas

I smirked. "His po-lice buddies can't save him now. He embarrassed 'em, went too far, fucked up one too many times, so they cast him outta their dirty rat cop club. Now he's our problem to solve."

East Vegas was a world away from the strip. It was sketchy at best. The seedy strip club we waited in was as rough as a hairy asshole. I'd seen four drug deals openly go down out by the bar, not a care in the world.

The stripper kept stumblin' over her ridiculous heels as she tried to dance to the electro beats thumpin' through the speakers. Her eyes were glazed, her head more than likely in a different dimension. Men threw curses and insults at her, along with the odd bill. Not that I took any notice. All my attention was on the guy with dark blonde hair who was piss drunk and falling asleep at the opposite end of the bar.

What was probably once a pristine blue shirt was now grimy, pants creased and unkempt. Price was probably a good-lookin' guy once, could even kinda understand what my woman must've seen in him. Her soft heart would've probably broken if she'd seen him propped up like that at the end of that bar.

But he wouldn't get the chance to break her heart again.

I'd make sure of it.

My heart leaped as the burner phone beeped with a text.

Colt: Eyes need testing. All good

I glanced at Breaker and smirked.

It didn't shock me that this place's cameras were fucked. The owner probably broke 'em on purpose so the

Jules Ford

cops couldn't ID all the drug deals that went on. Not that I was complainin'. It meant that nobody could trace us here.

Luke Price looked like he was gonna take a tumble from his stool any minute. I just needed to wait it out, follow him, and then we'd deal.

"Think we should wait outside," Breaker said from the stool beside me. "He won't last much longer. Nobody can ID us and say that we followed him out of the place if we disappear before he leaves."

Kit had a point. "Let's go," I agreed.

We got off our stools and made our way through the main doors.

Security was a joke. One guy opened the door for us earlier, but he was more interested in the stripper that hung off him than us. Now we were leavin', and he was nowhere to be found. Asshole was probably fuckin' her in an alley somewhere.

The stench of urine hit me as soon as we walked into the street.

Garbage blew across the road along with a cloud of red dust. Only one streetlight worked. It cast a shadow over us as we walked across the street and into the mouth of an alley.

Leanin' back against the wall, I breathed in through my nose and outta my mouth. I repeated the action, tryin' to calm the adrenaline that raced through my veins. I looked at Kit, who seemed unaffected by everythin'. "How do you do that?" I asked, tone curious.

"Do what?" he enquired flatly.

"How are you so unbothered?" I pointed to his chest. "I bet if I put a hand to your heart, it'd be beatin' regular. My ticker's goin' like a roadrunner on coke."

"I can switch off," he replied. "Shut it down. Don't feel a fuckin' thing. Honestly, half the time I don't want to."

Atlas

"Jesus," I grumbled under my breath. "Hugh Hefner one minute, Terminator the next. God fuckin' help me."

Kit's eyes never left the door of the strip joint that we'd just left.

"How do ya do it?" I asked. "Is it a military thing?"

Kit's eyes darted toward me, then back to the target. "I was in bomb disposal, brother—needed nerves of steel for that shit. The military officers trained us to shut it down as soon as the unit accepted us. What the instructors didn't teach me, the boys did."

My forehead furrowed.

Had to respect a brother who could turn it on and off like that. Maybe he could teach me a trick or two. I wasn't too proud to take tips from a decorated veteran.

"Can you show me?" I asked.

"Jesus," he snapped. "We're on a fuckin' job."

"Not now, ya dick." My eyes went to the door of the strip club, then back to Breaker. "When we get home. Teach me the-"

"-Showtime," Kit bit out, cuttin' me off.

My heart jerked, and my eyes whipped across the street.

Price was stumblin' outta the strip club and staggerin' slowly up the garbage-ridden sidewalk.

"We need to stay as far back as we can without losin' him," Kit instructed. "We don't wanna be ID'd."

We began to move out of the dark alley and into the muted street light.

My heart hammered, but I kept my focus on the mission. Losin' my shit wasn't an option if I wanted to do this and get the fuck outta Vegas without us bein' nabbed.

We pulled our baseball caps forward as we rounded the street where Price had disappeared seconds before.

Voices floated through the night air, and we dived into the alcove of the shop doorway that we were walkin' past.

Jules Ford

Two men started to converse. They were about thirty feet ahead of us. Luckily, they didn't pick up that we were there.

"You already owe me five-hundred bucks, Luke."

A whine, then, "Ritchie, man. You know I'm good for it."

"You ain't been good for it since you got kicked off the force, friend." The other guy's tone was jeering. "You don't earn yourself freebies anymore, so why you up in my fuckin' face askin' for favors? I ain't a charity."

A pause, then, "I did you a lotta favors, Ritch. You would've got locked up if it wasn't for me losin' prints and witness statements."

Breaker's eyebrows shot up his forehead.

I shook my head; jaw clenched so hard it ached. Fuckin' corrupt cops made me wanna hurl.

An audible sigh cut through the air. "This is your last one. Next time you wanna hit, you pay."

"I get my cheque tomorrow, Ritch man. You know I'm good for it. I'll come and find you."

My mouth twisted, chest tightenin'.

An ex-detective scorin' drugs on a street corner 'cause his ass was addicted to smack wasn't somethin' you saw every day. I wondered how long he'd been usin'. Was he shootin' up back in the day, then goin' home to Sophie and hidin' it from her? Was he puttin' her at risk without her even knowin'?

My lungs burned so hot that I had to suck in a breath.

Fuckin' dirty cop scumbag.

We heard the sounds of back-slapping and goodbyes. I ducked my head around the alcove to see Price headin' up the street. Another guy in a dark hoodie gave us his back as he jogged in the opposite direction.

"Come on," Breaker said quietly.

I followed him back onto the street until we were silently shadowing Price again.

Atlas

The area we were heading into was quieter, obviously residential. Price's official address was a few miles away, but he had another place that he used. We didn't know if it was a girlfriend's apartment or just a place he had on the lowdown that he used nefariously.

From what we'd discovered, there were two Luke Price's. The standup guy that had lost his way that he portrayed to his ex-colleagues, versus the drug-addled loser that would steal from his grandma for his next hit.

I was about to create a third version of Luke Price.

A dead man version.

We watched him stumble up some stairs toward an old, rundown apartment block. He fell several times, which allowed me and Breaker time to catch up. He was so out of it that he didn't even register that we were behind him when he pushed the main door open and almost fell inside.

Kit went straight into buddy mode. He walked toward Price and helped him up. "Hey, man. Are you okay there? You don't look too good. You sick?"

"I'm good, friend," Price slurred.

Kit wrapped an arm around his waist. "Where's your apartment? I'll get you inside."

Price was so out of it that he didn't even notice me in the foyer.

Close up, I could see him more clearly, grey skin, dirty clothes, and hair. His eyes were glazed and bloodshot.

He was a fuckin' mess.

Price raised an arm and pointed down the hall. "Over there."

Kit nodded, took the asshole's elbow, and began to half drag; half carry him down the corridor.

Music thumped from one of the apartments. Sounds of a fight rang out as a woman yelled at her man to get the fuck out. The place was a shithole that stank of piss and weed.

Jules Ford

So much for bein' a fuckin' cop, a pillar of the community. Asshole had turned into a goddamned gutter rat. Good enough for him too. I liked that karma had grabbed his ass by its jaws.

"Where's your keys, man?" Kit asked his new best friend.

Price rummaged in his pocket, eventually producin' a set. "Thanks for this. Got a bit too wasted tonight."

"All been there," Kit replied. "You're good. Let's get you inside, and you can sleep it off. Your woman gonna look after you?"

I grinned. Kit was workin' out if he had someone in the apartment.

"Ain't gotta woman," Price slurred. "Bitches are more trouble than they're worth."

Bingo.

The door swung open. Kit gestured for me to stay put and disappeared inside with Price.

My back hit the wall opposite the door.

Our original game plan was to break in and kill him in his sleep, but a new idea pinged. If we could stage it right, it would solve some problems. This shit could be easier than I thought. We'd be off the hook because it would look natural.

Kit appeared at the door and nodded for me to follow him.

I stepped inside and almost gagged.

Like the rest of the buildin', the place stank of piss. On top of that, the smell of rottin' food and pure filth assaulted my poor fuckin' nostrils.

"He's wasted," Kit whispered. "Left him passed out on a ratty old chair. Looks like a fuckin' drug den in there."

"Got an idea," I murmured and explained my idea to Kit.

Atlas

As he listened, a big grin took over his face. "It'll work like a charm," he agreed. "You know how to set up a hit?"

"You're the fuckin' party boy, brother," I argued. "Thought you'd be able to do that shit in your sleep."

"Never injected shit and never did heroin," Breaker explained. "Had plenty of shit up my nose and down my neck, but never in a vein." He thought for a minute. "From what I've heard, you dissolve the smack in water, suck it all into the needle, then inject."

My shoulder lifted into a shrug. "I can do that."

"Right." Kit scratched his head in thought, then nodded toward a doorway. "I'll go find the stuff."

I followed him into a room that I guessed was the lounge. There was an old TV in a corner, a beat-up coffee table covered in drug paraphernalia, and an old armchair where Price had passed out. The worn carpet was so grimy that my shoes stuck to it. The walls had been stained brown from years of cigarette smoke.

Breaker nodded to the table. "Looks like he mixes his shit on there." He walked over to Price and started to go through his pockets. "Fucker reeks. Needs a hot shower and a can of deodorant. He's ripe as fuck."

"Just think, brother. Not too long ago, he was one'a the men tasked with protectin' this town and its people." My face twisted with disgust. "He hoodwinked my woman. Made her believe he was somethin' he's not and never will be. Then he beat the shit outta her, probably because she started to clue in. Narcissistic piece of shit."

My chest fuckin' scalded with hatred for the poor excuse for a man who'd passed out before me. The bastard was a total fuck-up.

"Makes me sick, brother. Had everythin' because he had my Sophie. But instead of takin' care of her, he beat her black and blue. Fucker never deserved her, and he knew it all along. It burns me that he took hold of her

Jules Ford

anyway, then made it so she had to leave the only family she had left. It goddamned burns me up, Breaker."

His lips twisted. "Soph's got us now. She'll be golden."

I jerked a nod. "Yeah. And I *know* what I've got. *I'm* gonna take care of her, and *I'm* gonna nurture her. *I'm* gonna make it, so Sophie laughs every day and knows her worth. She's gonna be loved and adored every second for the rest of her days. I'll give her the life she deserves, and it's gonna be beautiful. She stands with me, and I stand with her too. No fucker will ever hurt my woman and live. Not when she's got me."

"I've got her too, Atlas," Kit assured me, still checkin' Price's pockets. "If you can't be there, I will." He pulled a baggie outta Price's inside pocket and held it in the air, examining it. "There it is. Time to die, motherfucker."

I grinned, and the burn in my chest turned to satisfaction. We were about to do the world a favor.

That grin stayed on my face as I dissolved every molecule of smack in the baggy before suckin' it into one'a the dirty old syringes from the table.

Seconds later, I took Luke Price's arm in my gloved hand and injected enough smack into his vein to bring down a horse.

My grin was still in place.

Minutes after, we watched his body jerk while he foamed at the mouth.

A newfound sense of peace washed over me as I watched Luke Price leave the world a better place for not havin' him in it. Every instinct inside my body urged me to spit in his face, but I held back. DNA evidence and all that.

I'd gotten retribution for my Stitch. That would suffice.

An hour later, we rode our bikes into the King's compound and briefed 'em on the night's events.

Atlas

Thirty minutes after that, we were past the city limits, and I was on the way home to the woman who I was gonna spend the rest of my days loving with everythin' I had.

We had a long and happy life to start living.

Five Days Later

I'd just finished fuckin' Stitch in her bed, which was now our bed, seein' as I'd moved into the house of cuteness. I was pullin' her into me and kissin' her thick, glorious hair when her cell phone rang.

My gut jerked, and a shiver ran down my spine.

I knew what it was about. I'd been waitin', and all day I'd felt it in my blood.

We were still in the afterglow of our orgasms, chests still heavin'.

Stitch had a thin sheen of sweat over her breasts; all I wanted to do was lick the salt from her skin and ingest it into my soul. I loved makin' love with my woman more than I loved anythin'.

I'd never called it that before - Love makin'.

To me, it had always been 'fuckin', or 'sex,' somethin' that I did to let off steam and release some tension. But not with Stitch. With her, it was somethin' intimate, somethin' beautiful and necessary if I wanted to keep breathing easy.

She rolled outta bed and rummaged through her jeans before grabbin' her cell and stabbin' at it. "Hey, Ned," she breathed, laying back beside me. "It's late. Is somethin' wrong?"

The sweet smile she'd had fixed on her face for weeks started to fade. Her smooth, tan skin turned pale, and she whispered one word.

"What?"

Her eyes immediately came to me, and my chest panged while I watched 'em well up. "I don't understand," she croaked.

I leaped into action. Sittin' up, I grabbed Sophie's cell from my woman and stabbed the loudspeaker icon. "Ned, you got Atlas. You and the kids okay?"

"Atlas. Thank God." Her voice held a tremor. "I've just gotten word from a friend at the DA's office. Luke Price, Sophie's ex-husband, died of a drug overdose."

My soul fuckin' sang.

All I wanted to do at that moment was punch the air, but I kept my shit together and instead muttered, "Fuck. When?"

"A few days ago," she replied. "I'm fucking furious about it. Luke Price's boss assured me they'd keep tabs on him and sort him out. They fired him a few months ago for being high on duty and fucking up an important investigation. Nobody told me."

"Jesus." I scrubbed a hand down my face for Sophie's benefit. "What happens next? You need us to fly down there?"

"Up to you." Her voice sounded almost bored. "His old colleagues have collected for the funeral, but it'll be a cheap one by all accounts. My guy informed me that he was a total embarrassment to the department by the end. I'm not going. I'm glad he's dead. I don't need to say goodbye to him; if I did go, there's always the chance that I'd spit on his grave."

I took in Sophie's expression. She looked shell-shocked.

"I'll talk with Soph and call ya tomorrow," I informed her. "Is it cool if I store your number?"

Atlas

"Well, duh," she said, her cockiness makin' me wanna smile. "Go into Sophie's phone and get my office number. I'll tell my PA to put you straight through when you call."

"Gotcha."

"Sophie." She called.

Stitch's shoulders stiffened.

"Babe, this isn't your fault. You *didn't* drive him to shoot shit up his arm. You did your best and didn't give up on him easily. You did the right thing in divorcing him, and you did the right thing in doing it in the way that was best for you. You didn't owe him anything, not your love, friendship, or care. If I hear that there's even a flicker of guilt going on in that genius brain, I'll take my kids out of school, fly down to bumfuck Wyoming, and kick your beautifully shaped but scarily toned ass. Now, that's the law according to Kennedy Carmichael, and if there's one thing I know, babe, it's the goddamned law. Do you hear me?"

Silence.

"Sophie. Do you hear me?"

"Yeah," my woman breathed. "I hear you."

"Good. Now, don't lose a moment of sleep over that prick. We'll speak tomorrow. Atlas, don't you let her talk herself into feeling bad. Luke Price got the exact ending that he deserved. Now I'm out. Get back to your man, Soph. Good - fucking - night, babe." A click sounded, and the line went dead.

I set the phone on the nightstand. Sophie looked as if she were in a daze. My chest jolted. "Baby," I breathed.

"He beat me," she whispered. "He beat me so badly that I fell and cracked my skull."

I felt my face twist.

I knew everythin', but her sayin' the words still made the burn set fire to my chest. That fucker put my woman through hell, and after years it was still affecting her.

"If he wasn't already dead, I'd fuckin' kill him," I whispered back.

"I know, honey, but it doesn't matter. I went through that, and it wasn't good, but you're my reward. I got you because of *him*." Her whole body jolted, and she leaped on top of me.

I didn't have time to brace before her body hit mine, and she buried her face in my throat.

My fingers trailed down her back. "Baby. I dunno what to say. I'm sorry for your loss."

Lie.

She sighed into my neck. "It's no loss, honey."

"Baby, what can I do? Want me to call Ned back? Or one'a the women? Cara'll know what to say." My hands went to her waist. I pulled her back and tipped her chin up with my finger. "You want ice cream? Donuts? I'll get you anythin' you want."

Her eyes locked with mine, and I stilled.

Sadness didn't pour from them like I thought it would; instead, they danced with relief.

A small smile crept over her face, and she let out a tinkling laugh. "Danny, you don't get it. I've lived in fear for three years. I've looked over my shoulder and had nightmares. Jeez, I left my only family to get away from him." She smiled brighter. "Don't you see? What he did brought me to you, to the club. I wouldn't have met you if it wasn't for him." Her eyes shone.

My fingers entwined with hers, and my thumb rubbed over the space where I intended to put my ring. Then she said the words that made my soul come alive, and my heart burst with love.

"Danny." She cupped the side of my face, her touch leaving a trail of heat on my skin. "Now I can move on with you, and I don't have to look back. I can look forward to our future together. We can have a beautiful life, honey. I'm finally free."

Chapter Twenty-Seven

Atlas ~ Ten Days Later

My head snapped back as Stitch's fist cracked across my nose.

"Fuck!" My eyes watered so hard that couldn't see shit. I felt a swift kick to the back of my legs, and suddenly, I was on my knees.

My cock thickened as soft little tits pressed against my back.

My woman tipped my face up, leaned down, and kissed me hard. She pulled back slightly. "That was for saying that I had no ass."

I staggered to my feet and lunged for her.

She let out a squeal and skipped away, giggling. "You think I'm gonna make it easy for you?"

I raised my hand to cover my grin, leveling her with a look. "Baby. When are you gonna realize? You make everythin' easy." I stepped toward her. "You easily make me happy. You easily make me hard as fuck, and you easily make my life more beautiful than I ever thought possible."

She stuck her arms out, grabbin' hold of the ropes. "And you said you weren't romantic."

Stalkin' toward her, I grinned. "I wasn't until I met you. Maybe you bring out the romance shit in me."

Jules Ford

"Well, duh," she sassed, channeling Kennedy.

I grinned, heart full of love for my beautiful, strong warrior of an ol' lady.

I thought the death of her ex would've affected her, but I called that one wrong.

She felt bad that it came to that. Felt terrible that Price's life went that way, but she didn't feel guilty. She knew that he got the endin' he deserved. It was like she said. She could sleep easier knowing he couldn't hurt anyone else.

And so could I.

My hand snaked out, and I tugged her into me, cock punchin' through my gym shorts. "Love you down in my bones, Stitch, baby. Love your face, your smile, and more than anything; I love your tiny little ass."

"Guess what's in my ass?" she whispered against my lips. "Remember that butt plug that you found in my box of tricks? The one with the pink diamond?"

I groaned as my cock hardened.

"Well." Her hand curled around my nape. She pulled my face down and kissed my nose. "I may or may not have utilized it this morning after you left."

My dicked went hard as a steel pipe. "Get outta the ring, Stitch," I ordered.

She smiled seductively before bending down, pullin' the ropes aside, and jumping to the ground.

I followed her down and began to stalk toward her. Bending, I grabbed the back of her thighs and hauled her up into my arms. Her legs snaked around my hips simultaneously as her hand slid across the back of my neck, and she pulled my face down for a kiss.

"Gonna fuck you good, Stitch," I murmured against her lips, walkin' us over to the wall.

She pulled her head back, flung her arms in the air, and yelled, "Yay."

I roared a laugh, and fine whisky eyes hit mine, conveying all the love in the world.

Atlas

"You make me so happy, Dan," she whispered. "I was lost for so long, honey, but you found me."

"No, baby," I croaked, throat suddenly thick. "You're the one who found *me*." I gently placed her on the floor and sank to my knees until my face was level with her pussy. I pulled her gym shorts down, and my breath caught when I saw she was commando. Her bare pussy glistened with her juices.

My mouth watered. "Fuck me." I got to my feet and lifted her arms to pull her gym bra off. My cock wept when I saw that she was as naked as the day she was born, all except for her sneakers.

It was hot as fuck, naughty as all hell, and my dick knew it too.

My hand went to back'a my neck, and I pulled my tank off. Then I bent at the knees and lifted my ol' lady back into my arms.

"Gonna eat my pussy, Stitch baby. You better hold on tight." I positioned my hands under her ass and lifted her high until her tight, wet, pretty little pussy was level with my mouth.

"Danny," she said with a moan from above. "What if somebody comes down?" She leaned her back against the wall to help support herself.

"They'll see us fuckin'," I murmured, "They'll see my tongue in your cunt and know that you and I are bound for eternity and that you're mine."

She let out a soft sigh.

I took in her pink folds and smiled as I caught a wink of somethin' from her ass. My dick kicked again. I'd never seen anythin' so fuckin' sexy.

Lettin' out a groan, I took a deep breath, leaned in, and ate my woman the fuck out.

Soft hands went around my head. "Oh my God," she breathed as I gently pulled her pretty little clit between my lips and sucked hard as my tongue lashed against it.

She tasted unlike anything I'd ever known, sweet and musky. Even her pussy held a hint of strawberries, and it drove me outta my mind. I groaned as she began to grind her soppin' wet cunt into my mouth, lettin' me now that she was already chasin' it.

I slid two fingers inside, and her cunt clenched as I fucked her with 'em, still suckin' on her clit.

Never had I wanted a woman the way I wanted her. I needed inside her so badly that my cock ached. I loved that she responded to me so fuckin' beautifully. She was an innocent who was down for anythin'. Sophie turned me on more than anyone had before.

She began to moan louder. Her pussy clenched harder as she began to climax in my mouth. I sucked harder on her clit until she screamed and came all over my face.

I continued to eat her through her orgasm, and her moans turned to soft whimpers.

Gently, I slid her down the wall until I lined her pussy up with my dick.

My hand went to the waistband of my shorts, and I shoved 'em down just enough to release my throbbin' cock.

"See what you do me, you hot little bitch." I growled, jacking myself. "You're mine, and I'm gonna fuck you so hard that you still feel me tomorrow."

"Yes, Danny," she cried, wrigglin' her hips. Her legs snaked around my waist until I felt her muscles grip my ass.

One hand kept her pinned against the wall while the other grabbed my hard length and lined it up. "Ready, baby?"

Her eyes went soft. "Yeah, honey," she whispered.

I gave one hard thrust and impaled her.

Her tight little cunt clenched around me, and I bit out a curse. "Tight-pussied little bitch," I said, groaning

Atlas

before my hips snapped back and thrust in hard again. "Gonna fuckin' ruin this cunt."

A strangled sound left her throat. "Fuck me harder, Danny."

My jaw clenched. I tamped down the urge to come already. "Jesus, Stitch baby. Love this pussy." I pounded into her hard, so deep that she squealed from the pressure of my fat dick.

My eyes rolled to the back of my head from the sensation of her tight little pussy gripping me.

She drove me fuckin' crazy.

I buried my face in her throat and bucked harder. My mind focused on the slickness of her swollen cunt, and the way she clamped onto me tightly. I groaned as the tell-tale tingle began to prickle in the small of my back.

Fuck. I wouldn't be able to hold off for long.

"Come, Sophie," I rasped. "Strangle my cock." But her pussy was already spasming around me. I shouted out my pleasure. "Tightest little pussy in the world," I rasped, and her cunt flooded. "That's it, baby, fuckin' soak me."

She threw her head back and shrieked as she started to come.

"Fuck," I shouted, poundin' harder. "Fuck. Fuck. Fuck."

Stitch writhed on the wall, lettin' out moans and groans as she orgasmed all over my dick, her pussy gettin' even slicker.

I couldn't hold off any longer. My cock erupted so intensely that lights danced behind my eyes. Every inch of my skin tingled, my back, my dick, even my thighs as I powered into her harder and harder, bathin' her insides with streams of my cum.

My mouth caught hers, and I sucked hard on her bottom lip, still moanin' with the force of my orgasm. I kept thrusting hard until, eventually, I started to come down.

Jules Ford

I buried my face in her throat and smiled as I felt her shiver.

My knees started to give way, but I kept her secure. My cock wasn't ready to be free of her cunt, not yet. I sank onto my ass and pulled her down, keeping my cock inside her warmth.

"Baby." I reached up and tucked a lock of her hair behind her ear. "My heart will give out one of these days."

"Don't worry," she breathed. "I'll save you."

Jesus, my woman was killin' me. She was so generous, so givin'. I was one lucky motherfucker.

My hand trailed up her spine. I cupped the back of her neck and pulled her down for a soft kiss. "You already saved me, Stitch baby," I whispered against her lips, etchin' the words into her soul. "I love you so goddamned much. Gonna give you everything. My heart, my soul, my babies. We'll have a long and happy life, and I don't wanna wait."

My free hand went to my shorts pocket, searching before it curled over cold metal. "I promise to love your tiny little ass until the end of time," I vowed. "If you'll have me."

Her eyes went soft and gooey. "I love you."

My fingers entwined with hers, and I slipped a diamond onto her ring finger. "Then marry me and do it fast. I wanna be your husband more than I've ever wanted anythin'." Emotion burned my throat as I watched my ol' lady hold her hand up to the light, admire her ring, and smile so fuckin' brightly that my chest warmed with love.

Fine whisky eyes hit mine, and my girl whispered the one word that sealed our fate.

"Yes."

Epilogue

Sophie ~ Two Weeks later

"You look beautiful," Layla breathed.
I gazed in the mirror, and joy filled my heart.
My wedding dress consisted of a scrap of white lace that skimmed the top of my boobs and stopped five inches above my knees. It molded to my body like a second skin. White strappy sandals adorned my feet, and my lips were red and glossy.

For a wedding dress, it was kinda slutty.

Atlas was going to love it.

We'd come to Vegas to get married.

It was where my family was. Ned couldn't take the kids out of school with their Summer break only weeks away. I wouldn't get married without her and the kids there.

Cash and Cara, Layla and Bowie, John, Breaker, Abe, and Iris had come for the wild ride. Unfortunately, we couldn't bring the entire club because the men had to protect the clubhouse.

"You look like a woman who doesn't intend on wearing her wedding dress for very long," Ned drawled. "I wanna do you, and I'm not even a lesbian."

"Thanks, Ned." I giggled. "You say the nicest things."

Jules Ford

Cara and Layla burst out laughing.

"Mama," Sunny piped up. "What's a lesbian?"

Layla got down on her haunches and tucked a loose lock of hair behind her daughter's ear. "A lesbian is a lady who loves another lady." She straightened Sunshine's flower girl dress. "You look gorgeous, baby."

"Will Daddy like my dress?" Sunny asked.

Layla smiled. "He'll love it." She stood and looked around. "I've got to say, ladies, we're all looking pretty damned hot."

Kennedy lounged back on the sofa, sipping her cocktail. "Well, duh."

Cara ran a hand over her belly. "I look like a fucking whale." She turned and glared at me. "Couldn't you have waited until I popped junior out? I'll look like Sigourney Weaver in Alien in all the pictures." She pointed at Layla. "We've got the pretty little mama here who looks like every adolescent boy's wet dream." She jerked her thumb to Kennedy. "We've got hotshot lawyer ex-stripper who looks like she's walking a red carpet every time she tosses her long, naturally blonde hair." She pursed her lips. "And then there's the bride-to-be. Beautiful, smart, and without an ounce of fat on her. She's also canny enough to lock down the one man in the MC who was unlockdownable."

I slicked on another coat of gloss. "Cara. You're not fat; you're pregnant. And let's face it, Cash Stone - who is incidentally one of the most beautiful men I've ever seen - is totally besotted with you and his unborn child."

Cara's eyes softened. "Yeah. I guess so."

Kennedy perked up slightly. "He's incidentally one of the what the what?"

I put my hand to my hip. "Down, girl. He's in love with Cara." My eyes swept over Ned's fire engine red tube dress and hair out there. "Though, I think Hendrix will love you."

She perked up even more. "As in Jimmy?"

Atlas

"He plays a mean guitar," Layla informed her. "That's how he got his road name."

"He's hot too." Cara waggled her eyebrows. "Over six feet tall with bright blue eyes, tan, and abs you could lick until your tongue dropped off. He's got tattoos and long dark hair that looks hot even when he puts it in a man-bun."

Kennedy visibly swooned. "I think my kitty just meowed."

"Do you have a pussy cat?" Sunny shrieked. "Can I play with it?"

Kennedy busted out laughing.

"Mom. We gonna be long?" A boy's voice called over.

Ned looked over at her son. "We're setting off soon, kiddo."

My lips quirked as I watched Sunny go and sit with the twins.

Little thumbs flew as they played quietly on their Switches. The kids had dressed up to the nines. Kadence and Sunny wore ivory flower girl dresses, and my nephew wore designer jeans and a button-down shirt.

I took in his handsome face, thick dark hair, and brown eyes.

He looked like my son more than he did Ned's. He had the same coloring as the Stone's, but I supposed I did too.

Kady, on the other hand, was all her mother. Big blue eyes, long blonde hair, and a face so pretty that she took my breath away.

I'd missed them all desperately.

I'd been trying to persuade Kennedy to move to Hambleton and set up her private practice, seeing as Mr. Stafford was talking about retiring. She just laughed and said she'd go crazy living in bumfuck Wyoming.

A knock sounded on the door.

Jules Ford

I looked up to see Iris poking her head around. "The cars are here. It's time."

Taking a last deep breath, I looked in the mirror, and my mind went to Danny.

Words from a year before made me smile.

I'll take one for the team, boss. She's easy on the eye but not enough ass for my likin'. She's got the body of a fifteen-year-old boy. Never stuck it to a prissy man-bitch with more muscles than me before.

He was an asshole for saying those words, but I'd never felt more beautiful or loved in the last few months. My self-esteem was finally sky-high, and it was all because of him.

Atlas was a crude, rude biker with no tact or manners. He was also protective, generous, kind, and beautiful, inside and out.

He was also the father of the child that I'd discovered an hour ago I was carrying.

I'd tell my ol' man after our wedding.

The week before, I'd brought him a silver skull ring to wear on his finger, but I knew for certain that the news I'd deliver later would be the best wedding present ever.

My heart was buoyant because I finally had the family I yearned for in Danny and the Speed Demons.

Our baby would make it complete.

Atlas

Of all the places to get wed, it had to be fuckin' Vegas. Not that it mattered; the coroner ruled Price's death accidental, and everyone had moved on. Nobody batted an eyelash seein' as he was a known drug user.

I'd have married Doctor Sophie Green in a fast-food restaurant if she had asked me to. I didn't give a fuck

Atlas

about the weddin'. All I cared about was makin' her my wife.

I'd always thought I'd die alone. I never thought there was a woman out there who could steal my heart the way my Sophie did.

I gave my neck a little scratch. My nerves were so bad they were makin' me itch.

The boys were waitin' with me in the Little Chapel of Love.

I was already waiting at the end of the aisle and didn't mind admitting that I was sweating like a quarterback in the cheerleader's locker room.

While the women waited for Ned and got ready at the hotel, the boys and I went for a beer before makin' our way to the venue.

Layla kept sayin' it was bad luck to see the bride before the weddin, but it was a moot point seein' as I'd had my big, fat dick in her tight little pussy that mornin'.

Still, I didn't wanna push my luck.

We'd flown in earlier that day and checked into the hotel. We were gonna get wed, fuck to make it official, get drunk, and gamble before flyin' home the next day.

Couldn't leave the club for too long seein' as were at war, but nothin' was gonna stop me marryin' my Stitch with my brothers by my side.

I looked up to see Cash bolt into the room with a huge smile. "They're here," he whispered, takin' his place on the seats behind us.

The Little Chapel of Love was cutesy as fuck, totally up Stitch's avenue.

The registrar covered the room in white flowers. He was dressed smartly, thankfully, and not like Elvis. Our ceremony would take about ten minutes from start to finish, which suited me down to the ground.

All I needed was that piece of paper, and I'd be golden.

Jules Ford

Out of all my boys, I'd asked Breaker to stand up with me.

He was turnin' out to be a good, capable brother.

I think Cash was pissed that I didn't ask him to be my best man, but he didn't need it as Breaker did. Plus, Kit had been my partner in crime, literally, so there was that to consider too.

Music came through the speakers. I snapped my back straight, and my lips twitched at Blur's opening bars of 'Tender' that played through the sound system.

My mixtape had become legendary.

It had gone down a storm, not only with my girl but also with the other ol' ladies. They'd all asked their men why *they* didn't do romantic stuff like I did, and it was funny as all hell.

Go fuckin' figure.

Kit stood to my right. My boys were at my back, and my woman was about to walk down an aisle and promise herself to me for the rest of our lives.

Nothin' could best that day or the way that my heart grew at the thought of spendin' the rest of my life with the pretty little doc, who had somehow burrowed her way down deep into my soul.

She was my partner in every way. I trusted her as much as I trusted my boys.

She'd get down and dirty at the drop of a hat, and I thanked God every day for bringin' such a loyal woman into my life.

Kit glanced behind us furtively and gave me a nudge. "She looks amazin', brother. Wait until you see her. She's sexy as fu…" His voice trailed off, and his whole body locked.

A shocked gasp cut through the air.

A breathy voice said, "Kyle?"

Breaker went white as a ghost. Casper had more color than him.

Atlas

I whipped around to see a blonde woman standin' next to Sophie.

She was starin' at Breaker as if she'd seen an apparition. Two kids were standing to one side of her. My eyes slid to the boy who was glowering at Kit with his arms folded across his chest.

My gut gave a hard jerk.

He looked just like a Stone boy.

My eyes slashed across to John, who was also staring at the boy, open-mouthed. His shocked eyes cut to Kit. "Jesus Christ. He looks exactly like you when you were a kid. What the fuck's goin' on?"

The woman had a hand to her throat, her bright blue eyes glassy with tears. "You're dead. I looked for you. I gave them your name; they told me you were dead."

"Whoa. Whoa. Whoa." Abe's wide eyes darted between Kit and the blonde. "Who the fuck's Kyle?"

Sophie's mouth dropped open, and her face fell slack as understanding dawned. Her eyes sliced straight toward me. "Shit. Breaker's Kyle?"

Kit stepped forward and his hands reached for the woman. "I didn't die, Kenny kitten. I can explain. There was a fuck-up. I'm not Kyle Simmons."

My gut dropped to my boots.

Kenny? As in Kennedy? Shit, fuck, shit.

My lip curled into a snarl. "Well, you've fucked up this time and at my wedding too. I'm gonna kill you, motherfucker."

Bowie's stare darted between Breaker, Kennedy, and the kids. "Oh shit," he bit out.

Kennedy's face twisted with somethin' akin to hurt. "What kind of mix-up are you speaking of, *Kyle*? There wasn't a mix-up when you told me your name was Kyle Simmons. There wasn't a mix-up when we met years ago, back when you were on leave from the army. There wasn't a mix-up when you kept returning to Vegas to see me. There wasn't a mix-up when you left the last time,

Jules Ford

and also left me knocked up." Her voice hardened. "And there certainly wasn't a mix-up when I pulled strings and tried to find you through military records. Your commanding officer told me you died in an explosion just after the twins were born. So tell me, *Kyle,* exactly what kind of mix-up are you speaking of?"

"Asshole," the boy rasped.

"Mom?" the girl squeaked.

John glared at Kit, "You fuckin' idiot!" he bellowed.

"Jesus, Bro," Bowie murmured.

Cash's lips twitched.

Kennedy's eyes cut to Prez. "Hey! My name's Kennedy Carmichael. These are my kids, Kai and Kadence."

"I'm gettin' that, darlin'," Prez muttered. "Seems we have a mutual acquaintance." His voice rose with anger. "And it just so happens to be my complete *fuck-up of a son!*"

Sophie's eyes bulged.

My gut rolled.

Jesus Christ. Breaker's got twins?

Ned popped a hip. "I can't believe this shit. I've come to my best friend's wedding only to discover that one of the groomsmen is my dead fucking baby daddy. And hallelujah. Praise the lord," she threw her arms up in the air, "he's gone and risen from the dead."

Breaker's face fell. "I'm not dead, Kenny kitten."

She strutted her ass over to Kit and got all up in his face. "Well, duh."

"Kit?" John bit out. "You're on my shit list, boy."

Breaker's stare fell over Kennedy's shoulder and onto the little girl, his daughter. "Fuck," he rasped, skin turnin' grey.

Cash began to laugh.

Cara slapped his arm.

Layla's eyes were so huge they took up most of her face.

Atlas

Mini-biker Kit boy glared up at Breaker. "Asshole!" he snapped again.

I grabbed Sophie and pulled her into me. Mouth on her hair, I whispered, "Why the fuck does shit have to hit the fan on our weddin' day, baby?"

She heaved a long, hard sigh, pursed her lips, and shrugged her shoulder.

"Everybody out," I ordered, pointing to the door. "Sort your 'Days of Our Biker Lives,' Maury Povich goddamned 'he *is* the father' shit out somewhere else. Me and my woman are gettin' hitched, and shock fuckin' horror, *your* fucked-up shit is screwin' with *my* fucked-up shit. How would you like it if I did a 'who's the daddy routine at one'a your weddings, huh?" I looked to the heavens and let out a curse.

Abe glared at Breaker.

Cash laughed again.

John shook his head, muttering obscenities under his breath. His thunderous stare fell upon the little Kady girl, then slid over to mini-biker Kit boy.

I watched, dumbfounded, as a huge grin spread across his face.

He puffed out his chest. "Kids. I'm your grandpop, John. Welcome to the fuckin' family."

I bit back a laugh and clapped Breaker's shoulder so hard that he winced.

"Yo, motherfucker." I nodded toward mini-biker Kit boy. "I think you've got some explainin' to do."

The End

Thank You for Reading.

If you enjoyed Atlas and Sophie's story, I would really appreciate you leaving a review on Amazon.
xoxo

Breaker, Kennedy (and the twin's) story is coming Spring 2023

Acknowledgements

I've learned recently that it takes a village… Or in my case a tribe.

Thank you for all of the ladies on my Facebook group for your enthusiasm and love. Your theories about the Speed Demons are truly amazing and I love that you love the brothers as much as I do.

Elizabeth N Harris, Jessica Ames and Madalyn Judge, thank you all for keeping me going, and for all of the laughs and chats along the way. And also Christy Rose, I love your hustle, thank you for hustling for me.

Christina and Rose, thank you for all of your help, you've been amazing.

Thank you Mylene and Victoria… The best alpha readers ever.

ARC Team, thank you for your time. You ladies rock.

And a special word of thanks to Jayne. You do so much for me and I appreciate you more than you know.

Readers, thank you for all of your amazing reviews and feedback.

You truly are wonderful.

Raise Hell.

Jules

XOXO

Stalk Jules

Jules loves chatting to readers
Email her
julesfordauthor@gmail.com

Join her Facebook Group
Jules Ford's Tribe | Facebook

Instagram
Jules Ford (@julesfordauthor) • Instagram photos and videos

Printed in Great Britain
by Amazon